"A sparkling, heartwarming [...] can't-put-it-down read—a her[...] twists, and dangerously good [...]

—Sarah Pekkanen, author of *The Perfect Neighbors*

"With lively humor, Ballis pulls together a diverse cast, evocative renovation details, and delicious food descriptions in this well-seasoned novel. Fans of Mary Kay Andrews will enjoy this."

—*Booklist*

"Ballis delves again into foodie women's lit with flavorful results . . . Honest and touching."

—*Kirkus Reviews*

"An absolutely charming read! . . . Equal parts heartfelt and hilarious."

—Harlequin Junkie

"Ballis's heroine is a perfect blend of tough and vulnerable as she struggles to straighten out her messy life."

—Heroes and Heartbreakers (A Best Read of the Month)

"A funny and heartfelt tale . . . This is Stacey Ballis at her witty and chef-tastic best."

—Amy Hatvany, author of *It Happens All the Time*

"Readers hungry for cleverly written contemporary romances will definitely want to order *Off the Menu*."    —*Chicago Tribune*

"Insightful and hilarious."    —*Today's Chicago Woman*

"Witty and tender, brash and seriously clever . . . [Ballis's] story-telling will have you alternately turning pages and calling your friends, urging them to come along for the ride."

—Elizabeth Flock, *New York Times* bestselling author of *Me & Emma*

BERKLEY BOOKS BY STACEY BALLIS

# How to Change a Life

## STACEY BALLIS

BERKLEY
New York

BERKLEY
An imprint of Penguin Random House LLC
375 Hudson Street, New York, New York 10014

Copyright © 2017 by Stacey Ballis
"Readers Guide" copyright © 2017 by Penguin Random House LLC
Penguin Random House supports copyright. Copyright fuels creativity, encourages
diverse voices, promotes free speech, and creates a vibrant culture. Thank you for buying an
authorized edition of this book and for complying with copyright laws by not reproducing,
scanning, or distributing any part of it in any form without permission. You are supporting
writers and allowing Penguin Random House to continue to publish books for every reader.

BERKLEY is a registered trademark and the B colophon is a trademark
of Penguin Random House LLC.

Library of Congress Cataloging-in-Publication Data

Names: Ballis, Stacey, author.
Title: How to change a life / Stacey Ballis.
Description: First Edition. | New York : Berkley, 2017.
Identifiers: LCCN 2017014900 (print) | LCCN 2017023064 (ebook) |
ISBN 9780698171268 (ebook) | ISBN 9780425276624 (paperback)
Subjects: | BISAC: FICTION / Contemporary Women. | FICTION / Humorous.
Classification: LCC PS3602.A624 (ebook) | LCC PS3602.A624 H69 2017 (print) |
DDC 813/.6—dc23
LC record available at https://lccn.loc.gov/2017014900

First Edition: August 2017

Printed in the United States of America
1   3   5   7   9   10   8   6   4   2

Cover illustration: fireworks above houses © Lee Hodges / Getty Images
Cover design by Sarah Oberrender
Book design by Laura K. Corless

For my grandmother Jonnie, who taught me that every meal is an opportunity to demonstrate love and care, that every dish is a creative expression, that the making of a meal is a passionate artistic endeavor. She taught me to own my culinary mistakes as much as I celebrate my successes and, as we discovered together, that the lemon cake is just as delicious even if it has completely fallen apart under its own weight. Everything I cook is seasoned with her love, and I will be ever mindful of all the lessons she had to teach me.

She is both deeply missed and deeply present every day.

In loving memory.

# Acknowledgments

As ever, I am awfully lucky to have my family to support me. First and foremost, to my husband, Bill, who is my muse and my cheerleader and my most favorite person, thank you for putting up with my crazy. To my parents, Stephen and Elizabeth Ballis; my sister and brother, Deborah and Andy Hirt; my in-loves, Jim and Shirley Thurmond and Jamie and Steve Surratt—having you all in my corner means the world to me. I am blessed with the best nieces and nephews, so thank you to Rebecca, John, Elizabeth, Oliver, Kalie, and Quincy for letting me be a part of your lives. To my ever-amazing goddaughter Charlotte "7" Boultinghouse, I love you more than anything, but please stop getting taller.

This book is a celebration of friendship, and I am more deeply blessed in that arena than most. You are all too numerous to mention here, but you know who you are. Especially my friends from grammar school and high school and college—it is beyond wonderful to have you all still in my life. A special shout-out to the Party Crew, reconvened, expanded, missing one piece of our hearts; it is a blessing to know you all, and I really look forward to seeing what the second thirty years of friendship will bring us. Dave Ray, we're trying to make you proud.

For the Sisterhood of La Pitchoune—Shannon Kinsella, JeanMarie Brownson, Bethanne Patrick, Betsy Andrews, and my roomie Catie Baumer-Schwalb—thank you for being. We are all always dancing with Julia and stronger together.

For my Lunch Bunch, Jen Lancaster, Gina Barge, and Tracey Stone.

For all my Goulds, near and far.

For my extraordinary agent, Scott Mendel. This is our tenth book and almost fifteen-year anniversary of working together, so I think I can finally say that we are officially old friends as well. Thank you for everything, always.

For my team at Berkley, especially my editor, Danielle Perez. All is deeply appreciated.

In the weird world of writing, especially writing about food, I rely on my compatriots for advice, inspiration, wisdom, recipes, and more than a few cocktails. Thank you to Kat Kinsman, John Kessler, Jennifer V. Cole, Jane Green, Elinor Lipman, Amy Hatvany, Sarah Pekkanen, Renée Rosen, Liz Brack, and Ted Goeglein. Thank you for getting it and for being there for me.

And, lastly, to my readers. You cannot imagine what it means to put these stories into the world like helpless children and know that there are strangers who will take them in and nourish them and keep them safe. Thank you from the bottom of my heart. I'll keep trying to do you proud.

# How to
# Change a Life

When the bell rings, we all shuffle inside the large corner classroom on the first floor in the old building of Lincoln Park High School. Twenty-six spotty, nervous, and hormonal freshmen, with quickly fading memories of being the older cool kids just three months ago at our various elementary schools, thrust into the lowest level of the social totem pole. Funny what a difference a summer makes. Some of us have grown new boobs, gained an inch or two; voices have deepened; skin has erupted in angry red pimples. Braces have been removed, revealing straighter smiles, or added, with annoying and embarrassing accessories like rubber bands that fly into the world of their own accord at inopportune moments, or headgear that makes us look like we're eating television components. We've gained weight or lost it. Gotten chic haircuts or mortifying ones. Some are hoping for a clean-slate do-over, losing the hurtful nicknames and bad reputations that followed us through the previous nine years, and wanting to remake ourselves in a new image. Preferably a cool, popular image. Some are relying on a previous ranking as A-listers to carry us through into an equally popular crowd. Many of us, on this first day, have already suffered the usual brands of freshman hazing: we've had various nonlethal items chucked in our general direction, like pennies, eggs, water balloons; we've been given directions to the nonexistent "fourth floor" or suggestions to use the equally absent "elevator." The pretty girls have already been hit on; the not-so-pretty ones have already been ignored, if lucky, or laughed at, if less lucky.

In Chicago, at a high-ranking magnet school like Lincoln Park, while there are some neighborhood-based feeder schools, a great majority of the students are in special programs that they had to test into. So the school literally draws from the entire city. There is a freedom in knowing that the entirety of your eighth grade colleagues are not in attendance, having scattered to the winds, enrolling in other equally good magnet schools as well as various religious schools and private institutions. It's only first period, but so far I've recognized just one kid from my graduating class, Benji Colson, and he and I, while not friends, were both solidly B-list at Oscar Mayer, and weren't enemies. Benji appears to have grown about three inches over the summer, which is good for him, because he was still just a hair shy of little person height when we graduated, looking much more like a fourth grader than an eighth grader.

I wish I could have gifted him some of mine.

As of my official prefreshman physical exam, I am five-nine-and-three-quarters, and I'm pretty sure there is more growth on the way. My doctor said jovially that all the supermodels are tall. Which was sweet and annoying. Because what was left unsaid is that supermodels are also thin and beautiful, which I decidedly am not. I'm not fat and ugly either, thank goodness. My weight is what one might call proportional. I'm well muscled, with boobs that I pray stop growing very soon, since I totally bypassed training bras for a B-cup when I was twelve, and my current D-cup is already more than plenty. I have hips that are beginning to widen, thick muscular thighs, broad shoulders. Nothing jiggles on me—well, boobs notwithstanding. I've always been athletic, so while I think of myself as something of a gargantuan freak, at least for the moment my delight in all things delicious is fully balanced by my high activity level.

I've been blessed with clear skin, if a shade more olive than I would have liked, pale porcelain skin being all the fashion at the moment; blue eyes of no particular luminance; and dark brown, nearly black, hair that is very thick and straight, but thankfully naturally shiny. I keep it long so that I can pull it into a ponytail or braid when I run. I'm also sporting some godawful bangs, which I thought might make me look cooler but instead are just an enormous pain in the ass. I immediately regretted them, and began growing them out the moment I left the salon five weeks ago, so now they are in the "constantly in my eyes" length. I do a lot of blowing them up out of my way with a quick and noisy blast of focused breath, which is apparently driving my mother batshit. I suppose if I were five or six inches shorter, I'd probably qualify as "cute-ish," but at my size, towering over most of the boys my age on the planet, let alone my school, I'm just lucky that my face is what my dad always calls striking, and my mom refers to as attractive. Neither of these is the same as beautiful, and I've always been grateful for them treating me like an intelligent being and not overpraising my looks the way some parents do. I know people think they are giving us self-esteem boosts, but mostly they are fine-tuning our teenage bullshit radar, and it makes them seem less honest than they probably are.

As we all enter the classroom, heads down, you can feel the nervous energy in our group. This is the first chance to make our first impressions in our first class on the first day of high school. There's a lot riding on it, and none of us look prepared. The woman at the front of the room isn't what I expected. The sign on the door said *Mrs. O'Connor*, and I was imagining a roly-poly woman with pale skin, red apples on her cheeks, gingery hair going gray, maybe one of those Irish crown rings that you are supposed to wear one direction if you are single and another if you are married.

So the very tall, broad-shouldered, elegant African American woman with the short little dreadlocks standing in front of the chalkboard is a definite surprise. As we enter, I notice that the room is ringed with desks, leaving a big open circle in the middle, and none of the desks are labeled.

"Well, hello there," Mrs. O'Connor says to me as I come into the room. She looks me dead in the eye, and might even have an inch on me. "What's your name?"

"Eloise."

"Don't slouch, darling Eloise. You own the space you take up in this world. Abraham Lincoln said, 'You have to do your own growing, no matter how tall your grandfather was.' You stand straight and proud in every inch of your magnificence. Otherwise you let me and all our blessed sisters of substance down." She stretched out her swanlike neck and seemed to get even taller. Then she smiled, even white teeth in her beautiful face. I stood up straight, and she nodded appreciatively. "You're going to love Maya Angelou when we get to her in the spring. She was six feet tall at fifteen, and she's as fierce as they come."

I blush. "She's one of my favorite writers. I read *I Know Why the Caged Bird Sings* last year."

"Well, then, Miss Eloise, let's do her proud this year."

I nod, and cross the room as she directs everyone to stand in the center of the circle of desks.

"So, my new little loves, my name is Mrs. O'Connor and this is Freshman Honors Literature, room 106." Some blond guy in the middle of the room says "Crap" and runs for the door, just as the bell rings. "There's always one," Mrs. O'Connor says with a smile. The rest of us laugh nervously. "So, before we get started, we need to have desk assignments. I know many of my colleagues will be arranging you in the very-convenient-for-taking-attendance alphabetical order, but I think Mr. Lewkey and Ms. Lewis will spend enough time in close proximity to each other this year, so I will do things a little differently. I want you to arrange yourselves in order of birthdate. Month and day only, please. You will now have to introduce yourselves to each other in order to ascertain this information; I strongly recommend that you also exchange names and general friendly words as you go along. Spit, spot, as Mary Poppins might say." She waves her hands with their long tapered fingers at us, looking like a ballerina finishing a pose. If I tried to do that with my mannish hands, I'd probably look like I was swatting at mosquitoes.

I mill around, saying "Eloise, May?" until I hear a voice behind me.

"Hey, May! Over here!" I turn around and see a short curvy girl with a mass of curly brown hair waving me over.

"Hi, I'm Eloise," I say. "May twenty-eighth."

"Oh my God!" she says animatedly. "I'm May twenty-fifth! We're practically twins!"

"Yeah, we look like Arnold Schwarzenegger and Danny DeVito from that movie."

She laughs and snorts. "*Totally.* I'm Teresa Caparulo. Where do you live?"

"Up in Ravenswood Manor. Where do you live?"

"Not far from here, actually, just a few blocks over."

"Lucky you, that's convenient."

"Hey, did you guys say May over here?" The question comes from a gorgeous light-skinned African American girl with almond-shaped hazel eyes and long, wavy, chestnut-colored hair.

"Yeah, totally. Are you May too?" Teresa asks.

"Yep. May twenty-third. You guys?"

"I'm the twenty-fifth and she's the twenty-eighth."

"We're practically triplets," I say, smiling. "I'm Eloise; this is Teresa. She's local; I'm in Ravenswood Manor."

"Lynne," she says, shaking the hands we hold out to her. "Hyde Park."

"You win for longest commute," Teresa says.

"Yeah, well, it was either here or U of C Lab School," she says.

"But that is such a good school," I say, puzzled as to why she would schlep all the way to the north side if she could have gone to one of the best private schools in the city right in her backyard.

"Yep. In part because my dad is assistant principal and teaches English."

"Oh, then, never mind," Teresa says seriously.

"Exactly," Lynne says.

"So how tall *are* you?" Teresa asks me.

"Almost five-ten."

Lynne whistles under her breath. "Damn, girl, you had better stop eating your Wheaties."

This makes me laugh, and then Teresa laughs and the three of us are quietly giggling in the corner of the room.

"You know what this means, our birthdays all the same week?" Teresa asks.

"What?" I say.

She links one plump arm through mine, and the other through Lynne's. "We are going to have to be best friends, the three of us." And the way she says it is so decisive, so matter-of-fact, that Lynne and I find ourselves just nodding along. "Best friends forever," Teresa says, as a proclamation, and so it was.

# One

Okay, Ian, here we go—open your surprise box and tell me what you have." I've got my finger on my phone, the timer set for thirty minutes, ready to go. Ian's little face is so serious. For a ten-year-old he has tremendous focus.

"Let's see," he says, furrowing his dark brows over huge green eyes, his dark curls a little unruly and popping out from underneath his black bandanna. He reaches inside the lidded wooden box that says *Darcy's Treasures* in faded pink lettering on the side, a loving donation to his training from his twelve-year-old sister. "I've got a leftover cooked pork chop from dinner last night, an acorn squash, pistachio nuts, and honey vinegar."

"Okay," I say, practically watching the wheels turning in his little head. "Time starts . . . now!"

Ian gets down to business, steeling his little chef's knife.

"Talk me through it as you go," I say.

"I'm going to do a pork chop and roasted squash quesadilla with pistachio chimichurri and honey vinegar crema."

"That seems smart. Tell me why as you prep."

Ian begins slicing the acorn squash into rings, laying them on a baking sheet and drizzling with olive oil. "Well, the pork chop is already cooked, and quesadillas are a smart use for leftovers because they cook fast so things don't have time to dry out or get tough. The squash has good sweetness, which will go well with the pork, and will also be friends with the honey vinegar."

"Good. Why not just toss the pistachios into the quesadilla?"

He seasons the acorn squash rings expertly with kosher salt, taking a pinch from the bowl and holding his hand at eye level, raining the salt crystals down evenly over the squash, and then pops the tray in the oven. "Because the heat of cooking would make them lose their snap and you need that textural element for contrast with the soft quesadilla."

"Excellent. Tell me about the chimichurri."

He throws the pistachios into a small nonstick sauté pan and starts to toast them. "Well, I'm toasting the nuts to bring out the flavor and intensify the crunch, and I'm going to chop them roughly and mix them with minced green olives, mint, parsley, shallots, olive oil, a touch of the honey vinegar, maybe some red pepper flakes for heat."

I'm so freaking proud of this kid, rattling off chimichurri ingredients like a boss. I know I inherited him with a heck of a palate, but in the last six years, I feel like I've practically raised him from a pup. "I thought you were using the honey vinegar in the crema."

He smiles wryly. "Judges love it when you use ingredients in multiple ways."

I laugh. "Boom."

Ian is training with me for *America's Junior SuperChef*. The wildly popular kids' version of the reality television culinary competition is holding Chicago casting tryouts in five months. Ian tried out last year and made it through the fourth round, getting cut before callbacks. But he's a champ and not a quitter, and they asked him to come back to auditions this year, which makes me think they are setting him up to be this season's comeback kid. I've been the personal chef for his family, the Farbers, since he was four. I spend three days a week with them, prepping breakfasts and school lunches for Ian and his brother and two sisters, filling the fridge and pantry with reasonably healthy, easy-to-grab snacks for the kids and their endless gaggle of friends who always seem to be hanging around the house, and cooking heat-and-eat dinners. One afternoon a week I train Ian after school. As a personal chef I hit the goddamn motherlode.

The Farbers are the kind of rich that would make the Koch brothers say, "Damn, that's a lot of money," and the kind of people who make sure you would never in a million years suspect that they have that kind of wealth. Shelby and Brad were college sweethearts, fell madly in love, and got married right after graduation, before he invented some super-secret something or other related to communications that he sold for a couple of billion before he was thirty. But unlike some of their much less flush contemporaries, they don't broadcast it. Brad runs a tutoring nonprofit that focuses on providing safe and structured after-school programs to underserved neighborhoods. He looks like your basic sweet Jewish dad, a little bit paunchy, a little bit balding, average height and looks. Shelby is tiny, maybe five foot even, and slim, with an appetite like a lumberjack and the metabolism of a hummingbird. I'd hate her if she weren't so damned nice. She keeps her dark hair in a pixie cut, lives in well-worn jeans, Brad's old sweaters, and ratty Converse All-Stars, and is beyond devoted to her family. She treats me like a sister. Their house, while in the tony Lincoln Park neighborhood not far from where I went to high school, is not on one of the main McMansion streets, but tucked away on a small side street on the northern edge of the neighborhood.

The former three-flat that they converted to a single-family home still has all of its turn-of-the-century charm and quirks. They personally drop their kids off at school and take them to soccer games and go to recitals. They have a couple of regular babysitters for when they go out evenings, just local teenagers picking up extra money, and a housekeeper who comes twice a week to keep the mess under control. Brad drives an ancient Wagoneer that he restored himself, and Shelby has an Infinity SUV that is five years old. I'd say ninety percent of their extensive philanthropic generosity is donated either anonymously or in honor of other people.

But most important is that the kids also seem to have no idea that they are the top one percent of the top one percent. They are really well behaved, and not entitled brats in the least. Sixteen-year-old Robbie is a junior at Northside College Prep, excelling in his classes, and just got moved up to co-captain on the lacrosse team. Darcy is a twelve-year-old eighth grader, in her last year at Catherine Cook elementary school with Ian, who is in fifth grade, and little four-year-old Geneva, who is in junior kindergarten. Darcy is the musician of the family, playing trumpet in the concert band and electric bass with her School of Rock after-school program. Geneva is the dramatic one, and we all joke that she is destined for the stage or screen. She's a lovable terror, like a tiny little Amy Schumer, who remembers fondly every vulgar or scatological thing that was ever accidentally uttered in her presence. Full of sass and attitude, with a raspy little whiskey-soaked voice like she's been smoking two packs a day since birth. They are as close to having kids as I am probably ever going to get, considering both my ever-advancing age and my permanent state of single. With the added benefit of not having to put any of them through college.

I watch as Ian pulls the cooked squash out of the oven and drops it on the part of the cooktop that is currently not in use to let it cool for a moment while he mixes honey vinegar and a touch of brown sugar into thick crème fraîche, tasting along the way with the spoons I keep in a little cup on the stovetop. Satisfied with the crema, he turns back to the food processor, where he has chopped the pistachios, shallots, olives, and herbs, and empties out the contents into a bowl, adding a splash of the honey vinegar, a pinch of red pepper flakes, and a healthy glug of olive oil. He tastes, adds salt and a good grinding of black pepper, tastes again, and nods, pleased with himself.

"Ten minutes to go," I say, checking my phone. "Keep talking me through things."

Ian reaches for a large flour tortilla and places it in a dry nonstick skillet. "I'm going to assemble the quesadilla now," he says, sprinkling shredded fontina cheese over the whole surface of the tortilla. He dots the shredded cheese with small bits of fresh goat cheese. "I'm using fontina because it melts well and is mild, and some chèvre for a bit of punch and creaminess. Now the pork." He has sliced the pork thin, and layers it over the cheeses, following with cubes of the roasted squash. He takes a second tortilla and places it over the whole thing, pressing down so that the cheese, which is already getting melty, will help stick the two halves together. He covers the pan with a lid, then turns to get three plates out of the cabinet. He places a spoonful of the crema on each plate and gives it a very professional smear with the back of the spoon.

"Five minutes," I say.

He turns back to the stove, removes the lid, and deftly flips the quesadilla over, revealing the well-browned and crispy underside. He presses again with the spatula, hearing the sizzle as a little bit of cheese leaks out the side. He pulls one end of the quesadilla up to check that it is browned underneath and slides it out onto the cutting board.

"I think I'm going to let it rest for a minute," Ian says.

"Why?"

"So all the cheese doesn't ooze out. Like resting a piece of meat so you don't lose the juices?"

"I think that is a good idea, and you still have two minutes to go."

"Is it time *yet*?" Geneva says loudly, walking into the kitchen and clambering up into my lap on the bar stool where I'm perched.

"Almost. Give him one more minute," I say, kissing the top of her curly head.

Ian cuts the quesadilla into six wedges, stacking two attractively on each plate. Then with a saucing spoon, he adds some of his chimichurri over the center of the wedges. He takes the towel that is tucked into the belt of his apron and gently wipes a couple of stray drops of oil from the side of one plate.

"And *time*," I say. "Hands up."

Ian raises his hands, grinning like mad.

"*Now* we can eat eat eat!!!" Geneva claps excitedly, bouncing in my lap.

"We need one more judge, Gen—"

"DAAAARRRRCCCCYYYY!!!" Geneva yells at the top of her lungs. Jesus, this kid has pipes. I think my ears are bleeding.

"Darcy's at her trumpet lesson," Shelby says, coming into the kitchen and kissing Geneva's cheek. "But something smells amazing in here. Can I be a judge?"

"Absolutely!" Ian says, coming around the island to serve us our plates. Shelby kisses him as well, reaches up to squeeze my shoulder and wink at me, and perches herself next to me on a bar stool. Geneva immediately clambers over to her mom, who receives her with a loud "oof." I miss the warm weight of her in my lap; she's a cuddly kid, and I'm her godmother, an honor I was beyond touched to take on when Shelby and Brad asked me. I'm close to all the kids, but Geneva is the only one I've known since birth, so I have to admit she's got an extra-special place in my heart. But this family? Any one of them has first dibs on my kidneys if they need them.

"Chef, can you tell us what we are tasting today?" I ask in my serious Ted Allen impersonation.

"Yes, Chef. Today I have prepared for you a pork and roasted acorn squash quesadilla with fontina and chèvre, served with a pistachio chimichurri and a honey vinegar crema. Please enjoy."

I take my fork and knife and cut off a tip of the quesadilla, dragging it through the crema, and using my knife to make sure I get some chimichurri on the bite as well. I close my eyes and taste. The tortilla is crisp; the pork surprisingly juicy, despite being a lean cut that was reheated; the acorn squash sweet. The fontina was a good choice. It's super gooey but has a mild flavor that lets the pork and squash shine. The slightly sweet-and-sour crema works well, as does the bright herbal crunch of the chimichurri. Frankly, if I'd been served this dish in a restaurant, I'd have been pleased.

"Wow, Ian, it's good!" Geneva says, now sporting a crema mustache, a huge wedge of quesadilla in her hands dripping cheese and chimichurri into her lap. She starts to wiggle and sing. "His name is I-an, he cooks so goo-oo-ood, and he's my bro-ther, so I get to eat every-thing . . ."

"It's delicious, sweetheart. You're going to have to make more for Daddy later—he would love it!" Shelby says, using her napkin to absentmindedly try to mop up Geneva, who is devouring the snack with continued abandon, humming her little song as she goes, dripping crema on her shirt, her chin slicked with chimichurri. Then, with a sudden crescendo, she drops the rest of her piece on the plate, slides off her mother's lap, and begins a series of pirouettes around the kitchen.

"Ian, give me your assessment," I say, pushing my plate in his direction.

He tastes a couple of bites and then looks at me. "It mostly works well."

"Anything you would change if you did it again?"

Ian chews his lower lip thoughtfully. "I think next time I would leave out the goat cheese?" He seems to be asking me instead of telling me.

"Why?"

"Um, too much stuff?"

"That's an interesting way of thinking about it. What makes a dish have a taste of having too much stuff?"

"If it all isn't in balance." This one he knows.

"So take me through your components, and tell me where the balance would be off."

"Tortilla, crispy. Pork, savory. Squash, sweet. Fontina, gooey and salty. Chimichurri, peppery and green and bright, with some acid. Crema, tart and creamy and cool. And goat cheese . . ." He trails off.

"What does the goat cheese bring to the party?"

"Well, it's creamy, but the crema gives enough creaminess. So the goat cheese fights with it a little bit, overwhelms it, sort of makes the flavor . . . blurry?"

He's such a badass. "That's a good word for it, Ian. Anything else?"

He takes another bite. "I'd probably do the crema like the chimichurri, just a last-minute drizzle on top instead of underneath with the schmear . . . it's making the underside of the tortilla lose its crisp."

"That's a good catch. What is our rule about presentation?"

He grins and recites it like a catechism. "Presentation is important, but our mouth better be the happy one in the end. It needs to taste even better than it looks."

"Perfect. But, Ian? This is all just nitpicky. This is a spectacular dish, and you should be very proud."

"Okay, what'd the squirt whip up now?" Robbie says, coming into the kitchen and dropping his backpack on the floor. He leans down to kiss Shelby on the cheek, while snagging a wedge of quesadilla off the plate. "Hey, El," he says around a huge mouthful.

"Hello, Rob. How was today?"

"Good," he says, chewing. "Hey, Ian, dude, this is pretty killer. Good job." He reaches over for a brotherly high five. Ian beams. Shelby and Brad got super lucky with the kids spaced as they are. The two boys and two girls are both far enough apart in age that there is very little rivalry, and both of the older kids are very protective of the younger ones. There is certainly a normal amount of sibling squabbling, but in general they get along pretty well and are hugely supportive of each other. They all have different interests, so there is no competitiveness.

Shelby hands Robbie a napkin as he reaches for the remainder of the piece Geneva has abandoned.

"Hey! You! I'm *eating* that!" Geneva stands at Robbie's side like a tiny little dictator, hands on hips, glowering. Robbie reaches down and sweeps his little sister up into his arms and over his shoulder like a sack of potatoes.

"Is that *right*, little Miss Bossypants? Looked to me like you were giving a dance recital to the kitchen chairs, and not eating Ian's delicious snack." He starts to spin her around a bit, and she squeals in delight.

"I'm telling you right now, Robert, if she pukes down your back you will get no sympathy or help from me," Shelby says, smiling at her brood and winking at me.

"I'm not gonna puke, Mom!" Geneva says loudly. "Wait, maybe I am . . ."

Robbie stops spinning at once and puts Geneva down quickly.

"Ha! Gotcha!" she says, grabbing the rest of her snack out of Robbie's hand and returning to the other side of the kitchen, dancing and singing and being generally hilarious. At least to me. I think deep down Geneva is one of those kids who is a hoot when she doesn't belong to you and you get her in small-ish doses. I would imagine that living with her energy full-time would be exhausting and maybe even eventually annoying.

"Eloise, what do you think? Do we have the next Junior SuperChef here?" Shelby asks me, as Ian begins to clean up. It's part of our rule. When I cook for the family, I clean up. But when we train, he is in charge of keeping his stuff clean and keeping his equipment in good shape. I taught him how to sharpen his knives by hand, how to clean the cast-iron skillet with salt and oil it before putting it away. He takes it all very seriously, which impresses me almost more than his natural cooking talent.

"Forget Junior SuperChef, your house might get a Michelin star before his voice changes."

"I don't know what you mean," Ian says in a voice an octave lower than his usual tone. Which makes Geneva lower her already basso profundo into an even lower register, making her sound scarily like the little girl in *The Exorcist*.

"Ian will get *three* Michelin stars before he has any hair in his pants . . ."

"Geneva!" Shelby says, trying not to laugh. "That is *not appropriate.*"

"Sorry, Mom. Robbie said it the other night. I don't know why Ian is going to get hair in his pants, but it sounds gross." Geneva rolls her eyes at Shelby and dances off.

"Robert Farber."

"Not my fault. She's always eavesdropping. I did not say it in front of her on purpose. She's only gonna get worse, mark my words . . ."

"That is not the point, young man." Shelby is barely containing her smile.

Robbie shrugs. "I'm going to do homework. What's for dinner?"

"Thursday night is pasta night," I say. "I left you guys a lasagna Bolognese, garlic knots, and roasted broccolini. Ian is going to make the Caesar salad table side." Thursday is the day I come in only to train Ian, so on Wednesdays I always leave something for an easy pasta night. Either a baked dish, or a sauce and parboiled pasta for easy finishing, some prepped salad stuff, and a simple dessert.

"Awesome. Does the lasagna have the chunks of sausage in it?"

I narrow my eyes at him. "Robert Adam Farber, would I leave you a lasagna *without* chunks of sausage in it?" I say with fake insult in my voice.

"No, El, you totally have my back on all things meat. What's for dessert?"

"Lemon olive oil cake with homemade vanilla bean gelato."

"Epic. Thanks, El, see you tomorrow. Good job, broseph." And he grabs his backpack and heads up the back stairs to his bedroom.

"Eloise, you've had a long afternoon, I'm sure, and Ian has the kitchen in hand. Why don't you take off?" Shelby says. "Tell me you have fun plans tonight—let me live vicariously . . ."

"Oh, I have a big night planned. First I'm going to stop by my mom's and have a quick cocktail hour with her and Aunt Claire, and then I have Marcy stopping by for a bit, and finally some quality time later with Netflix and a cuddly corgi."

Shelby sighs. "Simca might be the cutest dog on the planet, but she is no substitute for a person . . ." Shelby would love for me to be dating. Any time she meets a single man over six feet tall she tries to fix me up.

"Don't ever tell Simca she's not a person—she'll never forgive you!" I say in mock horror.

Shelby doesn't seem to get that, for me, alone does not mean lonely, and I'm really genuinely looking forward to the evening ahead. "But since all is good here, I do think I will head out, try and get my visit in before Mom and Claire are schickered." My mom and Aunt Claire have been best friends since kindergarten, so Claire never got the least bit prickly when Mom started dating Claire's older brother Louis when they were in high school. Or when she married him six years later.

Claire's husband, Buddy, died in a horrible car accident several years ago, followed by my dad barely a year later from a fast-moving, devastating pancreatic cancer. So Claire sold her house in the burbs and bought the house next to the house I grew up in, and they settled into their combined widowhood together. They pulled down the fence between their respective backyards to have one large backyard where they can garden and putter and entertain together. They are both a bit hippy dippy, occasional pot smokers thanks to Claire's convenient glaucoma diagnosis and Illinois' burgeoning medical marijuana industry, and they both love comfort food (and junk food, when they have the munchies). I've occasionally wondered whether there might not be something of an untapped lesbian thing happening there, but one night when they were stoned I got up the courage to ask them, and the two of them laughed so hard that Claire literally peed her pants a little bit.

"Sweetie, trust me, if your mom and I were thusways inclined, I'd just have moved in with her, and not gone through the hassle of buying that silly, expensive money pit of an old house next door with all the maintenance problems," she said. Claire's turn-of-the-century brick house is in need of constant repairs and upkeep, as all old houses are.

"All right, all right." Shelby throws her hands up in mock surrender. "Have a good night, Eloise. We'll see you tomorrow."

"I'm stopping for supplies on my way in. Any special requests for the weekend?"

"You know us, we love everything you do. But make sure we are good on kid snacks. I think both Robbie and Darcy have friends sleeping over this weekend. Lean heavy on salty stuff and not too much sugar—we want them to sleep eventually . . ."

"Will do. See you tomorrow. Great job today, Ian, you're really rocking it out. Next week we'll do a baking challenge."

"Thanks, Chef!" Ian always calls me Chef on the days we train, practicing for when he will hopefully need to respond to the judges respectfully. The rest of the week I'm just Eloise.

I grab my jacket off my hook in the mudroom and sling my bag over my shoulder. I peek back and see Ian scraping down the wood cutting board, to prep it for a beeswax and mineral oil treatment. Geneva is pulling Shelby down the hallway toward some adventure in the front room, yammering about something animatedly. As much as I love my little house and my little dog and my little life, for some reason I'm always the teensiest bit reluctant to leave the warm and loving chaos here.

I head out into the gangway and up the side of the long house toward the front. Just as I get to the sidewalk, I see Darcy coming up the street.

"Hey, Eloise! How did Ian do today?" she asks, breathless after jogging the last half block to come see me.

"He did great, Darce, just great. There might still be one

small bit of his masterpiece left in there if you hurry. How was your lesson?"

"It was cool. I finally hit a C above the scale!" she says, waving her trumpet case at me.

"Wow, you've been working at that for a while. Good for you!"

"Yeah," she says, brushing the fine hair that has escaped from her ponytail off her forehead, revealing her gray eyes with their long dark lashes. She's at that gangly stage between kid and teenager, all long legs and knobby knees. "I just really went for it and it was there, right up there!"

"So cool. When is the first band concert?" I try to come to the occasional after-school event for the kids, a recital, a game, a decent role in a play . . . not enough to be the creepy wannabe extra mom or anything, just about once a year per kid, enough so they know I care.

"Oh, Eloise, don't come to the first one, come to the one at the end of the year. By then my teacher thinks I might get a solo!"

"You let me know. I'll come when you want me there."

"Cool. And, Eloise?"

"Yes?"

"My friend Brooke is coming to sleep over this weekend."

"Is she the peanut allergy or the vegan?"

"She's gluten free." Darcy rolls her eyes. "I know, gross. But she's the real kind, the get-sick celery-something kind, not the fake 'I think gluten makes me fat' diet kind."

"Celiac."

"Yeah, that. Can you . . . ?"

"I'll prep everything separately and label it for you guys, and pick up some packaged stuff as well just in case."

"You're the best. See you tomorrow!" And she jumps up the front steps two at a time, her long legs accentuated by the hot pink leggings she is wearing under her black plaid skirt, with her new floral Doc Martens boots. For all the trumpeting and concert band, she wants to present herself as a rocker chick, and having seen her perform with her School of Rock band over the summer, my money's on rock and roll. I gave her the new Sleater-Kinney album for her last birthday, and now whenever I'm working, she steals my phone to scroll through my iTunes to see what other secret musical treasures I have. She hasn't found the Ani DiFranco yet, but it's coming.

I unlock my Acura MDX and slide in. The Farbers gave it to me a couple of years ago when my old Honda Accord finally gave up the ghost. Brad said it was important for me to have a vehicle for getting to and from work and schlepping all the groceries. I tried to tell them that they already overpaid me, and that I was fully capable of buying my own car, but Shelby shut me down. "This is Brad you're talking about. If you tell him you can't accept the Acura, tomorrow he'll buy you a Bentley just to spite you."

"Brad, I cannot possibly accept the Acura . . ." I said jokingly, and Shelby swatted me on the arm, and then hugged me.

"Eloise, you're family. Besides, when Robbie gets his license he'll need a car, so then we can trade you up and give him this one with some mileage on it, and it will be big enough for him to take over the morning drop-off for his siblings."

I tried to say that in that case, she should take the new Acura and give me her old car, but she said with all the kids she hauled around, the endless snack crumbs and Gatorade spills and occasional unexpected vomiting, she had no intention of having a new car until Geneva left for college. I never could argue with Shelby and Brad, especially over their generosity with me. They have taken me with them on vacations and gifted me fully paid-for vacations for me to take on my own. They pay full benefits, with killer private health insurance, and insist on getting billed for all uncovered out-of-pocket. My salary is double what a live-in full-time private chef would usually command, and I work only three and a half days a week. My last Hanukkah bonus paid for me to fully remodel my master bathroom. And last year, they brought in a kitchen designer and let me work with her to do a full remodel of the kitchen, no budget, top-of-the-line everything, and I was like a kid in a candy store. A German candy store. Every Gaggenau appliance imaginable, Poggenpohl cabinetry, twin Miele dishwashers with the really cool flatware rack on top . . . those Germans are amazing with precision appliances.

Aunt Claire once asked if my work was satisfying. After all, I only have the Farbers and one other client, Lawrence Costas, the famous interior designer, now retired, for whom I cook one day a week and one dinner party every few weeks. Lawrence predates the Farbers—he was my first private client, and so he is grandfathered in for life.

"Why wouldn't it be? I have clients that feel like family, I make far more money than I've got a right to, considering the workload, and I have amazing benefits. What could be bad?"

"I suppose I meant if you are satisfied creatively."

I'd never really thought about that. The Farbers give me free rein, but they have a repertoire of my dishes that they love and want to have regularly in the rotation, and everything has to be kid friendly; even if we are talking about kids with precocious tastes, they are still kids. Lawrence is easy: breakfasts, lunches, and healthy snacks for his days; he eats most dinners out with friends, or stays home with red wine and popcorn, swearing that Olivia Pope stole the idea from him. And I'm also in charge of home-cooked meals for Philippe and Liagre, his corgis, who like ground chicken and rice with carrots, and home-baked peanut butter dog biscuits. Simca was a gift from him, four years ago. She was a post-Christmas rescue puppy, one of those gifts that a family was unprepared for, who got left at a local shelter where Lawrence volunteers. He couldn't resist her, but knew that Philippe and Liagre barely tolerate each other, and he couldn't imagine bringing a female of any species into their manly abode. Luckiest thing that ever happened to me, frankly. She's the best pup ever. I named her Simca because it was Julia Child's nickname for her coauthor Simone Beck. She is, as the other Eloise, my own namesake, would say, my mostly companion. Lawrence's dinner parties are fun to do—he always has a cool group of interesting people, occasionally famous ones—but he is pretty old-school, so there isn't a ton of creativity in those menus, lots of chateaubriand and poached salmon with the usual canapés and accompaniments.

The most creative I get is alone at home, in my kitchen, developing new recipes. I've got dozens in my computer that are what I would consider finished, probably a couple hundred more in my notebooks in various stages of planning and testing. No one knows about them. They are just for me. Although I don't know what I'll ever do with them. I know I don't want the stress of a restaurant or catering business, and I wouldn't ever leave the Farbers or Lawrence. Adding another client would be technically doable, but since I don't need the income, I don't see a point in looking for one. I told Claire I was content.

"Content ain't the same as happy, muffin. I'm just saying."

Which may be true. But it isn't the same as unhappy either.

# Two

Claire's in the sunroom. I'll be down in a minute!" my mom calls down the stairs when I let myself in.

I hang my coat up on the coat tree in the foyer and drop my bag. The house has barely changed my entire life, with Mission-style furniture, tribal rugs, and eclectic art on view everywhere. I head through the kitchen, the site of my first culinary triumphs and disasters, with the old cabinets that slam and drawers that stick. The terra-cotta tile floor is hopelessly stained from years of spilled oil and wine; the butcher-block countertops are pocked with burn marks and water rings and nicks and scratches. Through the backside of the kitchen is the small den that used to be my dad's hangout, with French doors out to the back deck. Last year, when the old deck turned out to be rotted beyond repair, my mother replaced it with an en-

closed three-season room and turned Dad's den into a small
studio for her watercolors. The French doors are open, and I
walk through to the cozy sunroom, where Aunt Claire is sipping her signature margarita.

"Beanpole! Come kiss me. The heart would rise but the
knees have other ideas." She puts down her drink and opens
her arms to me. I lean over and kiss her soft cheek, her ash
blond curls piled in their usual messy bun atop her head tick-
ling me. Claire is still a beautiful woman, with fair skin, blue
eyes, and a wide, generous smile. She has sort of a Carly Simon
thing going on, and she is aging just as beautifully. She gestures
to the table where there is a pitcher of drinks and nods for me
to grab one for myself. I'm just taking a cold, refreshing sip of
her famous concoction when my mom flies into the room. Her
small, trim figure is clad in cotton pedal pushers and an old
long-sleeved thermal Blackhawks shirt that belonged to my
dad, her trademark white Keds on her feet, and her graying
auburn hair twisted up into a hair towel, a few damp, curled
tendrils peeking out.

"Hello, dumpling, how are you?" she says, her voice full of
kind concern, reaching up for a hug. My mom was probably
five foot five at her tallest, but I'm pretty sure she has begun
the inevitable shrinking process, so at my five-eleven-and-a-half
she is about eye level with my chest.

"I'm good," I say. "Drink?"

"Absolutely." She plops next to Claire on the deep love
seat, leaving me the cushy club chair facing them. I hand her a
glass, top off the one Claire is waving at me, and sink down myself,
grabbing a pretzel stick out of the bowl on the coffee table.

"So, did you hear the news?" my mom asks with her brows
furrowed in a way that lets me know the news isn't good. These

days, between Mom and Claire and their group of contemporaries, I now refer to catching up with them as the "death and
dying update."

"Probably not. I was training Ian all afternoon, and wasn't
listening to the radio on the way over. What happened?"

"Oh, honey. Mrs. O'Connor passed away."

The piece of pretzel turns to lead on my tongue, and I take
a deep swig of margarita to dislodge it.

"Sorry, kiddo, I know she meant a lot to you," Claire says
sympathetically.

"I saved you the obit." My mom reaches into her pocket and
hands me a slip of newspaper.

The photo shows the elegant woman I remember; the only
difference is that her locs are longer and grayer. But the slim
neck, the regal bearing, the beautiful smile, all still there. I
read the brief paragraph.

Helene O'Connor, née Weber, passed away peacefully in
her sleep after a long and heroic battle with breast cancer.
She was 73 years old. A retired English teacher who spent
the bulk of her career at Lincoln Park High School, she also
volunteered for literacy programs with the Chicago Juvenile
Detention system and was a board member at Rivendell
Theatre Company. She is survived by her husband, Glenn
O'Connor, two brothers, Morris and Joseph, and a sister,
Athena. Viewing will take place Wednesday and Thursday,
September 21 and 22, from 2:00 to 8:00 p.m. at Leak and
Sons Funeral Home, 7838 South Cottage Grove. Funeral
services and internment will be private, for the immediate
family only. In lieu of flowers the family requests donations
be sent to Sisters Network (sistersnetworkinc.org), Rivendell

Theatre (rivendelltheatre.org), or Trinity United Church of Christ Social Justice Team (trinitychicago.org).

My heart hurts. Mom reaches over and squeezes my hand, and Aunt Claire refills my glass. There is tightness in my throat, but no tears are coming. I'm sad, but mostly ashamed. It's been over three years since the last time I saw her.

"She was so lovely when your dad passed," my mom says, not letting go of my hand. "What a classy lady."

And she was. Coming to the shiva all three nights, each night bearing a different delicious offering: baked macaroni and cheese and a pot of slow-simmered greens, a huge casserole of chicken and rice, a massive three-layer chocolate cake. Soul food, to be sure.

She came to the funeral with her husband, a sweet man straight out of central casting for South Side Irish Chicago. She towered over him by at least three inches, and he was as barrel-chested and thick as she was lithe. His hair was a salt-and-pepper Brillo pad and his eyes a piercing blue, and he stayed at her side with the bearing of a man who was born a farmer and chosen consort to a queen. He looked at her with powerful love and a clear sense of his own good fortune.

She held me in a tight embrace, stroking my hair as I wept for at least five minutes, never letting go, never stopping the humming murmur in my ear telling me that my dad was out of pain and in his glory surrounded by the ancestors and friends who had been waiting to receive him. I have never been a religious person—my faith is in science and butter and people who have earned my trust—but Mrs. O'Connor was a woman of deep conviction and when she said it, I suddenly had a wave of profound peace wash over me and I knew that my dad was okay, and that we would be okay too.

But more importantly? Two weeks after he was gone, she stopped by on a random Wednesday evening with a pot of beef stew, a bowl of liberally buttered egg noodles, a pan of lemon bars dusted in thick powdered sugar, and two bottles of zinfandel. The three of us ate and drank and caught up, and never once talked about my dad or the loss. She just came and fed us and was good company. I went to the kitchen after dinner to make coffee, and when I heard murmuring in the dining room, I peeked around the corner. Mrs. O'Connor had both of my mom's little hands clasped in her long ones, and both of them had their heads bowed, foreheads nearly touching. Mrs. O'Connor was saying something I couldn't hear, and my mom had tears running down her cheeks. I let them be; I loaded the dishwasher and cleaned Mrs. O'Connor's serving pieces to ensure that they had ample quiet time together. When she left, she hugged us both very tightly and told us we were warrior goddesses and that she would check on us again soon.

Later, I asked my mom about it and she said that they were praying together, that Mrs. O'Connor had offered prayers for my dad in his peace, and for my mom and me. She said that it was so comforting, not overtly religious as much as it was a prayer to the universe that we all move forward with as much ease as possible. She came by again about a month later with another dinner, and she dropped off a sweet potato pound cake a few weeks after that, and then for rest of the year, she would check in with us every other month or so, to see how we were faring. It always seemed to magically coincide with a difficult time: a holiday, Valentine's Day, one of our birthdays, or Mom and Dad's wedding anniversary. On the first anniversary of his death, my mom and I each got a note in the mail saying that she was thinking of us.

It had meant so much to us both how quietly present she had been, not just in the immediate chaos of loss when all friends and family are on deck, but for that extended time when everyone goes back to their lives and forgets that the ones left behind grieve through that first year in a roller coaster of emotions.

For a while I would check in with Mrs. O'Connor fairly regularly, but when I started with the Farbers, the first year flew by in a whirlwind of figuring everything out and building those new relationships. I remembered to send her a batch of the Brazilian caramel fudge balls I was gifting people that year for the holidays, and I got a lovely note back. That was the last time I saw her or reached out. There is not a decent or justifiable excuse in the world.

The idea that she had been so amazing to us, to me, ever since I was a kid, and I let it just fall through my fingers out of laziness makes me so deeply ashamed. The thought of her suffering, of her poor lovely husband suffering, and that I didn't know and wasn't able to make her soup or send him cookies, or support either of them in any way, the very idea of it makes the tears finally come hot and fast and my mom pulls on my hand and moves me out of the chair and onto the love seat between them, where they can both rub my back and comfort me.

Good God, woman, what happened to your face?" Marcy says as she comes through my front door and thrusts a pastry box at me, leaning down to give Simca a dog biscuit. My little fluff monster takes the treat delicately in her mouth and trots down the hall to eat it in her dog bed in the kitchen, her wide tush swaying side to side with the gait of her stubby little legs. "You're welcome, Simca," Marcy says, and the dog stops in her tracks, turns around briefly, and then heads back up the hall. "Cheeky bitch," Marcy says.

Marcy was my best friend in culinary school. I was top of our class in all the savory courses and she took top honors in all the pastry and bread work. Marcy is also small, not quite tiny, but maybe five-three, and slim as a whip. Considering the amount of baked goods she consumes on a daily basis, she must have a helluva metabolism. She's as fair as I am dark, with strawberry blond hair that she keeps shoulder length, often with streaks of hot pink or teal blue running through it. Pale jade green eyes with nearly invisible blond lashes, and masses of freckles. We love to dress up together for Halloween. One year we were Fiona and Donkey from *Shrek*; the next, Xena and Gabrielle. Last year we went all out and were Brienne of Tarth and Tyrion Lannister. We both hate the whole "sexy/slutty" Halloween costume thing and prefer to make a hilarious tableau. Plus, she, like me, is solidly single and not really looking. So we spend Halloween with Lawrence and his friends, who love a good costume and don't intend to get drunkenly lucky. At least not with us.

Marcy is the pastry sous chef at the Astor Place Hotel, working under the amazing Sophie Langer. She will be the head pastry chef at the new outpost bakery café, Sophie's, that Sophie and the hotel are opening in Logan Square in a few months. It will be part of Little Astor, the small boutique bed-and-breakfast they are creating in a historic six-flat just off the square on Kedzie. So Marcy gets the whole married-to-your-job thing, and while she is four years younger than I am, she is middle-thirties enough to own the part of her that likes being a homebody for the rare hours she isn't working.

Unlike me, she also has a healthy and active sex life, and has confessed that for every third or fourth wedding they cater at the hotel she ends up with a groomsman or single guest. Since my boy options at work include one elderly gay man, one happily married father of four, a sixteen-year-old, and a ten-year-old, I am both a homebody and a celibate one. Marcy disapproves, but accepts this about me and doesn't nudge, unlike my mom and Claire, and Shelby. And Lawrence.

"I've been a little upset," I say, weighing the box, which is labeled with the Astor Place logo and is surprisingly heavy for its size.

Marcy looks puzzled. "Crying upset?"

"Yeah." I hate crying. In no small part because I am an ugly crier. Like, off-her-meds-Claire-Danes-in-*Homeland*-on-steroids ugly crier. My whole face gets red and splotchy, my eyes swell up like a pug with a thyroid condition, and my nose runs with thick trails of snot, and I end up spending the better part of six hours looking like I've been hit in the face with a bouquet of poison oak.

Marcy follows me into the kitchen, where I put the box on the island, and Simca, having finished her treat, comes over to Marcy for petting. "Oh, now you love me, do you?" Marcy says, hoisting my beastie into her arms, getting some delicate face-licking and ear-nibbling love, and perching them both on the love seat bench I have at the counter. Simca finishes her snuggling for the moment and leaves Marcy's lap to curl into a pile of fur on the bench beside her, while I open a bottle of pinot gris. I toss Simca the cork, since she loves to chew them, and she catches it deftly in her mouth, then clasps it between her paws to get some purchase for good gnawing.

"I don't think I've ever seen you cry in all the years I've known you," Marcy says, reaching over to the bowl of giant green Cerignola olives I have put out and popping one whole in her mouth, looking like a chipmunk smuggling an acorn.

"I try to avoid it if possible." I pour us two glasses. We clink and take a sip of the cool, crisp wine.

"I mean, you didn't even cry that time you took the whole underside of your middle finger off with the mandoline and bled all over your mise en place," Marcy says, matter-of-factly.

Ugh, that was an awful wound and a long recovery. I instinctively run my thumb over the slightly shiny underside of the middle finger on my right hand, devoid of all fingerprints and only barely creased at the knuckles. "Nope, and you can see why." I gesture to my face.

"What happened?" she asks, taking a small piece of the Parmesan that I have broken into craggy shards on the small wooden board I've laid out, with a wedge of triple-crème Délice de Bourgogne Brie, some nuts and dried fruits, a homemade quince and plum membrillo paste, and some tiny little German wild boar sausages that I've been hoarding since my trip to Berlin last year.

I take a breath. "My favorite teacher from high school died." I can feel the tears wanting to come back. I don't cry often, but when I do, it's like breaking the seal of something ponderous. The emotions stay right at the surface, threatening to bust through at the slightest provocation.

"Oh, honey, that sucks, I'm so sorry. Had you stayed close?"

I shake my head, knowing if I tell her about how shitty I was to let the relationship die on the vine for no good reason, I'll lose it all over again.

Marcy seems to sense this and shifts tactics. "What made her your favorite?"

I tell her about freshman year, and how she made me feel good about being tall. About how it was her class where I met and bonded with the people who became my most important friends in high school. I tell her about Mrs. O'Connor also being the assistant track coach, where I was a presumptive Olympics-bound shot-putter until I blew out my knee junior year and ended my athletic career. I tell her about how Lynne and Teresa and I were so lucky and got her again for English senior year, and that she was the one who convinced me to go to college even without the athletics, to test the wide world instead of just going straight to culinary school, even though I suspected it was what I would want to do with my life. That she wrote the most amazing letters of recommendation for me with all my college applications, and then again when I applied to culinary school after graduation. I stop there. I can't tell her about what happened after Dad died; it would be too much.

"Wow. Cool lady, sounds like. I'm so sorry for your loss. So did you talk to them? Your friends? Are they in town?" She plucks a sausage from the platter and peels the powdery white skin off before popping it in her mouth.

"I don't know. We haven't seen each other in . . ." I start to do the math. "Seventeen years?" God, that sounds like a long time. Too long to even be possible. But that is about right. Teresa's wedding was New Year's Eve 2000, and that was the last time we were all together. Lynne was on the West Coast full-time by then, and I was in France until my dad got sick in 2009.

"Damn." Marcy spreads a piece of baguette with the gooey Brie and then adds a thin slice of the membrillo and chews it thoughtfully. "Think either one of them will be there? At the visitation?"

I haven't even thought of that. "No idea, frankly. I presume Teresa is still in Chicago. I was at her wedding a zillion years ago, and I'd have to guess that by now she has a houseful of kids. Lynne was living in L.A. then, and seemed really happy, so I doubt she would have come back here. I don't even know if either of them would know that Mrs. O'Connor has passed."

"Someone must have let them know on Facebook."

"Possibly. You know I'm not on it."

Marcy shakes her head. "I know. I just still can't really fathom why."

"You forget I was abroad for nine years. Most of it in a town where we were lucky to get the landline phones to work consistently, let alone Internet. When all this social media hooey really hit huge, I was working my ass off in a flyspeck village in Burgundy." My standard excuses. Why am I so skittish about social media? Because the one time I toyed with the idea of Facebook, the first thing I did was look up Bernard and saw a picture of him with three kids in his lap, all of them the spitting image of him, and my heart shattered into a zillion pieces and I had to call in sick to the Farbers, because I couldn't stop crying for three days and in those days I ate three huge bags of Doritos and a box of Ho Hos and mashed potatoes and an entire gallon of ice cream washed down with a bottle of bourbon.

I left Chicago with the ink barely dry on my BA in English lit from Northwestern, the week after Teresa's enormous wedding, and headed straight to Paris for culinary school, having done a semester abroad there junior year and fallen in love with the city. I did the Grand Diplôme at Le Cordon Bleu, and then staged around France for a year at various Michelin-starred restaurants. Michel Troisgros recommended me to a friend of his who had a small Relais and Chateaux property in a little town in Burgundy, near Beaune, that had a restaurant shooting for its first star, and a sous chef who had announced an imminent departure to open his own place. On Michel's recommendation I was given a one-week tryout at Chez L'Ami Bernard in the Auberge D'Ortolan, and by the end of the third day had been offered the job. And there I stayed until my mom called to tell me Dad was sick.

"Okay, but you've been back for, like, seven years? More? Pretty sure the Wi-Fi works fine here."

"I hate the idea of all that shit. All the time suck, the inane crap that everyone seems to get obsessed with. What am I really missing, Candy Smash?" I have to admit to myself, my lack of computer participation has much more to do with my being something of a technophobe. But it sounds so much better to just be dismissive of the negative aspects of such a plugged-in life, kind of like those people who say they don't have a TV because they love to read. Not nearly as worldly to say you don't have TV because you don't know how to work a remote control and would be too afraid to try to hook up a DVD player.

"Crush. Candy Crush. You're a wonder, my friend, a true wonder." Marcy stayed in Paris after graduation to do extensive continuing pastry courses and then worked at the legendary Patisserie Stohrer before moving to Chicago to work at the Peninsula Hotel, partially because I had always raved about how much I loved the city. While she was still in Paris, I would always go back and stay with her in her little flat in the 9th between stages, and she would always take her holidays to come see me wherever I was. Sometimes we would meet for weekends in other European cities, exploring the markets in Amsterdam or the food halls in London together, sharing pitiful tiny rooms at shitty hotels so that we could afford to eat at the best restaurants. I was sad when she left Paris, but relieved she landed in Chicago, and we were fairly good about staying in touch in the years she was here and I was still there.

"Speaking of wonders, what's in the box?" I say, desperate to change the subject.

"Some testers Sophie and I are working on for the new place. Want your opinion," she says, pulling the box over and slicing the tape open with her thumbnail.

I look inside. There is a large roll, a miniature pie about four inches across with a golden crust that is sprinkled with large crystals of sugar, a stack of cookies, a square of what looks like bread pudding, and a small tub.

"Okay, what am I looking at?" I say.

"This is the rustic roll I was telling you about last week, the one based on the classic Poilâne bread." My favorite bread of all time, with its dark, almost burnt chewy crust and the tangy, fermented chestnut-colored crumb.

"Yum, very excited about that."

"Us too. I think we've finally nailed it. This is what we are thinking for pie service, all individual whole pies instead of slices. This one is classic apple."

"Because you still can't stand it when the servers don't get the pie slices out of the pan perfectly."

"True. The cookies are cornflake snickerdoodle, Black Forest, and ginger lemon cream."

"Cornflake snickerdoodle?"

"Sophie's thing. She wanted a cookie that tasted like the top of a good noodle kugel."

"She's fucking brilliant, that woman."

"I know, right? This is a piece of the palmier bread pudding, and that is the vanilla semolina pudding."

My mouth is watering.

"Is this an official tasting?" I ask. Marcy and I often just cook for each other, and might offer some generic notes and suggestions on things after, if the other asks for feedback. But officially tasting during recipe testing is a whole different beast.

"Yep, if you are up for that."

"Of course. Let's finish our wine and snack and then we can get to work."

I'm relieved, since if we do a tasting officially, we are doing it by essentially competition standards. We take sips of water and nibbles of plain bread to clear our palates between bites, and we make careful notes about every aspect of the item: texture, flavor, balance of elements. Looking for anything that can help take the recipe into the realm of perfection. This means there will hopefully be no more talk about the various important relationships that I have let simply fall like so much sand through my open hands, and I won't have to think about why it never occurred to me to simply close my fingers and try to save at least some of them.

# Three

"El-o-eeeze," Geneva singsongs as she hops into the kitchen. "Why are you so faaannncccyyy?"

I look down at myself. I'm wearing a gray pencil skirt that pulls a little too tight around my midsection, but my black wrap-style sweater covers that part fairly effectively. Black tights, and my tallest pair of shoes, a wedge-style black suede, because Mrs. O'Connor was the first person to make me feel good about owning my height, and I want to be as tall for her as possible. My hair is twisted up into a chignon, slightly more polished than my usual messy bun, and I'm wearing a little bit of makeup. As soon as I finish dinner for the Farbers I am heading straight to the funeral home for the visitation. Mom will meet me there.

"I have to go somewhere after work, peanut," I say to her

as she climbs up onto one of the stools, and I reach over the counter and tweak her nose.

"Where you goin'?"

I think about this. The Farbers are pretty honest with their kids about most stuff, but in the time I've worked for them there has not been a death to deal with, as far as I know, so I err on the side of caution. "I'm going to a kind of a party."

She looks me up and down and makes a face. "You don't look like a party. You should have *pink*!" She throws her arms open wide to indicate exactly how much pink she thinks I should have. Geneva loves pink.

I laugh. "I probably should, kiddo, but I'm afraid all of my pink was in the laundry."

She nods solemnly at me. This is something she understands, because whatever Geneva really desperately wants to wear at any given moment is likely to be in the laundry, much to her consternation. Shelby has often said that she is going to start just buying two of everything for her so that she doesn't have to endure the exasperated lectures from her four-year-old on her substandard laundry habits.

"Geneva," Shelby says, coming into the kitchen. "Leave poor Eloise alone, she needs to finish."

"To go to her paaarrrtttyyy!"

Shelby looks at me with a wink. "Yes, honey, to go to her party. Why don't you pop back downstairs and practice your letters." The hours between when the kids get home from school or their various activities and when dinner is served are generally relegated to homework or reading. Shelby says once they get dinner in them, it is hard for them to focus, so as soon as everyone is home from school they are banished down to the basement rec room, which has one wall set up with a long table that serves as four side-by-side workstations. The older kids help the younger ones, sort of, and Shelby checks in if things get noisy. Geneva doesn't exactly have homework from pre-kindergarten, but Shelby wants her in the habit as much as possible, so she has some worksheets and books down there and G is supposed to keep herself occupied like the rest. She is not so good at that, and most days will eventually find her up in the kitchen yapping at me for at least some part of "homework time." I can't say it disappoints me.

"Okay. 'Bye, Eloise! Have fun at your party!" She skips out of the room, and Shelby takes up residence in the abandoned chair.

"You know you didn't have to be here today," she says, her meaning clear.

When I told her Monday that I would need to leave a little early she tried to get me to just not come in, but I need to be working and keep my mind off of things as much as possible. I'm still feeling enormously sad and guilty and ashamed, and I'm not so good at dealing with deeper feelings. I've spent the last few days working on recipes at home, testing things late into the night, thinking up new challenges for Ian's training, and relying on a nightly small glass of warmed bourbon with a trickle of honey to help ease me into sleep.

Lawrence wasn't home when I went to drop off his weekly rations yesterday, so instead of the two hours of chat I usually get with him, I had eerie and unsettling quiet. It kind of paralyzed me for a moment. I didn't really want to go home and I didn't have any logical errands to do, so I just organized everything in his fridge and freezer, threw out anything that was old enough to be questionable, and made a list of basic pantry items that he was running low on. Once I ran out of busywork at his house, I went home and took Simca on as long a walk as her tiny little stumpy legs would allow, then had a long wallowy afternoon at home. I binge-watched the original British *House of Cards* and ate my way through my fridge, well stocked with the detritus of my recipe testing. Not coming to work today was not an option.

"Oh, no, I definitely did. This is exactly where I needed to be today."

I don't say more and Shelby doesn't push. "Okay, well, then, what do I need to know about dinner? Something smells amazing."

"You've got braised short ribs in the big oven, and that potato, leek, and prune gratin that Brad loves in the warming drawer underneath. There is asparagus prepped in the steamer—Ian can just turn it on and set it for eight minutes." When I helped redesign their kitchen, the Gaggenau rep convinced me to put in two warming drawers, since I'm usually leaving them food that is fully prepared but won't be consumed immediately, and an in-counter steamer, which has been a total game changer when it comes to getting a simple green vegetable on their plates every night, not to mention making the weekly pasta night a cinch.

"The perfect thing for a chilly fall night like tonight."

"That is what I figured. And there is a chocolate ginger sticky toffee pudding on the counter for dessert. The coffee caramel sauce is in the other warming drawer."

"That sounds interesting, a new one?"

One of the recipes I've been working on this week, sort of an update of the English classic. I'm loving how the dark chocolate and sweet heat of the ginger take the cake out of the cloying realm, and the bitterness of the coffee in the caramel sauce sets it all off beautifully. "Something I've been playing with."

Shelby gets a look in her eyes, and I know she is just gearing up to say something. "Look, I know you don't like to talk about your personal life too much, and I completely respect that, but I know that this must be a difficult time, and if you need a break, or someone to talk to, or . . ." She trails off, probably because she can see the look of embarrassment on my face.

"Thanks, Shelby, really, I'm fine." I'm not, and she knows I'm not. But we both silently agree to pretend that I am, because to do anything else would cross a line neither of us wants to cross.

That is one of the things about my job, the danger zone. Because when you feed a person day in and day out for an extended period of time, you get to know them sometimes more intimately than friends or family. You know their deepest wants and desires, the things they crave, what heals them when they are sick, and what soothes them when they are sad, and what makes a celebration a celebration for them. But while you might feel like a weird combination of friend and family, you are neither. Not really. You are, at the core of things, the help.

"Personal chef" has the word "personal" right in there, and it is the personal part that can make things awkward. Shelby might think I need therapy—clearly does think it if she is bringing it up—and probably not only wants to find the therapist but also to pay for it. But this is not a discussion we can appropriately have, and while she is devil-may-care enough about conventions to attempt to open the door, she is smart enough to shut down those impulses when I close it. Which is the hardest thing to do. Because there is a huge part of me that wants to bust out crying, and collapse in her arms the way I've seen her kids do, and let her comfort me. To let her be the sister I never had growing up. But for all of our sakes, one of us has to be strong about keeping some boundaries, and lucky for all of us, I'm really, really good at boundaries. Which, while I know in my heart is good for my work, is starting to feel like it might just be the way I am in my life in general, and I'm not really sure that is a good thing for my life, however much it might suit my livelihood.

I think we are both grateful for the sudden eruption of loud chaos from downstairs, some yelling and a crash, and Geneva's air-siren wail. The kids might be pretty great, but they are still kids and siblings, and when World War Three launches, as it does with all the frequency one might expect of a large family, it is passionate and loud. Shelby shrugs in a resigned fashion, gives my hand a quick squeeze, and winks at me, then heads downstairs to wipe tears, soothe bruised feelings, make people apologize, and supervise the cleanup and reconciliation processes. I take a relieved breath and wipe down the counter so that I can leave before I have to feel one more damn thing today of all days.

check my face in the visor mirror, reapply lipstick, tuck a wayward piece of hair back into place, and take a deep breath. I've been parked in the parking lot for fifteen minutes, waiting to see my mom's car pull in, but then my phone pings with a text from her saying that her meeting is going to run really late, and that she will probably just plan on going to the second visitation tomorrow. Crap. Now I'm on my own.

I get out of the car, straighten my skirt, and brace myself as I head into the funeral home. The reception room is packed, and there is a small side room where I presume the viewing is, for those who want to have a quiet final moment. I can see a small throng near the viewing room where Glenn is standing, surrounded by a bunch of men who all look like him. If they aren't his brothers, then there is a South Side Irish convention happening. I take a deep breath and cross the room to him. When he spots me, not difficult in a room where I tower over all the women and almost all of the men, his face lights up and he holds his arms open. I fall into them and he hugs me tightly.

"Thank you for being here," he says into my hair.

"Oh, Glenn, I'm so sorry, I didn't know . . . and I should have . . . and I . . ."

"Hush, lass. No one knew—she swore us all to secrecy. She had 'too much to do to be ready to go, and didn't want to deal with any nonsense.'" He does a great imitation of her, and hearing a perfect replica of her voice come out of his rugged face makes me giggle. "There you are. Don't you feel bad for one tiny moment. You'll dishonor her memory. She knew you loved her, and she knows it still and that is everything. The rest is just noise."

He reaches up and wipes the tears off my cheeks.

I can't believe he is the one making me feel better at a time like this. "Thank you for that. Is there anything you need? Anything I can do?" He seems so strong, but I know his anguish must be nearly unbearable. It feels lame to ask, but I don't know what else to say.

"Can you make my blockhead brothers and their fussing wives go back to their houses and stop occupying mine?" he asks with a wink. "The boys are decimating my liquor cabinet, my sisters-in-law are uniformly terrible cooks, and their hellion children are destroying all the breakables and leaving sticky handprints everywhere."

"She would have hated that."

"She hates it now, trust me. She always said you all were her kids, the perfect kids, ones that lived in other people's houses and didn't require college funds. I was just always happy to have our own little bubble, the two of us."

"I can't make your brothers sober or their children well behaved, but I could stop by next week with something edible."

He smiles. "That would be good for my soul, sweet girl. You are welcome anytime." He squeezes my hand and we hear something crash and then a deep voice scolding someone in not-so-hushed tones, and Glenn rolls his eyes and leaves my side to see which niece or nephew has done what sort of damage. I make a promise to myself: What Helene did for me, for my mom, I will do for him. I will honor her memory by being there for Glenn, by feeding him and being good company. I'll find out all the important dates, their birthdays and anniversary, and put reminders in my calendar to reach out, and I'll ask about his favorite foods and cook them for him. My heart feels lighter, and the tightness in my throat releases for the first time since I found out she was gone. I turn to go, but then I see them.

Lynne and Teresa.

The two of them are standing near the door, signing the guest book. Lynne looks amazing—the years haven't touched her. Her shorter hair is a new, slightly more golden shade that flatters her caramel skin and hazel eyes, and she is dressed in an impeccable navy suit that shows off her trim physique. Teresa is rounder than she was, wearing a drapey black dress with an equally drapey gray sweater over her curves. Her beautiful face has lost its childlike look and is now unmistakably the face of a woman, and her black curls are accentuated with the beginnings of a white streak over her left eye, right where her mom had one. When Lynne finishes signing the book she looks up, spots me, and raises a perfectly groomed eyebrow and shakes her head. She elbows Teresa, who looks up to see me too, and her mouth turns down and her brow furrows and her chin begins to tremble as I cross the room to them. By the time I reach them, all three of us are crying and we fall into each other's arms, holding tight, and something deep inside me breaks open and I don't know if I am the happiest girl in the world or the saddest, or maybe both, but I know that I feel safe.

A nother round, please," Lynne says to the young woman who stops by our table to check on us. After our emotional meeting at the visitation, Teresa, Lynne, and I headed back north, to the lobby of the Drake Hotel for drinks. In high school we would go once a year for high tea the week of our birthdays. It seemed an easy choice, right off Lake Shore Drive and still a relatively quick trip home for all of us. Teresa now lives in Oak Park and Lynne moved back from California a few months ago and has a condo in the Gold Coast.

"So, our little ghost, where have you been?" Lynne asks me pointedly. We've already caught up on the basics. Teresa is the proud mom of three enormous Italian man-children, sixteen, fourteen, and twelve, each taller and broader than the next, and has been a stay-at-home mom since her first was born, nearly nine months to the day after her wedding night. Lynne is still a PR guru, divorced from a guy she refers to only as Mr. So-Very-Wrong, and was wooed back to Chicago from L.A. late last spring to take over as head of PR for a major Chicago marketing firm.

"Seriously, El, you just completely fell off the face of the earth," Teresa says. I'm feeling slightly defensive. To hear them tell it, they have been friends "on Facebook" and have gotten together just once, for lunch, since Lynne came back. It isn't like they have been hanging out all this time since we were last together.

"I was in France, until my dad got sick in '09, and then I came home and just stayed with him and Mom till the end. Thought about going back, but didn't want my mom to be here alone, and realized I didn't have much to go back to . . ." When I left for Chicago, Bernard made it clear. If I couldn't give him a specific time frame, he could not promise that my job or his bed would be left open for me. "So I got a job, and have just been lying sort of low, working, living quiet."

"But why no word? It makes me feel so bad that your dad was sick and I didn't know, and I didn't know you were back. Why didn't you call or something?" Teresa looks deeply wounded.

I wish I had some good reason to give her, but the truth is all I have, and it sounds so stupid and small when I hear it come out of my mouth.

"I think I felt mostly embarrassed. I mean, I was living so far away, and it wasn't like e-mail and all that was a part of our lives when I left."

"And you always hated all technology," Lynne says pointedly. "I thought those word processor typewriters in school were going to be the end of you."

"Yes, I confess. I actually went to college with my mom's old Selectric and managed to avoid all things computerized until the last possible moment. I had a flip phone until about two years ago when it died and my boss made me get a new iPhone on his family plan. I'm old-school."

"You're a dinosaur," Lynne says, as the waitress brings our second round of French 75s.

"Hey, I didn't exactly see the two of you frantically searching for me either . . . My mom is in the same house with the same phone number I had when we all talked every night. If you had really wanted to contact me, it wouldn't have been hard." Deflection seems the best way to go here.

"She's got us there," Teresa says.

Lynne puts her hand up. "Okay, look, we are grown-ass women. We are all going to name it and claim it. We were lazy bitches and got swept up in our lives and work and time went by and then it seemed too much effort to try and get back in touch. It was never for lack of love, just lack of initiative. Agreed?"

"Agreed," I say, relieved.

"Agreed," Teresa says, grinning.

"But now we are all back together, can we please not let a damn decade and a half disappear on us? Because, as we have been reminded tonight, life is short and fucking precious," Lynne says.

"Girls' night? My house? Next week?" I ask.

Lynne pulls out her enormous iPhone. A few clicks on the screen with her impeccably polished nails, and she nods. "I'm good any night except Wednesday."

Teresa checks her own phone. "I can do Tuesday or Thursday."

"Thursday it is," I say. I'll have time during the day to prepare a bit before Ian's coaching session, and after it I'll get home in plenty of time to pull dinner together. "Let's say seven." I give them my address, ask about any dietary restrictions, and we toast the plan with the tart, fizzy cocktails.

"The Three Witches, together again," Lynne says, using the

nickname we gave ourselves when Mrs. O'Connor cast us as the three witches in *Macbeth* at the end of our first semester with her.

"Never to be parted," Teresa says.

"Watch out, world, the coven is complete," I say, and we toast and laugh and sink back into the deep chairs, and suddenly we are eighteen again, being fancy at a downtown hotel, full of the confidence that comes when you are part of a group, and you love them and trust them and know they have your back and keep your secrets and that as long as you are together, nothing bad can happen.

I get home just before ten and let Simca out in the backyard for her evening toilette. I don't have the energy for a real walk tonight—all these hours in tall heels after a full day of work have my poor feet, used to abuse, screaming in pain. I shimmy out of my skirt, hopelessly creased into a million wrinkles around the top, and then wrestle my ample hips out of the Spanx that were the only reason it even zipped up. I pull on a pair of jersey pajama bottoms and one of my dad's old concert T-shirts that he saved from his years as a rock aficionado, this one from Beatlefest in 1980, signed on the back by Harry Nilsson, who was there to promote an end to handgun violence and signed the shirt for a ten-dollar donation. My dad took the shirt to a local tailor and had the signature embroidered over so that it could be washed but not lost. It's one of my favorites, and I only wear it on special occasions. Tonight, full as it was of emotion and memories and happy and sad, feels like an appropriate night to have Dad and Harry with me.

Simca follows me up the narrow staircase to the big attic.

Bungalows like mine were designed with sort of easily remov-
able roofs, and stairs to the attics instead of ladders. The attics,
which are usually well insulated, have underlayment flooring
instead of bare joists, so that as families grew, the roofs could
be raised up or dormered to create a second floor of living
space. Someday I would love to make a great master suite up
here for myself, but in the meantime, it is terrific storage. I
walk past all my luggage, the tubs of summer clothes, boxes of
notes and books and things from college and culinary school,
and there in the corner is a small Rubbermaid tub labeled
*LPHS*. I grab it and head back downstairs.

Suddenly starving, I root around in the fridge to see what
I have lying about and find the heel of a meat loaf I made a
couple of days ago when Brad mentioned he was craving meat
loaf sandwiches. It had suddenly sounded good to me too, so I
made a small one for myself. In the breadbox, a couple of slices
of the brioche loaf I made last night when I couldn't sleep; a
little smear of spicy Korean gochujang paste on the bread; some
thinly sliced cucumber salad, a little wilted in its rice-wine
brine but still crunchy; and the meat loaf. I take my sandwich,
a canister of potato sticks that I bought in a fit of nostalgia the
other day, and a bottle of Coke, and head for the living room.
I put the plate on the coffee table and the tub between my feet
on the floor, and eat with one hand while I go through the box
of memorabilia. Folders of old papers, report cards, envelopes
of photos . . . I find what I'm looking for in the very bottom, the
yearbook from 1995, our senior year.

*Lions' Pride.*

I eat and flip through the pages. How young we all were.
How dated and embarrassing our hair and clothes. A picture
of me with Mrs. O'Connor, me on crutches from right after my

surgery, my Olympic dreams dashed. Me and Lynne and Teresa sitting on the hill by the little amphitheater in front of the
school, wearing matching Ray-Ban sunglasses. Lynne sported
a "Rachel" haircut and a small plaid miniskirt with a cropped
sweater, over-the-knee socks, and penny loafers. Teresa wore
denim overalls over a thermal long-sleeved shirt, with a boys'
oxford shirt tied around her waist and Doc Martens. Her curls
an enormous mass. I was in black leggings with a huge plaid
flannel shirt and clunky bright blue wingtips with no laces. We
look like extras from the *Clueless* movie set.

As I turn the last page, a piece of paper falls out of the back
of the book. I pick it up.

*Fabulous at Forty*, the header says in my own unmistakable
scrawl. I swallow the last bite of my sandwich and take a long
draw on the icy Coke.

Mrs. O'Connor gave us an assignment right before finals
senior year. Write a list of the things we wanted to accomplish
by the time we were forty. Not a bucket list, not the things we
thought we should experience, but more who we wanted to be,
what we wanted to achieve. When we finished, she had us pick
a partner in class, to trade lists with, and to have the other
person annotate the lists with what they saw us achieving.
Lucky for us there was an odd number of students in the class,
so she let the three of us work on it together.

"Here are the things that I will accomplish before I am
forty," I wrote. "I will be a well-respected chef, with two restaurants in Chicago, one fancy and one a small, casual, diner-
type neighborhood place for comfort food. I will have published
at least one cookbook so that people can make my recipes at
home for their families. I will make sure that all the recipes
really work perfectly like those of my hero, fellow tall cook

Julia Child, but maybe without so many steps. I will have a husband (who is at least 6´3˝) and maybe one kid. I will own a home with a really amazing kitchen, and on my nights off from the restaurants, we will have fabulous dinners with my family and our friends—our house will always be full of happy people eating well and laughing. I will do a lot of charity events, and support causes for underprivileged kids and the hungry." Wow. Don't think I'm going to be called Nostradamus anytime soon. The only thing I've actually done off this list besides being a chef is owning a home with a pretty amazing kitchen. But the rest? Phooey. On the back, I read Lynne's and Teresa's notes.

Lynne says that I will also have a weekend place in Michigan for escaping, that she will be the PR person for all my restaurants and that my fine dining place will have at least one Michelin star and my casual place will become a chain, that my multiple cookbooks will all be bestsellers, that I will have my own foundation for feeding hungry children, and that I will have won many awards both for my work and my philanthropy. Teresa notes that I will have two or three children with my tall, successful husband, and that once a year she and Lynne and their husbands will join us for an exotic couples' vacation without any of our kids. And that once a week we will get together for a girls' brunch or something that fits into my work schedule, and that we will always celebrate our birthdays together.

So typical. Lynne sees tangible markers of success, made possible by her guidance and input. Teresa is all about family and friendship and personal connection. And I have dreams that seem somewhat achievable, but are missing a bit of the oomph that real dreams should incorporate. Why did I need Lynne to predict wild success and fame, even if she was helping make it happen, and I didn't imagine it for myself? I wonder if losing the Olympic dream made me a little gun-shy on the whole big-picture thing. Especially since, if I'm honest, despite my drive to get to the Olympics I never really imagined I would win any medals. I never pictured myself on the Wheaties box. I just wanted to be part of the team and have the experience. I tend to dream on the more realistic side of things.

I pack most everything back into the tub, but leave the yearbook and the list on the table. Who knows, maybe when the girls come over next week it will give us a giggle.

Simca uses her little step stool to come up beside me on the couch, curls her body next to mine, and rests her regal head on my knee. I scratch between her ears.

"Get ready, old girl, you are going to meet my oldest friends next week." And in a weird way, I think, so am I.

# Four

tear in through my front door like a bat out of hell. I'm late and more than a bit frantic. Ian's coaching went totally sideways today, Geneva had some sort of four-year-old meltdown the likes of which I've never before been privy to, and by the time everyone figured out how to calm her down, Ian's beautiful chocolate soufflé had collapsed into a sticky, sweet, rubbery Yorkshire pudding and his caramel had burnt to an acrid layer of superglue in the bottom of the skillet and set off the smoke alarm. Then Ian cried, which he almost never does unless he is in pain, and then Geneva cried again because she made Ian cry, and Darcy stomped around full of preteenage indignation about how the littles just have to come up with some tears to get all the attention.

Shelby and I did not have enough arms or soothing words

to appease them all, and right in the middle Brad came in and, without really jumping in to help, asked if Shelby had picked up ink for the printer, and the two of them got all snippy with each other, which made me very uncomfortable. By the time we got everyone mostly returned to emotional equilibrium, and Brad and Shelby disappeared into his office to talk, I didn't have the heart to let poor Ian clean up the epic mess alone, so I was over an hour late getting out of there.

By the time I got to Whole Foods it was jammed with the after-work crowd, and the ten-items-or-less line was occupied by a woman of supreme entitlement insisting that the ten items meant ten different *types* of things, so that her overflowing cart was fine, because multiples shouldn't count.

I'm sweaty, my pulse is racing, Simca is in need of a pee, I'm in desperate need of a shower, and Lynne and Teresa will be here in less than an hour for our reunion girls' night. I drop the bag of groceries on the counter, turn the oven on to 350 degrees, toss Simca out into the backyard with a promise for a real walk before bed, and take the stairs two at a time to the bedroom, stripping off my clothes as I go. I take the world's fastest shower, throw my dripping hair into a bun, pull on a pair of jeans and a sweater, and run back downstairs.

At least I know better than to plan an after-work dinner that requires last-minute preps. I did almost everything for tonight yesterday, including setting the table, so now that I'm clean, I can take a deep breath. I take the roasting pan of braised chicken thighs with shallots and tomatoes and mushrooms in a white wine Dijon sauce out of the fridge and pop it in the oven to reheat. I dump the celery root potato puree out of its tub and into my slow cooker to gently warm, then grab the asparagus that I steamed yesterday and set it on the counter to take the chill off. I pull the butter lettuce I bought at Whole Foods out and separate the leaves into a bowl, filling it with cold water as I go, and when they are clean, I pop them into my salad spinner and whizz the crap out of them. They go into the big wooden salad bowl I got in Morocco. When dinnertime comes I'll chop the asparagus and add it to the salad along with some tiny baby marinated artichokes, no bigger than olives, and toss with a peppery vinaigrette. The sourdough baguette I picked up goes on the table intact; I love to just let guests tear pieces off at the table. The three cheeses I snagged at the cheese counter get set to the side so that they will be appropriately room temp by the time I serve them after dinner. I might not be French, but all those years there have stuck, and I simply cannot have dinner without some cheese after.

In a way, I'm kind of grateful for the urgency. I don't have to think too much about tonight and the girls, and wonder how things will go. Beyond the quick bullet points of our current status—happily married with kids, happily divorced without, contentedly single and not looking—we didn't do a lot of real sharing last week. I'm not really sure of either of them. I woke in a cold sweat in the middle of the night wondering if the person I have become is remotely as interesting as the teenager I was. When they knew me, I had athletic drive and passion. Even after the injury, I was focused on my recovery and on figuring out what to do with myself, determined not to be one of those sad-sack former high school star athletes who spends all her time bemoaning what might have been and resting on laurels. I finished strong, got into Northwestern, got accepted at the toughest culinary program in the world, and headed off to a glamorous life abroad.

But they don't know about Bernard, or how I let myself sink

into believing that I wasn't destined for a relationship after him, or how I fell into my current career and have been treading water ever since. They don't know how hard it was to help take care of Dad as he fought and lost his battle. How awful to see what it did to my mom. They don't know that outside of Mom and Aunt Claire and my employers, I pretty much have only one real friend, and my social life consists primarily of hanging out at home with my dog. My job is reasonably active, but I haven't done anything remotely athletic since the day my physical therapist pronounced me healed.

Lynne and Teresa are living their dreams. Lynne, as far as I can tell, is insanely successful, and Teresa is raising her family, and I'm . . . what? Cooking. Not famously, not publicly, not in a way that will win any awards. Just cooking. Professionally, personally, this is what I've got. I don't ever really think about it, but tonight, with the two of them rematerializing before me imminently, my life suddenly seems so minute and unimpressive.

I shake my head, push the thoughts out, and focus on setting out the predinner nibbles I picked up when I went to get the lettuce and cheese. Olive-oil-roasted Marcona almonds, crunchy fried Peruvian corn kernels, some fat olives. Teresa said she wanted to bring something for dessert, and Lynne said she would bring wine, so we should be in good shape. I've got a few bottles of sparkling water in the fridge, as well as some carafes of filtered still water. I let Simca in and get her dinner organized.

"I know, Sim, I'm sorry. Mama's a bit up under it tonight," I say as she gives me her patented world-weary look. I sneak a spoonful of peanut butter into her kibble, an extra treat for putting up with me. I could swear she winks at me before tucking in. She has finished her dinner and is delicately cleaning her paws when the bell rings.

"Okay. Ready or not, here we go," I say to her and head to answer the door.

Wait, wait . . ." Teresa says, ripping off another piece of baguette and dunking it directly into the puddle of sauce at the bottom of the chicken pan. "He had a *wife*?"

Apparently, two bottles of wine in, dishing about Bernard seemed like the thing to do. It started easy enough; we decimated a bottle of champagne with the nibbles and fell back into the where-is-so-and-so and did-you-hear-about-what's-her-face. This was followed by a really spectacular bottle of Côtes du Rhône with the chicken, plenty of praise for my cooking, and sharing about jobs and children and family stuff.

With the warm food and wine filling us up, Lynne started questioning me about my love life. At first I waved it off, like I do with everyone. "If he is out there, I'll be delighted to meet him, but I have a wonderful full life without him, and if he never shows, I'm okay with that too." A very empowered speech, I've always thought. A good sound bite, even if a part of me I don't really like to acknowledge thinks it may be false bravado. But Lynne narrowed her eyes at me, and Teresa sucked her teeth in that classic Italian Mama way.

"Bullshit, baby girl, I call Bull. Shit," Lynne said, dividing the last of the bottle between us.

Teresa raised that animated eyebrow, and it all just spilled out. How I got the job at Bernard's restaurant. The easy camaraderie between us. The night he stopped by after closing while I was working on some new items for the menu and made me a perfect, fluffy fresh-herb omelet swimming in butter and poured me Armagnac older than me and made passionate love to me, telling me I was a goddess and that I tasted like the finest wine and that our sex smelled like truffles. We ate an entire bowl of chocolate mousse naked on the kitchen floor. That we kept the affair a secret for months, as his ex-wife, Claudine, was still part owner of the restaurant. Despite the fact that their breakup was due to compulsive adultery on both their parts—for him an endless assortment of women of all ages, shapes, and sizes; for her, a string of much younger men—from the moment he moved out of their cottage and into a small town house near the restaurant, her jealousy had amped up, and it was easier for him to just keep his relationships a bit on the quiet side. She was volatile and violent, with a midday cocktail habit that didn't look good on her. Once we went public, she became a constant thorn in my side, showing up at the restaurant with her girlfriends to poke fun and be snarky and complain and send every dish back twice.

I told them how I had never been in love like that. The longer Bernard and I were together, the more beautiful and sexy and special I felt, and the more I imagined a lifetime with him. I told them about the week my period was late, and how he kissed my belly and called it Bouboune, a nonsense endearment, and said that we would have the most beautiful girl. And how he cried in my arms when I eventually got my period, like a dream had died for him.

"Ex-wife," I say, taking another sip of wine. "Sort of. But not from how she behaved. She was a jealous nightmare."

"Well, just because she let him go doesn't mean it wasn't hard to have his new girlfriend right in front of her," Lynne said, picking some asparagus out of the salad bowl with her tapered fingers.

"I wasn't flaunting anything, just living my life," I say, scooping up some of the velvety celery root puree on my last crust of bread. "Small town, impossible to disappear."

"Well, I think it sounds awfully *French*," Teresa says reverently, which makes us laugh.

"Oh, it was French, all right. Passionate, fabulous, perfect. Right up until my dad got sick. And then it was all, *mon amour*, it's been nice, don't let the door hit you . . ."

"He did not," Teresa says, her mouth hanging open.

"He most certainly did. Said that he was sorry for my dad, but if I left without a return ticket, I wouldn't have anything to return to."

"Ouch," Lynne says.

I shrug. "What could I do? I couldn't just come for some sad good-bye visit, and I couldn't in good conscience just leave him there without a sous chef for an indeterminate period of time. I had to give him leave to replace me professionally, and unfortunately, he was not the kind of guy who could be expected to not replace me personally as well. Then, of course, it turns out that the whole thing was a lie. He and the ex had never officially filed the paperwork—some sort of tax issue; just told everyone they were divorced. And they never stopped sleeping together, not even when he was with me. Then, within months of when I left, he knocked up my replacement."

"What a jerk," Teresa says.

"What an asshole," Lynne says.

"Whatever," I say. "Who needs a French man when there is French cheese? Half as stinky and twice as smart." I bring over the cheese platter, moving the chicken out of the way. I'm already regretting telling them about Bernard. He is something I don't like to think about, let alone talk about. When I heard from my friend Jean-Marie the truth about his nondivorce and infidelities, it tainted every good thing he'd ever made me feel about myself. She said everyone presumed I knew, since it was, after all, Bernard. Lawrence is the only other person who knows the whole story, and his reaction was that Bernard made me completely distrust not men, but relationships and my own judgment. He had his own Bernard in his past, and said we were peas in a pod. That I should do as he has always done, take companionship and sex when it presents itself, save love and long-term relationships for friends, family, and dogs. Easier that way, and not without its benefits. Except that Lawrence gets laid fairly regularly, and I do not.

"I'll drink to that," Lynne says, raising her glass.

"Me too." Teresa winks.

We demolish the cheese, and huge slices of Teresa's cornmeal pound cake, perfumed with vanilla, crunchy on the outside, and meltingly tender on the inside, and repair to the living room with little glasses of Madeira. We look through the yearbook, laughing till tears are rolling down our cheeks at some of the less flattering pictures of our classmates, remembering the good times and us. Then Lynne picks up the Fabulous at Forty paper off the table.

"Oh, hell no! I remember this assignment," she says, shaking her head. "I can't believe you saved it."

"Me too!" Teresa says. "That was a fun one. I have mine, in my memory box."

"Of course you do," says Lynne. "I threw all that shit away. Just boxes of crap."

Teresa shrugs. "I thought it would be nice for my kids someday."

"Yeah, not anything I will ever have to worry about," Lynne says, reading the list, and then turning it over to read their notes. "We were sure something."

"Teresa, I don't remember your list, what was on it?" I ask her, sipping the sweet wine.

"Nothing surprising." She chuckles. "I wanted to have a great husband, four kids—two boys, two girls—a nice house. I wanted to take over family holidays from my mom, do some volunteer work for the church, maybe work part-time when the kids were in school. And the two of you said that you couldn't think of one thing to add for me, by the way!"

"You failed so miserably!" Lynne says sarcastically. "Three boys and no girls?"

Teresa's face gets a bit sad. "We lost a little girl second trimester about a year and a half after Antony was born, and then two more first-trimester miscarriages. Decided our blessings were plenty, and stopped trying." Her eyes shine a bit brighter.

"Oh, honey, so, so sorry for that. It must have been so hard on you guys," Lynne says, squeezing her hand.

Teresa shrugs. "I have three healthy boys who are turning into lovely young men. They are plenty. Someday I'll have daughters-in-law and maybe granddaughters. What about you, Lynne, do you remember anything on your list?"

"I think I said I would go into advertising, make my first million before I was thirty, and marry Wesley Snipes. And, Teresa, you said Wesley and I would have three goddamn kids, and, Eloise, you said I would open my own firm."

"Mmm. Wesley Snipes," Teresa says. "Blade. I mean, damn. These children and their Robert Pattinson nonsense, they do not know from sexy vampire."

We laugh. "Well, Wesley aside, things seem to be going well for you," I say.

Lynne shrugs. "I beat my million deadline by a year, and perhaps if I had married Wesley instead of Mr. So-Very-Wrong I wouldn't be single now. But I can't complain."

"So funny. The way we thought things would be by the time we were forty, and now, we just have eight months," Teresa says. "Things are so different."

"We should make new lists!" I say, joking, refilling everyone's glasses. "What we should do before we turn forty."

"Yeah," Lynne says, laughing. "And add in our stuff for each other like we did last time."

Teresa smiles. "And then we should make a bet that we have to do it all before we actually turn forty or . . . or . . ."

"Or we have to run naked down Michigan Avenue," I say.

"Or we have to donate a lot of money to something!" Lynne says.

Teresa suddenly gets a look on her face. "We should do that."

"What?" Lynne asks.

"That. We should remake our lists together, and have to do them before our birthdays or we should have to donate, like, five grand. In Mrs. O'Connor's name."

"You're serious?" I say, suddenly thinking this isn't funny anymore.

"Why not?" Teresa says. "Look, my life is good, but there is stuff that could be better, and things that I want to do but don't ever bother to start. I presume you both have some things you could see improving upon. Why not try together? Why not use each other to get motivated? Maybe God gave us back to each other because we are stronger together, because we have things to do and become that we need each other for. What's the worst thing that could happen? We'll hang out a lot; do some things that scare us a little with some good friends at our backs? One or more of us will be a little poorer to the benefit of something good?" Her face suddenly goes from serious to sly. "You ladies chicken? Know you can't beat me?"

Lynne makes a clucking noise. "I do believe this crazy bitch has just thrown down a gauntlet. It's like she doesn't know us at all." Her mouth twists into an evil grin.

"You people are drunk," I say, a pit opening up in my stomach.

"Prolly," Teresa says. "But that sounds like you are a wuss."

"Well, you know, all that competitive fire went out of her back in the day," Lynne says wickedly.

"Fuck you both. You're on." Good Lord, why did I say that? Because it's what I would have said twenty years ago. When you are with the people who knew you twenty years ago, a part of you reverts to being that girl. And right now, I wish that girl would shut the hell up.

"Okay, bet. How many things have to be on the list?" Lynne asks.

"We each have to do three things for ourselves, and one from each of the others," Teresa says. "That is only five things to accomplish in eight months, which should be doable."

"Okay. If we all get it done before the birthdays, no one has to be out of pocket. Anyone who doesn't make it in time has to write that check. But we each have to make a list of six things for ourselves, and two things for each other. We each get to pick which of the things from the other girls we have to do, but the other two get to pick from our list the other three things, so that we can't set ourselves up for easy stuff, and we can't sabotage each other." Leave it to Lynne to establish rules and prevent cheating.

"The other two get to vote whether something can get crossed off the list, so there has to be some sort of proof," I say, head spinning.

"This woman is having *Sixteen Candles* flashbacks," Lynne says. "Gonna make us show her someone's underwear in the bathroom for a dollar."

"No, that's a good idea," Teresa says. "And we have to have a joint birthday party of some kind—that is the deadline for the lists. Checks get written that night."

"Go get some paper, El, this thing is on," Lynne says, and in a daze I walk over to the sideboard and get some paper and pens. "You can't think too much, and you can't couch this shit in surface crap. We'll know. Deep-down, serious life goals and dreams and things that need doing, or it won't be worth it." She holds out her pinky. Teresa links her forefinger around it and sticks her pinky out. I link it with my forefinger, and Lynne connects us with her forefinger around my pinky.

"Three-way pinky swear," Lynne says. And we each make eye contact with the two others and shake. And then we start to write.

I wake up shockingly early in light of the fact that the girls didn't leave till nearly one. I'm also surprisingly not really hungover—just a little dry mouth and the slight twinge of a headache. I get dressed, and Simca and I head out for her morning walk. We get home, and I grab a yogurt and fill her bowl with kibble. And then I look at the sheet of paper on the kitchen counter.

### To Do Before Forty—Eloise

1. *Find a new hobby that has nothing to do with food or cooking.*

2. *Create real book proposal for cookbook, and send to at least ten literary agents.*

3. *Find a new athletic endeavor that doesn't hurt my knee, but keeps me more active.*

*From Lynne for Eloise: Do something social out of the house at least once every other week, and at least once a month it must be something with strangers . . . a tour, a class, places to potentially broaden your circle of friends.*

I picked that one since her other suggestion was to join some sort of women's networking group, which sounded awful.

*From Teresa for Eloise: Start actively dating . . . at least fifteen real dates total.*

Since her other suggestion was to look into maybe freezing my eggs, it was like choosing between root canal surgery and food poisoning, but Marcy keeps telling me how easy it is to get dates these days with all the online options, so I figure I can suck it up and just get through them.


G od help me. I push the sheet aside. I can't even begin to think about what I've gotten myself into.

"Simca? Your human is a complete moron."

And my pup looks up at me as if to say, "Well, duh."

# Five

M y girl, it's too, too wonderful!" Lawrence says, sipping from a mug of Japanese honey ginger tea. "I adore everything about it." He runs an elegant hand through his thick, wavy salt-and-pepper hair, ice blue eyes twinkling behind glasses with thick black rims.

"Of course you do. Because you know you'll hear all the downsides of my dating foibles, you evil thing."

His corgis, Philippe and Liagre, come trotting into the dining room, and as usual, Philippe curls up at Lawrence's feet and Liagre comes to sit with me. I reach a hand down and scratch between his soft ears. Lawrence's corgis are of the pale, apricot-colored, stumpy-tailed type so often seen with Queen Elizabeth, while my Simca is a tricolor who never had her tail docked. More of a peasant corgi, if you will. But they are all adorable.

"Well, one must have some small bits of joy in one's dotage, darling." He winks. "I can't say I'll be disappointed to hear how that part of your challenge is moving along. I'm happy to help, you know, plenty of fix-up opportunities." He grunts as Philippe insists on being pulled up into his lap. They might look small, but they weigh a ton.

"Yeah, I'm going to have to take you up on that, scarily enough. Because I cannot begin to think about what online dating would even look like." The idea of dating at all makes my stomach turn over. But at least if Lawrence is fixing me up, there is a bit of safety net. Liagre sighs and rests his head on my foot.

"Done. I will reach into my little black book and you should expect your phone to begin ringing tout de suite! What about the other girls, how do their lists look?"

"Well, Teresa wants to bring a little bit of the fun back to her marriage now that her boys are old enough to fend for themselves most of the time, so one of hers is about doing one thing a month to spice up her marriage. She also wanted to find some stuff outside the home to work on, so she has to volunteer once a month for something, and she has to find a part-time job before the time is up."

"All seems smart and positive." He takes a sip of the hot, spicy, sweet tea.

"My goal for her was to broaden her palate, since ninety percent of what she eats and feeds her family is Italian, and the rest is burgers and American fare. Apparently her eldest went to a friend's house for a sleepover and they went out for Thai food and he ordered a burger. So I'm going to take her on some foodie adventures around town and teach her to cook some fun stuff."

"An open mind and an adventurous spirit are gifts you can give your children. I like that one. What was Lynne's for her?"

"To get more involved in the financial end of her life. She is one of those wives who has no idea how much money her husband makes, where their investments are, or how they are doing on saving for retirement and the kids' college, so she has to take a course on basic household finances and financial planning and learn how to fully participate in managing those parts of their life."

"Very practical. A good list. And for Lynne, queen of all the massive successes?"

"Well, for herself, she of course wants her business to grow, so she set a goal to land at least one seven-figure client. She also has been thinking that she should put down roots, since she hasn't ever owned her own home. In California she rented; then when she was married, she moved into his house; and now she is renting again. So she has to buy a place. And she wants to give back more, so she has to join the board of a charity."

"Wow. I like it—make no small plans."

"That's Lynne. But I think she has some of the hardest stuff. Teresa has her signing up for one of those top-end executive matchmaking firms, and I have her getting a dog!"

"You didn't." Lawrence claps his hands in delight.

"I did. I said she needs someone to be accountable to, and some source of unconditional love in her life while she is waiting for the matchmaker to find her a man."

Lawrence whistles under his breath. "These lists of yours certainly are ambitious. You couldn't have thought of anything simple? A bit of dandelion fluff on the wind?" He does know how to turn a phrase.

"Well, each of us at our own level. Lynne will probably have her whole list knocked out in the next month, knowing her. More tea?"

"Please." He hands me his mug and I take it into the kitchen. I love this kitchen. It is small but perfectly appointed, with a stunning Aga range and hood in a lovely pale lavender, with charcoal gray cabinets that have polished-nickel hardware and white marble counters. I refill both of our mugs with the spicy, sweet elixir and rejoin him at the dining table.

"Okay, down to business," I say, handing him the mug and pulling open my notebook. "What are you thinking for Halloween this year?" We just have a couple of weeks till the holiday, and Lawrence is famous for his Halloween parties. I get to plan and execute all the catering prep, but then hand it off to hired help the night of so that I can be a guest at the party. He always hires Marcy's friend Alex to do the night-of cooking, and he and I work really well together, so I never have to stop enjoying myself to help in the kitchen.

"I think last year we went for spooky elegant. We should go the opposite direction, and instead go for fun versions of street food! What do you think?"

"I think I love you. Especially since I won't have to make eight thousand black blinis with orange salmon roe."

"They were delicious . . ."

"Of course they were. They were also a pain in my substantial ass. How many are we this year?"

"Probably thirty to forty over the course of the night."

"Okay, and is there a costume theme?"

"Classic Chicago. Whatever that means to someone, from Al Capone to Michael Jordan to Marshall Field and the Everleigh sisters, to dressing up like one of the lion statues from the Art Institute."

"Terrific. So we should celebrate Chicago street food. Mini Chicago dogs, mini gyros, mini Italian beef sandwiches, little deep-dish pizzas . . ."

"Exactly my thinking, smart girl. But be sure to acknowledge the diversity of our fair city—we have Chinatown and Pilsen and Little Italy and the South Side . . . with street food we can do little tastes from all of our wonderful cultures."

"True enough. Let me play with some ideas and send you a menu to look at in the next day or so."

"And dear Marcy will come, yes?"

"Of course. She and I will have to figure out our costumes."

"Well, for once, maybe be a pretty girl? Your costumes are always hilarious, but now that you are on the dating market, it wouldn't kill you to wear a dress. Just for practice."

"I'll think about it. Anything else you want me to do for the party? Special requests?"

"Not that I can think of."

"Will it be the usual suspects?" Lawrence has a wide rotation of friends that he cycles through for his monthly dinner parties, but Halloween is special. I often think he uses it as punishment if someone has offended him in some way; it is a clear dig to not get an invitation. And he is always gathering new people, so sometimes there is fresh blood to liven things up.

"Mostly. You'll probably recognize at least three-quarters of the guests from the dinners or last Halloween. I'm not inviting any of the ones with the boring spouses this year . . ." Last year there was a strange black hole of boredom right at the center of the party where a group was gathered making awkward small talk and listening to one wife monologue about her terrible job, while someone else's bland husband talked about

lawn maintenance. I myself was cornered for the better part
of an hour listening to some blowhard who fancies himself a
natural-born chef tell me about all the amazing twenty-course
dinner parties he is always having, where everyone tells him
he is better than any fine-dining tasting menu in town. Lawrence told me later he got sucked into one of the ghastly events
last year, and that the guy's food is as inane as his conversation.
Guess the fun ones will have to stay home with their dull spouses
this year.

"Can't say I'll be disappointed with that."

"None of us will, darling, none of us will. Good Lord, dog,
you are giving my lap pins and needles." He puts Philippe back
onto the floor with a thud. "What do you have for the rest of
your day?"

"I'm taking dinner to Mrs. O'Connor's husband tonight—
just going to check in on him."

"You are a kind girl. I know he will be glad for the food and
the company."

"I hope so."

"Well, I think we have all we need here . . . thank you as
always for the provisions, my darling. I will look forward to the
menu for the party, and will see you next week, same time?"

"Same Bat-time, same Bat-station," I say with a grin. Lawrence once confessed to a fantasy about Adam West in his blue
Batman outfit.

"Scoot, you evil girl, or I will give your number to every
single man I know under five foot five."

I throw my hands up in surrender and gather my notes. I
give him a kiss on his cheek and head out of the gorgeous
apartment into a perfectly sunny and brisk fall day, thinking
about what I should make for Glenn for dinner.

* * *

That, dear girl, was the best meal I've had in months. Bless you," Glenn says, rubbing his little belly with a satisfied grin.

"Glad you liked it!" I say. "Sure you don't want another helping?"

I made a classic French blanquette de veau, an old-school veal stew with a white wine sauce, served over wide pappardelle noodles that I tossed with butter, lemon zest, and chives, and some steamed green beans. I also made a loaf of crusty bread using the no-knead recipe that everyone is doing these days and is so simple and so delicious.

"I think three plates is plenty!" Glenn laughs. "Besides, I'm pretty sure I saw some dessert in there, so I had better leave a sliver of room."

"You got me there." I made a fallen chocolate soufflé cake filled with chocolate mousse. Mrs. O'Connor always talked about being married to a chocoholic: apparently Glenn believes that if it isn't chocolate, it isn't dessert. While he will happily eat any dessert placed in front of him, from fruit pies to vanilla ice cream, if there is no chocolate, he will literally stop on the way home for a Hershey bar or a drive-through chocolate milk shake.

He stands, and the two of us clear the table. He moves in his kitchen like a man who is still finding his way, opening two or three different drawers or cabinets to find the Tupperware containers or plastic wrap. It breaks my heart a little bit.

"Don't look at me with those puppy eyes, you enormous goddess. I had no idea where anything was in this kitchen when Helene was alive. I cultivated very carefully my ignorance of where everything goes, as well as a complete inability to load a dishwasher the way she wanted, which kept me from having to do very much in the cleaning-up department. Frankly, I'm very tempted to load in a massive stash of paper and plastic and call it a day."

"Don't get sassy with me, mister, you are perfectly capable of putting things away in your own home. Kitchens are only intuitive for one person at a time. Next time I come, you and I will reorganize so that things go where your intuition thinks they should go."

"Fine. If you insist on my self-sufficiency, you are going to have to get that dessert out sooner rather than later."

"Deal." We pack up the rest of the stew and side dishes, and Glenn puts on a pot of coffee while I cut generous slices of the cake. We sit back down at the cozy little kitchen table and clink coffee mugs before digging into the cake, which is at once light and rich. We finish our plates in companionable silence, and sip the bitter coffee, his light and sweet and mine black.

"So. How are you doing? What has been going on with you?" he asks.

I think about this for a moment. "I've mostly been just cooking for my clients, spending time with my mom and aunt, nothing terribly exciting." I pause, thinking about the bet. "And I've been reconnecting with Lynne and Teresa, you know, since . . ."

"Since the memorial."

I nod.

"It's okay, you know. To talk about her, to talk about her absence. I sort of like it, in a way, how big the space is that she left. It would be so awful if she went away and left some minor hole, like a rock dropping into a pool of water. She was too monumental for that. What we have now is something of a crater. So we can celebrate that a bit, you and I, the enormity of the void."

I love him for thinking of it that way. "She was larger than life in life; it isn't surprising that she remains so after."

"Exactly. And she would love that you girls rediscovered each other through her. She took special pride in your friendship, back in the day, in being a small part of that."

"She was a huge part of that. I don't know if we would have ever found each other if not for that class." The truth of this seems somehow shocking when I say it aloud. When I think about what we were to each other, what we might be becoming to each other again, for it all to rest on the tenuous thread of coincidence, of ending up in the same English class in high school, of Mrs. O'Connor deciding to organize the class by birthdate, of all of us being born the same week . . . it's just all so flimsy.

"I think the universe sends us the people we need. You would have found each other one way or another, but Helene always did like watching the three of you grow together. Maybe you can bring them by one night?"

"Of course! I know they would love that." But deep down, it lands weird, this request to bring in Lynne and Teresa. I wonder why I have to fake enthusiasm for this. Especially since my goal is anything that will make Glenn happy, and clearly he wants to see them.

"Wonderful! That will be something to look forward to."

"Indeed. And my mom wanted to come by sometime, if you were up for that."

"Hmmm, let me see, filling the house with an endless string of smart, beautiful women? Well, I will suffer if I must . . ." His blue eyes twinkle mischievously.

"Wicked man." I chuckle. It is clear why Mrs. O'Connor loved him so much. "Is there anything else I can do for you?"

"Your coming means the world, and your cooking is a gift from the gods. Why no restaurant? Helene and I both assumed you'd open one of your own after running that place in France. We were hoping to have a regular table!"

"That is sweet, but I don't have the mentality for restaurant work, not for the long haul. I know so many chefs who burn out, who eventually dread the kitchen. I love the work I do. I think because I started cooking for my friends and family, doing it as an act of love and nourishment . . ."

"And comfort and healing," he adds seriously.

I nod. "And that. My job is as close as I can get to that feeling. Yes, I'm doing it for money, but I genuinely care about my clients and I feel a part of their lives. If I had a restaurant, I might know if it was someone's birthday or anniversary, but I wouldn't know what their favorite dish was, or what childhood memory I could cook up. This way, I can make a living doing what I love, and I feel like I'm making a difference in a really personal way."

"That makes a lot of sense. Being on the beneficiary side, I can tell you, you do make a difference."

"Thank you." I pause, wanting to say the thing that has been lurking in the back of my mind all night. "Was she disappointed in me, do you think? Because I disappeared? Because I wasn't here for her when she needed me?" There is a little lump in my throat, but I'm determined not to cry.

"Oh, honey. Not in the least. You have to remember that with her career she had to be prepared to make connections that had time limits. Every year a new group of students, new faces in the teachers' lounge. She loved you, and always said how special you were to her, but she knew that in the times you weren't in touch, it wasn't because you didn't love her."

I lose hold of the tears in my eyes. Glenn reaches out and squeezes my hand. "I meant what I said. She didn't want people to know, when she got sick; she didn't want the attention. Trust me, if I had thought for one minute that having you around would have made things better, I would have been in touch myself."

"That makes me feel better." And again I realize how unfair it is of me to make this about myself and my own guilt. "How are you doing, really?"

"I'm okay. Good days and bad days. I joined a group down at the church, so that has been helpful. My buddies are good about making sure I have stuff to do, places to go. I'm thinking about doing some volunteering. The days can get a little long."

"My mom did that too. She does a great after-school program down at the Y a couple afternoons a week. She reads with kids, does arts and crafts, helps the older ones with homework. Parents who work can have a safe place for their kids to be between the end of school and the end of their workday, and parents who don't can have a little break to run errands or get in a workout."

"That sounds like a great thing—do you think she would talk to me about it?"

"Absolutely. They always need more people, especially since it runs five days a week. I'll have her give you a call."

"Thank you. And I think I will take you up on that kitchen organization. I can never find the thing I need when I need it. Suppose I'm going to have to navigate those things a bit more proactively."

"How does Saturday look?"

"Wide open."

"I'll bring lunch."

"With brownies?"

"Absolutely."

When Simca and I get back from our walk, I make a small pot of tea and settle in on the couch with my laptop. Simca hauls herself up next to me, snuggling her warm weight against my hip. I rub her head with my left hand while scrolling through e-mail with the other.

From: Mamaltalia2734@gmail.com

To: LynneRLewiston@HampshirePR.com;
    ChefEloise@gmail.com

Subject: Getting it done!

Ladies,

Find attached a photo of my nametag from my first volunteering effort. I spent the afternoon at the local senior center giving manicures to the ladies. It was a HOOT. Those old broads have some stories to tell, and apparently, the nookie opportunities are rampant over there. Let's just say I used up a whole bottle of Jungle Red.

How is everyone else doing with their projects?

Also, I'm getting us tickets to the special showing of *The Breakfast Club* at Webster Place for the 24th, so save the date for movie night!

T

Lynne has already replied.

Nice job! I had a meeting with my new Realtors over at Coldwell Banker. We are going to start looking at properties this weekend. I'm for the movie for sure. El? What do you have for us?

LL

I hit reply all.

Well, I have officially told my client Lawrence that I am available for fix-ups, so he promises that I will have horrible dating stories to regale you with very soon. And I'm going to tour Midtown Athletic after work tomorrow to see if maybe they have some options for me.

In other news, I had dinner tonight with Glenn O'Connor and he requested that we set a date for you guys to come with me, so let's look at calendars and find a night to go keep him company.

Count me in on the movie.

XOE

Then I shoot a quick e-mail to Marcy.

To: MarcyBakes@gmail.com
Subject: Halloween

Well, we have the theme . . . classic Chicago, whatever that means to us. And Lawrence has requested we be pretty girls, any ideas? The good news is he wants me to do street food,

so let's be sure whatever pretty girls we are going to be don't
require Spanx!

XOE

I start looking through my recipe files in search of some of
my street food recipes, when my e-mail pings with Marcy's
reply.

Easy. You be Daryl Hannah in *Splash* and I will be Jennifer
Beals in *Flashdance*. Chicago girls, and their most famous
classic roles. We can dress up like them in the two famous
fancy restaurant scenes, which puts you in a flowy floral dress
and me in cuffs and a dickey, neither of which requires Spanx,
and both of us have to carry plastic lobsters. Done.

M

I love that little pixie. Now I just have to get a wig.
And a flowy dress.

# Six

love Wednesdays. Wednesdays are blissfully quiet. The older kids are at school all day and they all have after-school programming. Geneva and Shelby have their weekly group. The four moms and their kids all met in a Mommy and Me class, and now they take every Wednesday afternoon for group playdates. They go to museums or to the zoo or to a pottery-painting place, something active and interesting. The house is peaceful, and all I have to do is cook. Since tomorrow I will only be here to coach Ian, I have to get them set for dinner tonight and tomorrow, as well as lunches and snacks to get them to Friday dinner.

I set up my insane mise en place, all my prep work, as soon as I arrived this morning. I have a lot to do, but if I stay focused, I should get it all done and cleaned up and still be out by four when everyone starts getting home. For tonight, I've got a bacon-wrapped pork loin roast, which I will sear crispy, and then leave for them in a slow oven, so that it is hot but not overcooked when it is time for them to sit down to dinner. Sweet potato, pear, and parsnip gratin is the perfect foil for the pork, and a crunchy, simple salad of sliced celery, fennel, green apple, and shaved Parmesan, dressed in lemon juice and olive oil, will keep things from getting too heavy. I'm making lemon cream squares for dessert, a special thing for Darcy. I know she had a math test today that she was really anxious about. They are her favorite. I figure it will either be a reward or a comfort, and will let her know I was thinking of her.

The work is easy, recipes that are second nature, the slicing and dicing and chopping. I've got this kitchen set up just the way I love it, everything in easy reach, plenty of prep bowls and containers and sheet pans for keeping it all organized. The night before, I make my time and action plan, what to do in what order to keep me working as efficiently as possible. While it all requires a certain amount of attention, it does allow for my brain to wander more than a little. Usually, it would be thinking of new recipes or techniques, wondering about how to take a dish that often requires a lot of last-minute attention and convert it to something that can be done in advance. But these past few weeks, since reconnecting with Lynne and Teresa, since the bet? My head is swirling with ideas that make me at once anxious and excited.

I've always deep down wanted to do a cookbook, as it seems that most of my free time is spent developing recipes and imagining how the photographs would look, how people at home might cook my dishes for people they love. So the butterflies about having to actually pull a real proposal together are welcome and sort of joyous. To kill two birds with one stone, I've signed up for a drawing class, as my potential new nonfood hobby, thinking that maybe I could do some cool line drawings to incorporate into the cookbook, to elucidate the more complicated recipes. I loved to doodle and draw when I was a kid, and still fill any handy piece of paper with intricate scribbles when I am on the phone or bored. Marcy got me one of those adult coloring books—it has very elegant detailed graphics of profanities—and I like to work on them while I watch TV. I'm even glad about the new exercise program, since that will be good for me in the long run, even if I'm a little nervous to see how much I've really let myself go physically.

But the dating. That is when those butterflies turn into pterodactyls, and those bitches have a temper. Sharing my Bernard story, or as much of it as I felt up to in the moment, with Lynne and Teresa, got my head in a bit of a swirl. My mom doesn't know; it felt too unfair to dump it on her when I came back, with everything she had to manage with my dad's illness. It would have only made her feel worse. Marcy knows, but we don't ever speak of it. Even my conversations with her about it have always been mostly on the surface. She doesn't know that he was the only man I've ever been in love with. She doesn't know how badly he broke me. That deep down, where I don't ever like to look, I don't know if I even have it in me to ever let another man in, not that deep, not for real.

Which is why I am so grateful for the quiet today. Because tonight?

I have a goddamned date. And thinking about food, about feeding my Farbers, that is the only thing keeping me from total panic.

I pull the chocolate chunk cookies out of the oven and slide them on a rack to cool, and I turn off the blackberry balsamic sauce I've made to top ice cream, to let it cool. I load the second dishwasher with the gear from this last round of cooking. The first one is already well through its cycle. I check my watch. It's 1:45, so with the two-hour dishwasher cycle, I will be able to finish up here in plenty of time to get out the door before the hordes arrive. And to get home and figure out what on earth to wear. Thank God Marcy has the night off, so she can help me get ready. And since her cable is on the fritz for the ump-teenth time, she'll hang out with Simca at my place while I'm on my date, and be ready for a good debrief when I get home.

Jack, my date, is a friend of Lawrence's, recently divorced and an architectural photographer. He is forty-five, has two kids, and lives in Albany Park. We had a very pleasant phone call—he certainly sounds nice enough—and I agreed two days ago to meet him for drinks tonight at the Violet Hour. And promptly threw up.

I never throw up. *Ever.* I once legitimately picked up *E. coli* in Mexico, and only found out because I had a bad enough case of the runs to call my doc, and she said she could not believe I was even standing, let alone not puking my guts out with the levels in my system. My stomach? Iron. Lined in Teflon. And kryptonite. But within forty seconds of agreeing to my first date in nearly a decade, I was hunched over the toilet like I'd been eating yesterday's bargain-bin sushi dipped in raw chicken juice. Poor Simca didn't know what to do, so she climbed up onto my back and sat between my shoulder blades chewing my ponytail and licking the back of my neck as I retched.

I sit down to quickly write my note to the family:

*Hello, Team Farber! Hope you are hungry.*

*For tonight, there is bacon-wrapped pork loin in the first oven. Take it out to rest at 5:30, and you can carve at 5:50. Ian, if you are feeling ambitious, reduce the pan juices, mash in the cloves of garlic, monter au beurre, and season to taste to make a pan sauce. There is a sweet potato gratin in the first warming drawer; should be ready to slice and serve. The celery fennel salad is in the white bowl in the fridge with the damp paper towels on top and the dressing is in the jar next to it. Take the bag of Parmesan shavings that are on top of the salad and sprinkle over before dressing.*

*Lemon cream bars are in the fridge drawer in the butler's pantry.*

*Ian—tomorrow is going to be a dessert challenge, and there will be at least one or more savory ingredients in the box, so bone up on some creative nontraditional dessert ideas tonight.*

*Happy eating!*

*Big love,*
*Eloise*

I finish wiping down all the counters just as the dishwasher pops open to indicate that it is finished. One of the many things I adore about these Miele units: they make everything easy, including knowing when your cycle is done. I pull open the door and quickly unload the dishwasher, putting everything back into its place. I gather up my stuff, shut down all the lights, and head out the back. It was a long day, and my feet and lower back can feel the time spent standing, despite the cushy gel mats they have on the floor. I should have just enough time for a hot bath before Marcy arrives, and I'm hoping it will soothe my nerves as well as my aches.

Help," I say, opening the door for Marcy, my hair in a mad nest on top of my head, one fake eyelash stuck to my eyebrow.

"What the hell happened to you?" she says, dropping her bag on the floor near the door, slithering out of her black leather moto jacket, and leaning down to rub Simca's head.

"I tried to get pretty."

I thought it might be good to put my hair up; I have a habit of twisting strands of it when I get nervous, so I figured if it were up, I couldn't do that. I watched a video on YouTube that made this particular updo seem so simple: a couple of hair bands, three bobby pins—and a casual, slightly messy bun should have happened. But something went awry, and now my head looks like a deranged wombat is nesting on it. My eyelashes are stumpy, the result of a flambéing incident in culinary school (they never really came back the same), and suddenly it felt important to have nice ones, but those little suckers are slippery, and the glue dries faster than you might think.

"You have failed in a spectacular way."

"Can you please just help?"

"Oh, I can help. I can help a lot. Come on." She takes my hand and leads me to the stairs. "You too, Shorty. She's gonna need some moral support." Simca trots happily behind us.

A half hour later, the miracle is complete. Marcy has me in a pair of dark skinny jeans, which seems oxymoronic in light of my size 16 ass, but they have some good stretch in the mix, so everything is sort of locked and loaded. A black V-neck sweater with matte black beading around the neckline and cuffs and my flat zebra-pattern pony-hair slip-on loafers, in case he's short. We matched the outfit with a pair of black-and-white diamond hoop earrings that Shelby gave me for my birthday last year, and a bracelet made of ten thin strips of dark metallic pewter leather that winds around the wrist twice before snapping closed. My hair is in a high ponytail, with one of those cute little bumps at the top that make it more grown-up on a date and less cheerleader than my usual ponytails. And my makeup looks amazing, very natural: skin looks glowy, blemishes covered. She cut the fake eyelashes into small pieces with three or four lashes per piece and stuck them in strategically to boost my natural lashes and make me a bit more vamp and a lot less Vampira. A sheer shimmer on my lids, and a pale nude gloss on my lips, I look like me, just shinier. And for the first time in a long time, I hear Mrs. O'Connor's voice in my head. "Stand tall, like the queen you are; be your most present and authentic you. The rest will come."

"You are a godsend."

"I'm better than that. Here." She hands me a caramel.

"Yum, snacks! Just one?"

She puts up one finger. "Not snacks, edible. Eat half now. If things start to go sideways, eat the other half."

"Edible? Of course it's edible, it's candy. Why can't I just eat the whole thing?"

Marcy shakes her head. "Not edible like you can eat it. Edible like edible marijuana edibles. A guy at work has lupus, so he has a card and he gave me this as a gift to thank me for a favor I did him. I thought you could use it more than me."

"Seriously? Weed caramel?"

"Trust me. Very mellow. Takes the edge off. Half now, half if you need it later. You know, if the gibbering starts."

If I get really nervous, I can start running on at the mouth. I bite the caramel neatly in half, then return the second half to its wrapper and slip it into my purse. It is sweet and creamy with just a hint of bitterness, and a back note of something similar to rosemary on the finish. Not super delicious, but not terrible either. Mrs. O'Connor's mental pep talk notwithstanding, I'm all about doing whatever gets me through the night.

"Shall we call you an Uber, fancy-pants?" Marcy asks.

"I was just going to drive over, help keep me from drinking too much."

"Yeah, well, not anymore. You just ate half a weed candy, no driving for you."

"Oh, good thought. Uber it is." I pull up the app and enter my address. "Okay, Andre will be here in two minutes. Wish me luck."

Marcy reaches up and puts her hands on my shoulders. "You will be fine. The date will be great or horrible or mediocre or wonderful or whatever, but *you* will be totally fine."

I can feel an ease coming over me, and I don't know if it is the caramel kicking in or just Marcy's soothing words, but either way, I'm grateful.

"Thank you. See you in a bit."

And I head out my front door.

O kay, these are insanely delicious," Jack says around a mouthful of pork belly taco.

"Indeed," I say, reaching for a second taco al pastor.

After two very perfectly crafted cocktails at the Violet Hour, and some perfectly benign conversation, it became clear that Jack and I had absolutely no romantic chemistry. He isn't really over his divorce as yet and has something of a preference for small Asian women. He confessed this after he completely lost his train of thought in the middle of a story about his son, when a very pretty Japanese woman walked by our table en route to the ladies' room. I had already eaten the second half of the caramel before entering the bar, having frozen where I stood from the moment I got out of the Uber, so I was mellow enough to call him out on the obvious ogling. He blushed and admitted that he had agreed to call based on Lawrence's persuasive nature.

"He threatened to not invite you to the Halloween party, didn't he?"

Jack nodded sheepishly.

"It's all good. Between us, I think you are a very nice guy, but not really my type either." Which is true. While Lawrence did his best with the height—Jack is about dead even with me—he is also super skinny. I am not a delicate flower; I probably outweigh him by forty pounds. If I were even inclined to get physical with him, which I certainly am not, I'd probably break him in half.

"Friends, though, I hope," he said, raising his glass to me.

"Absolutely." I clinked his glass. "You hungry?"

"Sure, we can order something if you like."

"I have a better idea."

Which is how we ended up at Big Star across the street from the bar. Apparently the irony of edible weed? You still get the munchies. And now that we aren't concerned at all about making a good impression on each other, we've ordered half the menu and are eating with abandon. Jack has guacamole on his shirt, I have pastor juices running down my arm, and we are both having a very good time.

"So why is Lawrence doing the full-court press on you, if I may be so bold?" he asks. "I would think you wouldn't have any trouble finding dates. You're very attractive."

"Thank you. I've, um, been out of the game for a while, easing back in. Friends of friends seem like an easier way to get back into things. Safer, I guess." I dip a house-made chip into salsa. There is a hint of lime on it, and we've already been through two baskets.

"That makes sense. I would think it would be harder, as a woman, to feel safe with online dating. He didn't mention an ex . . ."

"It was a long time ago. Difficult breakup. And then more of a career-focus thing for me. Time just got away from me."

"But now you're ready to be back out there. That is great. Good for you. I'm working on it too."

"Well, don't praise me overmuch . . . the dating wasn't really my idea."

Jack reaches for a lamb and chorizo taco. "Yeah, I'm going to need more than that. Life coach recommendation?"

"Something like that." I give him the brief on the bet, and he laughs.

"I think it is a fun idea. Maybe in six months you can check in on me, dare me to get back out there."

"Only if I find a little Asian woman to offer you."

"I'll drink to that."

We clink our bottles of Shiner Bock beer and keep eating.


You'll like him," I say to Marcy, offering her the bag of marshmallows I found in my pantry. She waves me off with a sly grin, and I continue to eat the pillowy, bland, sugary sweets.

"I'm sure I will, dear heart. He sounds like a very great guy, what with his inattention and Asian-lady fetish."

"Don' be ssnmarky," I say, mouth full of marshmallow.

"I think it was good, you ripped off the Band-Aid and had an actual date. It was a date, right, please tell me he at least paid . . ."

"He was a perfect gentleman, paid for everything, and ordered my Uber on his phone."

"Well, he's earning more than a few points there. I've seen you chow down at Big Star when you're sober, you giantess. I can't imagine how many tacos you put away with the munchies."

"You don't wanna know." I shake my head. Marcy holds her hand out for the bag of marshmallows, and when I give it to her, she deftly ties the top in a knot. And makes the no-no finger at me when I make a pouty face.

Simca is snuggled on the couch between us in her favorite position, head on Marcy's lap for between-the-ear scratching, and her wide tush up against me for butt rubbing. She is a total hedonist, my pup.

"Well, I'm glad it was a nice night."

"More than nice—I killed two bet birds at once!"

"How do you mean?"

"Well, Violet Hour? That was a date, a real live date, so that checks one off the list. And I have the text message confirming it to forward to the girls. But, when we decided to go for tacos, we had already admitted we weren't into each other romantically, so that was a bona fide social event out of the house with a stranger, so I got my biweekly social thing checked off, and the monthly stranger part worked out. *Boom.*"

"Look at you, gaming the system."

"I know, right? Next week is the Halloween party, so that is this month covered on the social obligations."

"Except you need another date."

Damn. Forgot about that one. "Yeah. I'll have to ping Lawrence again."

"Nope, I've got you covered. You're gonna get a call from Ethan. New maître d' at the hotel." She raises her hand at me before I can protest. "He is six foot four, built like a lumberjack, and very nice. Just moved here from Portland, so he doesn't know many people. And Thursdays are his night off, so you should be able to sneak in something next week before the party, and get your October checklist fully completed."

"I love you."

"I know, baby."

"There's only one thing."

"What's that?"

"I might need more of those caramels."

# Seven

Marcy slides out of her coat in Lawrence's foyer, revealing her homemade dickey. She couldn't find one like the one in *Flashdance*, so she took a white button-down tuxedo shirt, removed the sleeves and back, and added an apron tie around her waist. Like a shirt mullet. She kept the cuffs and is wearing them like bracelets, snappy black bow tie around her neck. Wide-leg tuxedo pants and shiny patent leather lace-up wingtips finish the look. Her brown curly wig is teased into a halo of curls, and she is carrying a large plastic lobster that matches my own.

I found an end-of-season boho-chic floral chiffon dress for practically no money at Nordstrom Rack, over which I am wearing a loosely knitted ivory shawl, and flat lace-up sandals. Marcy found me the most incredible long, wavy platinum blond wig, which she has styled to perfectly match Daryl Hannah's from the movie, twisting two strands and pulling them back to keep it out of my face. She's done my makeup again, very shimmery and ethereal, and while I'm definitely not going to go blond anytime soon, it is kind of fun to see myself looking so different. And she owed me after the whole Ethan thing.

He did indeed call, and we made a date for Thursday night. We met at Billy Sunday for drinks, and he was indeed tall and good-looking. He was also, as I was deftly and fairly casually informed in the first ten minutes of our date, a gluten-free vegan CrossFit pansexual submissive.

"How was I to know?" Marcy said as we were getting ready tonight and I was raking her over the coals.

"Well, considering the speed at which he shared it all with me, I'm astounded that he didn't mention any of it to you. I mean, look, I was an athlete, so I can deal with the whole CrossFit thing. I'm not a sexual prude—let your freak flag fly. I'll learn some spanking techniques. And I don't particularly care about the brand of people who have preceded me. But *gluten-free vegan*? Hell no. I mean, really."

Marcy snorted with laughter. "Can you imagine? It's inhuman. I'm so sorry. If I had any idea, I would have never . . ."

"At least it was a good story for Lynne and Teresa." They roared when we did a three-way phone call to hear about the world's shortest first date. I claimed a fake emergency and bolted in exactly eighteen minutes. I can handle a lot, but if I can't make you carbonara, we're done for. "They want to meet you, by the way."

"In an alley with torches and pitchforks?"

"In a restaurant with cocktails."

"Done."

* * *

The two of you are gorgeous!" Lawrence says, greeting us in his eggplant silk pajamas covered in an olive green velvet smoking jacket and embroidered velvet slippers. He is drinking a martini and carrying a pipe. "I might have to take your pictures later for my magazine!"

"Why, Mr. Hefner, you wicked man!" Marcy says, kissing him on the cheek.

He winks at her, and then looks me up and down. "Spectacular to see you looking like a girl, my dear. Jack said you had a convivial evening, but no sparkle. Pity. But I'm terribly proud of you for getting back on the horse, and have many, many more eligible bachelors in my little black book for you, not to worry. In the meantime, why don't you take your glorious self inside and see if blondes have more fun!"

We clink our plastic lobsters with his martini glass and head into the party, which is in full force. There are several different incarnations of mayors wandering about, a Rahm, two Daley Juniors, a Daley Senior, a Harold Washington, and a Jane Byrne. Poor Michael Bilandic doesn't even make the cut. We spot some famous sports figures, the Blues Brothers, and a spectacular incarnation of the big Picasso statue downtown. I see Jack across the room, dressed as a Chicago Blackhawk, but he is in deep conversation with a guy dressed as John Cusack in *Say Anything*, complete with black trench coat and boom box, so I decide not to distract him. I'll say hi later.

"I believe it is cocktail o'clock, my little mermaid. Have to keep you lubricated!" Marcy says, steering me toward the bar. But halfway there, she gets sidelined by a guy, dressed like Ferris Bueller, she randomly knows from her gym, and in ten seconds they are trying to figure out how they both ended up here. I keep my path and head to the other side of the room, where the bar is set up.

"What can I get you?" the bartender asks me. I vaguely remember him from last year's party, but have forgotten his name.

"Can you do a Negroni?"

"Absolutely. Up?"

"On the rocks."

"What's a Negroni?" I hear a deep voice say slightly above my head, which is a place I rarely hear voices. I turn and am looking directly into a clavicle. A very smooth, well-defined clavicle, the color of French roast coffee. It is centered between shoulders of nearly impossible width, and clad in a Bears football jersey, which I recognize as Mike Singletary's number from back in the day. I look up into a handsome face, square jawed, much like Samurai Mike himself, with liquid brown eyes. His hair is cropped tight to his head, and he is smiling at me with even, white teeth. He looks like Idris Elba and Morris Chestnut had a baby. A really tall, broad-shouldered baby.

God bless Lawrence, he does love to fill these parties with the prettiest boys. Water, water, everywhere, as they say. At least not if you're a girl. But it does mean that one can flirt shamelessly all night with darling men who tell you how fabulous you are and don't try to take you home, which is just my kind of scene.

"A Negroni, Mr. Singletary, is equal parts gin, Campari, and sweet vermouth. Served either up or on the rocks, with an orange twist or slice."

"That sounds delicious—make it two," he says to the bartender. Kyle? Craig? Damn my memory. Kevin?

"I wouldn't think a lovely mermaid like yourself would rec-

ognize me . . . what with no football out there in the ocean."
He is still smiling at me, and with the close proximity I can
smell his cologne, something spicy, almost like cinnamon.

"Not even the ocean could protect us from 'The Super Bowl
Shuffle.'" I know it is something of a cliché, but I just adore
hanging out with gay men. I get a little bolder, a little wittier;
they bring out the best in me.

"Yeah, sorry about that."

"You're forgiven." Our cocktails are handed over, and we
clink glasses and take a sip. Whatever-his-name-is knows his
business: the bittersweet liquid is perfectly balanced, perfectly
chilled, and perfectly delicious.

"I might have a new favorite cocktail. The Negroni. Who
knew?"

"You just have to hang out with more mermaids. We have
all the best stuff."

"I don't doubt it. So, should I call you Madison, or try and
make dolphin noises?"

I laugh. "Eloise. Eloise Kahn."

"Nice to meet you, Eloise Kahn. I'm Shawn Sudberry-
Long." Of course he is hyphenated. His husband must be
around here somewhere. Probably equally gorgeous.

He takes my hand in his enormous paw and kisses my
knuckles gently. I really wish that straight guys would take
classes from their gay brothers on how to make a lady feel like
a lady.

"So, Eloise Kahn, are you an actual football fan? I'm impressed you recognized the jersey. Most of the guests here
wouldn't know Mike Singletary from Mike Douglas."

"Yeah. My uncle and my dad shared season tickets when I
was growing up, so I got to go to a lot of games."

"Anything after October?" This is a total Chicago test. Soldier Field, where the Bears play, is an outdoor stadium. If you go to games in cold weather, that is the mark of a die-hard fan.

"You mean like Christmas Eve Day against the Packers in a blizzard? You are talking to a woman who knows how to layer . . ."

He laughs. "Good girl."

"I take it you're a fan?"

"Lifelong. Football in general and the Bears specifically."

"I'll drink to that."

"I'll tell you one thing about these Negronis, they do make a guy hungry. I've seen the buffet stations and things are looking pretty delicious over there . . . and I think your lobster isn't going to cut it for real sustenance, so can I escort you around the nibbles and see what tempts us?"

"Absolutely." I know what is on the buffets and I'm hungry as a real bear.

Shawn takes my elbow and deftly guides me through the crowd of revelers. Alex has done a great job, as usual, of setting everything up, and all of our prep of the last few days is out in its glory. Mini Chicago hot dogs, with all seven of the classic toppings for people to customize. Miniature pita breads ready to be filled with chopped gyro meat and tzatziki sauce. Half-size Italian beef sandwiches with homemade giardiniera my mom put up last summer. We did crispy fried chicken tenders atop waffle sticks with Tabasco maple butter, and two-inch deep-dish pizzas exploding with cheese and sausage. Little tubs of cole slaw and containers of spicy sesame noodles. There are ribs, chicken adobo tacos, and just for kicks, a macaroni and cheese bar with ten different toppings.

"One thing about Lawrence, he does know how to put out

a spread," Shawn says when we have filled our plates and found a quiet corner to eat in.

"Well, I suppose I should thank you."

"Why is that?" he says, deftly stripping a rib bone of its succulent meat and rolling his eyes in pleasure.

"I'm his chef."

Shawn raises an eyebrow at me. "I'm pretty sure I saw some guy in the kitchen barking out orders and sweating over a pan when I got here."

"Yeah, that's Alex. Lawrence is very nice about letting me be a guest at the party, so I do all the menu planning, prep, and setup, and Alex executes night of."

"Be still, my heart, the woman can cook. This mac tastes like love from my aunties."

"Thank you, that is the best possible compliment."

Marcy plops down next to me and picks up half of a taco off my plate. "Great food, El, as always." She turns to Shawn. "Hi, I'm Marcy." She puts out her hand, showing an epic amount of side boob in the process. She should know better than to bother at a Lawrence fête; she could probably be doing naked jumping jacks and Shawn wouldn't bat an eye.

"Shawn. Pleasure." He shakes her hand, but I notice does not kiss it.

"So, Shawn, you've been monopolizing my date."

"Sorry about that. I didn't realize she was spoken for." A strange look comes over his face.

Marcy laughs her throaty laugh. "Not date-date—good Lord, no. You know how Lawrence feels about 'the lesbians.' Just my bestie and wing girl." Sad but true, for all his wonderful qualities, Lawrence does seem to have very old-school queeny ideas about lesbians and can let slip little phrases like,

"They're great if you need your landscaping done, but not really fun at parties." I let it go, considering his age, although it does make me a bit uncomfortable.

"Yeah, I have heard him mention something about the 'comfortable-shoe, Subaru-driving girls.'" Shawn makes air quotation marks and does a passable impression of Lawrence's lilting speech pattern, complete with a femme-y eye roll.

We all laugh, and Marcy continues to pick things off my plate, while the three of us hang out. Shawn, as it turns out, is a former client of Lawrence's; he had him design his condo when he moved to Chicago three years ago from California. Shawn is also a doctor, orthopedic surgeon to be specific, and apparently one of the go-to guys for not only the Bears but the Bulls as well. He is part of a sports medicine private group operating out of Northwestern. Very impressive. This is his first Lawrence party, so he really doesn't know anyone here, and seems grateful for me and Marcy and a quiet place to hang out. Guess the husband couldn't come.

"I have to go check on Alex, I'll be right back," I say, figuring the two of them can manage without me, and I head to the kitchen.

"Chef," I say to Alex, who is sending out a server with a fresh batch of chicken and waffles.

"Chef, you look awesome!" Alex says, winking at me.

"You are killing it in here," I say. "Everything is completely soigné." Alex laughs at my use of the French term, which means cared for, and which for a while was terribly overused by chefs to mean that food was really on point. I had a professor in culinary school who said it probably forty times a day.

"I'm just your hands; you're the one who killed it with this menu. And I hope you know I'm stealing the mac and cheese recipe."

"I'm happy to share. You need anything in here?"

"I think I'm good. I'm sending out the Frango mint brownies and the Dove ice cream sandwiches in a little bit."

"Perfect. Just yell if you need me."

"Stop. Go to your party. I got this."

"So you do."

I leave the kitchen and stop at the bar to get another round of Negronis, and somehow I manage to carry all three back to the corner we've staked out.

"My savior goddess!" Marcy says, accepting the glass happily.

"Thank you, Miss Eloise. You should have let me take care of that," Shawn says.

"Not a problem, I was right there at the bar."

Marcy gets pulled up to dance with a tiny little guy dressed as Al Capone.

Shawn and I make eye contact.

"I don't dance," we both say in near-perfect unison, which makes us crack up. We sip our drinks.

"Why don't you dance?" he asks me.

"Bum knee, Doc. Blew it out in high school."

He nods. "Basketball?"

The natural guess, given the size of me. "Nope, shot put. Pre-Olympic."

"Wow. You know, that is kind of badass."

"Yes, yes, it is. And you?"

"Two left feet. I have rhythm, you know, being a brother and all," he says in a jokey, extra-deep Barry White voice, "but I cannot seem to translate it to the dance floor."

"No dancing for us, then. What about you—dare I ask if you played football?"

"Guilty as charged. High school, college, got drafted, and then took a bad hit during preseason and busted out my shoulder. Two surgeries and a year of physical therapy and my time was officially done. Never played a single regular-season game in the big show."

"Ugh. Were you drafted here?"

"I wish. Vikings."

"Oooh. Rivals. Still, very impressive."

"Yeah, you've never heard the crunching noises my joints make when I move. Anyway, I really liked the docs who put me back together, figured it would be cool to do what they did, and I'd been a biology major undergrad. Thought I might do research stuff, when I was in school, you know, not figuring on football being any sort of guaranteed actual career path, but then the surgery made me think that maybe actual doctoring might be good."

"That is amazing. Seriously. I mean, I knew that a life of professional shot-putting would be glamorous and make me wealthy, so it was hard to let go of the dream, but I did have some cooking skills to fall back on."

"Hey, you knew how and when to pivot. That is half the battle in life."

Shawn is easy to talk to, and while periodically people come up to say hello to me or comment on my costume, and Marcy comes to check in between bouts of shaking her groove thing on the dance floor, we stick pretty much to ourselves. He just makes me feel completely at ease. So when he asks for my number, suggesting we hang out sometime, I'm delighted, figuring that a new friend will help me check off some of my social bet obligations. Shawn seems like he would be up for going to a class or something. He hasn't mentioned his significant other, so maybe things are rocky there. I don't feel like I should pry.

Marcy bops over. "Hey, my good man, can you cover me with this tall drink of water if I take off?"

"What, abandoning your date? I'm hurt and shocked." I'm neither, just mostly amused.

"Yeah, sorry about that, lovebug. But I just got a ping that there is some after-hours madness going down with the Bannos boys at the Purple Pig, and I know you are not going to let me drag you down there, no matter how I beg."

I shake my head. "You tell Jimmy Senior and Junior that I adore them, and that I am expecting an invite to ziti night at the house one of these days. Have a great time." I tend not to go to too many chef events around town. I think I'm always a bit sheepish that I have spent so many years away from restaurant kitchens, off the line, cooking quiet and private.

"Not to worry, Marcy, I've got you covered here. I will get your mermaid home in one piece."

"I owe you one." Marcy bows to him, nearly having a wardrobe malfunction, and kisses my cheek before heading out.

"She seems fun," Shawn says, watching her take three twirls across the dance floor during her exit.

"She's a great girl."

"And you really didn't want to go out with her? I go to the Purple Pig all the time—the food there is amazing. I would have thought you'd want to go, especially if you know the chefs there."

"Yeah, the late-night chef scene can be a little much—too much booze, too much food . . . I'm sort of a boring house mouse, really. I love this party of Lawrence's. It's a fun night, but really, I'm a total 'Netflix and hang out with my dog' kind of girl."

"I appreciate that. My ex was very much about the social scene, the right parties, endless charity events. I have to say, I don't miss that about L.A. at all. I'm glad to be back in Chicago, where people like dinner parties better than house parties, and I only have to break out my tux for rubber-chicken dinners three or four times a year instead of three or four times a month."

Hmmm. So it's an ex after all. Poor guy. Wonder if he left the former hubby in sunny California.

"Was it the breakup that brought you back here?"

"Sort of. My ex was very committed to staying in L.A., but I had an offer from my current group in their San Francisco office that was really appealing, especially since I have a lot of friends in the Bay Area and some family. And they said that if I joined the group in San Fran, I would have first dibs on any job that opened in Chicago, which I knew was ultimately what I wanted, a chance to really come home. The vibe in Northern California was much more my personality. When I said I wanted to seriously consider the job and the move, that was the end of the marriage."

Poor guy.

"I'm so sorry. That must have been really hard."

He shrugs. "We'd been growing apart for a while. Probably got married too fast to begin with, and probably for the wrong reasons. One of those good-on-paper situations, looking back at it. The job offer just crystalized things for both of us."

"I get it. My last relationship ended because my dad got sick and I had to come home from working abroad to help take care of him and my guy couldn't come here, and said he just wasn't up for waiting for me."

"For what it's worth, I think your guy was an idiot."

"For what it's worth, I think your guy was too."

"What guy?" Shawn looks puzzled.

"Your ex."

Shawn barks out a laugh. "Damn, woman, so much for my game. Here I am giving you all my best charms, and you are sitting here thinking I'm gay?" He pauses. "Not that there's anything wrong with that . . ." And he winks.

I can feel all the color drain out of my face. "But . . . you . . . you just . . . I mean . . . Lawrence . . . and you're . . . so . . . I mean . . . you smell good . . ." I'm sputtering like a complete fool.

He laughs again. "Well, thank you for that. My mama is a very big 'cleanliness next to godliness' woman, so I'm glad I'm not some big stinky fool up in here."

I can feel the blush burning my cheeks, and I stare into my lap.

Shawn takes one finger and raises my chin to meet his gaze. "Let me start over, pretty lady. My name is Shawn Sudberry-Long. I am a good man who loves his mother. I am a doctor, and I have had a tremendously fantastic time getting to know you a bit tonight, and would very much like to take you on a date and continue to get to know you, if that is something you think you might be up for."

I nod and manage to choke out, "Yep. Yeah. Okay."

"Okay, then. Now, would you still allow me to escort you home, or at least escort you into a cab if that makes you more comfortable?"

I want to crawl into a hole. Ten minutes ago I had a new gay best friend. Now I have some ridiculously good-looking man who *likes* me. I have no idea what to do with that. Ten minutes ago, on Marcy's direction, I would not have thought twice about letting him take me home, but now, I'm just too mortified.

"A cab, a cab would be really totally fine, you know. I mean, you live downtown, and I'm all the way up north . . ." Now I sound like I'm making excuses to not have him take me home because, what, I'm afraid?

But he nods sympathetically. "I get it, no problem. Shall we get you organized?"

I nod my head yes, and we stand up. He places a firm hand in the small of my back, which now sends some very specific tingles to some parts of me that tend not to get many tingly times, and we wind our way through the crowd to Lawrence.

"Darlings, you found each other. I hoped you would!" He kisses my cheek and shakes Shawn's hand. "Thank you both for coming, and enjoy the rest of your evening, whatever that brings." He winks lasciviously.

I can feel the blush coming back. "I'll see you Tuesday, Lawrence. Thanks as always."

"Great party, Lawrence. Really appreciate the invite."

Shawn and I head out and downstairs and into the brisk night air. He pulls out his phone. "Address, milady?"

"Oh, you don't have to, I mean, I can Uber . . ." I'm fumbling in my purse for my own phone. Shawn places his large warm hand over mine.

"Allow me."

So I do. I give him my address and he plugs it into the app.

"Look, Eloise, I didn't mean to shock you, and if you don't want to go out with me . . ."

"No!" I say much more vehemently than I mean to. "I mean,

yes, I was surprised. I just assumed based on context that you were gay, but I'm really—I mean, I really had a good time tonight, and you are a very nice guy and I'm just—I mean, I really would very much like to go out with you." I'm not quite getting my sea legs back under me, but at least I'm not a complete drooling idiot.

"That makes me very happy. By chance would you be free this coming Friday night?"

I think ahead. The Farbers are going out of town, so I have the whole weekend off, except for brunch with Glenn on Sunday. "Yes, yes, I am."

"Wonderful. I'll pick you up, let's say, seven?"

"Sure. That would be lovely."

"Is it okay if I call you, between now and then?"

"Of course. That would be nice."

A black Lincoln SUV pulls up. Shawn goes to open the door for me. "I'm going to text you when you pull away, so that you have my cell number in your phone. Would you mind texting me back when you get home so that I know you are safe?"

"Sure, I'll do that."

"Well, then, I'll talk to you soon, and I'll look forward to Friday night. Good night, Eloise."

"Good night, Shawn."

And then he leans forward and kisses me very gently on the lips, closed mouth, firm and with definite purpose, but not aggressive. It makes my breath catch. He closes the door for me and taps the side of the car to let the driver know that it is okay for him to pull away.

My head is reeling. Nothing like this has ever really happened to me. It was never the really handsome guy who singled me out for attention at parties. I was sort of always the girl the nice average guys might end up with after the hot girls shot them down.

My phone pings.

Get home safe, and I'll give you a call tomorrow.

This makes me smile with my whole face.

And when I walk into my house, after giving Simca a good head rub, I text him back.

Home safe and sound with my attack corgi. Thanks for a really lovely evening. I'll look forward to talking to you soon. I think for a second and then add, P.S. In the interest of full disclosure, it is important that I tell you . . . I'm not really a blonde.

I see three little dots blinking right away.

Thank you for letting me know. In the same spirit, I should tell you that I'm actually a five-foot-two Vietnamese goatherd. I have a really great costume guy.

This makes me laugh. I reply, I love goat cheese, so that should work out fine.

Three dots again. Glad to hear it. Talk to you tomorrow. Sleep well, Eloise.

I swoop down and pick up Simca, cuddling her in my arms. I might not dance in public, but what no one knows? I'm a serious secret-solo-dance-party girl. I waltz my confused dog around the living room laughing, and wondering if maybe, just maybe, I'm more ready for this whole dating thing than I thought.

# Eight

knock on the door of number 1024 in the very chic Park Newberry building. It swings open and Lynne, somehow looking impeccable and stylish in a Lululemon workout outfit, with a cute bandanna over her hair, grins at me.

"Welcome to the new pad!" she says, ushering me inside. "Teresa is running late . . ."

"As always," we say in unison, since being late is one of Teresa's main occupations. I put down my large bag and hand my coat to Lynne, who hangs it in the entrance closet.

"I can't believe you bought this place so *fast!*" I mean, we barely made the bet a month and a half ago back in September, and she is already moved into her new condo.

"It was just good timing. The owners had already moved to Florida, so the place was sitting empty. I was prequalified for much more than they were asking, and it was in such impeccable shape that there was no need for contingencies. My place was month-to-month, so timing wasn't an issue on my side. Really, I had a team come in and paint for a couple of days, and voila! Obviously I still have a lot of work to do, but I'm pleased." The place is covered in boxes, with artwork stacked against walls, but she has set up her living room pretty well, and has a nice spread of cheeses on the coffee table and a bottle of wine open. She pours me a glass and gives me the tour. The condo is pretty straightforward: two bedrooms, two and a half bathrooms, living room–dining room combo, and a large den that will clearly be an office. There's a well-appointed eat-in kitchen, plenty of storage, his and hers walk-in closets off the master, and a spectacular master bath.

"I see you've taken over both closets . . ." I say, laughing.

"Seasons, darling. Winter and fall there, spring and summer over here."

"Not exactly taking the 'if you build it he will come' attitude, I guess."

"Hell no. This is my place. If he comes, and frankly I don't know that I even want to go down that path again, then there will have to be a new neutral place when the time is right." Lynne continues to be somewhat bombastic about her ex-husband, but I'm the last person to call her out on that. I certainly keep any of my Bernard references on the overblown side. Because it is always easier to shoot for funny than it is for truth.

"That makes sense."

"You have no idea. I mean, when that lummox I married decided that the whole life we had been heading toward and planning for should just up and go another direction? I was fucked. I'd given up the best rental condo in the history of L.A. rentals and moved into his house, so after the divorce I had to find a new place, which wasn't nearly as great as the one I had given up. So this condo is for me. If someone shows up who actually is worthy of permanence, we are going to buy something new together and start fresh. But for now I'm building my life around me. And this is a good start."

"Well, it is gorgeous, congrats." I can see what she means about wanting to put down some very independent and personal roots. It sounds like her marriage, brief and badly conceived as she makes it sound, really threw her for a loop. I know from Teresa that they met and were married in just the span of six months or so, and that it only lasted a year and a half. Lynne's been divorced for over four years, so while most might wonder why she is still so vitriolic about her ex, I get it. I know better than anyone that there is no real time limit on how much damage someone can inflict, or how long it can take to recover. I've been home from France for a long time. But the Bernard wounds, while technically healed, are still red on the surface and tender to the touch. For all her tough-girl exterior, I know Lynne, and I know if she is still finding reasons to denigrate the former Mr., then she too is dealing with some stuff that makes your breath catch if you turn the wrong way and aches when the rain is coming.

The bell rings, and Lynne goes to let in Teresa while I look out at the view of Washington Square Park and the Newberry Library. It's not the kind of place I would ever want for myself, too modern, too new, but it suits Lynne to a T and I'm happy for her, if a little chagrined at how easy it all seems to be for her.

I know she is going to be the first to complete this stupid bet. And I don't really know why that irks me—after all, we were very clear this isn't about winners or losers. We can all fulfill the bet and be off the hook. We could all fail and have to write three checks. And yet, there is some tiny part of me that just doesn't want Lynne to cross the finish line before us. Which is weird, because I don't feel the same about Teresa, who flies into the apartment in a whirlwind of excuses about why she is late, handing Lynne a platter of cookies and shimmying her curves out of her coat. Hugs and kisses all around and then Lynne takes her on the tour while I retrieve my package from the front door and unwrap the still-warm loaf. I've made their old favorite, pizza strudel, a recipe I invented in high school. It's essentially pizza dough rolled out to a long rectangle, covered in a combination of mozzarella and provolone cheese, studded with chunks of sweet Italian sausage and slices of pepperoni, and then rolled up strudel-style and baked. I slide it onto a cutting board and slice it into inch-wide slices, pour some chunky roasted tomato sauce into a bowl for dipping, and arrange it all on the white platter I brought as both serving piece and hostess gift.

The three of us settle into Lynne's deep couch, making small plates and sipping the dark red wine.

"Cheers to Lynne on her new place and on checking off the big item on her list!" Teresa says, and we all clink glasses.

"How about Eloise having two actual *dates*! That is pretty major," Lynne says. "Even if there wasn't any chemistry."

"Or bacon." Teresa chuckles.

I told them about Jack, and they both gave me permission to count the date as a two-parter to help with my other social obligations, which I thought was generous of them. And of course I told them about Ethan, since if I'm going to be dating badly, it might as well provide some amusement.

I did not tell them about Shawn.

After all, Shawn and I aren't having our real first date till tomorrow night. So there is nothing to share, not yet. And for some reason, it was really easy to share about the Jack night, the blind date that turned into nothing, a funny story, what with me half-baked and him ogling the waitress. But meeting Shawn feels somehow different. Less funny and more un-nerving.

We've spoken on the phone every day since Saturday, talking as easily as we did at the party, and during the day he will send little funny texts or ask me what I'm cooking. Every time I get off the phone with him I'm really happy—for about three minutes, and then I get a pit in my stomach, and it sends me into something of a tailspin. I don't want to hope, or think great things, or imagine that he is going to be something or someone for me. It's been so long since I even entertained the thought; I feel like if I even dare allow the tiniest imaginings about him, it will pull some muscle. I realized that while I hadn't been looking forward to the dating part of the bet, it was because I was anticipating a series of dates sort of like with Jack—benign, of no consequence, all one-offs with no actual romantic pressure. They told me I had to date, not that I had to find a relationship. The idea of actually liking someone never occurred to me.

He called earlier tonight while I was in the middle of coaching Ian, and while I didn't take the call, apparently just seeing his name on my phone made something change on my face, because Ian stopped frosting his chocolate beet cupcakes with his vanilla goat cheese frosting.

"Why is your face all red and happy? Was that a boy?"

I'm mortified. "It was a friend. Less chat and more work, there, Chef."

"It was a boy," Ian said and then got back to work.

"I agree," Teresa says. "I think the dates are a big step. When is your next one?"

Sigh. "Tomorrow night," I say.

"Ooh. Do tell. Who is this one?" Lynne says, dunking a slice of pizza strudel into the tomato sauce.

"Just another Lawrence fix-up. Former client," I say, brushing it off. After all, it's true, and I don't need to tell them about the party or the communications that have occurred since.

"Well, I think you should broaden your horizons beyond just Lawrence," Teresa says. "So I hope it's okay, I gave your number to my cousin Joey. His best friend is divorced and a really nice guy, so expect a call from Angelo!"

"And Milo," Lynne says with a grin. "He's a marketing guy for a restaurant group."

Oy. So not excited about the coming deluge of new boys. But I suppose, for the bet, if everyone keeps sending me dates, I can get it all out of the way.

"Great, ladies, thank you for the assist! Enough about me. I want to hear how your stuff is going. I mean, obviously we are sitting in the first major hurdle for Lynne . . ."

"She's totally going to knock her whole list off in, like, two seconds," Teresa says.

"I know, right? Very annoying."

"Hey, I can't help it if I'm Just. That. Fierce." Lynne snaps up in the air with every word, the way she used to in high school when she was feeling proud of herself. We all laugh.

"Well, I'm not exactly having the same luck as the two of you," Teresa says. "I signed me and Giorgio up for a salsa-dancing class at the Park District, you know, heat things up a bit . . ."

"That sounds like fun," Lynne says. I think it sounds like a nightmare, but then again, I can't dance.

"That's what I thought! But the teacher was really annoying, and the class was way overcrowded, and we didn't really do much except step on each other's feet and then Gio got mad at me . . ."

"Why did he get mad?" I ask.

Teresa looks at her hands sheepishly. "I couldn't stop leading."

Lynne and I look at each other and bust out laughing.

"It's not funny! I was really trying, but when I tried I would just go all noodle legged, and then he would step on my feet and get madder . . . We ended up leaving class during the bathroom break and just going home."

"Well, at least you tried?" I say, trying not to laugh, since Teresa is clearly upset.

"Right, the bet isn't that you have to be successful at spicing up your relationship, just that you do things that show you are trying!" Lynne says. "After all, we didn't tell El she had to find a boyfriend, just that she had to be dating!"

I can feel myself wanting to grin, so I stuff half a piece of strudel into my mouth to hide my secret bit of happy.

"Well, I hope the next thing works, or I don't know what I'm going to do," Teresa says.

"Wha's the next thnngg?" I say, chewing the cheesy, meaty pastry.

"I signed up for a pole-dancing class," she says with a wicked gleam in her eye.

"Ha!" I say, almost spitting out my mouthful.

"Don't laugh too hard, I signed you up too," she says, making Lynne snort. "*Both* of you." Teresa looks at Lynne and nods determinedly.

"Hell to the no, woman. I am not getting up on a pole," Lynne says.

"Yeah, that is just not going to happen," I say, grateful for Lynne putting her foot down. If she had agreed, I would have been in trouble.

"Oh, yes, it is. Eloise, it is a social night out, so it checks off a box for you, and maybe you can find some hidden rhythm in your no-dancing body. And, Lynne, you are coming because you are way too fancy for your own good, and it will be fun. It's like a whole burlesque thing. You don't have to do the pole; you can do fan dancing or even belly dancing. The class is, like, ten girls and four instructors, and there will be cocktails." She holds her hand up as Lynne and I gear up to protest. "You. Are. Both. Coming." When Teresa puts her foot down, there is no point in arguing. I can kind of see Gio's point about the whole leading thing.

"Fine," Lynne says, throwing her hands up in surrender. "We'll come. What the hell."

"This should be seriously embarrassing," I say, imagining my enormous, ungainly self attempting to dance seductively while tripping over my own feet.

"Yep," Teresa says and winks lasciviously at us, and we all reach for more wine.

So I said, could you please take a break from Pokémon Go to perhaps do your job?" Lynne says, while Teresa and I make meaningful eye contact. The past hour has consisted of essentially a monologue about everything that annoys Lynne about people in her company. Teresa and I haven't gotten a word in edgewise, not that we need to, since neither of us would have any idea about any of the people she is referring to. Of the three of us, Lynne was always the really big talker, never shy about telling someone their story was annoying or making snoring noises while someone else was saying something she found boring. Teresa was plenty chatty, but never seemed to mind when Lynne interrupted or talked over her. I was always the good listener: my vocabulary of ums, mm-hms, oh nos, and of courses were well matched with my full cadre of head nods, shakes, brow furrows, and shoulder shrugs. When Teresa and I were alone, we were fairly evenly matched, especially since she was always good at asking people questions about themselves. But when the three of us were together, Lynne definitely took the conversational lead. Although I don't remember it being quite this egregious. It's like we could be anyone; we are just sitting here to be the vessels to receive her endless verbiage.

"Wow," Teresa sneaks in while Lynne takes a sip of wine.

"That's a lot," I say.

"Right? Seriously, these damnable Millennials are going to be the death of me. I told the rest of the partners, if they insist on bringing in all of these baby-faced interns, then part of the program should be to be sure they tell them to speak when spoken to, and do the job so I don't have to babysit. This is *work*. This is a j-o-b. You need a participation trophy and a twenty-four-hour Snapchat news cycle about your life and what kale-based products you ate for lunch? Go be a barista. Mama Lynne does not have time. Do the work, people, do it right so I don't have to come back after you and clean up your mess."

On and on she goes. This intern accidentally copied a client on a snarky e-mail that was supposed to remain internal. That partner dresses like she thinks she is Linda Evans on *Dynasty*.

This client is an idiot, that one is a misogynist, the other one might be a closet racist. Lynne went to her first condo association meeting and is clearly going to have to run for president next year if anything is going to happen. I check my watch.

"Um, Lynne, I have to go let the dog out," I say, unable to sit any longer.

"Oh, yeah, I should get back to the boys, didn't realize how late it's gotten," Teresa says, standing up along with me. "Do you need help cleaning up before we go?"

"Nah, I got this. Thanks for coming over to christen the place."

"Our pleasure. Congrats, sweetie. Enjoy it," Teresa says, pulling on her coat.

"Really a great place, Lynne, so happy for you," I say, and we hug and Teresa and I walk out and down the hall to the elevator.

"Holy crap," I say when the doors close.

"Yeah," Teresa says. "She was really wound up."

"I know she was always a talker, but that was weird and manic."

"I dunno, maybe she's just nervous. She's only been back a short time, and she only came back because she was hitting a ceiling at her L.A. firm and she had an iron-clad nonpoach clause, so she couldn't leave them and open her own shop, even though her clients loved her. She's in a new company, and now she's purchased a new home, which makes it all real. I guess it is a bit overwhelming for her."

"I guess," I say.

The elevator opens on the ground level, and we walk outside to go to our cars. Teresa gives me a hug. "I hope your date tomorrow night is really wonderful. Will you call me this weekend and tell me how it goes?"

I smile, thinking that actually, I hope my date is really wonderful too. "Yeah, I will, I promise."

"Okay. Drive safe. And, El?"

"Yeah?"

"She's still our Lynne."

I sort of know what she means. "Yeah. She is."

# Nine

This is one of the most delicious things I have ever eaten," Shawn says, finishing his first bite of lamb and immediately cutting me a piece and offering it across the table to me on his fork. I take it, reveling in the perfectly cooked, medium-rare, juicy meat.

"Yeah, well, wait till you try this . . ." I put a piece of my duck breast on my fork, being sure to get him some of the braised beluga lentils on top for a perfect bite. He accepts the mouthful and rolls his eyes happily. "I know, right?"

"Damn."

We are at Brindille, enjoying a spectacular French meal. And I really do mean enjoying. After a week of fairly constant communication, I was somewhat less nervous than I thought I would be for tonight. I mean, I was still a little agitated, but I managed to get myself dressed and made up without Marcy's help or gifted pharmaceuticals. Shawn picked me up in a huge black Uber car, looking even more handsome than I remembered him in a pair of well-fitting dark jeans, a deep eggplant shirt, and a black cashmere sport coat with a jaunty gray and black herringbone pocket square. He came to the door to fetch me, immediately complimented me on my brunetteness with a wink, and kissed me on the cheek before offering his arm and escorting me to the car. He asked if Brindille was okay—he figured French was a safe bet since I had lived in the country—and I admitted that I'd wanted to try it for ages.

"You know," he says, "we are really doing a job on the little ones tonight . . . veal, lamb, duckling, bunny . . ."

This makes me laugh. "It is a terrible thing, but the cuter the protein, the more delicious I find it!"

"I'm just so delighted to be with a woman who will eat."

"Well, you'll never get an argument with me. I've never been able to feign a birdlike appetite. As I'm sure is not a shock."

This is true. Even in my limited dating experience, I was not the girl who ordered light fare while on dates. Food is just too important to me, and it was always the thing Teresa and I both thought so weird about Lynne. She is super picky about her food in general, will eat some meat, but not on the bone, so she usually just gets fish or boneless chicken breasts, and always orders things with sauces on the side or no oil or limited salt, and almost always will send things back at least once. On dates, she would order salads with lemon and no oil and then push them around her plate. Teresa and I are both eaters, and our philosophy was always that while we didn't use dates as a place to pig out, at least we ate like normal people.

"Not a shock, just a very welcome observation. I love good

food, and frankly, I hadn't ever thought it was important as a quality in a date, but then . . ."

"You went out with someone who thought food was fuel?"

"Exactly! The worst. The ones who wish . . ."

"There was just a pill to take!" we say in perfect unison, and laugh. I take a sip of the rich wine, smooth with a hint of red fruits and a smell like old leather.

"Yeah. These days the whole food thing is just a Pandora's box," I say, remembering Ethan and his gluten-free vegan admission and how it completely shut me down where he was concerned.

"Exactly! Between people's sensitivities and preferences and the diet fad of the moment . . . it used to be that politics and religion were the hot-button issues. I'll be honest, I haven't really dated that much since my divorce, but now I feel like it is the first thing I should ask a woman . . . because I'm too old to manage someone's food neuroses. I mean, if you are allergic to something medically, no worries. If you have some preferences? Not a big deal, we all do. But some of this stuff these days? I'd take a Tea Party Republican Christian Scientist if she'll just eat gluten and bacon."

"I know, the whole paleo or raw diet or juice cleansing . . . Food shouldn't be hard. It should be a celebration."

"What about in your job—do you ever get clients who have those kinds of restrictions? I would imagine that would be really frustrating as a chef."

This strikes me as a very thoughtful question. "I'm super lucky. My main clients are a wonderful family of normal eaters, with a couple adventurous ones in the mix, and no restrictions or allergies. The usual personal preferences, of course—a couple of them don't love things too spicy, the dad isn't a huge fan of puddings or custards, and the smallest girl will not eat any condiment besides ketchup. And they all hate bell peppers."

"Well, I'm with them on that—bell peppers are not exactly my favorites either."

This makes me happy. I hate bell peppers. "Mine either. Were you beaten with stuffed peppers as a child?"

"Worse. My dad loved them on and in everything. In meat loaf and hamburgers and meatballs, stuffed, sliced on salads . . . on pizza."

"Oh, no! Not on pizza! It poisons everything!"

"See? You feel me. It's like grapefruit in a fruit salad. I love grapefruit, but it makes everything around it taste like grapefruit. I want grapefruit on its own, and I want melon to taste like melon, and I want no bell peppers anywhere near me."

"I'll drink to that." We clink our glasses, as the waiter clears our plates.

We order desserts and decaf espressos.

"So, Eloise Kahn. A gorgeous, smart, native Chicago girl who can cook, is a Bears fan, hates bell peppers, and likes to eat. You know, you make a guy start to believe in unicorns. I have to ask, how it is possible that you haven't been snapped up by now?"

I can feel the flush start in my neck and move up to my face, and I'm sure I'm now the color of a beetroot. "You are very sweet."

"I'm just honest. You seem so—I mean, please take this the right way—normal."

This actually makes me laugh, because it is the adjective most of the guys I have dated have always come up with. "By which you mean not obviously crazy and reasonably not high maintenance."

"In all the best possible ways. I think I mean that you appear to be a rational grown-up. A rare commodity in the dating world."

"Thank you, then, for that. I guess I just never really did enough dating to learn all the weird games and things people are supposed to play. I always mostly started as friends with guys, and then at some point something would just nudge us in a more romantic direction, and it never occurred to me to be anyone except myself. And since we were friends first, they already knew me, so it would have been weird to just change all of a sudden. I think you might actually be the first guy to ask me out in a traditional way!" I hadn't really thought about that, but it is true. All of my dating life has been either ending up in bed with a friend and waking up in a relationship, or blind dates that went nowhere. No middle ground. I'm thirty-nine years old and Shawn Sudberry-Long is the first guy to ever meet me, ask for my number, and ask me on a real date. It's exhilarating and sad all at once.

"That is an honor I will own happily. Makes me feel smarter than your average bear. I know what you mean about relationships of proximity. I had two girlfriends in high school and a couple in college. Mostly cheerleaders, since that was who was around with all the football. I rarely met many other girls. I dated a couple of fellow med students, out of desperate convenience, and a couple of nurses during my residency. It's probably why I ended up with my ex, Linda. She was different, not in the medical game; we met at a charity event and hit it off, and that was that."

I'm dying to know more, but I have to let him share on his own, at his own pace. I want to know what she looked like, what she did for a living, who she was and why it really ended.

I realize that I want to know all of this so that I can be everything she wasn't, because this is a really great guy and I'm liking him. Really liking him.

"That would make sense. My history is much the same; substitute fellow track-and-field guys for cheerleaders and culinary students and chefs for doctors and nurses and you've got it in a nutshell."

"And the last ex? The idiot that let you leave and didn't come with you?"

"The chef-owner of the last restaurant I worked at in France."

"Hmmm, maybe I shouldn't have gone for French food after all . . ." He has a twinkle in his eye.

"Oh, no, I still love all things French. Can't let one bad apple spoil the most glorious country and cuisine—that would be a much bigger tragedy."

"I've never been."

"To France?"

"Nope. Spent a bunch of time in Italy, some vacations in Spain, Germany, Austria, and a great trip to Amsterdam once, but never made it to France. Yet." There is something about the way he makes eye contact with me when he says "yet" that makes my heart skip a beat.

"You'll love it."

He doesn't break the gaze. "I believe I will."

I'm grateful for the arrival of our desserts and coffees. We place both plates in the middle and share them equally, a tangy lemon tart and a deeply flavored hazelnut cake.

When dinner is finished, he helps me with my coat and we head out to where another car is waiting for us. Shawn opens the door for me and then walks around to the other side and gets in. As soon as he sits down he takes my hand in his and I love how my fingers, always large and, to my mind, somewhat manly, feel dwarfed and delicate. His hand is huge and strong, and I can immediately feel my heart race and every nerve in my body is suddenly alive. The best way I can describe it is to say that I feel electric. As if he could touch me anywhere on my body and see visible sparks. He turns to look at me and gives a small tug on my hand, and I take his cue and shift toward him as he lifts his arm and slides it around me, pulling me close against his side. The warm length of him next to me is exquisite, and his arm around me makes me feel so safe. He leans over and kisses my temple as the car drives through Lincoln Park.

I turn to look at him and he kisses my mouth, very gently, like he is savoring me. It is so different from any first kiss I've ever had. There is no driving urgency, no devouring need behind it, and not a hint of insecurity or tentativeness. He kisses me as if kissing me is what we were made for, as if he knows that he has all the time in the world to just kiss. It isn't the fumbling, curious kiss of high school or college, where the kiss itself is a question. It isn't the kiss of two exhausted culinary students or chefs half-drunk and falling together to scratch an itch. And it certainly isn't the all-consuming kiss that started my affair with Bernard, who grabbed me with force and determination and kissed me like he was staking a claim. Shawn kisses me like kissing me is his most favorite thing to do, and the kissing is for its own sake and not a part of something else. Then he stops, just as gently as he started.

"My goodness," he says, his voice low. "I hope that wasn't too . . . I mean, I don't want you to feel . . ."

"It was lovely, thank you."

"Eloise, I hope it isn't too soon to say that tonight was

maybe one of the most enjoyable nights I've had in recent memory, and I would very much like to do it again."

"For me too. And yes, I would love to see you again." I love that he is doing this now, here, in the car. It is almost as if he is assuring me that he isn't going to pressure me to continue the evening, to go further. It is a gentleman's ask and I'm enormously grateful. Because, as much as my body is responding to him in all sorts of flashy ways, I know I'm not ready for more. Not yet.

"I've got some family obligations the rest of this weekend, but maybe Monday or Tuesday night?"

I think quickly. Monday will be chaos with the Farbers just getting back. But Tuesday I have Lawrence, which is pretty easy, so I can use the rest of that day to prep some stuff for Wednesday so that I won't have to get up quite as early.

"Tuesday would be perfect."

He smiles. "Wonderful. Can we keep the time a little flexible? I have an afternoon surgery that should be done by five, and I should be able to do the paperwork quickly, but just in case, can we say I will pick you up somewhere in the six-thirty-to-seven-thirty range? I'll text you when I am out of surgery with something more precise."

"Of course. That would be fine."

The car pulls up in front of my house. Shawn holds up a finger to me to indicate that I should wait for him to come open my door. He gets out of the car and walks around to get me, then escorts me up my front steps.

"Thank you again for a wonderful night," I say.

"Thank you. I'll give you a call tomorrow, and look forward to seeing you Tuesday." He leans down and kisses me one more time, his hands in my hair, holding my head to his. Then he takes my key from me to open my door, kisses my hand when he gives me the key back, and heads back to the car.

I head inside, drop my bag on the console table by the door, and, with my feet barely touching the ground, go over to the couch in the living room. I flop down, and Simca hops up beside me. She looks at me with her head tilted like she doesn't recognize me at all. I can't blame her, I barely recognize me either. Unable to wipe the grin off my face, I reach for my laptop. There are several e-mails from Teresa and Lynne.

From: MamaItalia2734@gmail.com
To: LynneRLewiston@HampshirePR.com;
    ChefEloise@gmail.com
Subject: Sunday is the big day!

Hope you girls are ready for our burlesque class! El—how was date #3? Horror show? Joey says Angelo will be in touch soon . . .

T

Lynne has already replied.

I am only doing this for moral support.
    Yeah, El . . . how did it go tonight? Short? Comb-over? Milo is out of town this week, but I know he will be in touch when he gets back.

L

_____

Yeah, well, Milo might be out of luck if Angelo gets there first . . .


T

_____


Cousin Joey's bestie? Doubtful.


L


It is sort of annoying that they both appear to be assuming my date would be a disaster. But now I have a problem. Because for some reason, I don't want them to know about Shawn. I don't want to hear their opinions; I don't want to solicit their information. I weirdly don't even want to tell Marcy quite yet. He feels like a delicious secret that is just for me. Like the little treat chefs hide in the kitchen for themselves for after the party is over . . . the oysters of the chicken, the ends of the brisket, the last piece of bacon, the corner brownie. Kissing Shawn feels like licking the bowl of frosting once the cake is finished, or eating the last spoonfuls of still-warm risotto in the pan while you are cleaning up. Extra special, private, the littlest bit naughty.

I hit reply all.


Date was fine, not horror show, neither short nor bald nor unpleasant, nothing much to report, dinner was good. I feel like I am going to get the hang of this dating thing. Will look forward to hearing from Angelo and Milo to see which of them can win my love.

Speaking of which . . .

T—Anything heating up at your house besides lasagna?

L—How did the meeting with the matchmaker go?

Oh, and by the way, signing you guys up to come to a glassblowing class with me as part of my list.

XOE

I shut the computer down and let Simca out into the backyard for her nightly business. My phone pings. I have a text from Shawn.

It's going to be really hard for me to fall asleep with this grin on my face. You are delicious. I hope that is okay to say. Sleep tight.

I type quickly.

It is very okay to say. Thank you for such a great evening. Sleep tight yourself.

I head upstairs, get ready for bed, let Simca come cuddle up beside me, and find that despite Shawn's worry, you can actually fall asleep smiling after all.

# Ten

pull into the parking lot behind the nondescript building on Diversey with the discreet signage: *L'Amour Dance Studio.* Good Lord. I'm wearing a new workout outfit: black leggings and a black fitted tank with built-in bra, a zip-up fleece jacket, a new pair of trainers on my feet. My recent bet-related embracing of a fitness regimen required the acquisition of some gear, since, while chefwear is comfortable for a lot of things, working out isn't on the list. I've been testing the options at various facilities around town, and so far I enjoy the water classes best because they are easiest on my joints. I've also had a test session with a personal trainer who specializes in sports injury recovery, working on building muscle mass specifically around supporting old injuries and protecting the body from future reinjury. It was strange to be back in a gym, lifting weights again after over thirty years. But the trainer seemed impressed. "The body remembers form and breathing and technique." She said I wouldn't have as far to go as I think to get my body back into better condition. Pilates and yoga have both been recommended to me, but I'm hesitant. They feel a little too earthy-crunchy to me, but I haven't ruled them out yet.

The studio is dimly lit with pink and lavender lighting, and the walls are upholstered in tufted magenta velvet. There is a vague scent of gardenia in the air, which I'm presuming is meant to be romantic but reminds me vaguely of a perfume my grandmother wore. There are some other women milling around, looking at photos on the walls, cases of costume items, feather boas, corsets . . . I look around and spot Lynne across the room in a quiet corner sitting on a huge antique settee, immersed in her phone. When I step toward her she holds up a finger to let me know that she wants to finish what she is doing. The gesture is a little self-important and more than a little dismissive, and it lands badly with me. It reminds me of when we were kids and if anyone ever said anything she disagreed with, she would hold up her hand in front of their face. She did it with a smile, like it was a joke, but it never felt like much of a joke on the receiving end, and it always took most of my willpower not to swat her hand away. Teresa and I used to call it the Edicts of Lewiston, the way Lynne always presented her opinions as if they were indisputable facts, in a tone that indicated that if your opinions differed, not only were you wrong, but you were also an idiot. It makes me think about me and Lynne making fun of Teresa's constant lateness, and I wonder what the two of them as a duo find annoying about me.

Lynne finally looks up from her phone and smiles at me. She pats the seat next to her, and I plop down into the deep cushions. "That crazy woman has precisely six minutes to show up to her own stupid dance class, or you and I are getting out of here and finding the nearest Bloody Mary."

"No argument from me."

A scantily clad trio of women appear in the lobby, opening a large set of double doors into the studio space. The other women start to head inside. Lynne checks her watch again and raises an eyebrow at me. "Four minutes."

"I'm sure she'll be here."

"We shall see." She turns back to her phone just as Teresa comes flying through the door.

"Hi, hi, I'm here . . ." she says breathily. "Traffic, and just, crazy at home with the kids . . . and you know, me!"

"Whatever," Lynne says. "Let's get this fiasco over with, shall we? I feel a thousand years old. All the girls that just went in there look about twelve."

We head into the studio space and drop our bags on some chairs in the corner of the room.

A heavily made-up woman in a black brocade corset, platform stilettos in red satin, and a long purple feather boa strides to the front of the room.

"Hello, goddesses! Can everyone gather around, please?"

Lynne looks at me with pure disdain on her face as Teresa grabs our hands and pulls us toward the front of the room.

"So, today is going to be fun! This class is about being loose and free and in our bodies and celebrating the fabulous sensual power that we all have within us. Everyone will get a chance to do all three techniques that we are exploring here today: fan dancing, chair dancing, and pole dancing. We'll be working in small groups. We'll get started in just about five minutes—in the meantime, you'll see some costumes and accessories on the racks and bins in the back of the room. Deck yourselves out in something that makes you feel sexy!"

"I hate you," Lynne says to Teresa.

"C'mon, it will be fun, we'll just stick together," Teresa says, pulling us both over to a bin and draping a blue boa around Lynne's shoulders.

"Yeah, Lynne, it will be fun," I say, pulling out a pink satin stretchy waist cincher and snapping it around my thick middle.

"What the hell. Let's get this over with." Lynne hands Teresa a sheer silver scarf and we all head over to the other side of the room where there is a set of shiny chrome poles calling our names.

Well, this is not exactly how I had hoped to spend my Sunday," Lynne says, handing me a cup of coffee.

"Yeah, me either." I take it gratefully.

"Nurse says she should be in recovery for about another hour before we can see her."

Giorgio comes flying into the waiting room, trailed by three enormous dark-haired boys. He comes over and hugs Lynne and turns to me.

"It's so good to see you, Eloise, really, Teresa is very glad to have you both back." He gives me a powerful hug. He's just as I remember him, dark hair now sparkling with gray, and thinning a bit around the hairline, but still a big handsome guy with a broad smile. "Come meet the boys. Gio Junior, Francis, Antony, this is your auntie Eloise." They all shake my hand deferentially. The honorific sounds strange since I've never met any of them.

"Boys, here's some money, go find yourselves a snack or

something." He hands over a handful of bills to Gio Junior, and the three boys head off down the hall. Giorgio turns to us. "What the hell happened?"

"She fell. Broke her ankle in a couple of places. They are putting in some pins," Lynne says matter-of-factly.

"She's going to be bionic!" I say, in a very lame attempt at humor. Lynne and Gio both look at me awkwardly.

"How did she fall?" he says.

"We were in an exercise class," Lynne says pointedly, sending me a message that I shouldn't elaborate. After all, while Teresa wants to spice up her marriage, she wants it to be organic, and she certainly would not want to embarrass Gio by talking to us about feeling neglected. I suddenly realize that Teresa likely hasn't told Gio about the bet at all, let alone that part of it.

"Yep," I say. "My fault, trying out some new things, wanted to get back into shape."

"Well, I know she was looking forward to hanging out with you girls."

Lynne snorts. I can't look at her or I'm going to laugh.

Because hanging was exactly what got Teresa in trouble. She was very enthusiastically executing a spin in a pair of borrowed Lucite heels when she tried to put down her foot at the end of the spin, the heel caught, the ankle turned, and she lost her grip on the pole, and her full weight just snapped the ankle with a loud crunching noise.

"Well, we are having a good time reconnecting, but obviously we'll have to plan some less athletic events in the future," Lynne says.

"I'll bring over some dinners and things this week," I say, my first impulse always to cook for someone.

"I can help with shuttling the boys to things if you need," Lynne says, in a way that makes me think she is more likely to give them all access to her Uber account than actually take them anywhere.

"Not to worry, ladies. Between the women at the church and the PTA girls, not to mention my aunts and sisters, we'll have the home front covered. You can be on cheering-up and keeping-company duty. Because if my T can't cook and keep the house and run our boys around, she's gonna go sixteen types of crazy. So plan on some quality time, *capeesh*?"

"Of course," I say.

"That goes without saying," Lynne says.

A doctor comes out. "Teresa Minetti?"

We all wave.

"She did great. Surgery went perfect, and the ankle should heal well. She's in the recovery room, and a little loopy, but you should be able to take her home in a couple of hours. She'll have a sheet that tells you everything you need to know about caring for her. She'll have a boot on and I'm giving her a prescription for a medical knee walker so that she can get around. There are a couple of places to rent them if you prefer—might want to ask your insurance what they cover. But you can go in and see her in a moment."

"Thank you, Doc, really appreciate it," Gio says.

"She's requested the ladies first . . ." the doctor says. "A nurse will be out soon to escort you in."

You dinn't tell him . . ." Teresa says groggily when Lynne and I come in the room.

"Of course not," Lynne says.

"I said it was my fault, I was trying out some new exercise programs, and you guys were just helping me out."

"Did he asssh what kind of class?" she asks.

"He didn't, but we should know one, just in case . . ." Lynne says, turning to me.

"I'm signed up for Zumba at Lakeshore Fitness tomorrow morning?" I admit sheepishly.

"Perfect," Lynne says. "Just the kind of fast dancing old klutzy here could injure herself on. T? That registering with you?"

"Yesh. Zuuuumba. We were Zumbaing and I twisted my ankle and fell on it," Teresa says sleepily.

"Excellent. We're gonna let your boys in. We'll check in tomorrow," Lynne says, leaning over to kiss her cheek.

"Try and get some rest. Talk to you later," I say, squeezing her hand, and Lynne and I leave the recovery room and head out to send in her family.


Ouch!" Shawn says when I relate the details of her injury on the phone. "That is a bad one. Ankles are hard—however optimistic the doc was, they often never really fully heal. She's likely to have some residual pain and weakness pretty much permanently. How did she do it?"

I pause. I think about telling him about the bet, but then I think it might make it look like I'm only going out with him for that, so I chicken out. "Exercise dance class. I'm trying out a whole bunch of new things to try and get into better shape, and they were keeping me company."

"I like your shape just fine, doesn't look like it needs any improvement from where I sit."

I blush. "Well, thank you, but I'm sure you understand as a

former athlete, when you start to think you've really let yourself go, it doesn't feel great."

"I know what you mean. You spend all those years focused on your body, conditioning it to do what you want it to do, and when that stops being its primary function, you have to figure out how to feel healthy while balancing that with more normal life."

"Exactly! At first it feels like getting away with something to not work out as much, or as hard, but for me it was too easy to get out of the habit altogether."

"When I was in med school, it was okay, because I could study on the treadmill, and I had a buddy who was a gym rat too, so we would quiz each other and do flashcards as part of our weight reps. But when I got into my residency? The only exercise I got was running around the hospital. I took the stairs, biked there when the weather was nice, but getting to the gym? Didn't happen."

"You were better than me. I finished physical therapy, went to college and did just enough to maintain my recovery, and then I moved to France and most of my exercise was walking somewhere close to eat something delicious!"

He laughs. I love his laugh. Deep and resonant. "Well, if being healthier is important to you, as a medical professional, I support all of that. You said you are trying a bunch of stuff—anything you like so far?"

"I seem to do the best with swimming and water-based activities. I know water aerobics sounds like the most popular class at the senior center, but I love the weightlessness, and how easy it is for me to stretch in the water."

"I recommend water classes for a lot of my patients. Just swimming in general is a great workout. I enjoy it myself. In fact, if you like, I'm a member at East Bank Club and sometimes I do their Power Circuit Pool Workout. It's really good. Only on Wednesdays from six to seven in the morning. Want to meet me and we'll do it together and then have breakfast before work?"

My heart stops. East Bank? The city's toniest health club, full of hard-body trainers and tiny little exercise-obsessed women who glow instead of sweat? Morning isn't exactly my best time, plus, water? This means a bathing suit and no makeup and wet hair and . . .

"No pressure, I mean, if you don't want to . . ." he says.

"I do!" I don't! Why did I say that?

"Great! It's a really fun class, challenging, but the instructor is cool. And the Grill makes some very tasty omelets."

"Sounds like fun, thank you." Sounds like a nightmare. And it sounds like I have to buy a new bathing suit ASAP.

"I'm just excited that I get to see you two days in a row. What do you think about steak for Tuesday night? Since we're going to be all athletic Wednesday morning . . ."

I can't be too upset when he is already locking down a third date before our second date even happens. "I never say no to steak."

"Have you been to Boeufhaus yet?"

"Not yet, but I hear great things."

"Well, then, let's give it a shot!"

Simca gives a little bark at the door. "Speaking of exercise, looks like someone is in need of a walk before bed."

"I will let you go. Busy day tomorrow?"

"Yep, groceries bright and early and then at the Farbers' all day getting the week organized."

"I'll let you work, and check in tomorrow night if that is all right?"

It's more than all right. "Sounds good."

"Have a good night, Eloise."

"You too, Shawn."

I get up off the couch and put Simca's leash on her. We head out into the brisk November air. It's hard to believe that Thanksgiving is just two and a half weeks off. Just thinking about it puts a little spring in my step. I love Thanksgiving. It's my favorite holiday. In the past couple of years, we've developed a ritual. Since the Farbers are the types who like to eat Thanksgiving dinner at around three p.m., and my family has always preferred Thanksgiving dinner at dinnertime, I get to work the morning and early afternoon, and still get to Mom's for family dinner in plenty of time. Since I'm prepping all week anyway, I do double prep at the Farbers', getting all their favorites organized, as well as the dishes that my family counts on. The menus are similar, but with some important differences. The Farbers like a corn bread stuffing with sausage; my family is an herb-and-onion, regular-bread stuffing group. They like their sweet potatoes mashed, with marshmallows on top; we go for sliced, with a praline pecan topping. They do green beans and we do Brussels sprouts. But both families like a classic roasted turkey with pan gravy, homemade cranberry sauce, soft yeast rolls, mashed potatoes, and apple pie for dessert.

Just thinking about Thanksgiving makes my stomach rumble, and I realize that with all the excitement of the day, I've pretty much forgotten to eat, which is very unlike me. Simca finishes her business, and I do my blue bag duty, grateful for a small neat dog that makes small neat poops. She looks up at me with her signature smile, and I praise her for being such a good girl, dropping the bag into the garbage can on the corner. We head for home, and I make a mental note of what is lying about my larder. It'll be pasta for sure, fast and filling. I know there are a couple leftover roasted chicken thighs from a recipe test I was doing yesterday. We head up the front stoop, and I slip off her leash, give her a treat from the jar on the console by the door, and head for the kitchen to wash my hands.

I shred the chicken with my fingers and put it into a small skillet to warm, separate a couple of eggs, and whisk the yolks quickly until they have lightened and thickened. Pour in a healthy glug of cream, then grate a flurry of cheese over the top, mixing it in. I zest a lemon from the bowl into the mix, and then squeeze in the juice. Some salt and pepper. I go over to the pots in my window and, with the scissors I keep there, snip off some parsley and chives, which I chop roughly and add to the mix. When the pasta is al dente, I drain it quickly, reserving a bit of the cooking water, and add it to a large bowl with a knob of butter, mixing quickly to coat the pasta. I add in the lemon sauce, tossing with a pair of tongs. When the whole mass comes together in a slick velvet tumble of noodles, I taste for seasoning, add a bit more ground black pepper, and put the shredded chicken on top with a bit more grated cheese.

A fork and a cold beer out of the fridge, and I take the bowl out to the living room, tossing Simca a piece of chicken, and settle in on the couch to watch TV, twirling long strands of the creamy lemony pasta onto my fork with pieces of the savory chicken, complete comfort food. I realize that while this is something I make all the time, I've never really written down a recipe for it, but maybe I should. I wish I could say that I have the willpower to leave half of the enormous bowl for my lunch tomorrow, but it doesn't take long for me to be dragging the last forkful through the dregs of sauce in the bottom of the dish. I'll have to make it to bring to Glenn this week.

I put the bowl to the side and reach for my laptop, opening a new document. I write down the ingredients and my best guess of the amounts in the delicious meal I've just thrown together. In order to turn a last-minute jumble of stuff into an actual recipe, I'll have to go back and measure everything precisely, while making very specific notes about techniques, timing, temperatures, and the like. What was the effort of about fifteen minutes will become several hours of testing and retesting so that someone who isn't a chef can still make it with the same yummy results. I know a lot of people would dread the process, purposely complicating something that started so simply. But I love it.

It makes me think of Julia Child and her compatriots, testing over and over to make my favorite cookbook work so perfectly. It's why my heart has always wanted to do a cookbook, so that everyone gets the scrumptious things they want when they want them and also the satisfaction of doing it themselves. That pride when you cook something and it is so satisfying; it is love on a plate.

Hmm. *Love Plates.* That actually might be a good title for the cookbook.

"What do you think, my little fur nugget?" I reach over to scratch between Simca's ears. "How does *Love Plates* sound?"

Simca gives me a wide grin, and then settles her sweet head onto my knee. My phone rings and I reach for it, hoping it is Shawn calling to say good night, but I don't recognize the number.

"Um, Eloise? My name is Milo. I'm a friend of Lynne's— she said I should give you a call?"

My stomach turns over. I'd forgotten about Lynne and Teresa being so helpful with the dating part of my list. "Sure, hi, Milo, yes, Lynne mentioned that she had given you my number." I don't exactly know what to do with this. On the one hand, I have no real interest in dating anyone besides Shawn; on the other, we've technically only had one date, and while there are two more on the books, the presumption of exclusivity would be completely insane, on either side. And I do have the bet to think about. But I'm dreading having to meet yet another new person.

"Great, well, I was wondering if you might be free for drinks sometime this week," Milo says.

I think about Tuesday night, and my date with Shawn. Thursday night, I have a drawing class, Wednesday night I'm bringing dinner to Glenn, and I want to save the weekend for Shawn should he want to lay claim to either Friday or Saturday night. "Um, I appear to be free tomorrow evening, if that would work?" I say, hoping that he is busy.

"Darn, I've got an event tomorrow night. Nothing else this week?"

I scroll through my calendar again. "Sunday might work?"

"Yeah, I can probably make that work on my end as well. Should we say sixish? Webster's Wine Bar on Kedzie?"

"Yes, that sounds good. I look forward to meeting you."

"Me too. You've got my number if something comes up?"

I check my phone. "Yep, right here in my phone."

"Terrific. I'll text you a picture so you know what I look like."

"That sounds great."

I hang up and put the date into my calendar. I feel conflicted. I do like that it helps check a date off my list, and at least it is a Lynne connection, so he probably won't be horrific. But my head is obviously elsewhere.

I pull up the chart I made for my list. So far, I'm on track for the dating part of the bet. I've got my drawing classes, so the nonfood hobby is underway, ditto the athletic endeavors. I'm slowly pulling together the recipes I think would be the best examples for the cookbook proposal, but I still have no idea how to write the proposal itself. I mean, who the hell am I? Some non-famous, non-restaurant-owning, non-blogging nobody who cooks for one family, one septuagenarian, and my family. Who am I to think that anyone would care about a cookbook I've written? I'm feeling a bit behind on the whole socializing-with-strangers thing, but I've done some research and found some classes that seem like they could be fun: wine tasting, a special movie screening event at the Xfinity store, and the glassblowing and such. So strangely, I'm doing okay with the whole thing. My anxiety about it has definitely diminished.

I feel like Mrs. O'Connor would be a bit proud.

Because I can write that check if I lose this bet fair and square and after giving it my best shot. But I know I wouldn't be able to honor her memory with less than my best effort. So I have to keep plugging away. I have to have drinks with Milo and find more social activities, and I have to figure out how to write a cookbook proposal that at least fakes a belief that I have something of value to add to that oversaturated marketplace.

And if I'm going to do all of that? I'm going to need chocolate. Lots and lots of chocolate.

Since tomorrow is my free night, I figure I will swing by Teresa's and visit, and as I recall, she always loved chocolate too. So tonight? I'm going to do a final test of my triple-chocolate chewies, dark chocolate cookies with white and milk chocolate chips, one of the recipes I'm thinking of including in the proposal, and I just want to make them one more time to be sure they are perfect.

"C'mon, girl. Come keep Mama company while she makes some cookies for Teresa." Simca and I both haul our carcasses off the sofa and head for the kitchen, where nothing is confusing and everything is safe and I know with total certainty who I am and what I am supposed to do.

# Eleven

W hat time tonight?" Lynne asks when I put the phone on speaker so I can keep working. I'm just crimping the top crust over a mound of apples on the second pie.

"Six thirty for cocktails. We'll probably sit down for dinner around seven thirty."

"And you're sure I can't bring anything?"

"Lynne, you are a horrible cook. Besides, between my prep, and my mom and Aunt Claire baking and filling in with the old family favorites, we already have enough food for a dozen people and there are only the four of us!"

"Sounds more like a coven meeting than Thanksgiving," Lynne says. I had been surprised to discover while we were visiting Teresa over the weekend that Lynne didn't have plans for Thanksgiving. Both of Lynne's folks are gone, and while she has open invitations from her aunts, she says that Christmas with them and the extended family is plenty of quality family time and that Thanksgiving would just be too much. Teresa and her brood go to Gio's sister's house, and she immediately invited Lynne to join, but I saw the panicked look on Lynne's face and jumped in to cajole her to join me and my mom and Aunt Claire. She accepted gratefully.

"Yes, it does at that. But it is a nice quiet dinner, and we'll all get ample leftovers."

"Wine at least?"

"That you can do." Lynne keeps a very well-stocked wine fridge and has impeccable taste.

"Okay, just one more thing . . . A friend of mine from California just got an extended consulting job here, doesn't know anyone, thought I'd give him your number . . ."

"Yeah, I think your matchmaking days are over. I can't believe you'd even suggest it after the Milo debacle!"

"He still feels terrible," Lynne says, snorting.

"As well he should!" Milo did, indeed, text me a picture as he said he would. But it wasn't of his face. I was shocked. Then I was disgusted. Then I quickly replied to cancel the date.

"It was an accident, he just clicked the wrong picture," Lynne says.

"Okay, the mere fact that such a thing is even *possible* completely squicks me out. You get that, right?"

"Completely. But at least he wasn't trying to send you a dick pic on purpose."

"Oh, yeah, that makes it *so* much better. No more fix-ups from you for now; lady, you are on probation."

"Well, at least he didn't take you on a date to his *mother's house*." Lynne is really laughing now.

Sigh. Cousin Joey's friend Angelo called shortly after the Milo incident and was so respectful and sweet that I agreed to a date. And he did indeed take me to dinner at his mother's house. It felt like an arranged marriage. It was the most awkward evening possible, with Angelo and I trying to get to know each other while his mother kept shoveling more masses of gummy, congealed lasagna onto our plates. Teresa was almost as mortified as Lynne was about the pornographic accident, and apparently Cousin Joey got quite the piece of her mind.

"Yeah, *both* of you are on the no-fly list for fix-ups. I'll see you tonight."

This doesn't bother me in the least, because Shawn and I have had five more dates in the past two weeks, and it just keeps getting better and better. He took me for steaks at Boeufhaus, followed by ice cream sundaes at Margie's. The next morning I met him for the swimming workout class and I was stunned at the sheer glory of his body, his muscles beautifully defined under smooth skin, with just the tiniest bit of softness over his abs keeping him at least a bit human. And, despite my concern about the form my own form is in, my new Miraclesuit bathing suit with a zillion internal panels kept everything reasonably locked down and Shawn's gaze was all I needed to let the self-consciousness melt away. He looked at me the way I look at chocolate cake.

Our mutual competitive natures kicked in as soon as the class started, both of us working hard, encouraging each other, and pushing ourselves to the limit. Showered and changed, we had a hearty breakfast at the club café before heading to work, and Shawn, as I had hoped, asked me out for that Saturday night. We went to dinner and a movie, and made out like teenagers. We both had busy schedules last week—I had to begin

Thanksgiving prep and spend some time keeping Teresa company while her sisters-in-law went through her house like cleaning machines, but we talked on the phone every day. We went to a play Friday night and on Sunday we had brunch and walked the 606 trail.

Today he is with his family, but he is coming to my house later tonight for a nightcap after we are both done with family obligations. Which has me all freaked out, since I'm pretty sure tonight is the night we are likely to actually fully consummate this relationship. Because I like him. I really like him. And I trust him. He has been such a gentleman, has taken the physical part of our relationship so gently and slowly, that now, instead of being nervous about going to bed with him, I'm beyond ready, I'm eager. I haven't been eager since Bernard. And it is that very eagerness that scares me most.

I still haven't told anyone about him. I mean, Lawrence knows, and has been wonderful about not prying. He is glad we connected and doesn't push for information. Teresa and Lynne know I'm generically "dating," obviously, for the bet. I send them pics of movie and theater tickets and menus at restaurants so that I get credit, but all they know is that Lawrence is doing a good job of fixing me up. I haven't mentioned any of it to my mom or Aunt Claire. I've convinced myself that until Shawn and I are sleeping together it isn't a real thing, so I don't have to fess up to anyone about him. I don't know why I'm still so skittish about telling them I've met someone who has real potential, but I think in some ways I'm waiting for the other shoe to drop.

Or waiting for the sex to be bad.

I was never really the sexiest girl, never felt that comfortable with any of it, honestly. My high school, college, and culinary school dating was fine, but never really earthshaking. I never understood how people got all insane when it came to sex; when I was getting it I enjoyed myself, but when I wasn't, it never really bothered me all that much.

Until Bernard. Sex with Bernard was incredible, intoxicating, and likely the reason I was so blind as to who he really was. It was boundary shattering. Soul opening. I had no idea that two bodies could create that much intense pleasure. It was like I'd been eating basic roast chicken my whole life, sometimes dry and kind of unsatisfying, sometimes juicy and delicious, but never something that was much more than simple sustenance. Bernard was roasted duck. Skin crisp and crackling and fatty, meat succulent and the slightest bit gamy and exotic—everything that chicken, while the same general shape, isn't and never can be. I got addicted to him, to his touch, to the taste of him, to the feel of his body against mine, to the way he filled me up. He could just look at me a certain way across the room and my knees would go weak. He could whisper something in my ear on his way through the kitchen, and I would have to excuse myself to the bathroom to furtively give myself relief before I could continue to function. It was the most centered I ever felt in my body, aware of every nerve ending, every inch of my skin alive and craving his touch. And with that intense physical connection came the emotional one, as if breaking open that sexual barrier also broke open every secret chamber of my heart and soul, and I let him know me the way no one has ever known me, every deep dark scary part of me, and it was safe and I loved him and I believed it was forever.

I've convinced everyone, including myself, that sex isn't important to me. That relationships aren't important to me. But the truth is, I can't imagine myself being with anyone for any length of time who makes me feel any less than Bernard did, and at the same time, I can't imagine ever letting anyone else in that deep again. Because when they go away, if they go away, that wound is too big to heal fully. I've had plenty of injuries in my life, and usually, with proper care and time, it's like they never happened. But the damage Bernard caused was apocalyptic. The scars are numerous and varied and I keep finding them in the oddest places. They are still tender when pressed. Why haven't I dated? Because the only thing that scares me more than never feeling what I had with Bernard is the idea that I might indeed find that again.

So now I'm prepping Thanksgiving and keeping focused on a wonderful meal for the Farbers and then repeating a wonderful meal for my mom and Aunt Claire and Lynne, all the while trying to deal with the duality of being excited to see Shawn tonight, and nervous about what might happen. At least for the moment, it's quiet and I'm just concentrating on crimping a piecrust as attractively as I can manage.

Shelby and Brad and the kids are all at a local senior facility, serving Thanksgiving brunch to the residents who don't have family to visit them. It's the perfect thing to keep the kids aware of how important giving back is, especially during the holidays, and it keeps them all out of my hair so that I can get their dinner organized. Ian has been helping all week, and he is a more-than-competent sous chef, but to be honest, I really like the solitude of doing this work alone. It's my twentieth Thanksgiving, I realized earlier this week. I've officially been making this meal more than half my life, having taken it off my grateful mother's hands my first year home from college. I'd been missing having access to a kitchen, and came home from my first semester of dorm life ready to cook anything and everything. My mom, always a very good if not particularly passionate cook, was delighted to hand over the reins and we never looked back. Even in France, if I couldn't get home for the holiday, I always made as full a Thanksgiving dinner as possible for local friends and ex-pats.

I brush the tops of the two apple pies with an egg wash and sprinkle the tops with coarse raw sugar crystals and slide them into the oven. I set the timer, then check my list. The turkey is in, slowly burnishing to a golden brown. The stuffing and sweet potatoes are in their casserole dishes, ready to be reheated while the turkey is resting. The mashed potatoes are in one of the slow cookers, where they can reheat gently on low without collapsing. Green beans are prepped in the steamer; the dough for the rolls is in its second rise. Shelby set the table in the formal dining room, and Geneva and Darcy helped with decoration, and it is a lively riot of autumn leaves and gourds and cut-out crayoned turkeys. In the very center, an ancient wicker cornucopia, with real fruit spilling out onto the table. Everyone has a mini pumpkin with their name written on it to mark their places. They'll have their dinner at three, and then go to a movie, whatever animated movie has been released for the holiday weekend, and then come home for turkey sandwiches and cold stuffing and a night of board games.

I'm just pulling the pies out of the oven to cool on a rack in the butler's pantry when I hear the cacophony of Farbers coming in the front door. I smile, listening to the joyous noise of them. When I was growing up, our house, while no less loving, was a quiet place, just the three of us. We laughed long and loud, to be sure, but it was still the difference of a small chamber ensemble versus a full symphony.

*"Elllllooooiiiise!!!"* Geneva comes flying into the kitchen, her long chestnut curls a banner behind her, slamming her tiny body into me with the force of a miniature tank.

"Ooof. Hello, sweet girl. How was your morning?" I say, reaching down to pull her up into my arms and receive the loving kiss on my cheek and the tight little arms around my neck.

"It was *great*, Eloise! I gave them a show! I danced and sang and made everyone happy!"

"Boy, did she." Brad comes in and peels her out of my arms, dropping her unceremoniously onto her feet; she sprints off as soon as she touches the ground. "Happy Thanksgiving, Eloise." He kisses my cheek in the same spot as his rambunctious and affectionate daughter. "Smells amazing in here. Anything I can do to be helpful?" he says, grinning, as he snakes his hand out toward the casserole of stuffing. I swat at it and put on my angry grandmother tone.

"You leave that stuffing alone, Bradley Farber." My falsely stern tone makes him sheepish.

"Okay, Mama Bear. I'll wait." He wanders to the cookie jar, retrieving one of the almond apricot biscotti I filled it with yesterday.

"Brad, seriously? Dinner is in less than an hour and a half, and you already ate your weight in cookies this morning. Don't think I didn't notice," Shelby says to him, laughing. Brad has a hollow leg. I have no idea where he puts it, but his hunger is constant. I'd kill for his metabolism. Doesn't matter how much he eats, how active he is or isn't, he stays the same weight. Not thin like Shelby, but never more than the littlest bit poochy in the middle.

"Hey, Chef, I'm ready for work!" Ian says, heading straight to the sink to scrub his hands in the simple, unconscious habit of a real chef.

"Glad to hear it. I've got a list for you." I made Ian his very own time and action plan. He is going to be in charge of some of the last-minute stuff, making the gravy, for starters, as well as turkey carving, which we've been practicing on chickens for the last few weeks. Shelby has requested a brief poultry moratorium for the foreseeable future as a result, but the kid is great with the knife and I have total faith that he will get the bird to the table in good form.

Ian and I go over the details, and then I have him grab the rest of his siblings for roll time. Every year we do this together, the kids and me, shaping the soft yeast dough into rolls. The kids each get their own sheet pan and lump of dough, and they can make whatever shapes they like and top them with anything from sesame seeds to toasted pumpkin seeds to little bits of onion. I've got their trays all set up on the kitchen table, along with individual bowls of egg wash, and the center of the table has bowls of possible toppings. It's always been my little parting gift to Shelby and Brad: I keep the kids fairly well occupied for about a half hour so that the two of them can sit and have a glass of wine and some peace after their hectic morning before I leave them to a weekend full of activity.

"Hey, El," Robbie says, Geneva pulling his arm practically out of his socket. "Happy Thanksgiving."

"Yeah, happy Thanksgiving, Eloise," Darcy says.

I pull the soft, pillowy dough out of the warming drawer where it was proofing and cut it into four equal portions. I'll help Geneva with hers while the rest work on theirs. We cut and shape the dough, each pan reflecting the maker. Darcy's are all fanciful, intricately braided designs with meticulous application of toppings. Robbie's are rustic, essentially just random lumps of dough, indifferently egg-washed, and sprinkled with whatever toppings are nearest to hand. Ian's are perfect and chefly, rolled under his small hands to identical taut spheres, the toppings blended for flavor: fennel seed and onion; poppy seed and lemon zest; pumpkin seed and Espelette pepper. Geneva and I make flowers and butterflies and other artistic applications of dough, using the toppings like colors in a palette. We get the trays in the oven to bake, and Shelby sends the kids downstairs to play. Ian sets his phone with a timer to let him know when he needs to come upstairs to get his list started. I go over what is left to do with Shelby as I pack up one of the now-cooled apple pies into my pie carrier.

"I can't believe you have to go home and do this all over again," Shelby says, shaking her head. "It must be exhausting."

"I love it. Besides, everything is pretty much prepped over at my mom's house; most of it just needs reheating. I'll put the turkey in as soon as I get there, and then we'll relax and have cocktails till dinnertime." It's true—even our gravy is made ahead, since for my family I do Julia Child's deconstructed turkey recipe, which cooks in pieces on top of the stuffing, so it cooks quickly and evenly and makes the stuffing dense and moist. But because of that, there are no pan juices, so I made the gravy earlier this week from some extra wings and the giblets. There is very little to do for tonight beyond reheating and carving the turkey once it is done.

"Better you than me!" Shelby says. "But it does sound nice, a small quiet dinner. A nice long weekend."

Always funny how the grass is greener. I'm so envious of Shelby's brood, of the long table set today for this family, including both Brad's and Shelby's folks, who will be coming in soon.

Jealous of the potluck party they will have tomorrow with Brad's sister and her family, and some close friends. A big house full of happy people eating well and sharing stories. And she envies my simple quiet dinner, and the rest of my weekend, which she and Brad always insist on my taking off, full of long days with no responsibilities.

"Well, you should be all set for the weekend. I've got plenty of snacks and stuff laid in for you, Ian has a bunch of recipes for repurposing leftovers when you get sick of turkey sandwiches if he wants to play in the kitchen, and I've got all of Brad's Sunday supplies in the second fridge." Brad does a big breakfast for his family on Thanksgiving Sunday: eggs and pancakes and bacon and sausages and hash browns.

"You're the best."

I pull the trays of rolls out of the oven and set them on racks to cool on the island. Shelby laughs when she sees them.

"They are really their own people, my kids."

"Yep. Certainly are."

"Okay, well, you've done enough for a holiday, I'm officially kicking you out. Go home. Be with your family."

"Thanks, Shelby. You guys have a terrific weekend, and I'll see you on Monday."

"You too, El. And just know, we are very thankful for you." Her generosity of spirit is always deeply touching and makes me smile. She reaches up to hug me, and I hug her back.

"I'm thankful for you guys too," I whisper into her hair.

S top, I can't . . ." Aunt Claire says, pushing her plate toward me for another sliver of pie.

"Claire, you cannot bitch about this tomorrow," my mom

says, reaching for a divinity cookie, one of Claire's specialties, a light meringue cookie filled with mini chocolate chips and walnut pieces.

"I don't bitch," Claire says, dolloping a generous spoonful of vanilla whipped cream on her second helping of pie.

My mom rolls her eyes and starts whining in a mockery of Claire's low voice. "Oh, Hollis, I'm just so bloated, and you cannot imagine what the scale said this morning . . ."

Claire puts a huge piece of pie in her mouth and then opens it to show my mom.

"Girls, do I have to separate you?" I say, their antics getting more ridiculous than usual after indulging in Lynne's glorious old Riesling all night, not to mention the predinner Boulevardier cocktails, and now a lovely Madeira with the desserts. They're both hummingly buzzy.

"Bless their hearts," Lynne says, waving off my offer of the cookie plate. She's eaten small, rational portions of everything, praised all the deliciousness, and deftly skipped any second helpings. It seems so controlled, and, to be honest, I feel bad for her, that she can't just let go, let herself overindulge, embrace abundance.

I, on the other hand, have had seconds of everything, and thirds of stuffing. It's been lovely, if a bit quiet. Lynne and my mom got caught up, chatting about the old days, while Claire helped me in the kitchen, and we've talked politics and television, and all of the surface, small-talk things that one covers in casual conversation.

I keep checking my watch, which sometimes seems to have gone backward since last I looked, and sometimes seems to have leapt forward in a shocking manner. I know I'm preoccupied. I'm supposed to text Shawn when I'm gearing up to head home—he's requested that he be able to join Simca and me for our evening walk. They met last weekend when he dropped me off, and when I say that it was an instantaneous love match, I'm not exaggerating. He picked her up and she licked his entire head like he was a naughty puppy, and he spoke to her in some gibberish language and she yipped happily in reply.

"I always wanted a dog, but my ex patently refused, and they don't allow them in my building unless they are under twenty-five pounds," he said wistfully.

"I can't exactly picture you with a little purse dog," I said, imagining him with some Yorkie or Chihuahua.

"Well, I never would have thought about a smaller dog—I always wanted a mastiff or a Greater Swiss Mountain Dog or something manly. But this sweet girl could make me change my mind, yes, she could!" He snuggled into Simca's neck. "She smells like graham crackers!"

"She's a taut and trim twenty-four pounds, right under the wire," I said, and then stopped when I realized it might sound like I was moving my dog, and by proxy myself, into his condo.

"Well, then, she can come visit me anytime, can't you?"

We took her for a walk around the neighborhood, and she trotted proudly at his side and he even insisted on doing blue bag duty, which alone would be enough to fall for him.

"So, Lynne, you're happy to be back in Chicago?" Aunt Claire asks, sticking a finger in the whipped cream bowl.

"Well, I'm very happy with the job change. I realized in L.A., there was just too much dealing with the hot new thing. They are all magpies, anything new and shiny can distract them, so I had to spend almost more time coddling existing clients so that they felt appropriately attended to than I spent

actually doing my job. They all want to think that you are personally handling every piece of their business, when actually
your time would be better served handing off most of it to
underlings. It was fine when I was younger, but I wanted to
work with grown-ups, and stop being everyone's dancing monkey. Plus, the firm I was with had a daughter coming up
through the ranks, the heiress apparent, so I knew there was a
limit to how far I could go there. Here I can focus on landing
the big clients, and they all seem to understand that there is a
team approach to execution, so I can be more of a manager and
less of a worker bee." I wish there were slightly less imperious-
ness in her voice.

"I can't imagine you being a worker bee," my mom says.
"You were always much more of a leader, as I recall." She isn't
wrong there. If Lynne joined a club, they made her president
almost immediately. When she joined cheerleading, they made
her captain. As a sophomore. She was class president for all
four years of college, something that hadn't been done since
the university's inception.

"Yeah, it's not really my nature." Lynne laughs. "I miss the
L.A. weather, as you can imagine, and the social scene was
easier for me there, but I finally decided that if I was going to
be a focused career woman, and the career had more potential
here, then it was okay to come back."

"Well, it would probably be good to have some balance. All
work and no play, and all that jazz." Claire pauses. "We were
sorry to hear about your divorce; that must have been tough."

Lynne makes a face. "Mr. So-Very-Wrong? It was fine. Not
a big deal really. Sort of a momentary complication." She pauses
in a way that makes me think it was much more than that. She
shrugs. "We had a good thing for a minute, but ultimately I

think sometimes when you are dating someone they only show you the person they think you most want and need, and then once you are locked in, they relax into being who they really are, and sometimes that just doesn't fly. Mine was a classic case of good on paper, bad in practice. I don't know if we were really aligned on the big stuff in the beginning or if he was just pretending to be aligned because he knew it was what I wanted. But everyone ends up being themselves in the end. And if you tell them you need them to be the person they promised you in the beginning and they don't want to be that guy, you have to just move them along."

My mom and Claire both look a little taken aback. There is a coldness in Lynne's tone that doesn't belie hurt or a broken heart or betrayal. She is essentially talking about her marriage like it was a car she leased that didn't have the gas mileage they claimed in the commercials.

"How long were you together?" Mom asks.

Lynne thinks. "Two years, married for one and a half."

"Well, at least it sounds like it was somewhat amicable," Claire says.

"It never got ugly, not in the ways it could have been. We had a prenup; he owned the house; we hadn't really done much in terms of joint investments or anything. He wanted to go to counseling, but I knew we were done, so I kept it simple, moved out while he was out of town for a conference, and got the paperwork all organized. He wasn't happy, but he didn't fight it."

This gives me shivers. She just moved out while he was out of town? He wanted to go to counseling to try to save the marriage and she didn't want to bother? I love my friend Lynne, but at the moment, I'm finding it hard to like her very much. And I can't stop myself from asking.

"Why wouldn't you want to try counseling? I mean, you must have really loved him—you married him. It seems like if things got off track maybe something could have been fixed."

"Now, Eloise, how long have you known me? How good a problem solver am I? When I tell you that it wasn't fixable, trust me, it wasn't fixable. We didn't want the same things out of life, we didn't have the same priorities, and I had been clear about mine from the beginning, so when his changed, he really couldn't expect that I should change mine just because he did, could he?"

"I suppose not," I say. "I guess, not if they were fundamental."

"Trust me, girlfriend, they could not have been more fundamental."

My mom and Claire get up and start clearing dishes. "You girls sit," Mom says. "Eloise has worked enough for one day. We have cleanup covered. Lynne, would you like coffee or tea or something?"

"Tea, but only if you are making for yourself," Lynne says.

"Absolutely. How about you, muffin?"

"Sure, Mom, thanks. Yell if you guys want help."

"Will do. Lynne, will you take leftovers?"

"Thank you, but no," Lynne says, patting her flat stomach. "I don't dare." Which isn't surprising; she barely dared during the meal.

Lynne and I get up from the table and go into the living room to sit on the couch.

"I assume they don't know about the bet," Lynne says.

"It hasn't come up." Because I haven't brought it up. It would be the central focus of every conversation; they'd both be trying to help and support and encourage and advise, which is so lovely and sweet, but I'm just not up for it. It's all plenty at the moment, and I don't need a cheering section, at least not yet.

"Well, I'm proud of you," Lynne says in a serious tone. "Really, El, super proud. I know the dating thing is hard for you, and the whole social thing was never your jam, but you've embraced it all, and I think that shows some serious backbone."

"Thank you." I'm sort of startled by the intensity of her statement. "I figure go big or go home, right?"

"Right, but look, I mean, I know we had a lot of years go by, but I was always in your corner, you know? I feel bad that you went through a bunch of crap and handled it alone. Made me have to think about my own stuff, you know, my baggage. I know I'm not the warmest, the fuzziest, but when I heard that you came back from Europe, that your dad died, that you were here and suffering and struggling and you didn't reach out, that was a wake-up for me in a way, you know? Like, it is one thing to be tough, to be independent, to be confident, but it is something else to not be the person someone reaches out to when they are in the shit."

I feel bad. She thinks that it was some flaw in her that made me not reach out, like maybe I didn't think she would be good support for me, and now I feel bad for having been thinking ill of her earlier. "Look, Lynne, I didn't reach out to anyone. You might not be the cushiest place to land, but Teresa couldn't be more of a nurturer, and I didn't call her either. I felt shitty that I had let so much time go by, and it seemed even shittier to come back and reach out because I needed something. What could I say? Hi! It's been over a decade since I bothered to be in touch, but I've moved home from Europe, my asshole boyfriend dumped me, and my dad is dying, so maybe you could be focused on being nice to me! I didn't have the energy to even think about finding something for myself. My sole focus was on my dad and my mom and Claire, who had barely gotten her head above water from losing her husband and now was losing her brother, and then finding a job and trying the whole time to get over Bernard. Trite as it is, it wasn't you, it was me."

She nods and looks me in the face. "Well, never again, okay? We have each other's back. I do not have time or energy to train up a bunch of new bitches to put up with my sorry ass."

I shake my head and laugh. "Deal. You met with the match-maker yet?"

"I interviewed two that I didn't love, but at least one of them signed on as a client, so it wasn't all bad. I've got another meeting this week."

Only Lynne would go to interview a possible matchmaker and land a new client. She's a wonder. "That's cool. Was it really so simple, your divorce?"

"Is it ever?" Lynne sighs. "I dunno. I thought marriage was a box I would check appropriately when the right guy came along, and he seemed like the right guy. When it turned out I was wrong, that *we* were wrong, I needed to uncheck the box. Which is both simple and complicated. Simple in action, complicated in emotion. I don't think of it as a failure, per se, but it does feel like, I don't know, a black mark. It's on my permanent record. It doesn't embarrass me, but it does bother me a bit."

I reach over and squeeze her hand, understanding what she means. My mom comes in with two mugs of tea for us. We sip the hot, sweet beverages and shift talk to Teresa, who requested that we adjust her bet list to accommodate her injury, realizing that until she was more mobile, a lot of her items would fall by the wayside. We said she could take her financial class online; have a reduction on the number of things she had to do in the spicing-up-her-marriage and finding-a-part-time-job departments; and meanwhile focus on researching the non-Italian foods she wants to learn to cook and do volunteer stuff that can be done at home. Apparently next week she is stuffing envelopes for her neighborhood association fund-raiser, and she's signed herself up at Antony's school to manage the phone tree for the whole seventh grade. By the time our tea is finished, my mom and Claire come out with a huge bag of leftovers for me and a small one for Lynne.

"We just put in white meat turkey and cranberry sauce and Brussels sprouts and some of the sweet potatoes, and a couple of rolls. None of the really unhealthy stuff." Aunt Claire winks at Lynne. "You have to have leftovers from Thanksgiving, otherwise it's un-American."

"You get the works," my mom says, handing me a bag that weighs roughly forty pounds.

There are kisses and hugs all around, and a promise to come back to visit from Lynne. I kiss her good-bye, then claim the need to pee before leaving, and sneak off to the bathroom to text Shawn.

Just gearing up to leave my mom's house, should be home in about 10 minutes.

By the time I'm washing my hands my phone pings.

On my way! See you in 20.

Suddenly the butterflies, which had been somewhat distracted by good food and good wine and conversation, are back with a vengeance. I look in the mirror. I think about what Lynne would say if she knew what I was about to do. I can hear her voice in my head.

"You've got this. You are a badass. He is a nice man. He is a good person. He is goddamned fine as hell. Go get him and change the color of his sky."

And she's right, of course.

Lynne always is, just ask her.

So let's do this.

Good girl," Shawn says to Simca, unhooking her leash. We've had a great long walk, exploring the neighborhood and talking about Thanksgiving and family and memories and food. The evening is actually beautiful, crisp but not horribly cold and with minimal wind.

"Can I get you something to drink?" I ask, pulling off my coat and hanging it on the rack by the door.

"Sure, what are you thinking?"

"I was thinking maybe calvados. It's good for settling the stomach."

"Sounds good. I'm just going to wash my hands." He heads for the powder room, and I go to the kitchen to grab the bottle and some glasses. I pour us each a couple of fingers with a single ice cube and get back to the living room just as he is settling into the couch, with his new girlfriend Simca at his side. I hand him the glass and sit on his other side. We clink and I sip the strong liquid, making a smooth, fiery hole in my full belly. It never ceases to amaze me how this stuff can cut through a huge meal.

Shawn pulls out his phone and shows me his photos of the

buffet at his aunt's house, and I'm instantly jealous. It looks like magic. Turkey and a huge glazed ham. Mashed potatoes and potato salad, candied yams. Two kinds of stuffing, macaroni and cheese, green bean casserole, and a huge pot of greens. Something called green salad, which appears to feature lime Jell-O, and a bowl of ambrosia. A huge basket of biscuits, apparently his aunt Elsie's specialty, and another basket of his mom's rolls. The dessert table has four different pies on it— pecan, sweet potato, apple, and banana cream—as well as a towering coconut cake, a chocolate cake, and a huge platter of cookies.

"I'm so jealous. That looks amazing," I say when he finishes scrolling through the pictures and pointing out his family members with little funny stories about each.

"I dunno, there is something about a quiet dinner without a million people that sounds kind of nice."

I laugh. "That's the same thing my boss said this morning. I guess we always want the opposite of what we have."

"I don't want anything other than what I have right here," he says, leaning in for a kiss. I feel the electric shocks all the way to my toes.

We kiss for what seems like an hour before I can't stand it anymore. I pull away. "Did you want to come upstairs?"

He looks me in my eyes and nods. "Yes, Eloise, I would like that very much."


I open the fridge and start grabbing tubs. Mashed potatoes, stuffing, the bag of turkey.

"I'm gonna need sweet potatoes too," Shawn says, snuggling up behind me and kissing my neck.

"Well, naturally," I say, reaching for the tub of sweet potatoes.

We stand at the island, me in my robe, Shawn in his boxer briefs, and eat as if we've been starved for weeks. Feeding each other turkey with our fingers, chunks of cold stuffing dunked in cranberry sauce. I microwave the two kinds of potatoes while Shawn opens the bag of rolls, making us little sandwiches with a smear of gravy on the bread. When we have feasted on leftovers, Shawn reaches for me and kisses me hard—he tastes of sage and cranberries—and he pulls me back upstairs, where, fortified by our midnight snack, we show each other how very thankful two people can be.

Just before I fall asleep I think that there are two very important things I know for sure. Number one, Shawn Sudberry-Long is a spectacular and generous lover, and if there is a shoe that is going to drop, it is not going to be in bed.

And two, there is going to be pie for breakfast.

# Twelve

'm checking the cooler bag against my list. I've got a baguette, a chunk of a triple-crème Brie and a slab of aged Gouda, a tub of cold fried chicken legs, a green bean salad with new potatoes and roasted cherry tomatoes, a bunch of grapes, and a thermos of white gazpacho. Plates, plasticware, napkins. Marcy is bringing desserts, Lynne is bringing wine, and Teresa is just excited to be getting out of the house, now that she can drive again. Her ankle is healing slowly, but the doctor said that as long as she uses the big hard boot for walking or doing anything where she is exposed, she can use the smaller fabric boot for driving or hanging out in the house.

We celebrated her freedom on Tuesday night with a visit to Opart Thai House, where I introduced her to the magic of brilliantly prepared Thai dishes for the first time. She really loved the appetizers, especially the Tiger Cry, a marinated grilled beef with a spicy dipping sauce, as well as the chicken and eggplant in oyster sauce, and pad kra praow, a ground-pork dish with basil and peppers, which felt almost familiar to her— it has a background that tastes a bit like crumbled Italian fennel sausage. She liked the pad Thai, which she thought her youngest would really enjoy, and was sure that Gio would at least get into the various satays and embrace the broccoli and beef. She didn't love the curry, but that is advanced reading. I was delighted that she was so open to tasting and that she had a good time. Lynne had a business dinner, so it was the first time Teresa and I had been alone together, and it struck me how easy and comfortable it was just to be with her, with who she is now. We didn't really speak much about the past, just about current stuff, and I have to say, she is exactly who I would have hoped she'd be as a grown-up, and I know if I met her today I would want to be friends with her.

Simca gives a little yip as she always does when she hears the front gate unlatch. In ten seconds my doorbell is ringing.

"Hello, ladies!" Marcy says, coming in and shaking the light snow off her head. "It is like a snow globe out there." She hands me a bag that contains a large box. "Desserts."

I peer inside, but the box is sealed. "What do we have?"

"Toffee chip cookies, pine nut shortbread, raspberry oatmeal bars." She rattles them off. "Sophie says hi and thank you for the onion kuchen recipe, she really appreciated the share. Sent you a Nutella babka as a present." Marcy hands over a second, smaller bag that feels like a brick. Sophie Langer's Nutella babka is about the most perfect food I've ever put in my mouth. It will make for a wonderful breakfast treat the next time Shawn sleeps over, which he has done three nights out of the past six. We cannot get enough of each other, both in and out of bed, and I've just given myself over to enjoying his company and carnal attentions.

"It was my pleasure, and I never say no to babka. My grandmother would be very excited that someone wanted her recipe."

"Are they meeting us there?" Marcy asks. I think she is very curious about Lynne and Teresa, especially since she knows about the bet. She also knows about Shawn—not that it's feeling serious to me or that we've slept together, just that we have seen each other "a couple of times" and that I find his company enjoyable. Not ready to let that cat out of the bag, and have sworn her to secrecy for tonight with the girls.

"Yep, Teresa is picking Lynne up on her way down to the studio." Tonight the four of us are doing a glassblowing class as part of my bet obligations. We're allowed to bring in food and drink. The class will be about twelve people altogether, so I get to check the "socialize with strangers" box, but still have my peeps as backup. I'm more nervous about the wine tasting I've scheduled for next week, since that one I have to do all on my own. At least there will be drinking.

"Well, let's get this party started!"

t looks like a vagina," Marcy says to Teresa, looking at her paperweight cooling in the asbestos-lined box with the rest of the class's efforts. There is indeed an internal design of somewhat Georgia O'Keeffe sensibility.

"It's a flower!" Teresa says, grabbing a piece of shortbread, laughing at her handiwork.

"Sure it is, T, sure it is. Might be time to get back to the sexy part of your list!" Lynne says, looking at her own paperweight, with a perfect purple swirl in the middle and a netting of air bubbles over, as if she had been a glass artist her whole life.

"At least yours looks like something. What the hell am I going to do with this?" I say, gesturing to mine, which essentially looks like a solid green lump.

"Give it to your mom for Hanukkah," Lynne says. "Parents have to love the handmade gifts from their offspring, right, Teresa?"

"No. No, we don't have to love them. We have to *accept* them. We have to praise them, and express gratitude and excitement, but we don't love them, we love the intent of them. The actual reality of them is a huge pain in the ass, and frankly we count the days till our offspring move out of the house so we can box them all up and stop looking at them."

We all laugh at her vehemence. "Duly noted, Mama," I say, making a mental note to give my mom permission to get rid of all the various art projects I foisted upon her over the years, many of which still grace the shelves and display spaces in her house.

"Well, I like mine, it's a keeper," Marcy says with thick sarcasm. Hers isn't as bad as mine, but it is a close second. She was going for a colored internal sphere inside a clear one, but it isn't really round, so it looks more like a deep red, misshapen blob encased in glass.

"And it's benign, which is a relief," Lynne says snarkily.

"It's not a *toomah*!" Marcy says in a perfect Arnold Schwarzenegger *Kindergarten Cop* imitation. The two of them have been sparring a bit all night. It has been sort of friendly, but there is an undertone of something else that I can't put my finger on. Not quite a pissing match, but close. Lynne keeps making jokes from high school, and Marcy retaliates with stories from our culinary school days and our European adventures. It all seems good-natured enough, but I won't know for sure until I hear privately from each how it was to meet the other. I'd say it seemed a bit like they were jealous of each other, but for the life of me I can't figure out what that would be about.

"Oh, God! I love that movie," Teresa says, clapping her hands in delight. "I have got to show it to my boys on our next movie night!" Teresa and her family have been having movie nights of the classics from the 1980s and '90s ever since Antony turned twelve and was deemed old enough to handle John Hughes.

"Remember when we went to see it?" Lynne snorts. "Peter's Purple Puke!"

Teresa starts laughing. "I forgot about that."

I turn to Marcy, as I have been doing all night when Lynne tosses out these references. "We went to see the movie and ran into some other kids from school, one of whom was this guy Peter that Teresa liked. He had snuck in some booze in a huge bottle of grape pop, and then ate an enormous bucket of popcorn with extra butter, and as we were leaving the theater, he projectile-vomited purple across the parking lot. That was the end of Teresa's crush."

Marcy nods, with a look on her face that indicates this is not exactly the hilarious amazing tale that Lynne's tone implied. I immediately try to forget it, since I cannot handle puking of any kind. The first and only time Simca yakked up some foam and fluff from a chew toy she had destroyed when she was three months old made me gag over and over as I cleaned it up. She's been very accommodating to my sensitive stomach by not ever throwing up again. I appreciate that about her.

"Meanwhile, who is up for a nightcap at my place? I have some good news that I want to celebrate, and some really yummy bubbles!" Lynne says, changing the subject.

"I can do just one," Teresa says.

"We're in?" I say, confirming with Marcy.

"Great, let's get out of this hot box!"

We gather up the remains of our picnic and leave, headed for Lynne's apartment.

"So, what do you think of the girls?" I ask Marcy when we get into the car.

"Teresa is a sweetheart, such a classic Italian mama, I just want her to adopt me."

"Don't worry, she will. Wait till summer when her whole family starts putting up gravy from the tomatoes in her aunt's garden. You won't have to make pasta sauce for yourself all year!" I used to get invited to sauce day when the big harvest came in, fifteen loud, lovely Italian women covered in tomatoes, busting one another's chops, sharing recipe secrets, interrogating the single ones and poking at the married ones about childbearing, and drinking more red wine than would seem rational. I loved those days.

"I'll take that!" Marcy pauses. "Lynne seems, um, very sure of herself."

I laugh. "Large and in charge, we always said."

"I feel like I don't really know anything more about her than you shared with me before we met, you know? Like all her stuff is very surface." Marcy pauses. "I mean, she's totally nice, I don't want you to think . . ."

I hold up my hand. "I get it. She's sort of a closed system. But it's just how she is before she knows you. I think it's because her job means that she is endlessly meeting new people that she has to feign interest in, and so she is really practiced at the whole small-talk thing. Once you spend some time with her, she will open up a bit." It is interesting, Marcy picking up on some of the stuff that bothers me about Lynne, but my impulse is still to defend.

"Yeah, that's probably it," Marcy says in a tone that says that she doesn't really think that at all.

What are we celebrating?" Marcy asks when we are all sitting in Lynne's living room, glasses of Krug rosé in our hands, since clearly Lynne is waiting for someone to broach the subject.

"I have officially landed my first seven-figure client!" Lynne says proudly. "Here's to Angelique Morris!"

"Wow, the fashion designer?" Teresa asks. "That is huge!"

Angelique Morris went from local Chicago fashion staple to international fashion star when Michelle Obama wore several of her dresses over the course of a weekend trip to London, including a spectacular navy evening number that she was photographed in with Princess Kate. Angelique's career blew up. And being a Chicago girl, she's kept her headquarters right here at home. It's a huge get for Lynne, and I'm really excited for her.

"Signed this morning. We are taking over every aspect of her outside PR, and I'm her account director. I'll be transitioning off of my other clients slowly as we ramp things up for her, and then focus on her work exclusively. I even have an office at her building!" Lynne is actually nearly giddy, and we all toast and sip the delicate bubbles. "I met her at a meet and greet for the DuSable Museum—Theaster Gates is trying to get me to join their board—and we hit it off. When she mentioned she was in need of a PR firm to do a bit more than her in-house team was able to do on their own, and she didn't want to take on the care and feeding of new people for that department, I finagled a meeting and then went Full Lynne Lewiston on her. The lady didn't have a chance!" Lynne has just managed in one breath to praise herself and her work prowess, indicate that the "join a charitable board" piece of her list is also practically locked up, and name-drop not one but two local celebrities. She is astonishing in her efficiency.

"Congrats, honey, that is just wonderful. Good for you!" Teresa says.

"Yeah, wow, that is major," Marcy says. Marcy couldn't care less about fashion labels, cobbling together her nonwork wardrobe at vintage stores and cheap boutiques in Wicker Park, and she has already cooked for more famous people than Lynne will ever meet in a lifetime, so she just doesn't get fazed by it. "Congratulations."

And then, there is an awkward silence as we sip our champagne.

"So, I guess you'll win the bet, huh?" Marcy asks to break the quiet.

Lynne and Teresa both snap their heads around to look at her, somewhat shocked.

"So, you know about that, huh?" Lynne says, narrowing her eyes at me.

"Um, yeah, well, Eloise mentioned it, you guys helping each other get inspired to do some new stuff . . ." Marcy is stammering. Apparently the wine at glassblowing and now the champagne has loosened her tongue more than a little.

"Yes, well," Lynne says, faking nonchalance. "We all have

always supported each other in our endeavors. This seemed a fun way to spend the last months of our thirties."

"It doesn't matter, Marcy, of course you know, you're El's best friend! And it has been a good way to get us all out of our ruts. I'd say you should jump in and join us, but . . ."

"But you aren't turning forty this May," Lynne says, shutting Teresa down.

"Nope!" Marcy says. "I've got four more years for that." Unlike me, who did a regular college degree before culinary school, Marcy went to culinary school right out of high school.

"Well, from what I've seen, you won't need any bet to get you to do the stuff you need in your life. You seem to just really go for things. I really envy that," Teresa says. She is great about seeing the best in people, and her impulse is dead-on. I can't think of one thing Marcy ever wanted that she didn't just go after.

"Aw, thanks, Teresa, that's so sweet. I think because I lost my mom so young, and she was such a go-getter, I've always just had that drive to not waste any time questioning stuff, you know?" Marcy's mom died of cancer when Marcy was twelve, but the whole time she was in treatment, she was still living life to the fullest—getting her pilot's license, learning Spanish, raising money for medical research. Marcy said she never once wallowed or acted like a victim, she just tackled her treatment and her bucket list with equal passion, and instilled in Marcy a sense of appreciating life and being willing to take on a certain amount of risk when necessary to achieve your dreams and make sure that you are living your fullest life.

"Anyway, thank you all for celebrating with me. There will be a little party in a few weeks for Angelique's housewares launch. Everyone who is anyone will be there—it will be celebrities galore! I'll put all of you on the list!" And now we are back to talking about Lynne.

"Sounds fun," says Marcy in a tone that indicates that it doesn't sound like anything of the sort.

"Awesome, thanks, Lynne, that will be great," I say, waving off Lynne's proffering of the bottle to top me off. "It's getting late, and I've got a big day at work tomorrow." I just want to get out of here and call Shawn.

"Strenuous cooking to be done?" Lynne asks. "I'd imagine you'd be slammed with the season."

"Yep! The family is hosting their annual holiday party this weekend, and while they cater some of the big parts of the meal, I'm in charge of all appetizers and desserts and a few of the side dishes."

"Ugh, that fiddly stuff is so much harder than the big-ticket items," Marcy says, immediately having my back. "I'd rather do a ham or a turkey than a ton of apps any day!"

"Yeah, I should go too, get home before my menfolk tear the damn house to bits. Great night, and congrats again, Lynne, super proud of you, girl," Teresa says, hoisting herself up with the help of her cane.

"Well, thanks, everyone, for coming over." Lynne gets up to walk us all out, and we head downstairs, where our cars are parked in the circle driveway of the building. We make sure that Teresa is all set before we get into my car and I head for Marcy's Wicker Park apartment.

"Thanks for including me, El. I had fun," she says as we pull up into an empty parking spot in front of her building on Evergreen.

"Sorry if Lynne was a little prickly."

"It's all good. I get it. She predates me and wants me to know where I stand."

"Yeah, it's weird. I mean, she's known me longer . . ."

"But I know you better?"

"I think that's probably it. She knows the me that I was, but you know the me that I am now, and you have been there for all the important stuff—my becoming who I am, my dad's illness and death, the whole Bernard debacle."

"Speaking of which, how goes your fledgling romance?"

"It's fine, thank you."

"Cagey. And why don't you want them to know? I mean, Lynne is a tough nut, but she really seems to care about you, and Teresa would be planning your wedding."

"Exactly. I want to know what I think and how I feel before I get any input from other sources, if you know what I mean. I don't want Lynne to have her opinions, I don't want Teresa pushing it to be more serious than it is or should be. I need to just be in the moment with him and see where it goes and how I feel about that before I have to listen to any voices besides my own, if that makes any sense."

"It does. For what it is worth, I thought he was really awesome, and the two of you seemed to have very genuine and positive energy. I'll wait to hear from you on how it's going and if you decide it is time to go public."

"Thank you. And thanks for coming tonight. Hopefully it wasn't too weird. Maybe we can all hang out again. Lynne really is a good person. I think if she gets to know you, it will be less awkward."

"Hey, I'm all in with you, my tall friend. That now includes these two women from your past. So no worries." She winks and pops out of the car, heading into her building, taking the steps on the front stoop two at a time. I check my watch. It's almost ten. I do have a long cooking day tomorrow at the Farbers'. I should probably go home, walk the dog, and have an early night. But then my phone pings.

> Hello, sweet girl. Hope you had a good night. I'm about to leave my pal Freddie's now that the game is over. Should I go home or come to your place?

And suddenly all thoughts of an early night fly right out the window.

> I have a fluffy beast that needs a walk and a Nutella babka that isn't going to eat itself for breakfast. What do you think?

> I think I will see you in 15.

Looks like the night is about to take a turn for the better.

# Thirteen

t takes me most of the morning, but I get Lawrence's kitchen cabinets, fridge, and freezer completely cleaned out and purged of expired goods and items otherwise past their prime. He's in Palm Springs with pals for the next two weeks, and it's always easier to take care of this when he isn't around to see that I've relieved him of ten-year-old cans of foie gras paté and dusty jars of jams and pickled walnuts and such that he brought back from travels abroad. I wipe down the shelves of the fridge with a mild bleach and water solution, put new paper pads into the drawers, and put back the condiments and beverages that are still fine. I'll restock him with staples and basics for breakfasts and lunches before he returns. I replenish his spice jars with fresh contents, having done my end-of-the-year trip to The Spice House on Wells Street. Some people believe in spring cleaning, but when spring finally arrives in Chicago I want to be outside enjoying the weather and getting some much-needed vitamin D, not stuck inside. I do a purge between Thanksgiving and Christmas, so that I start the new year with a clean house and a freezer and fridge free of old sad items, ready to be refilled with delectables acquired during the festive season. I dump all my herbs and spices and replace with fresh, making for some very fragrant garbage.

This past weekend I finished the work at my house. I packed up all my spring and summer clothes into their tubs, looking wistfully at my old tub labeled *Bearaphernalia*, the serious cold-weather gear I collected over the years that allowed me to attend the December and January Bears games with my dad and Uncle Buddy.

Shawn and I are going to the game this weekend with some friends of his, but we'll be in a skybox, well insulated from the whipping Chicago winds off the lake and any snow that might arrive, so the tub is staying untouched for another season. Although I did dig out my Jimbo Covert jersey to wear, a real one that he wore in a game, which my dad got me. I swapped out my light cotton sheets and blankets for the flannel sheets and down comforter that will get me through the winter. Took down the light sheer curtains and replaced them with the heavy velvet ones that block the drafts. It felt so good that I came over here today to take care of Lawrence's kitchen so that he will come back to some of the freshness I'm enjoying at my house, and the place will be in perfect shape for his annual New Year's Eve celebration.

I love this time of year. For most people in the food industry, the holiday season is fraught with horrors. Demanding clients, missing your own celebrations to attend to the celebrations of strangers, long hours and short days making for depressing weeks. You leave the house when it is still dark and go home in the same gloom and it is as if there is no sun to shine. I probably won't see Marcy at all till the new year; her time will be so overbooked that any hours she isn't working she'll be sleeping.

But for me, this is my favorite time of year. Thanksgiving started the fun, my holy grail, and now I've got the Farbers' holiday party this weekend to prep for, after which they will head out of town for winter vacation for two weeks. This year they are going to visit Shelby's folks in Miami, with a detour for a few days to Disney World. They invited me to join them, but I declined, saying that I had promised to help Teresa do Christmas in light of her injury. Shelby didn't pry, but I know she suspects there is more to my sticking around than that, and she isn't wrong. Shawn will be in town until Christmas Eve, and then he will be in North Carolina visiting his folks until the thirtieth, but he is coming back for Lawrence's party.

When everything is squared away, I settle down at the kitchen table to make some notes. This year Lawrence wants to go small and elegant for New Year's. He has invited my mom and Aunt Claire, me and Shawn, his dear friends Michael and Jerry, who are currently hosting him in Palm Springs, his other dear friends Todd and Joel, who will be hosting him in Sedona in January, and his best girlfriend, Esme. He said I'm only allowed to cook if I can do stuff that allows me to be more guest than chef, so I've been working on a menu that relies heavily on items that are served cold or at room temp, or can be made ahead and reheated. Lucky for me, some of my favorite things can be done this way, and I think I have a fun retro-inspired menu that should please Lawrence and keep me from being a slave to the kitchen. We'll start with oysters on the half shell and homemade salt-and-pepper potato chips, just to whet the appetites. Then a wedge salad with homemade ranch dressing and crumbled peppered bacon. For the main course, a slow-roasted prime rib, twice-baked potatoes, creamed spinach, tomato pudding baked into tomato halves, and fresh popovers instead of bread. For dessert, the world's most perfect chocolate cream pie.

Marcy and I went on a Sunday boondoggle to Milwaukee last year and had lunch at this terrific gastropub called Palomino, and while the whole meal was spectacular, notably the fried chicken, the chocolate cream pie was life changing for us both. Marcy used her pastry-chef wiles to get the recipe, and we both love any excuse to make it. It's serious comfort food, and I can't think of a better way to ring in the New Year.

We'll serve buffet-style, so other than carving the meat and cutting the pie, I'll have very little to do except sit at dinner and hope that this is the right way to introduce Shawn to my family. I got very nervous when Lawrence said he wanted to include Mom and Aunt Claire, since it will mean fessing up to having a dating life. But then I decided that a small group of loving friends on a festive night would make for some good buffering so that poor Shawn doesn't end up feeling like he is being interrogated too much. I'm going to tell them when I see them tonight.

My phone pings just as I am locking up Lawrence's apartment. It's Lynne.

**I need you. Can you come to the apartment?**

Uh-oh. That doesn't sound good. Lynne *never* asks for help.

**Are you okay?**

My mind races. I wonder if she is injured or sick or something.

Yes. But I could use another pair of hands.

Curious. That sounds less like an emergency and more like work is in the offing.

I'm on my way.

knock on Lynne's door and hear a flurry of activity and the unmistakable sound of barking. Suddenly things are starting to make sense. The door swings open and there is my elegant friend Lynne, sweating and looking panicked, her hair a rat's nest, holding a wiggly Dalmatian puppy, who is chewing on Lynne's ponytail and scrabbling at her arms, already covered in red welts, with his rear paws.

"Hi," she says. "This is your fault."

I try to prevent myself from laughing.

"Well, hello there. Who is this?" I say, coming inside to see that her apartment looks like a crime scene. There are feathers everywhere, presumably from a destroyed throw pillow, unmistakable pee stains on the rug, scratches on the hardwood flooring, and what appear to be the remains of at least two different shoes.

"This is Ellison. Who I am about to fucking kill. Can you take him for a minute?" She holds out the beastie to me as I put my purse safely on the counter. I receive the warm weight of puppy, cooing to him softly, and hold him tightly with his back nestled against my front and his legs supported from underneath. I spot a small bully stick on the side table and pick it up, holding it while he chews it, and he calms immediately.

"Hello, Ellison. Are you a terror?"

"He's a fucking terror*ist*." Lynne begins to pick up the detritus from her little Tasmanian devil. "Look at my house! He's gonna destroy everything!"

"Well, yeah, he's a puppy. When did you get him?" I say, settling into one of the club chairs in the living room. Ellison readjusts himself on my lap and accidentally nips my hand, and I adjust the bully stick to keep his razor-sharp puppy teeth farther from my tender flesh. He snuggles into the wide expanse of my thighs, using his front paws on my hands to help hold the chew toy.

Lynne collapses on the couch, where I can see that one corner of the arm closest to me has been well chewed. "Over the weekend. I picked him up Friday afternoon. Took yesterday and today off to get him settled. He was so sweet. Calm and quiet, just spent the last four days as a lovely, mellow little guy. Then I went upstairs to the workout room this morning after his walk and came home to this!" She sweeps her hand around the apartment.

"Didn't you have him crated?" I can see the large black crate in the corner of the room.

"He was sleeping on his little bed when I left. I was only gone forty minutes."

I chuckle. "Yeah, that's all it takes."

"Clearly."

"How old is he?"

"Twelve weeks. He's had a month of puppy training at the breeder, so he can handle the leash, and knows 'sit.' But I would have thought he would be more housebroken than this."

Oh, Lord. "Lynne, I know I said you should get a dog, but didn't I specifically say you should go to the pound and get an older rescue dog?"

She narrows her eyes at me. "Don't go all 'I told you so' up in here. I'm aware of what you suggested."

"So how did you get from older rescue mutt to purebred Dalmatian baby?"

When Lynne blushes, her caramel skin deepens to a lovely mahogany. "Angelique."

"Angelique Morris?"

"She has Dalmatians. Three of them. I mentioned I was thinking of getting a dog, when I was meeting with her to try and land the business, and she immediately called her breeder and pulled strings."

I start to laugh.

"It's not funny! She got all excited that our dogs would be cousins and that would make us like family and I thought if I didn't go that direction I might not get the account and it all just snowballed!"

"Wow. You are committed to your work, I will give you that. Have you done any research on the breed?" Dalmatians, while lovely dogs in personality, are high energy, not particularly well suited to apartment life, and can be difficult to train.

"I have now. God help me."

Ellison has fallen asleep on my lap, such a sweet warm weight; you'd never know he was a one-man demolition crew. "I presume there is no going back on this, you can't return him?"

"Are you crazy? Angelique would think I'm a monster. Plus . . . I sort of like him. When he isn't munching my Prada and peeing on my silk rug."

"Good. He's a sweet boy, and Dalmatians *are* trainable, you just have to get serious. And you have to crate him when you aren't here, always."

"Yeah, that part I learned."

"Let's put him in there to nap and I'll help you clean up." I stand slowly, and the puppy squirms a bit, but doesn't really wake up as I put him in his crate and gently lock the door. I grab the throw blanket off the nearest chair and drape it over the crate to provide some darkness and sound buffering, and Lynne and I get to putting her place back to rights. I grab her iPad and put in a Petco order with some essentials for her, and schedule delivery within two hours. I forward her the contact info I have for Bryant, the trainer who helped me with Simca, and my dog-walking service.

By the time we've cleaned up the destroyed pillow and shoes, and cleaned the rug as best we can, it feels late enough that we can indulge in a drink and Lynne opens a bottle of wine.

"Cheers. Thanks for the save."

"Well, it is partially my fault, but I don't take full blame on this one."

"Fair enough. I totally get why you thought I should do it. You know, when he was so calm these past days it was amazing to just have this adorable little guy who loved me so much and just wanted to be with me. What the hell happened?"

"When you bring puppies home, it can take a few days before they feel comfortable enough to be themselves. The move from the breeder to your house is emotionally trying and it makes them exhausted and super docile. When they get comfy with you and their surroundings, they just become normal puppies, and everything that goes with that. Simca was an angel for the first three days, just padding around after me and snuggling with me whenever I sat still. And then she became a tiny little maniacal furball full of teeth who peed constantly. My arms looked like hamburger, and my rug wasn't salvageable. But nothing was more adorable than the sweet parts, the quiet, sleepy parts."

"That's how they get you."

"Indeed."

"Somewhere right now my ex is really smug."

"Why is that?"

"He wanted dogs. Dogs and kids. Not, of course, when we met. When we met he was all, I'm too busy, too much of an impact on lifestyle, too hard to travel, too much hassle, yadda yadda yadda . . ."

"Like you."

"Exactly! But then a bunch of his buddies all had kids at once and suddenly his biological clock started beeping, and when I said that he had always known kids were not my thing, he started insisting that then we should get a dog, because that would at least be a compromise."

"Wow, that must have been hard." I know Lynne—she has never wanted kids, not ever, and she has never been shy about it. I've always really respected her for that. She always said that she was in the Oprah mode, that she thought she couldn't be the woman she wants to be and the mother children deserve at the same time, and that she would focus on being a great auntie and godmother when the opportunities arose. "Do you think he was lying when you met? Saying what he thought you wanted to hear and figured you'd change your mind?"

"I dunno. He said that when we met he wasn't in that head-space, but that something changed. Tried to tell me that it was just because we were so great together and he loved me so much that it made him think we should be parents."

"Well, that is kind of sweet."

"That is kind of bullshit manipulation. And when I said that wasn't the arrangement and I hadn't changed my mind, it was the beginning of the end. Suddenly nothing I did or said was good or right, and every other word out of his mouth was a thinly veiled dig about my being selfish and inflexible."

I don't really say anything, since I also think Lynne can sometimes be kind of selfish and inflexible about some things. But she does not hide who she is, so if her ex married her, he should have known who she was, what she believed, how she wanted her life to be.

"And then he was shocked when I wasn't so keen on sex."

"Wait, you stopped sleeping with him?"

"Well, not entirely, but you know, we were busy and not really connecting, and I started to feel like he was disappointed in bed because it wasn't about making babies, you know? Like he was just scratching an itch, because if it wasn't going to have a higher purpose, there was no need to really be together." Lynne sounds hurt and I don't blame her. After all, she can't be held responsible for not changing her mind about something as fundamental as having children, just because her ex did a switcheroo on her.

Her tone changes, and there is a vulnerability that I've rarely heard in her voice. "I wasn't punishing him, you know? I kept trying, made jokes about how my body would always be slammin' with no stretch marks, tried to get busy in unusual places, be all spontaneous, but he wasn't really into it. Just turned into once a week or so, rolling over in the dark, not really being with me, just sort of going through the motions. Made me feel like I could be just anyone. It hadn't ever been like that, you know, we could always connect in bed . . . he was amazing—we were amazing together. Until we weren't."

"Wow. I'm so sorry. That is just awful."

"Yeah. I thought he would get over it, but he just threw himself into work and then he got a job offer in a different city and expected I would just pick up and move with him. He tried to say it would be a fresh start for us, but I said I would have to seriously think about it and while I was thinking he accepted the job and essentially said that he was moving and I was welcome to come with him if I wanted. I didn't want."

"That is so passive-aggressive."

"No, child, that is *aggressive*-aggressive. It wasn't even more money!"

This last part prickles a bit. After all, the focus here is that her husband was making very important life decisions without her. But she just kind of implied that it would have been more tolerable if there were bigger dollar signs involved. But Lynne is my friend, and at the end of the day, this man really hurt her, so I decide to shrug it off.

"Well, then, clearly he was not the right guy for you!"

"Nope!" she says, reaching her glass out to me for a toast. "Was then and will always be Mr. So-Very-Wrong!"

There is a yip from the crate and Lynne goes to get her pup, still a bit sleepy and back to sweetness mode. She coos and cradles him, kissing the top of his head and calling him a good boy and a sweet little man, and for a second I can kind of see where her ex might have thought she'd be a good mother. For all her hard exterior, there is a soft creamy center to Lynne.

"I'll walk you out and take this guy for a long stroll," she says, snapping on his leash. "Thanks for the save."

"Of course. He's adorable, and once he's trained, he'll be the love of your life, I promise. We'll have a play date with Simca maybe this weekend, okay? She'll help whip him into shape."

"Sounds good."

We head out, the pup prancing proudly in between us, and I hope that Lynne takes his training seriously, because if she doesn't, she'll be living with the enemy for the next twelve to fifteen years.

Thank you, lovey, this is perfect," Aunt Claire says, taking a sip of the Boulevardier I have poured her.

My mom comes into the living room with a tray of cheese and crackers. "Claire, put something in your stomach before you end up schickered," she says. Claire is famous for drinking without eating and getting loopy.

Claire snags a chunk of cheddar and two crackers, making a little sandwich. I pop a square of Swiss into my mouth as my mom settles into the couch next to Claire and reaches for an olive. I take a sip of my own Boulevardier; my mom is sticking to wine.

"So, are we doing Jewish Christmas this year?" Aunt Claire asks. The three of us usually go to a movie double feature and then out for Chinese food on Christmas Day.

"Can we do Jewish Christmas Eve instead? I'm supposed to help Teresa with her Christmas Day celebration, and I'm dropping off some dishes for Glenn to bring to his brother's big potluck."

"Of course! That is so sweet of you to give Teresa a hand, and that will be fun to have a big traditional Italian Christmas Day," my mom says. "Tell Glenn we send our love, and we're looking forward to seeing him next week." Mom and Claire are taking Glenn to a bowling event for one of their charities.

"Will do. I'm sure Teresa would love for the two of you to join, if you want."

"Thank you, but no. The two of us will find something fun to binge on Netflix," Claire says, answering deftly for both of them. My mom and dad and I used to do Christmas Eve and Day with Claire and Buddy, always something quiet and fun and intimate. I know both of them miss it, and even after all this time I think the idea of doing anything big or overly celebratory would feel too weird.

"Well, your choice. If you change your mind, lemme know."

"We will, thank you. It's lovely that you girls have reconnected. How special for you all. Will Lynne be at Teresa's?"

"Nope, she'll be with her family at her aunt's house. If she can leave her new dog!" I fill them in on Lynne's new family member and our afternoon activities. They think it is hilarious. I know I'm just stalling, I need to tell them about Shawn and I'm not really sure how to handle it. Aunt Claire tells a story about when Buddy brought home their bloodhounds, Bob and Bandit, and the neighbors threatened to call the cops if they didn't stop howling. My mom says that they were like the Bumpuses from *A Christmas Story*, and Claire sticks her tongue out. We never had dogs growing up because my dad was allergic, but now my mom loves when I go on vacation and Simca comes to stay with her. Spoils her rotten.

I take a deep breath and decide that casual is the way to go on the Shawn thing. If I talk about it like it is no big deal, maybe they will treat it like it is no big deal. "So, New Year's Eve, I'm bringing a date. Friend of Lawrence's that I've been seeing a bit."

Aunt Claire stops her drink halfway to her mouth, and my mom drops a cracker into her lap.

"Seeing romantically?" Claire asks.

"Yes. We met at the Halloween party and have been spending some time together."

"So a couple of months, then. Is it serious?" my mom asks, the cracker still resting on her left thigh.

"It's very nice, and we are enjoying each other's company. I don't know how you define serious, but we like each other and are seeing where it goes." This seems nonchalant enough. Except my mother's eyes fill with tears.

"Oh, honey . . . that is so great." She wipes her eyes, and Claire reaches over and squeezes her hand.

"Yes, it is, doll face, good for you. Tell us all about him."

"Hey, it's not a big deal, don't get all emotional. I'm just dating him." Oy.

"It's a *very* big deal," my mom says. "I thought that man in France ruined you forever. It makes me very happy that you are dating again."

This stops me cold. I never told my mom about Bernard, not once. He was a lot older . . . the whole ex-wife nightmare . . . he was my boss. I was pretty sure she and my dad wouldn't have approved, so I never mentioned him. "What do you mean the man in France?"

"Good Lord, Eloise, do you think we are all dumb? That we all just fell off the turnip truck? When you got home it was clear you had left someone behind, whatever brave face you put on it, and it was even more clear that whoever he was, he had broken your heart into a million pieces. And any suspicions have been amply confirmed by your patent refusal to have anything remotely resembling a romantic life ever since," Claire says pointedly.

"We have so hoped that you would get over him, get back out there. You deserve so much love in your life, sweetheart," my mom says through her tears.

"But you never said anything!" I feel like an idiot: of course they would have figured it out. My family is a lot of things, but stupid isn't one of them.

"Wasn't for us to pry. It's your life. You live it the way you want. But it's about time you were at least getting laid," Aunt Claire says, handing my mother a napkin and retrieving the cracker from her lap.

This makes me blush. "Well, I'm glad to oblige."

"Tell us the important stuff," my mom says, finishing her glass of wine, then blowing her nose loudly.

"His name is Shawn and he's an orthopedic surgeon specializing in sports injuries. He's from Chicago originally, divorced, no kids, lives in the Gold Coast." I pause. "He's very smart and kind and funny, he's forty-four, former pro football player, good-looking, and he's African American."

"Sounds lovely all the way around, dear heart. Is he tall?" Claire asks.

"Six foot five," I say.

"Whew. That is tall. The two of you must look stunning together!" my mom says. I love that neither of them are commenting on the race thing; not that I was really worried, but you never know.

"Do you have a picture?" Claire asks.

I pull out my phone and pull up the photo of him on his practice's website, and show them.

Claire snags the phone first. "Hot damn, girl, when you get back in the game you do not mess about. This man is gorgeous!" She whistles softly.

"Claire! Stop that. Gimme," my mom says and takes the phone. "Well, never mind. Your aunt is right, this man is delicious."

"Ewww. That is not appropriate, Mom!"

"Well, I'm just saying," my mom says, handing me back the phone.

"I'm glad you approve. Anyway, you will meet him New Year's Eve, and I'm counting on you both to behave yourselves."

"Oh we will, don't you worry," Mom says.

"Now, tell us everything from the moment you met and all the dates you have been on since. Don't leave anything out!" Claire says, snuggling back into the couch like a kid getting ready for storytime.

"Well, leave the naked bits out. I'm still your mother," Mom says, eyes twinkling.

I sigh. "Okay, well, when we first met at the party, I thought he was gay . . ." If they have been sad and worried about me all this time, and hurt that I never shared my secret Bernard pain with them all these years, then the least I can do is tell them the nonnaked details of the new man in my life. And as the story unfolds I realize two really important things. One, not only should I have been more forthcoming all this time, but I should be more forthcoming in general. My self-protective, secretive nature might suit my natural inclination to not have to listen to outside opinions, but it isn't fair to the people I love most.

And two? For all my protestations that my relationship with Shawn isn't serious, it is. It is very serious, at least to me, and that scares me more than a little bit. Because I can feel in the way I am describing him to Mom and Claire—the way I am presenting all the funniest things he has said, the most romantic gestures, the kindest actions—that I am really falling for him.

I want them to be predisposed to love him.

Because I love him.

Damn. That complicates everything.

But as I unfold the tale, I look at their rapt faces and at least I know one thing. If it all ends in tragedy, at least this time I'll have them to lean on. I promise myself that I will, if I need to, which is as big a step for me as falling in love.

When I get home, after the full tale has been told, and the three of us have decimated a pizza, the story being longer and more hungry-making than anticipated, I call Shawn.

"Hello, you, did you have fun with your mom and aunt?"

"I did have a lovely evening. They are both very much looking forward to meeting you on New Year's."

He pauses. "You told them about me?"

"I did."

"And they didn't disapprove?"

"Of what?"

"Of you having a black boyfriend." I can hear in his voice that this is actually something he was worried about.

"Do I?"

"Do you what?"

"Have a boyfriend." He said the word so casually, but it made my heart jump.

"Well, goodness, woman, I've been operating under that assumption. Do I have a girlfriend?" he says with a wicked tone.

"You do, of course you do," I say, the world's widest grin on my face.

"Good. Tell all your other boyfriends that they are off duty, will you?"

"I'll send out a mailing tomorrow, if you'll do the same with all your side-pieces."

"That's a pact."

I can't believe we've just had the exclusivity conversation in such a joking way; it is not what I expected at all, and yet, it is completely in line with how easy and free we are together. "And so you know, they don't care in the least that you're black, by the way. I hope nothing I ever said would have given you the impression it would have been a problem."

"No, nothing like that. I just noticed that you don't talk much about your family or friends, and I got the sense that you were playing your cards close to the vest on our dating, so I wondered what that was about."

Well, if I have a boyfriend and want him to stay that way, then my pact with myself earlier tonight about honesty and vulnerability needs to extend to him, especially to him. "Yeah, you know I told you about Bernard?"

"Yes, the French ex-boyfriend."

"Well, it was a truly devastating and horrible breakup, and in the aftermath I just closed myself off to dating and romance. I haven't dated in years, like, not at all, so when we met and it was so lovely and natural and fun, it was hard for me to trust it, and I kind of wanted to just keep it for myself for a little bit. But I'm really excited for you to meet my family, and they are really excited to meet you."

"Well, I'm very honored to be the man that you waited for. And I can't wait to meet your family, and to have you meet mine. Of course, you'll have to wait for Easter when my snow-birding parents get back."

The idea that he is presuming that we will still be together at Easter makes my heart skip a beat. "Sounds like a plan. Be fore-warned, Aunt Claire is going to flirt with you mercilessly, and probably inappropriately once the champagne starts flowing."

"Is that so?"

"I showed them your picture. They both went gaga."

"I am a fine brother," he says in an extra-deep voice.

I laugh. "Yes, yes, you are."

"Hey, girlfriend?" Putting emphasis on the word in the most wonderful way.

"Yes, boyfriend?" I think that may be the best word in the English language.

"Do you have an early morning tomorrow?"

"No more than usual. You?"

"No more than usual. I was thinking that perhaps I should come over, make sure you and the dog are safe on your walk?"

"I think that would be a very good idea."

"See you in fifteen."

"Yes, you will."

have a boyfriend. And my mom knows about him. Holy shit.

# Fourteen

Chicago is bustling. Nothing like December twenty-third. It is always crazy insane in this city. Last-minute gifts, last-minute trips, last-minute parties and gatherings. Usually I'm hunkered down, cozy at home, relaxing, fully stocked with food and drink and not thinking a thing about the season, except what to binge on, both food-wise and entertainment-wise. Since the Farbers are always traveling this time of year and I don't always go with them, we have an annual holiday dinner celebration together, usually around the second week of December, where they all cook dinner for me and we exchange our gifts. It is very sweet, and I look forward to picking out special things for the kids, and receiving their expressions of love, usually hilarious.

This year Robbie gave me a bottle of Jean Naté perfume, which I did not know they even made anymore, but which smells exactly like my childhood, since I gave it to my mom when I was about seven. Darcy made me a mix CD of her School of Rock band playing some of my favorite hits from the '90s, which was super sweet. Ian gave me a bottle of birch syrup, a rare sweet elixir that is similar to maple syrup but more complex and interesting. And Geneva made me a calendar, with every month a different picture that she drew. Of herself. Shelby and Brad gave me my usual generous holiday bonus, and a pack of ten massages at Urban Oasis, since I confessed to Shelby that my return to a more athletic lifestyle has been okay, but that the aches and pains of almost-forty are very different and harder to shake off than the ones I remember from my teens.

I gave Robbie a wallet, to show off his new driver's license. I enlisted Marcy's help on a fun and funky shirt and some cool tights for Darcy. I gave Ian his own professional knife roll, with a couple of new knives. And Geneva got the full set of Eloise books. It seems appropriate to introduce her to my literary namesake, although I'm a bit worried that she might find them a little too inspiring. For Shelby and Brad, a really special old bottle of Armagnac, one of the last bottles that I brought back from my time in France. Something for them to dole out in little nightcaps when the kids are all in bed. We ate a great dinner and watched some of the old Christmas specials and had a wonderful celebration before they left for Miami.

So usually, on the twenty-third of December, I'd be anywhere but out. Tomorrow night I'll do movies and Chinese with Mom and Aunt Claire, and Sunday will be Christmaspalooza at Teresa's. But today I am running around like the proverbial chicken because tonight is Shawn's last night in town before he leaves to see his folks, and we are spending it together. He wants to cook for me. Which is both wonderful and nerve-wracking. I am freaked out about finding a present for him. On the one hand, what if he isn't bringing me a present? After all, we've only been together, like, two months, so I certainly wouldn't expect one. But we are officially boyfriend and girlfriend, so that seems like gift exchange wouldn't be unexpected either. And then there is the level of gift . . . what if I get him something nicer than he gets me? Or much less nice? I haven't had to think about this sort of thing in so long, and I was never terribly good at it to begin with. It's a family trait. We're historically sort of terrible gift givers. The kind of gift givers where husbands give wives vacuum cleaners for their birthdays, and wives give husbands tickets to avant-garde Bulgarian dance productions for anniversaries. Kids who get socks and underwear at Hanukkah do not grow up to be awesome present pickers. Trust me, when a Kahn or a Rosen gives you cash or a gift card, that is actually showing wonderful thoughtfulness and not indifference.

I've been in and out of every store in the Water Tower on Michigan Avenue. Everything seems either too generic, too expensive, or not expensive enough. My hands might know the contours of Shawn's body, but not enough for me to feel confident about guessing his clothing sizes. Jewelry is too much, a scarf too little. Cologne too Father's Day, and besides, I love what he smells like already and wouldn't want to change it.

Exasperated, I pick up the phone.

"Darling!"

"Lawrence, I need help."

"I'm here for you, you know that. What do you need? Bail money? Rent boy? Kidney? Name it."

"I have to get a Christmas present for Shawn."

"Ha! Delightful, so delightful. If he were on my team, I'd fight a duel with you over him."

"Yeah, well, we're in a tricky spot. He's coming over tonight, and I'm pretty sure he is bringing me a gift, and I want to have one for him. But we haven't been together long enough for me to have a good sense of what he might want or what might be appropriate."

"Breathe, child, breathe, this is not complicated. The key is to get something sweet and adorable, something that would remind him of you in a playful way. That way it is truly the intent of the gift and not the extravagance that is the thing. I once had a lover for a brief time, and he would come over and I, being the consummate host, would ask if I could get him anything, and he would invariably say 'A pony?' So for his birthday, which came very early on in our romance, I bought him a small stuffed pony. It was only fifteen or twenty bucks, but he said it was the best gift I could have gotten him."

"That's a great idea, something cute and funny, instead of trying to go all elegant and meaningful. Thanks, Lawrence, you're the best!"

"Merry Christmas, sweet girl. I look forward to seeing you both to ring in the New Year."

I get out my phone and type in a query. It gives me exactly what I need, and I head for my car to go get it.

The kiss hits me right in the heart, and other parts southerly.

"Hello, you," Shawn says when we come up for air.

"Hello back. Can I help with those?" I reach for one of the grocery bags that he is carrying.

"Not at all," he says, heading for the kitchen and dropping

them on the counter. I head to the back door, where Simca is scratching to be let in, aware that her new favorite person is on the premises. I open the door and she scrabbles inside, her stumpy little legs going every which way on the hardwood floor.

"Hello, you glorious girl, you!" says Shawn, scooping up Simca in his arms and snuggling into her head. She yips and wiggles happily, licking his face. He gives her a loud smooch, and then drops her on the floor and reaches into his pocket to pull out a small deer antler. "Merry Christmas!" he says, handing her the treat, which she accepts daintily with a wide smile, and then trots over to her bed to have a good chew.

"My dog is madly in love with you."

"Well, who could blame her? Catch that I am."

"Indeed," I say, and we lean right back into another kiss. I cannot get enough of this man.

"And a little something for her amazing mom. Merry Christmas," he says, handing me a small box with a silver ribbon.

"Oh, Shawn, you didn't need to get me anything."

"It's just a little something to make you think of me," he says.

I pull the end of the ribbon and slide it off the box. I open the box, and inside is a thin silver chain, and on the chain two silver pendants. One is the number 50 with pavé white rhinestones, and the other is the Bears logo in blue and orange rhinestones. Fifty was Mike Singletary's number when he played, and the number on the jersey Shawn was wearing when we met. Turns out Shawn was number 50 in high school, part of why he always felt connected to Samurai Mike. I laugh.

"It's perfect," I say, attaching the clasp around my neck.

"Looks good on you." He kisses me.

"I have a little something for you as well," I say, walking

over to the sideboard and getting the bag I prepped earlier out of the cabinet.

"Well, now, we are all full of surprises!" He reaches into the bag and pulls out the small box. He opens the box to reveal my gift, a heavy brass key ring with a brass figurine of a mermaid dangling off it. He laughs and throws his head back.

"You called Lawrence," he says.

"So did you!" I say.

"Guilty," he says. "I'm pretty terrible at gifts. My ex-wife was always telling me not to bother, she would just go pick something out and put it on hold and have me go pick it up and pay for it. I really didn't want my first present to you to be a flop."

I shake my head. "I'm hopeless at gifts; everyone in my family is."

"Well, I'm grateful, because the necklace looks very sweet on you, and I absolutely love my key ring. Thank you so much." He kisses me.

"Thank Lawrence!"

"Oh, I do, believe me I do," he says seriously.

"Yeah, me too." I reach for him and give him a kiss to let him know how much I love my present, and how much it means to me that he wanted so badly to get it right.

"All right now, woman, don't distract me. I've got some serious dinner to make, and all of this pawing at me is keeping me from it," he says jokingly, and I put my hands up in surrender.

"What can I do to help?"

"You can pour us both a glass of wine, park your fantastic tush in that there chair, and keep me company."

"That I can do. Red or white?"

"Red, please. Something perky and insouciant with a hint of rebellious fruit and a subtle funk of old fencing mask." He fakes a snobby wine critic voice. It makes me laugh. I love that he can be goofy; I don't have a whole lot of silly in me naturally, but I respect it in others.

I open a bottle of Volnay and pour us each a glass.

"To our first Christmas," Shawn says, holding out his glass.

"I'll drink to that," I say, imagining that there might be another, but barely daring to hope, to think that far ahead.

We sip the wine, and he starts telling me about his plans with his parents at their winter place in North Carolina. His mom grew up there, so her sisters are still there with their families. There will be church on Christmas Eve and a big family get-together on Christmas Day, full of cousins and friends and amazing food. He'll get in some golf with his dad and do some light handyman stuff around the house for them. They are there every year from the beginning of December through the end of March, always back in Chicago in time for Easter weekend. It sounds like a lot of fun.

"Okay, now, I'm usually pretty confident in the kitchen, but I have to admit, I'm a little nervous to cook for you."

"Please don't be. I know so many people get all weird about cooking for a professional chef, but you know me well enough to know that half the time I eat a big bowl of popcorn for dinner. Anything you make will be great."

"That makes me feel better. But please be sure to stop me if you see me doing something egregiously wrong! I'm secure enough to be able to take some constructive advice."

"Noted."

While I sit and sip my wine, Shawn deftly unpacks the grocery bags. There is a pair of beautiful veal chops, some potatoes, thin French green beans. A foil-wrapped loaf. Shawn opens the veal chops and seasons them well, setting them aside on a tray, then puts the potatoes into a pot of water and sets it on the stove to bring it to a boil. He deftly snaps the ends off the beans, one by one, dropping them into a colander. I marvel at his ease in my kitchen. He won't let me help, beyond guiding him in the right direction for equipment. Simca, feeling left out and done with her new antler for the moment, paws at my ankle, and I hoist her up onto the seat next to me. She rests her chin on the countertop, watching Shawn put some heavy cream and butter into a small pan to warm.

I reach over and peek inside the foil loaf.

"Shawn, did you bring me a fruitcake?" Being Jewish, fruitcake has always been a punch line and never an actual food product. I've seen them, but never tasted one.

"Yes, ma'am. That there is my grandma Lou's recipe, sort of a cross between a Jamaican black cake and a southern fruitcake, and trust me, you are going to love it. It takes almost a week to make, and ever since Grandma Lou died, I'm in charge of the fruitcakes for Christmas. You're lucky Uncle Doug is on a Christmas cruise with his new flame; that would have been his loaf."

"Well, then, thank you, Uncle Doug. It smells good." There is a spicy aroma wafting up from the dark loaf, which doesn't look anything like the ones I've seen with their garish green and red candied cherries.

"It's shockingly delicious. I swear."

"I trust you."

Shawn pulls out a small hunk of cheddar and puts it on a plate, cutting off a slice and popping it in his mouth before sliding it across to me. I cut off a sliver and slip it to Simca.

"Woman, did you just give twelve-year-old cheddar to the dog?"

"Yep. She has a very refined cheese palate."

"Good to know."

I cut off a slice for myself, savoring the sharpness and the little salty crystals that pop on my tongue before the cheese melts into savory creaminess.

"So," he says, giving the potatoes a stir and setting the oven to 400. "Let me get this straight: you are going to spend Christmas Eve at the movies?"

"Yep. Traditional Jewish Christmas. We do it every year, either Christmas Eve or Christmas Day—movies and Chinese food."

"What do you see?"

"Well, when my dad and Buddy were alive, we'd always see whatever big action blockbuster was the holiday release that year, and whatever the big kids' movie was, the perfect double feature. Now that they're gone, we'll still do the kids' movie if it doesn't look too awful, and something chick-flicky."

"That must be hard, to have them both gone." Shawn drops the chops into a heated cast-iron skillet with a sizzle.

"Yeah. But it's been long enough that it is more wistful than devastating. The first couple of years were hardest, as you can imagine, but we hang in there."

"Wish I could have met them," he says, flipping the now-browned chops over. He slides the pan into the oven.

"Me too. Thank you." It is about the sweetest thing he could say to me.

Shawn drains the potatoes, takes the masher from the tub on the counter, and begins to slowly smash them while drizzling in the warm butter and cream mixture. When he likes what he sees, he reaches for a tub of sour cream and adds a healthy spoonful, gently folding it in.

"You've got skills, Mr. Sudberry-Long."

"Well, the women in my family believe in men who can cook. Especially big boys like me who eat everyone out of house and home!" he says with a laugh. "My mom always said if I was going to eat more than twice what she and my dad did combined, I'd have to pull my weight in the kitchen. My brother never really mastered it, but he's good at dishes."

"Will Ronald be there for Christmas?" Shawn's brother is apparently his polar opposite, a small, slight man with no athletic prowess, but genius-level brain; he's posted in Hong Kong at the moment, doing some sort of change management consulting for a major international corporation.

Shawn reaches across the counter with the spoon, and I taste the creamy potatoes, rich and delicious, with just the perfect amount of tartness from the sour cream. I roll my eyes in ecstasy. Shawn looks pleased with my reaction and winks at me. "Nope. He couldn't get away. But he said he might make Easter, so you'll meet him then."

"I dunno, that's, like, four months away. What if you're sick of me by then?" I say this in a very joking manner, but the little twist in my stomach belies my genuine fear that this might be true. Shawn and I are still in the early flush of exciting newness of our relationship, but we haven't had any serious discussions, not about the important stuff like money or religion or family. We haven't ever spent more than seventeen contiguous hours together. Neither of us has farted in front of the other. There are many, many milestones to get through to even see if this thing could be the real deal in some serious way.

But I want it. Deep down, as much as I have been trying to keep my heart in the moment, my head keeps taking flights of fancy into the future. You'd think that after Bernard blew up my heart all those years ago that the scars would be so old and faded that everything would be almost as strong as if nothing happened. But it doesn't feel that way. Everything that Shawn makes me feel, every layer of me that he peels away, it puts pressure on those ancient fault lines, and if I'm not cautious, if I don't tread very lightly, then the potential for Shawn to hurt me, maybe even more than Bernard did, is very real. I love Shawn, if I'm honest with myself, but I'm not ready to give him that power, to let him in that deeply.

Shawn looks up at me and directly into my eyes. "Let me be very clear about something, my darling girl. I could never get sick of you. Now, we are both grown-ass people, we know that in romance, there are a million things that can mean we won't be a forever love match. But we are friends, and I don't believe you could ever do anything that would hurt me in ways that would make me want to not still have you in my life as friends if it turns out we shouldn't be lovers. And I know for sure that I have no intention of ever hurting you in a way that would make you cut me out of your life."

He says this very matter-of-factly. "Look at you, all mature and stuff." I'm still keeping my voice light, but the simplicity of the statement, that he likes me as a friend in an important enough way to believe that even if we break up we would still be in each other's lives, this makes my stomach relax. I don't have that many friends, and other than Lawrence, who sort of doesn't count, no real guy friends. It's nice to think that if we don't make it romantically, I won't lose him entirely. And any woman is set at ease when the new man in her life tells her very sincerely that he isn't going to hurt her.

Shawn shrugs, chopping chives deftly. "I'm a hopeful romantic, but also a realist. We're off to a perfectly grand start. If I were a betting man, I'd bet on us. But you and I have both been here before; we know that it doesn't always stay that way. Eventually you are going to find out about my many flaws, and some of them might not be the kinds of things you can overlook. I'm going to put my trust in both of us to be adults, and if something comes up that is a deal breaker for either of us, then we'll talk about it intelligently. If it means we can't be together, we'll agree to stay pals. Because, to be sure, Eloise Kahn, I really like having you in my life, even if someday you can't be in my bed. Deal?" He sticks out his pinky like an old-school playground promise. I take it in mine and we shake. Then he puts down the knife, wipes his hands on a towel, and walks around the island to where I'm sitting.

"Many flaws, huh?" I say as he pulls me off of the bar stool and into his arms.

"I'm for sure not going to tell you about those until I've put you in a very forgiving mood." And he leans in and kisses me so hard and so long that any fears I have are just a little bit of noise in another room, faint and far away and really not scary at all. His hands hold my head to his, the kiss as precise and perfect as any we've ever kissed, and my hands slide around his back, feeling his strong muscles tighten as his arms move down to hold me firmly against the length of his body. He pulls away, and kisses my forehead gently. "But first, I'm gonna feed you!" This makes me giggle, and he rumples Simca's fur and sneaks her another crumb of cheese before going back to his side of the island to finish making me dinner.

Everything is delicious.

And fruitcake may be my new favorite breakfast.


'd like to propose a toast!" Gio says, standing at the head of the table. "To a wonderful Christmas for all of our friends and family. Thank you for celebrating with us! And to all of the chefs, especially my beautiful wife!" There are cries of *"cin cin"* and "hear hear" and plenty of clinking of glassware. Gio looks a million miles away from where I sit next to Teresa at the opposite end of the table. We've moved all of the living room furniture out to the garage in order to set up this massive long table that starts in their dining room and goes all the way out through their sunroom. There are thirty people here at the grown-up table, and at least fifteen "kids" in the kitchen.

The feast is family-style, of course. Every six-person section of the table has its own set of identical dishes: garlicky roasted chicken with potatoes, a platter of fat sausages and peppers, rigatoni with a spicy meat sauce, linguine al olio, braised broccoli rabe, and shrimp scampi. This is on top of the endless parade of appetizers that everyone has been wolfing down all afternoon: antipasto platters piled with cheeses and charcuterie, fried arancini, hot spinach and artichoke dip, meatball sliders. I can't begin to know how anyone will touch the insane dessert buffet . . . I counted twelve different types of cookies, freshly stuffed cannoli, zeppole, pizzelles, a huge vat of tiramisu, and my favorite, Teresa's mom's lobster tails, sort of a crispy, zillion-layered pastry cone filled with chocolate custard and whipped cream.

I got here bright and early to help out, right after I dropped off a big vat of macaroni and cheese and a chocolate sheet cake with pecans, both from Mrs. O'Connor's recipes, to Glenn. He was very grateful for my providing his potluck offerings; his family told him it wouldn't be Christmas without those dishes, and he is still pretty hopeless in the kitchen. We sat over coffee and a couple of muffins and I promised that as long as he needed me to, I would make those recipes for him every Christmas, and we held hands and he told me some fun Christmas stories from his life with Helene and I told him some about my dad and we both cried a little bit. I invited him to come to dinner with Mom and Aunt Claire New Year's Day and he readily agreed.

Teresa is finally out of the boot, but still can't stand or walk for very long stretches. The boys set up the tables and chairs, and I dressed them with Teresa's red tablecloths and green napkins and gold holly napkin rings. The plates and flatware are all plastic—it would be way too many dishes—but the glassware is real, rented from a local company, which will pick them up dirty tomorrow, so we don't have to worry about cleaning. Small centerpieces of mini rosemary bushes trimmed to look like Christmas trees and decorated with bits of tinsel are perfuming the whole room with a wonderful piney aroma, and all the aunts and sisters and sisters-in-law will get to take them home as parting gifts.

Everyone started arriving at about two this afternoon, laden with platters and bowls and cooler bags full of food, and the house became a riot of children laughing and stories being told in Italian and English, and copious eating and drinking. I had seventeen versions of the same conversation about where I had gone, and how special it was for me to be back in Teresa's life. I heard all about the accomplishments of all of the cousins, from dance recitals to Brownie badges to sporting triumphs to fabulously successful summer lemonade stands. And of course, being the trained chef in a room full of passionate home cooks, I was asked for opinions on every dish, seasoning, flavors, and, of course, whose was better than the others. Taking a cue from Teresa, who is very good at family diplomacy, I would wink at each sister or sister-in-law or aunt and say, "Now, you know I can't claim favorites, but you also know what's what." Giving each woman the complete confidence that I had just admitted that she was absolutely the best cook in the room without getting myself in trouble.

Mostly, I'm in awe of the dynamic of such a fabulous large and loving blended family. Teresa's mom laughing in the corner with Gio's mom, all the aunts taking turns attending to Gio's birdlike grandmother, ninety-five and a white-haired pistol, holding court in the corner and eating like a starved buffalo. The barely controlled chaos, the gentle ribbing, the constant hugging and kissing and ballbusting, and the enormity of the love in this house. I watch the little kids crawl into whatever adult lap is nearest for a snuggle, and it makes me think of Geneva and her affection for me, how nothing feels better than wee arms around your neck, or the feathery kiss of tiny lips on your cheek. The way they all have that kid smell. And my heart breaks wide open and all I can think is that it would be so nice to have family like this, big and brash and present.

We've always been a small clan. I never knew any of my grandparents, Claire and Buddy never had kids, and no one seems to be in touch with the extended family at all. We'd occasionally take in friends at holidays, to fill out the table a bit, but most often we were just the five of us. And then four. And now we are three. I tried again to get Mom and Claire to come today, but apparently there was a marathon on TCM that needed attending to. I promised to stop by on my way home with leftovers for them.

"I'm glad you're here, El, thanks for coming," Teresa says, watching me look down the table at the bacchanal. One thing about a dining table this long and this full and noisy, it creates little pockets of privacy and intimacy. Everyone else is engaged with each other, and we can sit in our own little bubble at the end, marveling at the astounding messy fabulousness of it all.

"Thank you so much for having me. Really, what a wonderful tradition."

"Yeah. It's endless, the cleaning and cooking and cooking and cleaning, but it's worth it. Do you ever think about it? Would you want this? Any of it?"

I smile at her. "I never really knew if it was for me, but now . . ."

"Now?" She looks at me expectantly.

"The idea is kind of appealing, to be honest. Not at quite this scale . . ."

She laughs. "Yeah, I'd keep it somewhat rational if I were you. But family, a husband, maybe kids?"

"It's not an unpleasant thought."

She narrows her eyes at me. "*You met someone*," she says.

I can't help it, I grin. "Maybe."

"O-M-G. Who? How?"

"A friend of Lawrence's. Very nice man. It's going well, so far. I don't want to jinx anything."

"Holy shit, that is so great. I'm really happy for you. But when do we get to meet him?"

"When I know for sure." Or as sure as I can know. When he's met my mom and Aunt Claire and they tell me that they like him. When the words "boyfriend" and "girlfriend" aren't still so foreign and exotic on our tongues. I want him to come back and ring in the New Year with me. Maybe tell me he loves me. I want to be really, really super sure before I let him meet Teresa and Lynne. Especially Lynne.

"Okay, okay. Can I have his name?"

"So you can go all stalkery with the Google and find shit out about him online? Absolutely not!"

"Damn. Does Lynne know yet?"

"No, she's been so busy with the new job and the new dog that I haven't seen her."

Teresa's face falls a bit. "That poor doggie."

"Oh, they'll be fine, just need to do the training."

"I meant spending Christmas in the kennel!"

"What?!" I hadn't heard anything about this.

"Yeah, she had church last night and family stuff today and then I guess she is leaving for the week to visit friends in L.A. through New Year's, so she boarded him starting yesterday. I feel so bad—he's so small and she just got him, and nine days seems like a long time to be apart."

"I thought she was staying in town!" I can't believe Lynne would just take off and leave her new puppy.

"Yeah, she was going to stay and work, but apparently Angelique closes all her stuff down between Christmas and New Year's every year, and some friend of hers reached out, so she just planned it last minute."

"That is so shitty." I can't help myself.

"Well, she deserves a vacation . . . I mean . . ."

"No, it's shitty, T. It's selfish. She has a brand-new puppy. That is a huge responsibility. Nine days is a really long time to be apart, to have training interrupted. It isn't fair to the dog. For what? Convenience while she goes to family functions? A vacation? She could have taken the gift of the week off to be here with him and training every day, to really bond and get him on a good schedule. Instead, she just drops him off like luggage with strangers and takes off? C'mon, Teresa, that is really self-centered behavior."

I can see the conflict in Teresa's eyes. Deep down, she knows I'm right. But her impulse to defend Lynne is strong. "I know he's a handful, and she's doing it all on her own . . . maybe she needed a break? She said the place she is boarding him will be doing training stuff with him while she's gone."

"T. There's no such thing as dog training. There's only *people* training. Yeah, anyone can teach a dog to sit or high-five with enough time and treats; that's tricks. But the key to puppy training is that it's essentially training the owner to behave in certain ways, to support the dog in being the well-behaved version of himself that he naturally wants to be. If your dog shits in the house, it isn't the dog's fault—the dog doesn't *want* to shit in the house—it's the owner's fault for not taking the dog out in time. If the dog is destroying stuff, it's because the owner isn't providing enough attention or activity. A dog isn't inherently destructive; he's just bored or understimulated. Lynne doesn't need someone else to train her dog, *she* needs to train herself to be attuned to the needs of the dog, to giving the dog a schedule to rely on. Jesus, T, how old were your kids before you left them behind for a week's vacation?"

Teresa blushes. "I'll let you know when it happens."

I shake my head. Of course she'd never gone on vacation without her kids. "Okay, then. Proving my point. Also, side note? You want a little more spice, maybe plan a trip for the two of you and let someone in this room watch your boys for a week. They'll be fine. Just saying."

"Noted. And you know Lynne. She's not instinctive about that stuff."

"No, she isn't." I can see on Teresa's face that the conversation is making her uncomfortable, and it's Christmas, so I pivot quickly. "Anyway, whatever. I hope she is having a nice Christmas and that she has a good vacation. More importantly, are you getting ready for your big teaching day?" I've got Teresa scheduled for a full day with Ian early in January to teach him some classic Italian dishes, including how to do pasta from scratch, basic Sunday gravy, meatballs, and a classic risotto.

"I hope so. I'm a little nervous. From your description he's a much more sophisticated chef than I am."

"He's got some serious skills, but he needs some of that Mama cooking in him. A little bit of the Italian soul food in his repertoire."

"Well, I can help with that!" She spears a chunk of sausage and pops it in her mouth.

"Yes, you can." I twirl a forkful of linguine and stuff it in my face, marveling at how the simple slick of good olive oil, a hint of garlic and parsley, and slippery noodles are so perfect.

"I keep meaning to tell you, I took the boys to that Mexican place you recommended!"

"Más allá del Sol? How did it go?"

"It was so much fun. I ordered just what you said, the melted cheese with sausage, and the little rolled-up chicken things, and then we got a bunch of stuff to share and taste. I promised them as long as they tasted everything, we could stop by McDonald's on the way home if anyone didn't like dinner and was still hungry. But they ate *everything*! It was really delicious."

"See? A little adventurousness can work sometimes. Plus, it keeps you out of McDonald's."

"Well, we still had to go to McDonald's. They didn't love the desserts so much, so they wanted McFlurrys on the way home." She laughs. "But change is slow, right? At least it was a start."

"It's a really good start." I wink at her and we drink our glasses of rich Chianti, and eat like it's our last meal, and let ourselves be swept into the loud wonderful din of the room.

And all I can think, for the first time since I thought I was pregnant when I was with Bernard, is that it's possible I do actually want some piece of this for myself. Maybe I really do.

# Fifteen

M m-mmm. Don'go," Shawn says, snuggling into my back. I wiggle back against him, feeling the warmth of him soaking into my body. We've barely been out of bed since he got home yesterday morning.

I did the girlfriendly thing and picked him up at O'Hare, shocked at the volume of luggage he had with him from such a short trip. Turns out between receiving a bunch of Christmas gifts and his mom sending him home with a month's worth of home-cooked goodies, he always leaves with one bag and comes back with three. We came straight to my house and had a lunch feast of his mom's amazing cooking: glazed ham, bread dressing, green beans she cans herself with salt pork, and a sweet potato pound cake that is beyond delicious. We took Simca on a walk to try to burn off some of the food, the whipping Chicago winds getting a chill well into our bones, came back to take a luxurious hot shower together, and fell into bed. We rose around ten p.m. to raid his goodies again, opting for a small pan of macaroni and cheese, which we ate in bed, one dish and two forks, and abandoned on the nightstand when we couldn't resist each other anymore, the sex playful and energetic.

I'm finding that the more time we spend together, the more fun I have. Sex with Bernard was always such a serious thing: long, deep, meaningful looks, strong eye contact, murmured phrases of love and longing. Sex with Shawn has that, but so much more. There is also talking and laughing and joking. We acknowledge the parts of lovemaking that are silly and funny and embrace laughing together. I only ever laughed with Bernard once, when he kissed his way up my body and said that I was the most delicious thing he had ever eaten, which was apparent from the glazed doughnut appearance of the lower half of his face, which I pointed out with a giggle, telling him he looked like a baba au rhum. He immediately lost his erection and didn't sleep with me for three days. That was the end of playful and funny with him.

Shawn can make me laugh in bed without it being a challenge to his masculinity, and I love the way we can start and stop and talk and not talk for hours. Just before dawn he reached for me again in the dark and we were silent and half-asleep as we came together, moving slowly, languidly, toward release and then slipping back into sleep without untangling.

"I can't stay. I have to go drop everything off at Lawrence's, get everything there all set up and organized so that tonight I don't have to abandon you too often to my mom and Claire's interrogations to putter in the kitchen."

"Okay, fine. But I can come help, right? Be your schlepper?"

This makes me chuckle, his use of Yiddish. "Yes, if you insist, you can be my Shabbas goy."

"Okay, I've been working on my vocabulary, but what is a shamus boy?"

"Shabbas goy. Technically a gentile man who does things for Jews on the Sabbath that they aren't allowed to do themselves, like turn lights off and on or carry keys."

"You can't carry keys?"

"Only if you're very observant."

"I've got a lot to learn," he says seriously.

"Not really. We're only culturally Jewish, not observant at all. Hence my ability to enjoy your mother's amazing ham yesterday."

"You did at that. I'm going to send her a note today telling her that you hit that ham like a shark hitting chum."

I swat his arm and sit up, stretching, feeling that wonderful feeling of delicate aches, my body reminding me of the endeavors of the night before, of this morning. He traces a hand down the length of my side, leaning forward to plant a kiss in the small of my back.

I turn to look at him and he throws his hands up in surrender.

"I give. Work it is. Can we shower first? Maybe eat something?"

"Yes and yes."

This morning's shower is much more functional than last night's, a perfunctory but loving mutual soaping up, with some strategic lather placement for entertainment value. We towel each other off and get dressed, and Shawn offers to take Simca for a walk while I rustle up some breakfast. By the time my man and my pup are back, there are scrambled eggs with some of the leftover ham and scallions and cream cheese, thick slices of sourdough toast lavished with butter, and freshly squeezed grapefruit juice. We tuck in, and I take him through what I need to do for the day.

"Sure you don't want to bail? I wouldn't blame you."

"Nope, I'm all in. I want to watch my baby work."

I wash up the breakfast stuff, and Shawn dries. Then I start to get all of the food that I've been prepping all week ready for transport. There is the standing prime rib roast, which I salted three days ago and have left uncovered in the extra fridge to dry out. I place the roast in a large Ziploc bag and put it in the bottom of the first rolling cooler, and then the tray of twice-baked potatoes, the crispy shells stuffed with chunky mashed potatoes enriched with cream, butter, sour cream, cheddar cheese, bacon bits, and chives, and topped with a combination of more shredded cheese and crispy fried shallots. My coolers have been retrofitted with dowels in the corners so that I can put thin sheets of melamine on them to create a second level of storage; that way items on the bottom don't get crushed. On the top layer of this cooler I place the tray of stuffed tomatoes, bursting with a filling of tomato pudding, a sweet-and-sour bread pudding made with tomato paste and orange juice and lots of butter and brown sugar, mixed with toasted bread cubes. I add a couple of frozen packs, and close the top.

"That is all looking amazing," Shawn says.

"Why, thank you. Can you grab me that second cooler over there, please?"

He salutes and rolls it over. I pull the creamed spinach out of the fridge, already stored in the slow cooker container, and put it in the bottom of the cooler, and then add three large heads of iceberg lettuce, the tub of homemade ranch dressing and another tub of crispy bacon bits, and a larger tub of popover batter. I made the pie at Lawrence's house yesterday morning before heading to the airport—it was just easier than trying to transport it—and I'll make the whipped cream topping and shower it with shards of shaved chocolate just before serving. I also dropped off three large bags of homemade salt-and-pepper potato chips, figuring that even Lawrence can't eat all of them in one day and that there will hopefully be at least two bags still there when we arrive. Lawrence insisted that he would pick up the oysters himself.

Once the coolers are filled and Shawn has loaded them into my car, I gather up the equipment I'll need, Shawn dutifully checking each item off the list as I put it in a bag.

"You're like a general prepping for battle," he says, looking over my time and action plan for the day.

"Yep. Have to be prepared. You ready?"

"I'm at your service, ma'am."

"Let's do this."

I check myself in the mirror one last time. My black jersey wrap dress hides a multitude of flaws, and more importantly will hide any accidental spatters that might occur while organizing the dinner. I've got my hair up in a tight, lacquered chignon so that I don't accidentally drop any in the food. I've been getting pretty good at my makeup with all the practice, and have kept it shimmery and simple tonight. I'm wearing my Christmas necklace from Shawn, my diamond studs, and a pair of black wedge heels that are fancy enough for a party but are also secretly super comfy.

I head downstairs and feed Simca and get my purse organized. Shawn dropped me off a couple of hours ago, after we got everything set up at Lawrence's, and then he went home in my car to unpack and get ready for tonight, and should be here any moment to fetch me. I'm still nervous about Shawn meeting my mom and Claire, but hopefully with the other people at the table, it won't be too bad.

I'm just swiping on a layer of gloss when the doorbell rings.

Oof. Never send to know for whom the bell tolls; it tolls for me.

Here. We. Go.



Darling, they're mad for him," Lawrence says, pinching my tush in the kitchen while I serve up slices of the decadent and silky chocolate cream pie onto flowery china plates.

"Stop that." I elbow him. Lawrence always gets weirdly handsy when he's had a lot of champagne, and tonight it has been flowing. But it is more naughty grandfather than truly lascivious. I peek around the corner into the dining room and can't help but smile. Shawn has my mom on one side, Claire on the other, and whatever story he's telling has them blushing and giggling like schoolgirls. I was originally mortified that Lawrence placed us apart, but he has a strict "no couples sit together" rule for dinner parties, so I was with him at the other end of the table with Jerry and Todd. Logical, I know. Todd is a major foodie and I suspect secret local James Beard Award voter, although he'll never cop to it. They are like the culinary Oscars and the voters are all sworn to secrecy. Jerry is just one of those guys who is at ease in any room, so there was plenty of good conversation at our end of the table, and, of course, Lawrence is always a good time. I spent half the time craning my neck around with my ears open to see what was going on at the other end of the table with my boyfriend and my family.

"Everything was delicious, my pet, truly. And don't you worry about that man of yours, he has them eating out of his hand."

"He seems to have that effect on people."

"You look happy, Eloise. Really."

"I'm tentatively optimistic."

"Why tentative?"

I lick a bit of cream off my finger after I slide the last piece of pie onto a plate. "Why do you think? It's too easy, too fun, too perfect. The sex is too good, he makes me laugh too much, he's charming the bejesus out of my family."

"How ghastly. Shall I kick him out immediately?"

"You know what I mean." Because he does.

Lawrence reaches up and places a finger under my chin, turning my head to face his. "Yes, I do. So listen good. Let your guard down. All the way down. Do you think that I of all people would put you in hands that I believed to be dangerous? If you break, you break, and I will make it my mission to put you back together again. But do not follow my very cowardly and bad example, my dear. I'm no role model. I let a deep hurt close me off from love forever, and I'm too old now to open myself back up. But it was a mistake and if I had it to do over, I would let myself get hurt again, even worse, in pursuit of love. Love is all, sweetness. And you deserve it."

There are tears swimming in his ice blue eyes, and such deep fervor in his voice that it lodges a lump in my throat. "Okay," I croak.

"Good girl." He wipes his eyes on a kitchen towel. "Now, for the love of Barbra, can we please eat this pie so that the queens in the other room can begin complaining about how many SoulCycle classes they are going to have to take to make up for tonight's indulgences?"

"Absolutely."

He reaches up and kisses my cheek, and we each take two plates of pie and head out to serve the guests.

The pie is gone in a flash, and we've barely gotten everyone a refill on champagne when it is time to count down to the New Year.

Ten!

Nine!

Eight!

Seven!

Six!

Five!

Four!

Three!

Two!

One!

HAPPY NEW YEAR!

We all toast and pull the cords on our confetti and streamer poppers, and then Shawn takes me in his arms and kisses me and whispers in my ear, "I believe this will be the best year ever." And then he lets me go, and goes over to give my mom a twirl, and dips Claire.

My mom comes over to kiss me. "Happy New Year, my wonderful girl. He's just everything I would have ever picked for you myself, and I can't tell you how much I like him, for himself and for you."

"Thanks, Mom, that means a lot."

"I invited him for dinner this week."

"Of course you did."

Claire walks over, fanning herself. "Good Lord, niece, please tell me his daddy is single. Maybe an uncle? Youngish grandfather floating around?"

"*Claire,*" my mom says, faking serious. "You leave poor Eloise alone."

"Just kidding, niece of mine. It's just my little stamp of approval."

"I know."

"Your mom invited him for dinner."

"She told me."

"I invited him to continue to put that shit-eating grin on your face, or suffer my personal wrath."

I smack my forehead. My mom shakes her head.

"Good to know."

Within twenty minutes or so, people begin making movements to the door, my mom and Claire first among them.

"Thank you, Lawrence, a fantastic evening, but the old ladies are turning into pumpkins at the ball," Claire says, giving him a hug. My mom leans in and whispers something in his ear that makes him smile and nod. They both receive hand kisses from Shawn, and then he leaves me behind to make sure they are deposited safely in the car service he arranged for the evening. He doesn't trust regular taxis on New Year's Eve. The driver will drop them off and then circle back for us; I'll have to pack up equipment and such before we can leave anyway.

The rest of the guests make their good-byes, some eliciting promises of shared recipes from me, and soon it is just me and Lawrence in the kitchen with Olga, his cleaning lady who always works his parties. She has done a miraculous job of stealthy silent cleaning as the evening progressed, and in the short time since dessert, she has loaded the dishwasher again and placed all of my spotless equipment back into their carrying bags. Always easier leaving than coming, with the food consumed. I load the bags of gear into the now-empty coolers for ease of transport.

"The driver will be back for us in about thirty minutes—he'll text when he's close," Shawn says, wandering into the kitchen and receiving the mug of tea I hand to him.

Olga shoos the three of us out of her kitchen, and we repair to the living room to sit.

"Well, dears, another year. Have we any resolutions?" Lawrence asks.

"Hmm. Good question. I think I resolve to make this lady here as happy as I can for as long as she'll let me," Shawn says.

"I approve of that one," Lawrence says.

"As do I," I say.

"What about you, my girl?"

I think about this. My bet list isn't exactly full of resolutions, per se, and it would feel like cheating to name any of those things. "I resolve to let him." This comes out more serious than I mean it to, but the look on both of their faces lets me know that it was safe for me to say.

"Another good one." Lawrence nods.

"And you, my little yenta? What do you resolve?" I ask.

"I resolve to take full credit for your love and expect that your firstborn café au lait baby will be named either Lawrence or Eunice, for my mother."

We laugh at his seriousness, and then Shawn looks at his phone and nods to me that the car is back. We thank Lawrence again for his generosity and hospitality, and I promise to see him Tuesday as usual. We both grab a cooler and roll them out and downstairs, and Shawn and the driver load them into the back of the SUV.

On the drive home, Shawn tells me all the silly things that he talked about with my mom and Claire, all the embarrassing stories they shared about me growing up, the touching stories they told him about my dad and Uncle Buddy. It means a lot that they were so candid with him, so I can forgive them for telling him about the time I pooped in the bathtub and completely freaked out the babysitter while they were having a dinner party downstairs.

At my house we load the coolers into the kitchen, let Simca out into the backyard for a quick evening toilette, and head upstairs.

"I think I'd better get started on my resolution," Shawn says.

"Well, then, I'd better get started on mine," I say, moving into his arms. We melt into the bed together, and it is sweet and deep and joyful. In the dark, just before we drift into sleep, Shawn murmurs to me.

"We are not naming our daughter Eunice."

"No, we most certainly are not."

"Happy New Year, Eloise. I love you."

I take the deepest breath I've ever taken, and whisper back, "I love you too."

I'm pretty sure he fell asleep without realizing that the dampness on his chest wasn't sweat.

# Sixteen

hand Shelby a cup of coffee, just the way she likes it, light and sweet.

"Bless you. How are they doing?" she asks me.

"See for yourself." I motion over to the island, where Teresa and Ian are separating eggs, dropping the whites into bowls and the yolks into the mouths of twin volcanoes of flour. There is a huge pot of Sunday gravy on the stove, a rich tomato sauce full of pork neck and sausage and oxtails, fragrant with onion and garlic, and hiding a pound of whole peeled carrots. The carrots are Teresa's family recipe secret for a bit of sweetness without grinding up the vegetable, which changes the texture of the sauce. They'll be fished out at the end, soft and imbued with the meaty savoriness of the sauce, and will serve as a special "cook's treat," drizzled with olive oil and sprinkled with coarse salt and ground pepper. In the oven, a tray of meatballs, roasting to browned perfection, to be simmered in the sauce and served on the side. Teresa starts to show Ian how to use a fork to gently begin to mix the egg yolks into the flour to get the pasta dough started. His apron is covered in meat juices and there is tomato in his hair, and I've never seen him happier.

"Look at that boy. Like a little bitty Bastianich."

I laugh. "He's taking to it like a fish to water. I'd be ready for some serious Italian feasts in the coming weeks."

"Perfect. Ingredients are plentiful, results are delicious and palate friendly for the other monsters, and frankly it's what I crave in the gloom of Chicago winter."

"Yeah, me too."

"So, date night tonight?" she asks with a sparkle. I finally fessed up to her after New Year's about Shawn and she is over the moon for me.

"Yes. He's taking me to MK."

"Ooh. Fancy."

"Well, we figured out that we both know Erick, the chef, a little bit, so we thought it would be a fun place for a date night." We've been staying in a lot, cooking together, for the past couple of weeks, but Shawn mentioned the other night that he doesn't want to get complacent with me, he doesn't want to stop planning special nights out, so I agreed to an upscale dinner. Besides, Erick is one of my favorite people and chefs, and the meal will be spectacular. And his pastry chef, Lisa, is one of Marcy's best buds, so I know that dessert will be a ruinous postdinner feast of amazing sweets.

"I think that is just so lovely. Thank you for bringing Teresa over—he's having such a great time. I worry sometimes that he takes it so seriously."

"Yeah, it's why I wanted T to teach him this stuff instead of me. She's a mom of three boys, so she has that nurturing energy and way of talking to him like a kid that I just don't have. I know I'm helping make him a great technician, but truly amazing cooking isn't really so much about technique, it's about heart and soul, and I don't want him to ever be missing that part of it."

"You have plenty of heart and soul, El. And you're great with kids!"

I smile at her and sip my tea. "I'm great with *your* kids. But that's because I know them so well. I know who they are and what they like and what their moods are. It's based in years of being with them. But I'm not a natural, not like you, not like Teresa." It's true. I might be terrific with the little Farbers, but put me in a room with anyone else's kids? I panic. I talk down to them or over their heads. Hand me a baby and I break into a sweat, sure that I'm going to drop it or let its neck snap back or, worse, that it is going to erupt some effluvia on me. Kids make me nervous as hell.

"I was terrible in the beginning," Shelby says.

"I have a very hard time believing that." She exudes the calm of the natural mom, the way Teresa does.

"Are you kidding? I was a hot mess for the first year of Robbie's life. I thought I was doing everything wrong, I overthought every decision, I thought Brad was going to divorce me. It took time and practice and recognition that kids are resilient and as long as you love them and aren't a complete idiot in the common sense department, everyone is going to be okay."

"Well, that gives me hope."

"Eloise, I know these things are inherently none of my business, but for the record, you'd be a great mom."

"I appreciate the vote of confidence."

"It's a little more than that. Brad and I have a favor to ask."

Uh-oh. "Okay . . ."

"Well, you know our folks are getting up there, and my dad has the heart stuff and Brad's mom has diabetes. Brad and I were talking over Christmas, and we were wondering if you would be willing to serve as guardian for the kids should something happen to us both."

I almost drop my tea mug. "Oh, Shelby . . . I . . ."

"Don't answer right now. Just say you'll think about it. It's just a legal protection, just in case of some insanely impossible tragedy. But when we talked about what would be best for the kids in that circumstance, it would be for them to be able to stay in Chicago, in this house, to continue to go to their schools, to keep everything as normal as possible for them. And to be sure that the person who would be taking care of them shares our fundamental values when it comes to politics and religion and all of the important things. We love you, and we trust you; you're family to us and the kids adore you. It's just paperwork, nothing bad is going to happen, but it would mean the world to us if you would consider it. Give us a little peace of mind."

"I don't know what to say. I promise to think about it. It means so much that you would even think of me, so thank you for that. When do you need to know?"

"You know, before that big bus crash in the next week or so." She grins wickedly.

"Oy! Stop that, don't even joke."

"Mom! Lookit!" Ian yells from across the kitchen. He is proudly showing off a deep golden ball of pasta dough, the flour volcano on the island completely gone.

"Good job, bud!"

"Are you sure there's no Italian blood in this young man? He's a natural!" Teresa says.

"I'm really doing it, Eloise!"

"Yes, you are, Chef. I'm super proud of you." I look at his gleaming face, at the way he is excited for my praise, and think that maybe, just maybe, in my new mind-set of embracing the things that scare me, maybe I should say yes to Shelby and Brad. It goes against my personal rules of keeping separation of church and state, work-wise. Complicates the relationship well beyond my comfort level. That worries me more than a little. But I don't know how I can turn them down without it being hurtful and, what's more, I don't know that I want to.

"This is so fun!" Ian says, and we all laugh at his exuberance.

I look at Shelby. She winks at me and squeezes my hand. "That's our boy." And I know exactly what she means.

Holy crap. What did you say?" Shawn says, as I tell him about Shelby's request over our pasta. Watching Ian all afternoon gave me serious pasta cravings, so Shawn and I decided to ask Erick to sneak us a small pasta course between our appetizers and entrées. As usual, he obliged us brilliantly, sending out a riff on cacao y pepe with a light but creamy sauce, crispy guanciale, shredded Brussels sprouts, and a fluttering of lemon zest, all punched up by the copious black pepper, which is somehow tamed of its acridness. I'll have to ask for his secret.

"I said I would think about it."

"It's a big honor."

"And a big responsibility. And it breaks all my rules."

"Well, of course, it isn't to be taken lightly. But from what you've told me, rules or not, you love those kids like family. Isn't it sort of late to try and pretend that they aren't all in your heart beyond being great employers?"

"I do love them, can't help it."

"Nor should you."

"What about you, can you imagine? If the worst happened?"

"Oh, baby. Talk about an hour-long dramedy waiting to happen! Can you picture it? It's perfect! Freshly in love, interracial, interreligious, middle-class couple suddenly find themselves with custody of four fabulously precocious rich white kids and their trust funds? The show would write itself. My mom will want Phylicia Rashad to play her, just be prepared for that."

I love how casual he is in his response, implying that we are in this together. As if it would be no big deal. "Ha! Yeah, and my mom will want Sally Field to play her, and Aunt Claire will insist on Carol Kane."

"I can see that."

"Idris Elba can play you," I say. "Or Morris Chestnut."

We keep laughing, casting our hypothetical blended-family comedy as we tuck into our entrées—veal for him, duck for me—feeding each other bites and reveling in the wonderful flavors. And then Shawn's face goes dark.

"Linda," he says, staring across the room.

"Linda who?" I ask.

"Linda, my ex-wife Linda. Just walked in."

Holy crap. I turn around to look behind me across the room and see the last person I expect. Lynne, with Angelique Morris, getting seated at a table about twenty feet away from us. Talk about coincidence. When she got back from her vacation, I finally fessed up to her about dating someone seriously, and I found her response to be less than energetic. She seemed to imply that it was good for me to have found someone I liked, but I should remember that I'm way out of practice in the dating arena and not to get too caught up in any one person. She implied that I would easily be prey to some guy with ulterior motives, and reminded me that I got snookered by Bernard. So I shared as little as possible.

"Well, that is a coincidence, because my friend Lynne just walked in too. Where is Linda?"

Shawn gestures to Lynne's table and a sinking feeling starts in my gut. When we were kids, Lynne, who always thought her name was an old lady name, used to say that she would reinvent herself as Lindsay or Lisa or Linda when she went into business. The California connection. The pasta turns to lead in my stomach. It's just not possible. I turn back around quickly before she sees me. "Maybe we should bail?"

"Of course not. We're adults; I'm sure she won't make a scene. Besides, what do they say is always the best revenge when running into an evil ex? To be madly in love with a gorgeous, smart, funny, spectacular woman on your arm?"

"Yeah, that's what they say." I down the rest of my wine quickly.

"Well, prepare yourself, she's coming over."

Maybe it isn't her. Maybe he was pointing at the table behind them, and it will be a funny story Lynne and I can tell Teresa later.

"Shawn," says Lynne's voice over my head. Fuck.

"Linda," he says, rising. "You look well."

"Visiting from San Francisco?" she asks, still not noticing me.

"I left San Francisco a couple of years ago, moved back here. You in from L.A.?"

"Nope, moved back myself a few months ago."

I can see the dark cloud move over Shawn's face, and I can't blame him. Since moving anywhere for his career was a big part of what broke them up, even just a few hours away from L.A., it must be a real slap to hear that she moved all the way back to Chicago. "How interesting," he says.

"Yes, well. And I'm sorry, so rude of me, who is your lady friend . . ." She turns to introduce herself to me and I look up at her. "Eloise?"

"Hi. Small world."

"How do you two know each other?" Shawn looks very confused.

"This is my friend Lynne. That I told you about," I say.

"More importantly, how do you two know each other?" Lynne asks.

"Eloise is my girlfriend. My interior designer fixed us up a few months ago. 'Lynne'? Back to your roots, are you?" There is venom in Shawn's voice.

"Figured if I was going to lose the last name, might as well lose the first as well." Never would have pegged Lynne for taking her husband's name. Maybe she's a little more traditional than I thought. Crap. Her husband. Shawn, my Shawn, was her Mr. So-Very-Wrong. "Eloise, this can't be the guy you were describing to me," Lynne says, narrowing her eyes at me. I think back to all my effusive praise of Shawn, especially his prowess in the bedroom, and I blush deeply. "Not the man I know so well—he isn't capable of it. At least it's early enough to save yourself. I'm certainly glad we ran into each other."

Save myself from the best relationship I've ever had? "I don't know what you mean, but I think we all need some air and some space." All I want is to get out of here.

"I mean that of course you aren't going to still date him, now that you know who and what he really is." Lynne says this as a statement of fact, and it burns into my chest like a laser.

"Linda, please do not make me forget my mama's careful upbringing," Shawn says with a low growl.

"For all her efforts, you'd think you'd have turned out better."

"Wow. I'd have thought after all this time, all this space, that I wouldn't be so much as a blip on your radar."

"And you're not. But if you think I'm going to just sit here and let you hoodwink my poor dear friend here, you have another think coming."

I can feel my face burning. "Lynne, can we all take a breath and talk about this?" This is the worst possible thing. I care about Lynne and her feelings, but I'm in love with Shawn, and while I'm a big believer in girl code, and never would have started dating him if I had known who he was, I don't think I can stop now.

"What on earth is there to discuss?"

"Lynne, I'm sure that this is shocking to all of us, but I'm not prepared to stop dating Shawn just because you used to be married."

"Well, that tells me where your loyalties are. For someone who hasn't had so much as a date for years, I find it fascinating that you will choose some new piece of boy over your oldest, dearest friend."

"That's unfair . . ." I hate how quiet and defeated my voice sounds. I was never able to stand up to Lynne, not when we were kids; she was always so sure of her rightness. The tone in her voice sends me right back to that place.

"Linda, so help me . . ." Shawn is livid. "That is enough."

Her whole face goes stony. "Fine. Enjoy each other. Eloise, don't say I didn't warn you. Really, good luck, both of you." She turns on a heel, heads back to her table, and whispers something to Angelique, and the two of them look over at our table and head for the door.

"I'm so sorry," Shawn says. "She's a nightmare."

"And one of my oldest friends," I say.

"Yeah. That too. Talk about your shit sandwich. I hope I haven't ruined your friendship."

I look up at him. "I frankly don't care a flying fig about my friendship, not when she was just so awful."

"She and I always did push each other's buttons, bring out the worst in each other. But that doesn't mean you throw away twenty-five years of friendship. Not over me."

I think about this. "Four years. Four years of friendship, twenty years ago. And a few months of reconnection. If you take high school out of the equation, I've only known her two months longer than I've known you, and you are a much better addition to my life." I've never been so angry, so hurt. That she would immediately go for the jugular with me, knowing my past, knowing how hard it was for me to open up to a relationship; I don't care that they had a bad marriage, that doesn't excuse her behavior.

"Thank you for that. I love you, El, I really do. I don't want anything to mess that up, especially not my ex."

"I love you too. I'm going to pretend for her sake that she was having an out-of-body experience, and give her some time to cool off and get her head right. But know this: If she can't get past it? I choose you." The words are stronger in my mouth than they are in my heart. I feel awful at this turn of events, and, what is worse, I feel awful that I am feeling so certain in choosing Shawn over Lynne. I should need some time, I should need to talk to Lynne alone when heads are cooler. But deep down, I know my heart won't change. And the idea that I don't feel worse about it makes me feel terrible. Like the worst friend on the planet. Teresa is going to freak out. I hope she will back me up, and if I lose Lynne, I hope I don't lose her too.

Shawn reaches across the table to take my hand just as a wave of five different desserts arrives at the table, courtesy of Lisa the pastry chef. "We're going to need a couple of bourbons, one cube each," he says to the waiter, reading my mind.

Armed with the strength of renewed commitment to each other, and a pair of forks, we reach out and choose the abundant sweetness that lies before us to erase the bitterness in the past. Whatever that choice may bring.

# Seventeen

waited two days to reach out to Lynne to see if we could have a rational conversation. We decide to meet on neutral territory, taking the dogs to Bark Park for a romp while we clear the air.

"You just have to know that I had no idea at all that the two of you were the *two of you*," I say as calmly as I can. "How could I? All I knew of him from you were his faults, and that he moved away from L.A. to somewhere else in California, and a snarky nickname. You never mentioned his career or background or anything—you never even said he was originally from Chicago. And all I knew of you from him was that your name was Linda, and that you guys had a really bad breakup."

"I know," Lynne admits. "I realized that it wasn't that you were keeping it secret because you knew who he was to me, but not till after I had already gone all Jerry Springer on you.

I'm sorry for that part. It wasn't a good look on me, and wasn't fair to you."

"Thank you for that. I think we can chalk the whole thing up to some brain spasm and let it go. Water under the bridge." I don't really mean this, to be honest; her words were deeply hurtful and it will take some time to forget the vicious way she went for our softest, tenderest parts. I also happen to believe that sometimes things said in spontaneous anger have a lot more truth in them than not, so the fact that she thinks I'm some sad sack who doesn't know how to handle herself in a relationship makes me feel awful. In no small part because I'm afraid she's right. But she does seem sincere, so I press on, desperate to have the whole thing on firmer ground. "Look, we just have to figure this out. You have to know that of course if I had been aware of the context when I met him, if I had known he was your ex, I would never have begun dating him, not without asking you how you felt about it before accepting. But I didn't know, and the fact is that now he and I have been together since Halloween and have developed very strong feelings for each other. I don't want to hurt you, it's the last thing I want, but I also don't feel like he and I should have to give up our relationship because of your history together. This is not a betrayal of you; I didn't steal him from you or sneak around. I just coincidentally met someone I really like who turned out to be your ex."

Lynne presses her lips together tightly. "I just don't know that I will ever be completely good with the two of you together, I have to be honest about that. I can try, but I can't promise."

"Okay, I get that, truly I do, trust me. So how do we move forward? Because the one thing that you know about me is that

I don't take any of this lightly. When I tell you that I really have deep feelings for him, you know what that means. And I hope that, deep down, you want that happiness for me. If I'm not going to stop seeing him, and I'm not going to stop being friends with you, how do we handle this? What do you need from me to at least be somewhat comfortable with the situation?"

"I think, for now, the less I know the better. You and I can just hang out with Teresa the way we do, and if you can keep happy, gushy boyfriend talk to a minimum when I'm around, that will help. I still think you should be careful, I still think that he is not a good person, so I can't really be a supportive girlfriend on this. But I can try to not say nasty things about him. I have to believe in my heart that you will see his true colors, and that the relationship won't last because you will discover that you deserve better, and then all will be fine. Please understand that I say this because I truly want to protect you. He is perfect in the beginning. Really amazing. I remember that part. That is why I agreed to marry him after six months of dating. But it isn't real, at least it wasn't with me, it didn't last, and I would help you avoid that if he hasn't changed. If he has changed, if he isn't the guy I remember, if he doesn't pull the rug out, good for you. If that doesn't happen, we can cross that bridge then."

I try to keep my face impassive, but deep down I'm fuming. The idea that she is essentially saying that I should just not talk about it and she'll wait till our inevitable breakup is so insulting. "Okay, well, for the time being, let's just agree that I will minimize boyfriend conversations when we are together."

"'Kay." She's quiet, and I feel like she wants to say more but doesn't know how to do it.

"Lynne, I know you are trying to keep me from hurt, and

I am so honestly grateful for that. I know it is possible that he might be everything bad that you say, and in a few months you can yell that you told me so. But I have to believe that it is possible he is different, that what we have is real, and I hope that you will support me however it ends up. I just got you back and I don't want to lose that again. So please just be honest with me—if I do or say something where he is concerned that makes you mad, don't let it fester, let's just keep talking it out, keep being honest with each other?"

"Fair enough. We will do the very grown-up thing. And for what it's worth, if it does go sideways, I promise not to say that I told you so. I'll just maybe think it a little bit." She gives me a little smile and I smile back.

"Deal. Okay, then. So, how are things going with you?"

She looks somewhat relieved to have the hard conversation over, and so am I, even though I don't really feel like anything has truly been resolved. "Good, actually. Work is great, Angelique is great, the beastie has mostly stopped destroying the house, although if I don't keep him out of my closet he is still an occasional shoe redesigner." Ellison and Simca are rolling around and playing happily together. He's already taller than she is, but she still outweighs him, so it's a pretty fair pairing.

"He'll grow out of that eventually, just keep plenty of chew toys around and make sure your closet door is closed at all times."

"Yeah. Oh, and since we aren't talking about your relationship, I suppose I should tell you that I have a date scheduled from that matchmaker."

"None of them are with a married French chef named Bernard, are they?"

Lynne laughs. "Not as far as I know, but I'll text you photos when I meet them just to be sure."

I laugh. We might not be back, but maybe we'll be okay eventually. "Sounds like a plan."

"Look, El, I'm not a total asshole, you know. I want to be happy for you, I really do. It's just a lot for me, you know?"

She seems sincere, and my heart softens a bit. "I know. For what it's worth, I'm really sorry for that part."

"Well, then, okay."

"Okay."

We can both say the words, but I don't know if we can walk the talk. Only time will tell.

I call Teresa on my way home.

"How'd it go?" she asks, worry clear in her voice. The whole situation made her really sad and uncomfortable when she heard about it.

"Okay, I guess. For now. We are going to move forward as respectfully as we can and take it a bit easy for a while. But I dunno, T, she sort of implied that she doesn't really see the relationship being successful, so she's just going to kind of ignore it till we break up. So she's rooting for us to fail, which makes me sad. I love him, Teresa, he feels like home to me, and I know I can't say that to Lynne, not right now, but I'm not seeing any red flags. I don't know if we'll be together forever, but I hate to think that she's always going to be against us."

"Just give her time to get used to the idea. Imagine if the situation had been reversed. I mean, Eloise, he wasn't her crush or her short-term boyfriend, he was her husband, they took vows. It might not have worked for either of them, and she might have been the one to leave, but damn. That has got to be a lot. It's hard enough when your ex dates anyone, but one of your oldest, dearest friends? Surely you get her side of things, even if she isn't expressing them terribly well."

"I know, I know, I keep trying to do that, otherwise I might say some stuff I couldn't take back."

"It's still really fresh. Give it a few weeks to let the initial dust settle, and know that I'll have your back when you aren't around. But be aware, be careful. Because there are only two outcomes here: either she is right and he isn't as amazing as you think, or you are, and he is perfect. If she is right, you are going to be devastated. And if you are, she will have to face the fact that maybe the failure of her marriage was more on her than on him. That's shitty all the way around."

She's right, and I hadn't thought of it that way.

"Just you be careful, of yourself and of her. And I'll pick up whatever pieces anyone loses along the way."

"Thanks, T, that means the world to me, and I know it would to Lynne as well."

"In the meantime, maybe you and Shawn and Gio and I can go out one night? I want to meet him, and I'm falling behind on some of the spicing-up-my-marriage stuff. Let's do some fun, silly, romantic thing—go to Geja's for fondue or something."

"Perfect. I'll talk to Shawn later and shoot you some dates; we'll get it on the books. I really think you'll like him."

"Any man who can make you as happy as you have been lately, I think I'll like him too. Even if Lynne thinks he's the devil in a man suit."

We laugh, and I realize that Teresa makes me feel so much better, about me, about Shawn and me. I know that I'll always have Teresa, and it makes me sad to think that, out of sheer laziness and stupid inconvenience, I let her be gone from my life for so many years.

'm taking Simca on an extra-long early walk today, and then dropping her off at my mom's, since I'll be with Ian at the *America's Junior SuperChef* auditions from seven thirty till God knows when, and I hate to leave her alone for so long. I'm rarely up at the ungodly hour of five thirty, but when Ian suggested in the most politic way that he would be much less nervous with me chaperoning him to the auditions instead of his parents, I couldn't very well say no. I think Shelby and Brad were a little bit hurt, but they would never show it, and just made me promise to text updates throughout the day.

"How is my sweet grandpup?" My mom has answered the door in her robe, her mass of curls piled on top of her head in a loose bun.

"She's excited to spend the day with you."

"Can you come in and get warm for a minute?"

"Just a minute," I say. The sky is just starting to lighten, and I still have to go pick up Ian and get downtown to the hotel where the auditions are happening.

"How is Shawn? We had such a lovely time with him last week."

Shawn came to family dinner last week and he fortified his good standing with a night full of family photo albums and shared stories, and his grandmother's recipe for homemade chocolate sour cream Bundt cake. It was a really fun and easy night, and I love how much he is himself with them, not trying hard or putting on a show, just comfortable in his own skin and letting them get to know him.

"He's good. He had a great time as well."

"We really like the two of you together. It seems like a natural fit."

"Thank you. It feels that way to us too."

"And Lynne is working through things?"

I told Mom about the whole debacle and my fears after Lynne and I talked the other day.

"I don't know. I think only time will tell. In the meantime, I can't let her feelings diminish my own, you know?"

"I do. For what it's worth, someone who really cares for you wants your happiness more than they want their own comfort in situations like this, so hopefully Lynne will come around once the shock wears off."

"Yeah, but still, I do get where she is coming from. It isn't like they just dated a little, they were married. That's a lot." Ever since I talked to Teresa I do keep coming back to that. Trying to keep myself mindful of how much that means.

"Did you ever think that some of this is fear? That by seeing her through his eyes you might think less of her? Lynne has many fine qualities, and I've always believed her to be a good person and she has been a good friend to you. But she's always been a little on the vain side, putting forward a very controlled and particular face and image. It's probably why she's so great at her job. But you have access to sides of her that she has no control over, that she can't spin, and that must worry her."

"I never thought of that."

"I'm sure you girls will work it all out."

"Thanks, Mom." I check my watch. "Gotta go."

"You have a great day and tell Ian that we're all pulling for him."

"Will do." I head for home, wondering about what my mom said. I've tried to take some of what Shawn has shared with me with a grain of salt since I found out that his Linda is my Lynne. It only seems fair since I'm giving him so much benefit of the doubt where her descriptions of him are concerned. Trying to hope that the years that have passed have allowed them both to become better people than when they knew each other. But if Lynne is really just trying to insulate herself? I don't know what to do with that. The people who know you longest and best, those are the ones who are supposed to love you, warts and all. Aren't we supposed to be able to just be ourselves and own our shit and still be okay?

I hate the feeling that is rising in me, and only for one reason. I see the same sorts of things in myself—the way I close myself off, the way I keep secrets, the way I keep people at arm's length. The way I have kept my world purposefully small for all of these years, telling anyone who asks that I'm content, and actively avoiding any conversation that implies that content is not the same as happy. They always say that the things that make you most annoyed in other people are the things you hate most about yourself. I wonder if my frustration with Lynne is as much about what I think of me as it is about what I think of her.

Ian is across the room, talking to a very adorable little freckled girl in strawberry blond pigtails and sassy cat-eye glasses. They seem to be becoming fast friends. I'm shocked at the number of kids who are here. I knew that the *America's Junior SuperChef* auditions would be a big deal—the show has become very successful very quickly—it just never occurred to me that there would be this many kids in Chicago who would qualify. The waiting room is packed to the gills.

"I think your son and my daughter are bonding," says a slight redhead at my elbow.

I look up. "Not my son, but my . . . charge, I guess. Your daughter is adorable."

"Thanks. She's a terror, but she's actually a good cook. So you are his nanny?"

I always hate to fess up to my position, especially since I don't want Ian to be set up as the rich kid whose parents could afford to get him private cooking lessons, the kid who has some sort of unfair advantage. "More like an occasional babysitter, and guinea pig for his cooking." I hate being evasive and dishonest, but I don't know this woman, so I'm not going to give her more info than necessary.

"Ha! I feel you. Our whole family is on the tester team. Ever since she got the call about the auditions, Audrey's been practicing. We're all five pounds heavier and somewhat bilious."

I laugh. "Sounds familiar. What is she doing for her signature dish?"

"Our family recipe for schnitzel with spaetzle and red cabbage with apples. My husband's family is German, and her grandmother taught her last summer." The producers said to do something personal, so that seems like a good choice. "How about your guy?"

"He's doing an old family favorite as well. Meat loaf with mashed potatoes and green beans." I leave it at that, neglecting to mention that his meat loaf features ground veal and pork and is wrapped in caul fat and basted with a homemade fig barbecue sauce, that the potatoes are more of a classic Joel Robuchon pommes puree of such buttery silkiness that you want to bathe in them, and that the green beans are blistered and charred in caramelized fish sauce with lime. Luckily, they were able to do a bunch of supervised prep when we arrived this morning, since he'll have only forty-five minutes for the actual cook. I know that his meat loaf mix is seasoned and formed and wrapped in the caul fat and he's done small individual-sized loaves so they will cook quickly. The barbecue sauce is made, as is the sauce for the beans. The potatoes are peeled and cubed and in a salted water bath, so everything should be pretty smooth sailing as long as he keeps to his plan.

"Sounds delicious. Hopefully they both make it through to the next round."

"Why stop there? I hope they both make it all the way."

"Cheers to that."

The two kids come over, and we make introductions all around. The little girl is Audrey and her mom is Catherine. Audrey is in need of a bathroom break, so the two of them head out, and Ian sits next to me.

"How you doing, kiddo?"

"I got this. I know my stuff. I'm not nervous, is that weird?"

"Nope. That's good. It means you're comfortable. Just be yourself, do what you do."

"That's the plan! Audrey is so cool, it's really nice to talk to another kid who has the food thing going on."

"That's great, Ian, she seems like a nice girl."

"Everyone seems pretty nice. I think it would be so fun to be on the show with all these awesome foodie kids!"

"Well, just remember, they are casting all over the country."

"Oh, I know. I'm just cooking for me."

"That's the spirit!"

A young woman in a headset with a clipboard comes over. "Ian Farber? You ready?"

"Yep," he says. He starts to go with her and then stops and runs back to me, throwing his arms around my neck. "Thank you, Eloise. I'm gonna go do it for both of us. Love you." Then he runs off, following the woman through the ominous doors at the back of the room. I smile and send up a prayer that this boy gets everything he deserves, everything he has worked so hard for, and then text Shelby and Brad that his first cook is underway and that I'll keep them posted.

Forty-seven minutes later Ian comes busting through the doors waving a blue ticket in the air. "I made it through! I made it through to round two!" All the kids in the vicinity start screaming and jumping up and down and patting him on the back and giving him hugs. It's about the cutest thing, how excited they all seem to be for him. Audrey grabs him in a huge bear hug and kisses him on the cheek.

"Good for him!" Catherine says.

"Look, it's her turn, I'm sure she'll do great too!"

Catherine gives Audrey a big double thumbs-up, and Ian whispers something in Audrey's ear that makes her smile as they lead her away for her cook.

Ian comes to sit with me and tell me the whole story. How the producers were there and a camera with a live feed to the judges and people back in New York. How he explained that meat loaf night was the only meal the whole family ever agreed on, and always looked forward to, and that last year he wanted to make it for his parents for their anniversary, but it didn't feel special enough so he figured out a way to take it up a notch and make it a little more elegant. Everything went well with the cooking, just like we had practiced, and he felt like it was just like breathing, like his hands knew what to do, and he had almost something of an out-of-body experience. He says he didn't get at all flustered that they were asking him questions while he was cooking. They praised the cook and texture on the meat as perfect and said that the spicy sweetness on the sauce enhanced it without overwhelming it. He says they really liked how the tart salty green beans brought a lot of brightness to the plate, and helped enlighten the palate, and they told him that the potatoes were the best thing any of them had eaten all day.

"And then the phone rang, and it was the judges in New York, and they put them on speakerphone and they all said they remembered me from last year, and how much they loved my food, and how they think I've gotten so much more mature and poised and that they were very excited to welcome me back!"

"That is so cool, Ian, that they remembered you after all this time!"

"I know! Wait, look!" He turns back to the big doors, and Audrey is coming out looking dejected.

"Oh, no," I say.

And then her face breaks into a grin as she pulls her blue ticket out from behind her back and waves it in the air. The room erupts and Ian shoots out of his chair and goes to congratulate his new friend. I feel full to bursting. Ever since I told Shelby and Brad last week that I would be honored to be guardian for the kids in case of an emergency, it's like my heart just got four sizes bigger.

The morning's blue ticket kids all get escorted into a big room after lunch to do the technical audition. They all get the same recipe and ingredients and have to execute it perfectly, a test of their knife skills and working off the cuff. Only half of the remaining kids make it through this round, and luckily both Audrey and Ian are in the group going through to the final round, a timed mystery basket challenge followed by an on-camera interview. It is after six o'clock by the time they are all finished, and we are told that they will get a call in the next two weeks to let them know if they are being invited to callbacks. The producers will be looking at tape from all of the day's activities, and, from what I gather, only four or five kids from Chicago will make it to callbacks, where they will meet the producers in person as well as the actual judges. This was the same place Ian got to last year, and we don't really know what part of his day was his weak link that prevented him from getting called back, but I know he is just happy to have gotten to the same round. He and Audrey exchange phone numbers so that they can make a cooking playdate, and I take Catherine's info to share with Shelby.

"Hey, Eloise?" Ian asks as I'm driving him home.

"Yeah, buddy?"

"Thanks for being my teacher. If I don't make it, it was still worth it to try because we got to cook so much together this year."

"Thanks, Ian. I really love cooking with you, and no matter what happens for the show, you and I can still cook whenever you want."

"Yeah? We can keep the lessons going?"

"Of course! You didn't think we'd have to stop just because the auditions are over, did you?"

"I thought maybe."

"Not a chance. I'll cook with you till you don't want to anymore, deal?"

"Deal. I want to do a little thank-you present for you."

"That is unnecessary, but I never say no to a present."

"I want to cook dinner for you and the whole family . . . and your boyfriend," he says with a wicked chuckle.

"What do you know about my boyfriend?" I'm shocked, but amused.

"I overheard my mom telling my dad that you were in love and she's so excited for you, and hopes that it's the real deal. Do you think it's the real deal?"

I laugh. "You know eavesdropping is rude, little man. But yes, it's possible that it might be the real deal. And yes, I'd be delighted to bring Shawn to dinner one night when you're cooking."

"Cool. You have to tell me his favorite stuff so I can learn to make it."

"I know he'll love anything you cook."

"Well, yeah, but it won't hurt to have a secret weapon!"

I reach over and ruffle his hair. "Nope, won't hurt at all."

# Eighteen

**From:** MamaItalia2734@gmail.com

**To:** LynneRLewiston@HampshirePR.com;
ChefEloise@gmail.com

Happy Valentine's, ladies! Thought it would be a good time to check in on our lists, and to start thinking about what we want the party to look like, since we are only a little more than three months out from our big week. As part of my online financial class, I've been learning how to do spreadsheets, so I've done one for us! Based on my calculations, here is where we all stand:

**TERESA:**
- Marriage heating up: 4 of 9 events completed
- Volunteering: in process—two things tested, still not committed

- Part-time job: not yet secured
- Learning to cook and eat non-Italian: check, doing non-Italian at least once a week
- Learn finances: course half completed, and Gio has promised to sit with me and take me through everything once the course is over in April

LYNNE:
- Land seven-figure client: check
- Buy house: check
- Join a board: in process—DuSable Museum—waiting to hear from nomination committee
- Hire matchmaking service and meet men: service hired, 1 of 5 men met
- Get a dog: check

ELOISE:
- Find a new hobby: check, drawing class
- Create cookbook proposal: in process
- Find a new athletic endeavor: check, swimming and training
- Social life: 12 of 18 events completed
- Dating: 18 dates completed

I'm really proud of us, and glad we made this bet, because it is definitely getting my butt in gear on some stuff I've been wanting for myself forever, and I hope you both feel the same. I'm also really excited that it looks like we are all going to complete everything on our lists, which is pretty cool. So for the party, I'm thinking we keep it fairly small? Nearest and dearest?

Something casual and fun, where kids can come? What do you guys think?

XOT

Lynne replies quickly.

Happy Commercialized Romance Day, girls. Good job on the lists, everyone. But since we are all going to really get this done, maybe we up the stakes a bit? I say that the first person to finish their list doesn't have to donate anything, the second person donates 2,500 and the person that comes in last does the full 5,000, and both of the losers have to donate in the name of the girl who wins! You guys ready to really throw down? Party details are really up to the two of you—my guest list is very small for this shindig, since most of my people are on the West Coast, so I'll go along with whatever you both want.

L

Things have been relatively okay with Lynne since our talk. She is clearly making an effort to just let me live my life, despite her objections. The three of us had brunch last weekend at Wishbone and it was actually mostly pretty fun, despite her making the occasional snide little comment, including one weird one about cultural appropriation when I ordered cheese grits. As I promised myself I would, I let the little digs slide, and Teresa, true to form, told Lynne that food is the great connector, and that we are at the restaurant as part of her own exploration of food outside her comfort zone, and then proceeded to order hoppin' John with a side of greens to make her point, and that shut it down.

Of course Lynne wants to up the ante, since she is about ten minutes from finishing her list. And as far as I can tell, Teresa is right on her heels. It feels like more of a way for Lynne to punish me than to reward herself.

> Happy Hearts and Flowers Day! And congrats, one and all, on what we have managed to accomplish so far. I know that I have done more in the past few months than I ever imagined possible. And Lynne? If you want to up the stakes, bring it. You might be a little bit in the lead, but the last five pounds are hardest to lose, am I right? Don't count either of us out—Teresa and I have some serious skills. I'm in if T is. And I agree on the party, something fun and casual works great. Why don't we get together in the next couple of weeks to really make a plan. Everyone can start thinking about idea and venues. My list is also really small. Teresa—I expect you to be checking another spicy marriage event off your list tonight!

> El

I shut the computer down, and text my mom to see if she is ready. She and I are taking a Valentine's lunch to Glenn. He has been working with her one afternoon a week at the after-school program, and when she mentioned to me that Valentine's Day might be hard for him, I said that I would definitely be up for a lunch. Lawrence is in Tucson this week, so I have today off. Shawn and I decided to avoid the amateur night that is Valentine's at most restaurants in favor of cooking together and watching movies. We planned the menu together: butter lettuce salad with a shallot, lemon, and caper vinaigrette, a huge tomahawk steak to share, wild mushroom risotto, and steamed broccolini, with a pistachio soufflé for dessert. Marcy dropped off some chocolate sablé cookies and caramelized white chocolate truffles last night to add to the party, as well as a gorgeous zucchini bread with chocolate chips "for break- fast," she said, winking. She is over the moon for Shawn and me and livid at Lynne.

"Seriously, Eloise, I know she's been your friend since the dawn of time, but that woman is awful to you. She's a classic mean girl."

"She's not, Marce—just think about it, that marriage is the only thing she has ever failed at in her entire life! Ever. She's always gotten everything she wanted, everything she ever worked for. She's got one black mark on her record, and her marriage to Shawn is it. And now one of her oldest friends is having a successful relationship with him. That has to be so hard."

"You're more forgiving than I could ever be. I think she is selfish and vain and doesn't care a whit about you or your hap- piness. Sorry, can't help it. For her to be so terrible to you for dating someone that *she* discarded? Especially after you told her the whole thing about Bernard and she knows that you haven't been dating since then. It'd be one thing if she left him because he was abusive or dangerous or a criminal or some- thing, and she was trying to save you from hurt. But from what you've told me, sounds like she dumped him because he de- cided he wanted kids and a dog and to take a better job. That is just shitty. You get that, right?"

I feel bad that I've probably done just that, made it seem like the divorce was all on Lynne. Teresa said something to me the other day about what a big thing the children issue must have been for Lynne. She told me that if Gio had said to her a year into their marriage that all of a sudden he didn't want to have any kids, it would have broken her heart and she would have probably left him, however much love there was between them. It made me think really hard about how difficult that must have been for Lynne, to marry someone she thought was in her corner on all the big stuff and then have him shift. I wonder how I would feel if suddenly Shawn decided that he wanted to be a raw-foods vegan, or that he never wanted to get married or live with someone again, or that he hated dogs. I don't know if we would survive any of that, and I do know that it would feel like he had sold me a bill of goods. And we are only a few months into our love. I really can't imagine how it would have felt to have such seismic shifts after already making things legal, and I feel really disloyal to Lynne for letting that go unaddressed with Marcy for so long.

"Marcy, it isn't that simple, not on either end. Shawn went through some stuff that changed his mind on a lot of fundamental big issues, and that really pulled the rug out from under Lynne. I love Shawn, and I believe he is in a much different, more settled place now than he was when they were together, that he isn't the same guy who did those things to her. But I also have to recognize that he is a person with faults, like all of us, and the end of their marriage was not one-sided. I believe that he handled a lot of things very badly in that relationship, that they both did, and all I can do is hope that the person I believe him to be today is in part because he learned hard lessons from that relationship ending the way it did. But it doesn't make it okay, his part of things. And it doesn't make it all Lynne's fault either."

"Okay, maybe, but she has to see how happy you are. That should count for something."

"I think it does. She is trying, Marce, I know she is, and when she falters I have to give her space to do that. I appreciate your protectiveness. Your points are duly noted."

But her points didn't really sink in until I was lying in bed, thinking about today and how Shawn and I had the exact same idea about how to celebrate Valentine's Day. How I feel like I'm the best version of myself when we're together and how happy he makes me. He's been a champ about letting the whole Lynne thing lie, hasn't said anything except that he was glad she and I had cleared the air and that he hoped it would all be okay with some time. And he hasn't made one negative reference about her since. I haven't told him about the little comments and snipes from Lynne, no point in poking the bear. I do wish he were a bit more forthcoming about the whole marriage thing, especially now that we know the connection. Four years is not such a long time, and I know that people can change a lot, but Lynne's warnings didn't fall on completely deaf ears. She said he was perfect, perfect for their six months of dating before they got married, perfect for the first six months of the marriage. And then it all went sideways really fast. A year of great and then a year of slow slide to over. He's never really acknowledged his part in it, never owned any of the end. That doesn't exactly sit easy with me.

My mom texts that she is on her way to pick me up, and I head to the fridge and pack up the food I prepped last night. There is curried chicken salad with grapes and walnuts, and small homemade rolls to make sandwiches, along with some pickled onions to perk up the combination. Israeli couscous salad with cucumber, tomato, feta, kalamata olives, parsley, and mint. A bag of chips, a batch of Glenn's favorite brownies, and a small bag of tiny clementines. I toss Simca a bully stick and get into my parka, since in true Chicago fashion, despite the brittle and bright sunshine, it is about four degrees out there. My mom honks, and I head out with the cooler bag.

"You should talk to Glenn about Shawn," she says when I mention Lynne's grits comment.

"Why?"

"Because no one knows more than he does about interracial relationships. If what Lynne said bothered you enough to tell me about it, you might want to unpack that for yourself. After all, you haven't met his family yet; he might have some words of wisdom on that. I know it's coming up and you want it to go well. And you said yourself that the few of his friends you've met so far have mostly been white. Maybe it is something of an issue, even a subconscious one, and it is just not on the front burner yet. Maybe it will never be an issue. Wouldn't hurt to be a little bit prepared, just in case not everyone in the world is going to accept you happily."

"Hadn't thought about that. Maybe, if it comes up organically. I also don't want to spend Valentine's lunch with Glenn waxing on about my new love when it is his first one without Helene."

"He's thrilled for you."

"Oh, is he?"

"He and I talk about you all the time, and he's delighted to know that you have found someone you like, and wants to meet him. You'll see, he'll bring it up way before you do."

Sigh. I suppose I can't begrudge her talking to Glenn about me. After all, besides dead spouses, I'm the other thing they have in common.

We pull up in front of Glenn's house, and I get the cooler bag out of the trunk.

"Now, this is every man's dream! Two beautiful women bringing him delicious food and good company." He comes out of the house to carry the bag for me, giving us each a kiss on the cheek. We head into the kitchen, and I start getting out serving platters and bowls for the food. Easy to do since I helped Glenn reorganize his kitchen to make better sense for him, so I know where everything is. Glenn has already set the table, and he and my mom set about pouring water and iced tea, all the while chatting easily. I set all the food up as a buffet on the kitchen island and call them in.

"Now, this is a true feast!" Glenn says. "Thank you, my dear, for all the hard work. You could have just picked up some sandwiches."

"And still sleep at night? Never! It goes against everything I stand for," I say in mock seriousness as we all fill our plates and head to the table.

"To two of the finest women I have ever known, thank you for coming to keep me company." Glenn raises his iced tea glass to us, and we all toast.

"How are you doing today?" my mom asks him, taking a small bite of the couscous salad.

"Pretty well, all things considered. I'm lucky—Helene never really liked Valentine's Day that much, always said that we didn't need the chocolate companies to tell us when and how to be romantic, so it wasn't something that we really celebrated. Sometimes we would get each other a card, the more over-the-top and sappy the better, but there were a lot of years we would sort of ignore it completely."

"That's good," I say.

"Indeed," my mom says. "Eloise's dad was a sucker for Valentine's Day, he would go all out. The first couple without him were really hard."

"I bet. I suppose it is all just a series of tests, the holidays and birthdays, the little moments that remind us of who's missing," Glenn says. "We're lucky to have friends and family around us to help us get through."

"How is your family?" I ask, remembering their good intentions and annoying results around the funeral.

"My family is fine. Fairly absent, to be honest. They are all really good at rallying around in the moment of crisis, but once they go back to their regular lives, they sort of disappear. To be fair, I'm not really disappointed—there is only so much time you want to spend with people who think you are broken."

"Oh, Lord, the head tilters!" my mom says. "For months and months, everyone you meet tilts their head to one side and furrows their brows and asks full of concern how you are holding up. The worst!"

"Exactly!" Glenn says. "My family is all those people. Every conversation is about reminding you how awful and sad you are supposed to be. God forbid you are having a fairly good day."

"Right! It's like, maybe ask me what I'm doing or how my work is going, what I've been reading or watching on TV or if I have any travel plans coming up. I've got plenty of times when the blues get me, no need to elicit them specifically." My mom laughs.

"Well, I'm a luckier man than most, for whatever failings my well-meaning family has in that area, Helene's family makes up for it. Her brothers keep taking me to sporting events and action flicks and to hear music, the women keep sending food and inviting me to dinners, and everyone is just utterly normal with me. They tell some of the old Helene stories, but nothing is ever morose or wallowing."

"It's wonderful that her family is so welcoming of you. Was it always that way?" My mom is opening a door on my behalf and it feels ham-handed and obvious, and I can feel the blush start.

Glenn chews a bite of his sandwich thoughtfully. "Pretty much. Don't forget, it was the seventies when Helene and I got together, and she was the baby of the family—her siblings had already brought home something of a United Nations of boyfriends and girlfriends. Helene's previous boyfriend had been black, and something of a tool, so I think they were just relieved that I was a nice guy and treated her with kindness and respect. Plus, this is Chicago. The most important thing is that I was also a South Sider and a Sox fan!"

We laugh, since in this town, neighborhood and team affiliation often do trump other factors when it comes to community bonding.

"I assume you are trepidatious about meeting Shawn's family?" Glenn says. "I hope you don't mind, your mother has been sharing some of your joy with me. I'm enormously delighted for you."

"Yeah, she mentioned that she told you. And yes, Shawn's folks are coming back from their winter place at the end of March and we are going to do a dinner with his parents to meet. Then I'm spending Easter with them to meet the rest of the extended family."

"Nerve-wracking under the best of circumstances, but potentially made more awkward by cultural differences?" He nods at me sympathetically.

"Something like that. Also, I have no practice in any of it. I met the parents of a couple of boyfriends in high school and college, but to be honest, Shawn is only the second real relationship of my adult life."

My mom reaches over and squeezes my hand. Slowly, tentatively, I've shared with her a little bit about Bernard and what happened. She has been really wonderful and supportive.

"Well, my dear, I will tell you what Helene told me before she brought me home. Be yourself. Do not alter, change, adjust, or in any way be anything other than who you are. Because two things are true: People can smell pandering and obsequiousness from a mile away, so anything you might do or say to try and bond on a cultural level will come across as disingenuous. And second, remember that this man fell in love with who you are, and they love him and want him to be happy, so by being your true self you are letting them see the person he loves."

"That is beautiful advice," my mom says.

"Thank you for that. It makes me feel better," I say, and it does. It is still a shock to me that who I am is the kind of person that Shawn could fall in love with, but he makes me feel so safe in that love that slowly I'm coming around to the idea that I'm worthy of it. I know that Glenn is right, you can't bond with people by attempting to force cultural connections.

"You're a wonderful girl, Eloise dear. Shawn's family will love you because Shawn loves you, just as Helene's family loves me because she loved me. Embrace your differences, let them be funny instead of fraught, and trust that these people raised the man who fell in love with you, so unless he is telling you that they aren't going to be comfortable, trust in that." Glenn grins at me.

I smile back at him and start clearing the plates. I load them quickly into the dishwasher and get the platter of brownies out to the table, then return to the kitchen to make coffee as my mom and Glenn chat.

As I wait for the machine to finish brewing, watching the dark liquid slowly fill the pot, I think about Glenn and Helene and everything they shared, the life they made together. And while his advice on how to handle meeting Shawn's family is good and makes me feel better, it doesn't fully alleviate my nerves. Because I know that Shawn is close to his family and if I want to stay with him, getting their approval is going to be essential. As much as Shawn makes me believe in his feelings for me, I'm still not so convinced that what he sees is going to be at all apparent to his family. Putting race and religion aside, who am I, really? I'm not particularly accomplished or successful, however financially stable. I know they won't think I'm a gold digger, but will they think I'm a good match for him? I have such a small little life. A little family, few friends, one of whom is his ex-wife. How does that look to people who want the best for their son?

I shake off the doubt; I've still got a few weeks to go. And suddenly it occurs to me. The bet. Since the bet I've got some hobbies and outside interests, and I'm working on my cookbook proposal, which shows some career ambition. Maybe, just maybe, this silly bet might be the thing that helps me be the kind of complete person that makes a decent impression. Who'd have thought?

t's like a cloud," Shawn says, digging into the soufflé.

"I know," I say, drizzling more crème anglaise into the crater I made in the center. "Old-school, but classic for a reason."

"Damn, that is so good," he says, rolling his eyes.

The whole meal has been spectacular, in no small part because we are good together in the kitchen. I stirred the risotto while he seared the steak. I made the salad dressing while he prepped the salad greens. He whipped the egg whites while I made the pistachio base. We operate in the kitchen like a well-oiled machine, which isn't always true of couples. Cooking well and easily together? It isn't instinctive and can't be taught. I've always been something of a loner in the kitchen, no surprise there, but I love cooking with Shawn.

We finish the soufflé and clean up the dishes, Shawn sneaking bits of steak to Simca at every possible moment. When the dishwasher is loaded and running, I pour us each a short calvados, and Shawn takes my hand and leads me out to the living room.

"I have something for you," he says, once I'm seated. "Stay right there."

He heads for the back door, so that he can go out to his car, which is parked next to mine in my garage. I sip the calvados, feeling its wonderful burn settling my stomach after the rich meal. I reach behind the couch cushion and pull out the small box that I hid there for him, and place it on the table. I hear the back door open again, and Shawn calls out to me. "Close your eyes!"

I shut them dutifully and hear him approach and the sound of something heavy landing on the coffee table. Then the weight of him sitting down.

"Okay, you can open them."

On the table is a large red bag covered in silver hearts, with silver and pink tissue spilling out of the top.

"Oh, Shawn! It's wonderful!"

"Well, let's hope you think so when you open it!"

I pull the tissue out of the top and look inside, and there is what appears to be a small silver metal suitcase. I lift it out of the bag. It is surprisingly heavy.

"What in the world?" I ask, unlatching the case and lifting the lid. My breath catches.

"You didn't."

Shawn grins. "I did. Did I do okay?"

My eyes fill with tears. "You did perfect. Thank you so much." Inside the case is the complete set of Copic drawing markers, over three hundred colors. I had shown Shawn some of the illustrations I've been working on for the cookbook proposal, and he really loved them.

"I went to the art supply store and asked what someone doing your kind of work would really love, and the guy said that this would be the end-all, be-all."

I throw my arms around his neck. "It is the most perfect thing." I love that it isn't jewelry or a spa gift card or flowers or anything expected for the Hallmark holiday. I love that it isn't something to do with cooking, which is everyone's go-to for gifts when you are a chef. It is the kind of gift that is a double whammy, first for its extravagance—I can't begin to imagine how insanely expensive this kit was—but mostly, because it means he sees me. It isn't something I mentioned wanting; he just knows me, knows how much I'm enjoying making the illustrations for the cookbook, knows that this is just the sort of luxury I would never indulge in for myself.

"I'm so glad you like it. I'm still new at this whole gift-giving thing." He laughs. "But I swear I didn't call Lawrence this time!"

"You did perfect. I'm afraid mine is a little bit small by comparison." I hand over the box, my stomach doing flip-flops. I'm taking an enormous risk, and I know that it could backfire, but like Shawn, I'm going with my own impulses, right or wrong, and if there are consequences, I have to be prepared to suffer them. If I'm going to live a bigger, fuller life, I have to own my feelings and not shy away from them.

Shawn pulls the ribbon and opens the lid of the box. He looks down, and then looks into my eyes, face serious. "Are you sure?"

I nod. "Yes." In the box is a set of keys to my house and an opener for my garage. "I love you, Shawn, and I trust you."

His face breaks into a huge smile. He leans forward, taking my face in his hands. "I love you, Eloise Kahn." And then he kisses me right into my bones, pulling me tightly against him, and I know that letting him in, to my life, my heart, my home, is both the bravest and the best thing I've ever done.

# Nineteen

check on the chickens, which are spinning in the oven on the rotisserie spit. I do love these Gaggenau ovens; they have all the bells and whistles. I've got a pan of fingerling potatoes with shallots and lemon underneath the chickens, soaking up all the delicious chicken juices and fat and crisping up beautifully. The first sweet asparagus of spring, thin as pencils and tender enough to eat raw, are prepped in the steamer, for last-minute cooking. And on the counter, a tall chocolate cake with billowy, vanilla-scented frosting, Ian's favorite. The whole meal is for him. Today he's at the callbacks for *America's Junior SuperChef*, and the production team requested the whole family be present for some background interviews, which makes me very hopeful about his prospects. In the meantime, this meal will be exactly what he will want, whatever happens, whether he wants celebration or comfort. And it is nice to have a quiet afternoon to cook and think.

The past few weeks have been both wonderful and confusing. Wonderful because Shawn and I have fallen into a lovely and comfortable routine. Most weekday evenings he will come over and we'll either make dinner together, order in, or go out for something easy. We're discovering our favorite casual places, the places every couple needs as a go-to. Opart for Thai food, Buona Terra for Italian, Mythos for Greek, Hachi's Kitchen for sushi. We'll eat and hang out; we've been discovering that our tastes in television are pretty similar, and have been introducing each other to our favorites. He's got me hooked on some of the darker, more obscure British procedurals like *Happy Valley* and *Broadchurch*, and I've turned him into a true fan of *The Great British Baking Show*. We've been bingeing on alternate nights, cuddled up close on the couch with a big bowl of popcorn, Simca snuggled in her new favorite place, next to Shawn with her head in his lap. I think she is as in love with him as I am.

He's taken to going home most weeknights, unless we really get into some hot and heavy bedroom play, just because it's easier for early mornings. But he always stays over on Tuesday nights so that we can get up and do the Wednesday pool class at East Bank together. On weekends we alternate planning dates and events. I'm still knocking social activities off my list, so we have gone to a trivia night, a special reception and showing of *Gone with the Wind* at the Studio Xfinity space, and a Friday night art opening at the Museum of Contemporary Art. We've had dinner with Teresa and Gio, my mom and Claire, and two couples that are friends of his, one of the other doctors in his practice and her husband, and an old college buddy and his wife. Both women pulled me aside to tell me that they are so thrilled for us and that they have never seen Shawn happier, so that made me all warm and fuzzy. And we are talking about planning our first joint dinner party, which should be fun— except I want to invite Teresa and Gio, and that would mean leaving out Lynne, which feels crappy, especially because not inviting Lynne would be something of a relief.

Everything couldn't be better or easier or more fun, and I'm less and less nervous about meeting his parents in a couple of weeks. But the other day Marcy brought something up that afterward kept bugging me. We were having brunch on Sunday, just the two of us to catch up, and she asked about the Shawn and Lynne thing.

"Here's the thing I can't stop thinking about," she said over scrambled eggs with chorizo and cheddar at Toast. "I know that Lynne was going by Linda in California, so you wouldn't have known who he was talking about when he mentioned her. But what about her mentioning you to him? Eloise is not a common name, and he knew she was originally from Chicago. You would have thought that when he met you and heard your name, he might have asked if you by chance knew a Linda? Chicago is a small town, and Chicagoans love nothing more than connecting the dots. Why didn't it ever occur to him that you might be the Eloise his ex had told him about?"

I didn't have an answer, and it nagged at my brain. I hadn't ever thought about it before, but it did seem odd. I'm almost forty, and I've literally never met another Eloise. It did seem strange that he could be married to her and never question if the Eloise he met in Chicago might be the Eloise he had heard about from his ex-wife. After a couple of days, I decided to be an adult, and just ask him.

"She never mentioned you," he responded. "Trust me, if I had known she had a best friend named Eloise and met you, I would have asked if you knew her."

"Never mentioned me? What about Teresa?"

"Nope. She never really talked much about her Chicago life at all. I knew she grew up in Hyde Park, but that was about it. I'm five years older than you guys, so it wasn't like we would have had any peers in common; I was already in college when you started high school. To be honest, she was always very much about the present, who she knew and was spending time with in the moment, and the past was just not a part of her life."

Never mentioned me or Teresa. I couldn't tell if I was more relieved that he hadn't had a reason to suspect the connection, or more hurt that our years of friendship hadn't warranted so much as a mention to the most important person in her life. When I called Marcy, she was perplexed.

"Wow. That is weird, no?"

Despite my wounded pride, I couldn't seem to help myself; I was compelled to defend Lynne. "Well, by the time she met Shawn, it wasn't like we were in touch. I wasn't exactly going to be invited to the wedding. It's not like she was obligated to reveal every friend she ever had in high school."

"Maybe. But I still think it is a little strange. I knew you for two days before you told me about Teresa and Lynne, your best buddies from high school. Just like you knew about Jackson and Tracy and Lily from my high school days. Casual mentions, but mentions nonetheless. Look at how you and Teresa have picked it back up, even though you are rediscovering each other as grown-ups—there is still that energy between you, that dynamic that says that you are super special to each other, with long and deep history."

"And I don't have that with Lynne?" This was more of a statement than a question, but my voice went up at the end anyway.

"Well, do you? Tell me this: Since she came back into your life, have you found her to be added value? Is she bringing anything into your world that is good or important?"

I thought about this. "The bet."

"The bet?"

"Look, I'm a formerly competitive person who lost her competitive edge over the years. I was perfectly contented in my life as it was, but that doesn't mean that there weren't things I wanted to be different. I was just paralyzed by inertia. So yes, the bet, the stupid bet, it got me off my ass, back into the world. Forced me to be open to meeting Shawn. And the bet would never have happened if she hadn't said so. When we were in high school, if Lynne didn't want us to do something, we didn't do it. She could shut down an idea in a snap. So yes, I have to say, whatever else she is or isn't, she could have said that the bet was just a dumb idea, Teresa and I wouldn't have pushed back, and we all wouldn't have agreed to do it—and look at how different and better my life is now!"

I didn't even realize that I felt this way, but in my gut I know it's true. We always went to the movies and concerts Lynne wanted to see, hit the parties she wanted to go to, and if either Teresa or I had an idea for something to do, if she thought it was stupid, we'd just let it go. I was always most comfortable with a guiding hand. I was a coach's athlete: tell me what to do and when and how and I would do it, no pushback, no questions asked. I was a good kid at home: if Mom and Dad set a rule, I was pretty good about following it. My professors in culinary school loved me: I followed all their teachings to the letter, turned out the food they wanted just as they wanted; I was never the hotshot in the back of the room altering recipes or tweaking techniques.

"I'll give her that, grudgingly. But I still think that she is sometimes awful to you, in ways that she doesn't appear to be awful to Teresa, and there is nothing wrong with saying that whatever she was to you back in the day is not something she can or should be to you now."

I didn't have an argument for that.

I'm pulling the chickens out of the oven to rest when the full cadre of Farbers come flying into the house.

"HE DID IT!" Geneva screams in her epic voice. "Ian is going to be a huge star on TV!"

Ian looks at me with a sheepish grin on his face. "They want me," he says, and then throws himself into my arms. I sweep him up into the air, heavy as he is.

"I'm so proud of you, bud, really, really proud. I knew you could do it."

"He was a champ," Brad says, beaming with pride. "You should have seen him, cool as a cucumber."

"He did you really proud, El," Shelby says, swatting at Robbie's hand as he reaches to open the cookie jar.

"He did himself proud, I'm just the coach," I say, so happy for him.

"Yeah, he was pretty good," Robbie says.

"I was super impressed, and my friends are going to freak," Darcy says. "We all got to give interviews and stuff, so we might be on TV too!"

"It was so cool," Ian says. "First they did all these interviews with us and our families, and then we did a technical challenge and it was making pasta from scratch!"

"Right in your wheelhouse!" I say.

"You have to call Teresa and tell her—I did it all the way she taught me, and Roberto Fiorini told me it was just like his grandmother's!" Roberto is one of the judges, a third-generation New York Italian chef, who is known for his gruff exterior and pulling no punches with the kids. So that is a huge compliment.

"That is amazing, Ian, really, he is a hard one to please!" I say.

"I know, right? And then they had us do a team prep challenge, and I got to work with Audrey and we killed it. Had to prep artichokes, supreme oranges, separate eggs, and fillet a fish! Beat the other teams by three whole minutes! Audrey has some serious skills, and she knew she could do the fish and oranges and I did the artichokes and eggs. She is so cool. And she made it through too! We said we have to go all the way to the finale together."

I love how supportive he is of his new friend. "That would be amazing. I'm glad she made it through."

"Yeah, it was really fun."

"Okay, team, let's get it together. Eloise made a great dinner for us and it's getting cold." Brad hustles the gaggle of kids to the front hall to get out of outerwear.

"Really, Eloise, thank you so much for all you did for him. You are a big part of why he made it."

"It's all his hard work. But I'm really pumped for him." I turn on the steamer to get the asparagus done, then pull the potatoes out of the oven and start to transfer them to a serving platter.

"The show films in New York over the month of July. How would you feel about being his chaperone?"

My hand stops in midair. "What?"

"Well, you know that summer is all hands on deck around here . . . Robbie has sports camp and Darcy has School of Rock camp, and Geneva has day camp, but only half days. Ian needs an adult to be there with him for the duration, and frankly, I think Ian would be more comfortable with you, for quality time with his coach. If you can't, or don't want to, we get it and of course we will figure it out, but to be honest, after seeing how important it was for him to have you go with him to the audition instead of one of us? He would be relieved to have you there with him."

"That is so sweet." My head is reeling. New York for a month? On the one hand, what a wonderful opportunity, so many things to do and see and places that have been on my list to eat at for years that I've never gotten to. On the other hand, a month is a long time to be gone. What would Shawn say? What about Simca? What about Lawrence?

Shelby seems to read my mind. "Talk to Shawn. We would be delighted to fly him out to be with you for the weekends. We've got plenty of time, just think about it."

"Will do."

"And, Eloise? If you think it would be too much of a hardship to be gone, we get it, there are backup plans we can pursue. Truly, don't think you can't say no."

And while six months ago I would never have considered putting myself or my life or my needs first, today I know that if no is the best answer, then that is the answer I will give. "Don't worry. If it isn't doable for me, then I will be honest about that."

"Great. Now get out of here. I know you have evening plans that are much more interesting. We'll clean up."

I almost say no, but then stop myself. "Okay. I'll see you

tomorrow." Apparently this old dog is learning new tricks all the time.

Despite the spring chill in the air, I decide to walk over to my mom's house for dinner. Shawn is meeting me there later. He has a late surgery, but says he isn't going to miss an opportunity to get good mom and aunt gold-star points, so I figured no need for us to have two cars there. By the time I let myself in, my face is frozen and my ears are tingling. March in Chicago is always deceptive; after the below-zero days of winter, it gets up into the forties and we all lose our minds and start to think it isn't really cold anymore.

"Goodness!" my mom says, kissing my icy cheek. "Did you walk over?"

"Yeah. It's chillier than I thought."

"Well, come in and warm up. We have to celebrate Ian's victory and his intrepid coach!"

Aunt Claire kisses me and hands me a Manhattan, the perfect warming cocktail, and I sit with her at the kitchen table and fill them in on Ian's day while watching my mom work on dinner. She is a good, solid home cook, nothing fancy, nothing innovative, just super normal, and the tiniest bit dated.

"Whatcha making?" I ask, sipping the drink, letting the smooth bourbon work its magic.

"Chicken Marbella," my mom says, and I stifle a chuckle. The ubiquitous 1980s dinner party favorite from *The Silver Palate Cookbook* is as old-school as it gets. Even I have to admit, it has its nostalgic charms. The savory chicken, punctuated with briny capers, salty olives, and sweet prunes, is one of those dishes that might not be ripe for a comeback, but it doesn't disappoint. It was always the recipe my mom pulled out when she wanted to do something impressive or celebratory, and it means the world to me that she is making it for Shawn.

"Yum. Haven't had that in a while."

"Well, I brought some to Glenn, and I had forgotten how delicious it is, so I thought Shawn would like it."

"When did you go to Glenn's?"

"Last week. I try and bring him dinner at least once a week; the man eats like a deranged college kid. You've seen his fridge—all cold cuts—and his pantry is full of cereal and canned soup and cookies."

"That is so nice of you."

"Well, it's only fair," Aunt Claire says. "After all, he takes you to dinner every time he comes to work at the after-school program with you."

I had no idea my mom and Glenn were spending so much time together, but it is nice. I assume the two of them have a lot to commiserate about, and it makes me happy that they are both getting out a bit. "That is so nice, Mom."

"He's a good man, and it is a sad time. No need for him to go through that alone. I had Claire to prop me up, and you and Helene. Seems like the right thing to do."

"Whatever the reason, it is very lovely."

"He wants to meet Shawn. If the two of you don't have other plans, maybe the four of us can meet up after we are done at the center one day next week? Grab burgers at the Orbit Room?"

Aunt Claire clears her throat loudly. My mom laughs.

"Sorry, the *five* of us."

"Thank you," says Claire, winking at me and plucking the cherry out of her glass. She pops it in her mouth with a grin.

"We can ask Shawn when he gets here."

My mom opens the oven and bastes the chicken, the sweet-and-sour scent wafting into the room. I notice the second pan in the oven and realize she has made her famous herb and onion stuffing, the perfect thing to soak up the sauce. She's really gone all out and it makes my heart swell with love.

"How is everything else going? The girls?" Aunt Claire asks.

I think about this for a minute and then tell them about Marcy's concern and my discovery about Lynne not ever mentioning us to Shawn when they were together, and my struggle with how I feel about her, how much I credit her with my recent growth, and my disappointment that it has been so difficult to really reconnect.

"That seems odd. Why do you think she was so secretive?" Mom asks.

"I dunno, to be honest. I mean, she changed her name, she stopped talking about her past. I have no idea what would have made her feel like she had to do that."

"Reinvention is an exciting thing," Claire says. "Wiping slates clean, becoming the person you always imagined yourself to be. If you're all the way across the country, not having to be face-to-face with your past on a day-to-day basis, it would be a little easy to fully commit to that new reality."

"I guess, but why? I mean, it isn't like she had some awful childhood to escape."

"Doesn't have to be escaping something bad, it can just be embracing something new," Claire says.

"Seems weird to me," I say.

"Me too. And frankly hurtful," my mom says. "As close as you three were, the years you spent together, you were like sisters. To erase that? As if it never happened? That feels cruel to me."

"It stung a bit," I say. "The whole thing is making me question whether it is worth it to even maintain the friendship."

"Oh, it's worth it," Claire says.

"I don't know, Claire. You know I like to see the best in people, but look at how Lynne has behaved. She's not really being a good friend," my mom says, ever my defender.

"I disagree," Claire says. "I think it is important that you keep her in your life, that you figure out what place she has."

"Why? I mean, I completely agree about Teresa—it has been so terrific to have her back in my life, easy and fun and, to quote Marcy, added value. But Lynne? She's been prickly and complicated since the beginning, and now, with the Shawn connection, and the fact that is it becoming completely obvious that she doesn't really consider our history together to be terribly important, why bother? I mean, I have to be honest, if I met her today at a party or something, I wouldn't choose to become her friend. So why should I keep putting in the effort just because we have some history?"

"Because we live in a disposable society," Claire says. "We lead busy lives and it is too easy to cut out people who challenge us or who are complicated personalities. I agree, if you met her today she maybe wouldn't be who you would choose. But you didn't meet her today, you met her twenty-five years ago, and for those years, she was one of the most important people in your life. Like it or not, she is a big part of who you are, of who you have become, and I think it is important for you to figure out how to keep her in your life in a meaningful way, despite the parts of her that are difficult. There are so few people who know us from those years, who remember who we were, who were a part of our becoming. She doesn't have to be your best friend or the first person you call, but I hope you'll really think before you discard her altogether. I believe that in the long run, you will be better off for having her in your life."

"Damn, Claire, you are getting very philosophical in your old age," my mom says.

"Middle age, thank you very much," Claire says.

"Um, unless you are planning on being a hundred and thirty, I'm pretty sure you are old," Mom says. "But wise. I have to say, it's possible your aunt here has some valid points."

"Yeah, I guess. I have to think about it. The whole Shawn thing is a complication that might make it ultimately impossible. If he and I stay together, and I dearly hope we will . . ."

"As do we," my mom says.

"Definitely," Claire says.

"Well, Lynne is his ex-wife and it was not an amicable split. If I am, as you say, going to benefit from having her in my life, how on earth do I manage that? How do I keep them both?"

"You'll figure it out," Claire says, as my mom wanders over to check on the chicken. "And be a bit soft with Marcy. She's been your one and only bestie, as the kids say, for a very long time. I suspect Lynne and Teresa being back in your life can feel a little threatening, and Lynne seems the easiest place to dump her jealousy."

"You think Marcy is jealous of Lynne?"

"I think Marcy fills the role with you that Lynne did, so if Marcy were going to feel pushed aside or replaced, Lynne would be the one to make her feel that way. I don't doubt her sincerity, or her protectiveness of you, but I also know that it must be hard on her. She had all these years of encouraging you to be more, do more, get out there, and then Lynne swans in and there is this bet and suddenly you are doing all the things she suggested and you ignored, and you are doing them successfully. Plus you have this wonderful boyfriend, which is another drain on the time you can spend with her."

"I never would have thought . . ." Marcy has always been so confident, so strong, in a million years I would not have thought she could be jealous, especially over me.

"I know. It's why I mention it." The doorbell rings. "Saved by the bell," Claire says, as I head over to let Shawn in.

"Hello, beautiful," he says, leaning in to kiss me.

"Hello, handsome. How was the surgery?"

"Long and exhausting. How did Ian do?"

I make it a habit never to call or text when I know he is in surgery. He mentioned that he hates to get out of a long procedure only to find a phone full of new obligations, and I try to be sensitive to that, even though I want to reach out a million times a day. "He made it through."

"That is so terrific, good for him. And congrats to you!"

"Yeah, we'll talk more about that later."

My mom and Claire come into the room to greet him, fluttering around him like a pair of excitable butterflies, taking his coat, asking about his day, handing him a drink. He handles it like a champ.

"Something smells amazing in here, and I'm hungry as a bear!"

"Come, come, dinner is ready!" my mom says, ushering us all into the dining room.

"You don't have to ask me twice," Shawn says, offering Claire his arm as my mom and I head into the kitchen to bring out the dishes.

"Claire is right about one thing, kiddo. You will figure it out. And whatever you decide, we'll support you," she says, spooning the rich sauce over the chicken. "I think you should talk to

Shawn about it. See how he feels, what he worries about. If you are a couple, then that takes precedence. It is possible to have friendships that don't involve spouses—Lord knows your father hated my girlfriend Allison, which was why I always spent time with her on my own and didn't foist her or her annoying husband on him. You can keep them both in your life if you choose and still be protective of him if he doesn't want to interact with her. But he is a good and smart man, and I believe he will help you figure out how to manage the whole thing if you let him in completely."

"I think so too." And I do. For all my nonconfrontational nature, as awkward as the conversation is likely to be, I also know that I want his advice, and to hear what he needs for everything to be okay.

"Now let's feed that poor man before he falls over."

My mom might not be a fancy cook, but I know I get my impulse to love people with food from her, and I'm so grateful for that gift.

"Yeah, let's do that." And we pick up the platters and head for the dining room.

Your mom is a good cook," Shawn says as we get back to my house after walking Simca around the block, bundled up against the cold, which intensified after I got to Mom's house.

"Yeah. You got all her serious specialties tonight, you know."

"The chicken Marbella. My mom used to make it all the time back in the eighties. It was total nostalgia."

"*Everyone* used to make it all the time in the eighties! It was exotic and fancy and fed a crowd."

"It was a lovely meal. Even if Claire did molest me."

I laugh. When we went to leave, he leaned in for a kiss and she turned her cheek the wrong way and ended up planting one right on his lips. "She was two Manhattans in."

"It was funny." Claire had blushed like a teenager and got all flustered. "I really enjoy them both."

"Well, at this point I'm pretty sure that they like you better than they like me, so that is good. They want us all to have dinner again next week with Glenn, but if that is a little too much family time, we can just say you have work."

"Not at all. Don't forget, I lose my family all winter; it's nice to have some time with yours. And I'm really looking forward to meeting Glenn."

I tell him about Shelby's request for me to chaperone Ian. "She knows that a month is a long time, and she offered to fly you out for weekends, but I want to know what you think."

"First of all, I'm not a part of this decision. If it is something you want to do, then you should absolutely do it. Of course if you do, I will come visit, and while Shelby's offer is very generous, I can fly myself to New York. Not that I want to be apart from you for a month, but it isn't forever, and we are grownups, we'll manage just fine. What does your gut say?"

I adore him. "I go back and forth. On the one hand, it's an exciting idea—there are a ton of things I could do and see and eat in New York. I've never really spent any significant time there, but I know a lot of chefs here who can hook me up with chefs there, so that would be amazing."

"But?"

"But . . . leaving you, leaving Simca . . . the Farbers and Lawrence?"

"Can I say something you might not want to hear?"

"Of course."

"Okay, first off, I will be fine. And I'll take Simca, so she and I can commiserate about our desperate loneliness without you, and when I come visit she will get time with your mom, who will spoil her rotten. I know there is a little part of you that thinks if you leave for a month the Farbers and Lawrence will somehow see that they can manage well without you, but I think that your being gone will just show them how much they love having you in their lives. I know it will for me. Absence does make the heart grow fonder, my love."

"Okay, that makes me feel better. But there is something else."

"What's that?"

"Ian. We're talking about me essentially playing surrogate mom, twenty-four/seven, for a little boy. I've never spent more than a few contiguous hours with any kid."

"Wait, you've been on vacations with them. That is twenty-four/seven."

"Yeah, but their parents were there. I was basically in charge of food! I wasn't in charge of kissing boo-boos or shutting down tantrums or delivering bedtime stories. What if he has a rough time being away? What if he gets cut or burnt on set or gets sick—kids get sick! What if he throws up? I can't handle the throwing up, Shawn, you know that . . ."

"Breathe, sweet girl, breathe. Look, you are strong and smart and kind and that kid loves you and trusts you. He will feel safe and you will be a rock star. And if something goes wrong, your natural instincts will kick in. What is the absolute worst thing that can happen? He'll throw up, and you'll sympathetically throw up, and the two of you will have a little vomit party, and then it will be one of those epic hilarious stories that the family will tell for years to come. It's New York. You aren't going to a third-world country. If something serious happens, one of his parents will jump on a plane and be there in a matter of hours."

"Vomit party?"

He smiles at me.

"You don't have to be a mother to be maternal. You just have to love him. Everything else will work itself out."

"I guess."

"I know. You are a natural nurturer, Eloise. You take care of people. You'd be a great mom, even a temporary surrogate one."

"You think?"

"I know." Then he grins wickedly at me. "After all, Lawrence is counting on our café au lait babies for him to give terrible names!" Lawrence does continue to tease with both of us on the child front, and Shawn and I have embraced it as one of our inside jokes.

I can't help but laugh. "Oh, really? How many of these babies are we talking about?"

"Five!" He pauses. "Or maybe even just one?"

I look into his face, and see that while we are joking, a part of him isn't really joking.

"Maybe one. To start," I say, not even believing the words coming out of my mouth.

"Maybe one, then. To start." He leans forward and kisses me deeply.

"I suppose then I should say yes and practice a little on Ian, huh?"

"Better to screw up with someone else's kid, is what I'm thinking."

I swat his arm. "You'd really want to take care of Simca?"

"I love that pup. If it will get you to do something that is good for you, I will happily take care of Simca, I will go over and make Lawrence's lunches, I'll fight off advances from your horny aunt, and I'll come visit you every weekend so that you remember who loves you and you don't fall prey to some famous celebrity chef's evil seduction."

"I love you."

"I love you too." He reaches for me. "Let's go upstairs and I'll show you how much."

"Not going to argue with that."

He takes my hand and we head up the stairs. Based on the efforts of the next few hours, he loves me very much indeed. I'm feeling so much better about everything, but then, just before I drift into sleep, one tiny little thing crosses my mind.

What do I do about him being at the birthday party?

# Twenty

'm just finishing up loading Lawrence's fridge when he breezes in with the boys. Luckily the new batch of peanut butter dog biscuits are cooled enough to treat them.

"Hello, Philippe! Hello, Liagre! Did you have a good walk?" I say, handing each of them a biscuit. They are both so different about treats. Philippe is a lot like Simca, takes it daintily out of your hand and goes somewhere quiet to eat it. Liagre, on the other hand, is like a whirling dervish. He snatches it up, devours it on the spot, and then spins and jumps and begs for more.

"Liagre! Stop the begging, it is unseemly," Lawrence says, kissing my cheek.

"How was the meeting yesterday?" I ask. Lawrence was meeting with a client who fired him midjob a couple of years ago and hasn't spoken to him since.

"Fine. Somewhat confusing, to be honest."

"In what way?"

"Well, you know, after the unpleasantness, we haven't spoken. So I thought perhaps she wanted to talk it through, maybe give me her perspective. But she sort of acted like nothing had really gone on, and just wanted to catch up."

"So, you are just supposed to, what? Forgive and forget? Pretend it didn't happen?"

"I guess."

"Would you even want that?"

"Not under this set of circumstances. If she had apologized, explained, even told me what she perceived that I had done to her to make her turn on me, and given me a chance to address it, then of course, it is always possible to move forward. But she didn't and I'm too old to play make-believe. So I wished her well, but won't be reconnecting with her again."

"How do you feel?"

"More relieved than I would like to admit."

"Why?"

"Honestly? Because as much as I was so sure that this meeting was about her apologizing to me, I was afraid it was going to be her telling me all the things I did or said that validated the way she treated me, and frankly, I'm judgmental enough about myself, I wasn't really up for hearing someone else tell me my flaws, because I might have agreed with them."

"Lawrence, you are one of the sweetest, kindest, most generous, most lovely people I have ever known."

"Thank you, my dear. I'm also catty, snarky, a bit superior at times, occasionally intolerant of other people's opinions if they don't jibe with mine. Yes, I'm charming company at dinner, and Lord knows I'll make your home gorgeous. But that doesn't mean I'm always a choirboy. No one wants to believe that someone else might see the parts of themselves they hate the most. The parts they're ashamed of. No one wants to listen to someone else lay out the litany of their faults, because then the blame lands squarely on your own shoulders and what does one do with that?"

I reach over and squeeze his hand. "One just remembers that the people who know him best and longest know that every human has flaws, but that his are far and away small and unimportant and that his amazing wonderful qualities outweigh them ten times over."

He squeezes back. "Thank you, darling girl."

"You're very welcome."

"And what do you have on your agenda the rest of the day?"

"I'm meeting Lynne for a puppy playdate, and then going to Teresa's to help her make a French dinner for her family."

"No Shawn tonight?"

"He's having boys' night out. One of his former teammates is in town, so there are a bunch of guys doing the chest-thumping, steak-dinner thing. If it doesn't go too late, he's coming over after."

"I love the way you glow when you talk about him."

"Me too. I don't know that either of us will ever be able to thank you enough."

"Well, all I did was put you in a room together, you did the rest. But I will take credit for the impulse."

"Good. After all, it makes up for all your other nasty traits."

"Evil Amazon. Get out of here and have your day."

I kiss him on the cheek. "See you next week."

On the drive over to meet Lynne, I think about what Lawrence said about not wanting to hear about your faults from other people. Because the more I'm getting out in the world, doing new things, meeting new people, the more I'm ashamed of how long I've been hiding from my own life. I look at Teresa and Gio and their crazy, sprawling family, at my mom and Claire and their girlfriends and volunteering and theater subscriptions, Marcy and her amazing wide circle of friends, with all their late-night adventures, and think that all of those things might have been mine. The years alone with no lover, no arms around me, no kisses, no hands on my skin. And what stopped me? Exactly what Lawrence said. Because deep down, I always sort of believed that I didn't bring much to the table.

Even back in high school, Lynne was the leader, Teresa was the social coordinator, and I went along for the ride and felt lucky to have them. I kept my circle equally small in college, and as soon as I went to France, I ghosted on them too. When I think back on my relationship with Bernard, I wonder if I really loved him as much as I thought I did, or if I just loved that he didn't seem to see the many flaws in me that I saw. I never stopped to wonder if he didn't see them because he was such a narcissist that he never saw much of anything past himself. And I let him break me so completely; it was a validation of all the worst thoughts I had about myself.

I think about what Mrs. O'Connor said to me when I came back to school after my surgery, with the full knowledge that my athletic career was over.

"You know what is amazing about women like us, Miss Eloise? We have so much magic in us, we contain multitudes. Did you ever know I was a dancer?"

"No, what kind of dance?"

"Ballet. And I was good, too. Thought a lot about trying to do it professionally."

"What happened?"

"I kept growing. Up and up and taller and taller and my shoulders and hips filled out, and my bosom decided to make an appearance and I stopped having the kind of body that you need to have in ballet."

"That is so unfair."

"True. But you can't ask some five-foot-nine ballet boy to hoist all of this fabulousness over his head like a feather. The audience would bust out laughing," she said, waving her arm over the length of her body.

I laughed. "I suppose not."

She reached out and took my chin in her hand. "You are so much more than one thing. You have so much more to give and be than just what you were. When I realized I couldn't be a dancer, I found out I could teach dance, and I did that to put myself through college. And I loved teaching so much that I thought maybe I could teach other things, and it turned out that one of my other passions, reading, could be something I could share with students. What is your other passion, the thing you like most to do?"

I thought about this. "I really love to cook. I read old cooking magazines and cookbooks and I love food writing, and I really just love playing in the kitchen."

"So perhaps you should see if maybe there is a way to let that passion take center stage for you, now that you will have time to explore it more fully. The hours you've just gotten back that you won't be spending in the gym, the days you won't be going to meets and practices, maybe that is time you can spend cooking and determine if that might be a new direction to go."

"I never thought about that." I always thought I would take the athletics as far as I could and then probably coach. As much as I loved cooking, I'd never thought of it being more than a hobby. But suddenly anything felt possible, because Mrs. O'Connor believed in me.

"You can be anything because you are *everything*," she said. "Don't you let anyone tell you otherwise."

In that moment I felt invincible. I felt powerful and possible. How was it that I let that feeling get so diminished in me?

I pull up in front of my house and go in to grab Simca. She gives me her special corgi smile and hops about excitedly.

"You love me despite all my many flaws, don't you, pupper?" Simca yips joyfully and does a spin.

"Well, girl, I'm working on loving me too."

They say that March comes in like a lion and leaves like a lamb, and that is almost always true in Chicago. The sun is shining in a very springlike way, but it is just in the upper forties, and the wind still bites. I'm bundled in a parka and scarf, looking like the abominable snowperson, at the dog park. But when I look up, Lynne, naturally, is in a sleek black shearling, with tall riding boots and a gray angora infinity scarf, looking like some movie star in Aspen.

"Oh my God, he's *enormous*," I say, as Ellison leaps up at me. He has more than doubled in size since the last time I saw him.

"I know," she says, leaning down to scratch between Simca's ears before joining me on the bench. "He's a monster. You have no idea how many times I've put him in the car to drive by Paws and make a drop-off."

She laughs, but the joke lands flat. I know how many people

buy dogs with no preparation and don't commit to training and then just hand them off to a shelter when it gets annoying.

"You can't give him up now, Simca would miss him." The two of them are playing happily and have found a Saint Bernard to join in the fun. The three dogs look like a Disney movie could break out at any moment.

"Well, then, for Simca's sake, I suppose I'll have to put up with him."

"Indeed. So it looks like Teresa has the party well in hand!"

"Leave it to T to just get it all organized," Lynne says. We got e-mails this morning saying that she booked the private room at Stella Barra on Halsted for our joint birthday party for the Saturday night of our birthday weekend. She sent us the menus so that we can start thinking about what we want to order.

"Well, I'm happy to let her handle it, aren't you?"

"For sure."

"Have you done your list yet?"

"Yep. Angelique, and my assistant. A couple other people from work. Theaster and another person from the DuSable board. I'm inviting some of my West Coast girls, but I have no idea if they'll want to make the trip in. What about you?"

"Mine is pretty easy and small. Marcy, Lawrence, Mom, Claire, Glenn, the Farbers, Shawn."

Lynne narrows her eyes at me. "Seriously? Shawn?"

"Well, yeah, of course, I mean . . ."

"You mean, what, exactly? That the most fun way for me to celebrate my fortieth birthday will be to watch my ex-husband paw you?"

"Come on, Lynne, he isn't going to paw me, he's not that kind of guy, but you can't really expect me to not invite my

boyfriend to my fortieth birthday party. How is that fair? You'll
be in a room of, like, forty people—it isn't like some small dinner party—you can just avoid each other."

"He's your 'boyfriend' for ten minutes." She puts air quotes
around the word and it makes something in my head snap.
"How important can it be? He can celebrate with you on your
actual birthday."

"He's been my boyfriend for almost five months, and we love
each other, and I don't think it's okay for you to expect me to
not have him with me at such an important event. I've been very
respectful of your past with him—I haven't talked to you about
him at all, or been gooey and glowy with you—but really, I
would think that maybe we could all just be adults about this."

She laughs derisively. "Adults? Since when are you an adult,
Eloise, really? You ran away from home to wander about Europe
like you were on some never-ending gap year, had a boyfriend
who was more a daddy figure, came back and hunkered down
with your mommy and your auntie and your little baking pal
Marcy, and essentially spend your life as a glorified au pair who
cooks and a part-time fag hag! Good God, even this stupid
bet! You needed to find a hobby and you picked up *coloring*, for
chrissakes. You're just an overgrown child, Eloise, always will be.
You haven't grown up at all since high school. Damn, the six-
year-old fictional character you were named for is more of an
adult than you."

A strange calmness comes over me. It's like the anger gets
into my blood and slows my heart and, despite the gut impulse
to just run away, I hear Mrs. O'Connor's words ringing in my
head. I can be anything because I am everything. And what I
need to be right now is my own best defender.

"I hope it feels better to have gotten all that out, because clearly, it has been festering. You done, or is there anything else you want to bring up? Maybe go at me for spilling the Coke on your pink cashmere sweater back in the day?"

"Whatever. You don't want to have a serious look at yourself, brush it off. Maybe I just won't come to the party at all. After all, it isn't like I'm not going to win the bet."

"I know that you hate that I'm having a successful relationship with the man you lost, but seriously, I thought we were past this."

"Lost? I never lost him, I kicked him to the fucking curb. Because I deserved better."

"Yeah, how's that working out for you? Oh, right, you haven't had a serious relationship since your divorce, and even a professional matchmaker hasn't been able to find someone who wants to be with you. Maybe it just really pisses you off that I'm in love and you're not. After all, you've always felt so above Teresa and me, the queen bee. But here we are and we have happy lives and loving partners and all you have is, um, well, what do you have, Lynne? Oh, yeah, money. With an opportunity for more money. Jesus, Lynne, you are so self-centered you don't even like your own *dog*."

Lynne's eyes are shiny with angry tears, and she opens her mouth and then closes it again.

I whistle and Simca comes running, and I snap on her collar. "You take a long hard look at who you are, Lynne Lewiston, and decide if she is the person you actually want to be. Because my life was fine when you were just a fond and distant memory. And if I met you tomorrow, I wouldn't be exactly keen to know you. You want to apologize to me for being a hateful, conceited, superior mean girl, you give me a call and we can talk like rational *adults*. Because it seems to me that the need to lash out and poke at what you perceive as my soft spots, just because you don't get what you want all the time, is about the most childlike behavior I can imagine."

Before she can say a thing, Simca and I leave the park. I just manage to make it into my car before the tears come.

I wait till the coq au vin is simmering away, the crème caramel is chilling in the fridge, and we are settled with a glass of wine in her living room before gearing up to tell Teresa what happened with Lynne this afternoon. I knew that if I told her right away, she would throw the cooking lesson out the window to just debrief, and I needed the soothing action of the cooking to calm me down enough to discuss it with her rationally. Because whatever is going on between Lynne and me, I don't want to use it to drive a wedge between the two of them. So I know I have to be able to share the story as calmly as possible and with little editorializing.

Besides, I want Teresa to have a shot at winning this bet, so teaching her this classical French dinner menu helps keep her on track. It's dead simple for a great home cook like Teresa, and it will have some familiar flavors to not scare the family: the rich chicken stew cooked with red wine, bacon, mushrooms, and onions isn't that far off from a chicken Marsala. Served over buttered egg noodles—getting a pasta in—with a bright salad of butter lettuce in a basic Dijon vinaigrette, and a perfect custard for dessert.

"Okay, that smells delish, my friend. I think my horde might actually love it. Thanks for the lesson. *Salute*."

"You're a natural. And I'm super proud of how much you have really embraced this whole thing. I love being able to have food adventures with you. Cheers."

"So, you wanna tell me what you have been wanting to tell me since you got here?"

Damn. "Lynne called you."

"You're darn tooting she called me. I've never heard her so upset. What the hell happened?"

I tell Teresa how it went down and what was said, to the best of my ability. She listens, nods, sips her wine, and doesn't say anything till I've finished.

"I am so, so sorry that you guys went through that. That is some awful nasty stuff to hear and to say, so that is a massive bucket of suck for both of you."

"But?"

"But what sucks most is that both of you are sort of right."

This stops me in my tracks. "What do you mean?"

"I mean that both of you are so touchy and angry, and said what you said because there are small elements on both sides of this where you are right."

"So you think I'm not an adult?"

"I didn't say that. I will say, wouldn't you have to admit that when she unleashed that nasty litany of crap at you, some of it stung because some of it wasn't entirely wrong? You did take off and hide; you did keep your personal and professional lives small and contained; you did not stand up to be strong and move ahead with big goals. You completely checked out of having a romantic life. Now, I don't mean that makes you somehow childlike; I don't think it does. But the facts are not entirely untrue, even if the accusation of what it means may be."

I think back at what she accused me of, and while I don't think she was right in the exaggerated way she portrayed it, a lot of what she said about my life isn't entirely off base. "Maybe," I say grudgingly.

"And don't you think that the stuff you said to her about her life—again, while delivered in a way designed to inflict the most hurt—still hit closer to home than she is comfortable with? I've said it before, you are asking a lot of her with the Shawn thing, and while I think you are within your rights to ask, it is too much to just expect it to be easy for her."

"Maybe. I don't know what to do, T. I really don't. I get that me and Shawn is a hard thing for her to get her head around, I do, but I'm not giving him up. And I'm not going to marginalize him in my life to manage her sensitive feelings. If she really thinks all those things about me, why would she want to be my friend? If she really thinks that about me, then why do I want her in my life? I'm sorry, I know that puts you in a terrible position, and I don't want to put you in the middle, but I can't see my way around it."

"Good Lord, woman, I've been the peacemaker between you two for our whole lives. Don't worry about me in the middle, worry about the two of you back together."

"Why? At this point, really? Why?"

"Because, like it or not, you guys are connected long and deep. And back in the day, when you got quiet or she got prickly, I'd tell you that you were amazing. I would tell her that she was amazing. And you know what? I was right on both accounts. You are both amazing. And you are both flawed and fucked up, the way everyone is flawed and fucked up. But you're better with each other than without. Because she pushes you to expect more of yourself and get out of your comfort zone, and you push her to be softer and less surface."

"God, have you been talking to my aunt Claire? She said it's important for me to have Lynne in my life too, not in spite of it being difficult, but in some ways because it is difficult."

"Your aunt is right."

"I don't know how to move on from here, though, after what we both said."

"Let it lie for a day or so. I'll figure something out."

"Are you a miracle worker now?"

"Wasn't I always?"

"Absolutely. For what it's worth, I have never had a moment's doubt about how amazing it is to have you back in my life, not since the first moment I spotted you at the memorial."

"Me either."

"Good." I check my watch. "I should get home before traffic is insane."

"And before Shawn gets there?" She winks.

"Nope, he's out with the boys tonight. I've got a date with Netflix and Simca, but he might stop by later."

"Are you going to tell him?" she asks.

I think about this for a minute. "Yes, I am. I know that he will be angry with Lynne, but at the end of the day, he is my boyfriend and I want to be completely honest with him about what is going on in my life. I don't want to hide things just because it isn't completely comfortable."

"Good. That is the right answer."

"Thanks, Teresa, I appreciate everything so much."

"Hey, it's taken me a lifetime to train you idiots to be my friends, I'm not letting all my hard work go to waste."

I laugh, and receive the hug she gives me with a heart that is the tiniest bit less heavy than when I arrived.

Simca's happy bark wakes me from my accidental nap on the couch. After the day I had, I ordered a pizza, washed it down with half a bottle of red, and finished up with a bowl of chocolate chip ice cream. Between the heavy food and the heavy day, I conked out before the end of my first episode of *The Missing*.

"Hello, Sleeping Beauty," Shawn says, leaning down to kiss me. "Naughty pup, waking your mommy."

"Hey," I say groggily. I love that he can just let himself in. "How was boys' night?"

"Good. Dry martinis, bloody steaks, lots of friendly ball-busting. They all want to meet you. Dave is still in town for a few days—you up for dinner? Maybe tomorrow?"

"Of course. Any friend of yours."

He smooches me again. "Wonderful. And how was your day?"

I think about this for a minute. "Hard."

He sits on the couch next to me, pulls my legs up into his lap, and starts massaging my feet. "Tell me about it."

"Okay, I'm going to, but you have to promise to wait till I'm all the way done before you say anything."

"Hmmm. Sounds serious. I'll put on my good listening hat."

I tell him about the fight with Lynne. And about what Teresa said. I tell him about the parts of what Lynne said that I fear are more than a little true, and where that comes from. He listened, never stopped rubbing my feet, and didn't make any faces or comments. He let me get it all out, and when the tears came, he just handed me a Kleenex. When I was done, he pulled me into his arms and held me close.

"My poor sweet baby, I'm so sorry that happened to you."

I sniffle into his shirt. "You don't think she's right?"

"Despite what she might tell you, Lynne is not always right. And while I don't see any of the things that she sees or that you fear, that doesn't make what happened today any easier."

"You don't seem very angry."

He laughs. "Oh, no, baby, I'm mad as hell. If that woman were in this room right now, I'd give her a piece of my mind that would make what you said to her sound like high praise. But I promised you that I wasn't going to let my history with her come between us, or between you two, and I intend to stick to that, no matter what." He pauses. "Look, El. It's easy to portray an ex as a villain. I've relied on that impression, maybe a bit too much, where she is concerned. But it takes two to tango, and I know that more than a little of her anger and lashing out at you is because of me. Of who I was then, of the part I played in our marriage failing."

Shawn has never really talked about this, and I want to hear it, so I don't speak, hoping he will just continue. And he does.

"I'm a people pleaser, El. Always have been. I liked being teacher's pet, mama's boy, coach's favorite. It's taken me more than a little therapy to recognize that in the process of wanting to make other people happy, I can sometimes gloss over my own needs or desires. I was always the 'go along to get along' guy—we'll eat at the place you want to eat, see the movie you want to see, be the couple you want us to be."

This makes my stomach knot up, because to a certain extent, it validates Lynne's impression that he wasn't his true self until after they were married. And it makes me question who he is with me. What is real and what might be an act? What can I trust?

"I want you to know that I'm not that guy anymore. I try very hard to own my thoughts and feelings and opinions, and trust that the people in my life can handle it if we aren't one hundred percent aligned on every damn thing."

"You didn't make any apology for hating my movie choices

last weekend." I was in the mood for some John Hughes, and Shawn suffered through both *The Breakfast Club* and *Pretty in Pink* before telling me in no uncertain terms that he found the movies unwatchable and making me promise not to make him see any more.

"Baby steps, but yes, that was Shawn 2.0 in action. That is who I am now, but while I still believe that the way Linda—Lynne—behaved at the end of our marriage was hateful, I cannot be my new improved self if I don't own that some of it was deserved. I genuinely loved her, but apparently not enough to let her really know the real me, not until I felt sure of her, of us. And the risk with that is that when you do reveal who you are, it can blow everything up, which is what happened with us. I should have been man enough to be myself from the beginning, and I wasn't, so a lot of it is on me."

"You can't take the blame for the whole thing."

"I don't. Just the parts of it that are mine to carry. But I know that it was wrong on both ends, and she does have a right to not want to be around me, to want to protect you, because she doesn't know who I am now, only who I was then. And who I was then, well, she would have been within her rights to warn you off. So I'm going to bite my tongue, swallow the nasty things I want to say, and put my energy into supporting you in whatever you decide to do."

"Wow. Now I know it's true, I'm definitely much less of a grown-up than you are!"

"I don't know about that. You seem to be all woman to me." He pulls me into a kiss. "Look, whenever the two of you figure this out, know this. If, this one time, it is easier or better for me to bow out of the party, for your sake, not hers, I won't fight you on that. I won't be happy, but I will manage. You and I will be celebrating on the day, and this one time, I will let that be enough. That is a one-time deal. I might be handling my anger right now and being as mature as I can be, but if you do decide to keep her in your life, it has to be with the caveat that she is accepting of you and me. One of the things I love most about you is that you do not bring drama. I am forty-four years old, and I do not have time or inclination to deal with that shit in my life. You feel me?"

"I do. Trust me, I don't want drama either."

"Good. We are understood. Now, what do you say we go to bed and skip pool circuit tomorrow and just sleep in a little bit and I'll make us omelets in the morning."

"That is, without a doubt, the best thing anyone has said to me all day."

# Twenty-one

"You did a great job today, Ian. Your sauce work is getting really terrific."

"Thanks, Eloise. And thanks for coming with me to New York. I'm so excited!" I told Shelby and Brad that I would chaperone Ian to New York, and they are going to come in for the weekends. They decided to trade off alternate weeks to have some one-on-one fun quality time with him, which will give Shawn and me the weekends to play. I know I'll be a lot more comfortable with it being just the two of us. It's one thing for us to talk semijokingly about our accidental family sitcom; it's another for us to act it out in real life.

"We'll have a great time, kiddo. Now I'm going to leave you to clean up, Chef."

"Are you seeing Shawn? He's the coolest!"

Last week Ian made good on his promise of dinner for us

and the family, a repeat of his winning dinner from the audition, to rave reviews all around. Shawn was his amazing self, engaging with the kids in a totally natural way, talking to Robbie about sports, and Darcy about music, and Ian about food, and Geneva . . . he never had to talk to Geneva about anything, since that kid doesn't stop talking herself. But by the end of the night, she was sitting in his lap, and he and Brad were making a date to go to a Bulls game, and Shelby was dragging me into the kitchen, on the pretense of making coffee, to gush about how fantastic he is.

"He liked you too, bud."

"Will he really come over and teach me some of his family recipes?" Shawn said he would do a soul food master class if Ian wanted to have some stuff up his sleeve for the competition.

"Of course he will. He already asked me to look at your weekends to see if there is a good one for you guys to play." Shawn is in surgery weekdays, but unless someone famous has an emergency, his weekends are pretty much his own.

"Awesome! Tell him I said hi!"

"Will do. See you tomorrow."

I head out and try to settle my stomach. Because tonight isn't just dinner with Shawn. It's dinner with Shawn and his parents, who got back to town earlier this week. He's given me the brief: His mom, Cheryl, grew up in North Carolina; his dad, Darren, in Chicago. They met at Northwestern, got married right out of college, and moved to Bronzeville. Cheryl was a curator of photography at the Art Institute, Darren was the president of a small independent publishing house, and they are now both happily retired and split their time between a condo in the Gold Coast and their place in North Carolina.

We're meeting them at Bavette's for dinner. Sort of a get-to-know-you before Easter next week at his aunt's house with the whole family. Shawn said Easter will be fun, but something of a madhouse, and he wanted us to have some quiet time to really get to know each other first. It's been interesting—things between us are really good, but also different since our big talk and his confession about his actions during his marriage to Lynne. Slowly, he has been opening up more and more to me about those days, and I've been doing the same about Bernard. We seem almost to be in a competition to show off our flaws to each other. Under different circumstances, I might see it as daring each other to flee, but there is something freeing about being completely honest, about just *being*. I get that he isn't communicative at all during work hours, so I don't reach out during the day unless absolutely necessary. He gets how close I am to Mom and Claire, and lets me know when he is up for family time and when he isn't, and I don't take it personally when he opts out. He's admitted that he really just prefers to sleep at his place on work nights, and I don't take it personally when he kisses me good night and leaves. Our weekends are spent together, and I don't worry that the weeknight separations are about me. He let me show him the way I like the dishwasher loaded, and doesn't get annoyed when I move stuff around after he does it. And I try to keep my navigation advice to a minimum when we are going places, because Lord knows that man can get prickly if I imply he isn't taking the best route somewhere. We are figuring each other out, in very real ways, and how to best be together, and it is new and a little scary, but mostly good.

Besides, if last night didn't make either of us run away,

nothing will. I made cassoulet, chock-full of beans and sausages and duck confit and veggies, and by nine o'clock, we were both so insanely gassy that we gave up on our polite habit of disappearing to the bathroom and just let it fly. The noise and horrific smells coming from both of us made us cry with laughter and made Simca, with her delicate sensibilities, leave the room, which made us laugh harder.

I guess the moral of the story is you don't know what love is until you are stewing in your mutual funk, and laughing about it instead of being disgusted.

I take Simca for a quick walk and then jump in the shower. I'm working on my makeup when my phone rings.

"What time is dinner?" Marcy asks.

"Shawn is picking me up at seven. Dinner is at seven thirty."

"How are you feeling?"

"Okay, I think. He's given me all the relevant prep info, and said that he's been talking about me for a long time and they're really excited to meet me."

"That is great! You sound pretty calm."

"Yeah, it's good."

"Do they know about the Lynne connection?"

"He told them just the basics, that she is my old high school friend and we didn't know about the connection until we ran into each other. They thought it was a crazy coincidence, but he said they weren't fazed and he certainly didn't add any other details."

"How are things on that front?"

"Teresa invited me over for brunch on Saturday and said she has a good plan and that all will be well, so I'm just lying low till I hear what she is suggesting."

"You know how I feel."

"You've made it abundantly clear."

"But if you decide you do want to repair that relationship, go forth with my blessing and I'll be a good girl."

"And?"

"And if she hurts you again I'm gonna turn her into mince pies."

"That's my Marcy." Ever since Claire suggested that Marcy might be feeling a little abandoned or replaced, I've been making a concerted effort to reach out more, to spend some quality one-on-one time with her, to show her that she is still super important to me. She seems a bit softer, so the charm offensive might be working.

"Go meet the parents, and have a great time. I'll be up late, let me know how it goes!"

"Will do."

I finish getting ready, keeping it simple: black pants, gray sweater, minimal makeup. Nice, but not like I'm trying too hard. I hear the door open downstairs and Shawn and Simca greeting each other. "Lucy, I'm hoooome!" he yells up the stairs in his best Desi Arnaz imitation.

I head down the stairs to where my handsome boyfriend is waiting for me.

"You look gorgeous, as usual," he says, after the kiss.

"Thank you. You clean up pretty good yourself, Doc."

"You ready for this?"

"Ready as I'm going to be."

"They're gonna love you."

"I'll settle for like and approve of."

"Nah, I aim high. Go big or go home."

I think about this for a moment. "Yeah, fuck it, they're gonna love me."

O h, Lord, this is the best chocolate cream pie I have ever tasted," Cheryl says. "There is not going to be enough yoga in the world to bounce back from this meal."

"You think that is good, wait till you taste Eloise's chocolate cream pie. Makes this look like Sara Lee," Shawn says.

"That is a pretty major claim, my boy. What do you say, Eloise, do you stand behind your chocolate cream pie?" Darren says with a wink.

"I'll bring one to Easter and you can judge for yourselves," I say, surprised at my own sassiness. The night has been amazing. Shawn suddenly makes perfect sense to me; he is the absolute blend of his folks. His dad is clearly an old-school gentleman, who treats his wife with equal parts respect, admiration, and deference, and looks at her like he cannot believe his great good fortune. His mom is intuitive, kind, genuine, and super quick-witted and funny. They are easy and loving together, and remind me of my mom and dad in all the best ways. They both ask me a lot of questions about myself without ever making me feel like I'm being interrogated or judged, and they pepper the evening with family stories and fun anecdotes about Shawn growing up, just the way Claire and my mom did when they met him.

"You'd better hide it from Uncle Foster if you want to get a taste," Shawn says.

"Oh, that is a good point," Cheryl says. "I think maybe you two should come to the apartment first and drop off the pie.

We can go to Jeannie's house together and then come back for pie and coffee. Or bourbon, depending on how horribly annoying the day is."

"Now, that is not fair, Cheryl. Jeannie does a lovely job," Darren says with a grin. Jeannie is his older sister and has inherited the role of matriarch since their mom passed.

"Oh, Jeannie makes a helluva ham, and I don't know what she does to those deviled eggs, but they are sublime."

"Sounds amazing," I say.

"Yeah, right up until Foster gets hammered and starts pinching everyone's butts, and her wannabe fake gangsta sons with their pants practically around their ankles start playing all that *bitch ho bitch ho* music, and then Liza will start making those faces . . ."

Apparently Liza is cousin Stevie's wife, a former debutante from Atlanta who tends to be something of a snob.

"Liza isn't so bad," Shawn says, barely containing a grin.

"Pfft." Cheryl turns to me. "That woman walks around like she has a potato chip between her butt cheeks that she's trying not to break."

I snort-laugh, and then clap my hand over my mouth in mortification. They all crack up, and Shawn puts his arm around me and kisses my temple.

"The ladies are going to powder their noses," Cheryl says, standing up. It seems more like a summoning than an offer, so I stand too and follow her to the bathroom.

"This might take a moment, Eloise, these Spanx are the devil's invention, but I just cannot bring myself to buy the ones with the split in them," she says, heading into the first stall.

"I know what you mean," I say, heading into the stall next to her. "The only thing I hate more than Spanx . . ."

"Is how I look without them!" She finishes my sentence, and we both laugh.

I'm reapplying my lip gloss when she comes out of the stall. Washing her hands, she looks at me in the mirror. "I like you very much, Eloise."

"Oh, Cheryl, thank you. I like you too."

"I mean, I like you for my son, but I knew that the moment I saw how happy you make him. I know Linda . . . um, Lynne is your friend, and that is going to take some getting used to, not gonna lie. But she never made him glow like he does these days, if you don't mind my saying."

"I don't."

"What I'm saying is that I like *you*. You are good people, Eloise, I'm good at spotting that. If I met you at some other function, for some other reason, I would want for us to know each other. Is that too much to say?"

I can feel my heart swell. "No, that isn't too much at all. I feel the same." And I do. If tonight had been some charity event or one of my new social activities, I would totally want to be this woman's friend.

"Good. It's been made clear to me that sometimes in an effort to be polite, I might not be as transparent as I think I am, and I know that at this stage of our lives, there is enough to annoy us without having to spend a moment worrying about whether we have made the connections we hoped we would."

This feels like perhaps Shawn has been sharing some of his truths with her as well, most likely including my nervousness at meeting her, and that feels really good. "Thank you for that. You're right, there is plenty to navigate around, and open communication makes things so much easier!"

"Well, then, we will make it our ongoing habit. Shall we go see what those rascals are up to out there?"

"Yes. And, Cheryl? Thank you for Shawn. He is a rare and extraordinary man."

"Yes, he is. Thank you for seeing that and making him a happy man. Happy is harder than extraordinary." And she takes my hand and smiles, and we head back to the table.

Oh, sweetie, I'm so happy for you. What a wonderful way to start off with them," Teresa says, handing me a coffee.

"It was amazing. They were just so warm and welcoming, they made me feel totally comfortable."

"As well they should!"

"So, I'm ready for the lecture. Let's get it over with, lay it on me."

"No lecture. Just some truth."

"Bring it." I've been readying myself for this all week. Teresa has some big plan to get Lynne and me back together. But I've been practicing having a spine these days, and I've come to the conclusion that while I don't want to dismiss the idea of Lynne and I staying friends out of hand, I am strong enough to let it go if she can't be supportive of my life and my love. Not just tolerant; actively supportive. Not fake and digging at me, but acknowledging the person I have become.

"Good. Think back to high school. What were the things you liked most about Lynne?"

I think about this for a minute, remembering the Lynne I knew back then. "She was fierce. She was fearless. She was a natural leader. She was funny, when she wanted to be. She'd be the first person to tell you privately that your outfit was horrible, but if some bitch in the hallway made a comment about it, she'd take her out with one of her quick, cutting remarks. She always had your back."

"True enough! What else?"

"She was the first person who showed up at my house after my surgery to decorate my cast."

"I was in church. But the rhinestones were my idea!"

"I know."

"Anything else?"

I think back. "It always felt like she was real with us. Like she was herself with us. She was always Miss Perfect with everyone else, but remember some of our slumber parties? When she would sing and dance along to all the Madonna videos? It was like when we were together she could let her hair down and be silly and not worry about how it might look."

"I remember that too."

"T, I just don't know that she still has that girl in her. I think the other one has taken over completely."

"And if she has?"

"Then I don't know that it's worth it to try. Maybe if we didn't have the Shawn thing hanging over our heads, but this is a serious thing. We really love each other and unless there is some shoe I can't see that is going to drop, this might be it, I mean really it. What do we do with that?"

"What if she agreed to let the Shawn thing go?"

"I don't know, I really don't. She said she'd be good about it before, and look what happened! It would have been easier if she'd just say that it's him or her, which is clearly what she thinks deep down. Then it could just be over."

"What if she meant it this time?"

"Did you talk to her?"

"I did."

"What did she say?"

The doorbell rings.

"Teresa! You didn't."

She shrugs. "We're getting down to business." She gets up to answer the door. I hear them greet each other, and Lynne say that yes, she'd love coffee, and then she walks into the kitchen and sees me. But instead of the daggers I'm expecting, the lower half of her face crumples and she comes over and throws her arms around me.

"I'm so, so sorry, I was horrible, you were right, I was being a major bitch."

She sounds so sincere, and I can count on one hand the number of times I've seen Lynne cry, and it makes me cry too.

"I'm sorry too. I didn't mean to say what I said."

"No, you were right. You were really right. I don't even know what I was doing."

"You're hurt and confused."

Teresa comes over and grabs us both in her soft arms. "All right now, ladies, we are going to sit down and get it all out, *all of it.* You are going to tell each other the truth the way we used to. Eloise, you are going to go first and Lynne is going to listen and not respond or react or interject until you have told her everything that is in your heart. And then Lynne will have her turn. Neither of you are going to lie or omit or gloss over, and you are both going to agree to really hear the other person. We never had secrets, the three of us, we never held anything back, and it's what made us strong and kept us together. So we are going to say everything that scares us, and then figure out how to move past it. Deal? Because I am not going to play monkey in the middle for one more day with you."

I look at Lynne, my eyebrows raised in query. She meets my eyes and nods.

"Okay," we say, and we follow Teresa to the couch.

The next two hours are brutal. By the time it is done, we are both wiping tears. I told Lynne every horrible thing I have ever thought about her, about her greed for money and position and power, and her obsession with the surface appearance of things. The way she is dismissive and superior. The way that I think she goes for the jugular and couches it in joking. That she is selfish, always guiding people to do the things she wants to do, go to the places she wants to go, become the people she thinks they ought to be. That I find her purchase of Ellison, and subsequent lackluster commitment to him, to be reprehensible. That I sensed that she had been knocking things off the list for the bet just to win, whereas Teresa and I were really working to improve our lives, using the bet as a bit of extra motivation. That she hadn't gotten Ellison to explore what it meant to have that unconditional love in her life, but because it would help her at work. That she hadn't chosen the DuSable Museum as a place to try to get on a board because she loved it and its mission and wanted to help, but because she knew it would look good and connect her to people who would be useful to her professionally. That she likes me better when she can pity me, and sees herself as some sort of great guru helping to bring me along. I give her credit, she sat there and took it. I told her that Shawn had owned up to his part in what went down for them, and that I was so deeply sorry that the person I met and fell for happened to be someone who had caused her pain. But also that there was a small part of me that wondered if her dislike of Shawn and I being together was because she didn't think that I should have something like that for myself before she does. When I finished, I felt desiccated, like all of my blood had disappeared. And then it was her turn.

I was surprised at how much of what she said had to do with being sad for me, disappointed for me. That she remembered someone with ambition and drive and fire in the belly, and that she would have expected so much more from me, in my career, in my life. That the girl she knew wouldn't have let Bernard get the best of me. But also that she was resentful of me because, as much as she saw my life as so much less than what she would have wanted for me, she envied how well I seemed to know myself, to know what I wanted or needed. The fact that I had Mom and Claire and she wasn't close to anyone in her family. That I worked for people who were also dear friends, and therefore it didn't really feel like work, and she worked for people who were superficial and who focused all their energies on manipulating other people to do and buy and be what they wanted. That she didn't trust anyone she had ever worked with or for, and she knows that part of her frustration with me is actually frustration with herself for in many ways becoming just like them. She said that she really had loved Shawn, and had wanted it to work, but that she had felt so betrayed by his sudden about-face when it came to their life together, because his changing his mind about wanting kids made her feel like she wasn't enough. That she felt so betrayed when he made her question her feelings about that, because society does a good enough job making women who choose not to have children look selfish and "less than," and she had been so relieved that they were on the same page. That he had never in the beginning made her feel like they were wrong to not want to be parents. So when he changed, she felt abandoned, like he had joined the masses in looking down at her for her decision. And then wanting to leave Los Angeles, knowing how much her career there meant to her, that she didn't know how they could ever get past it, not really, and it became easier to just pretend that what they'd had wasn't the real deal. So when she saw us together, saw me so happy, being successful at the one thing she'd never been successful at, with the one person she'd ever really wanted to be successful with, it just snapped something in her. She admitted it was made even worse by her low opinion of me, of my ability to have a relationship, because if I could make it work with him, broken as I am in that area, what did that say about her?

What she said to me made me cry, not just for the parts that rang so true, but for how much sadness and hurt she has about who she is and what her life is about. It made me cry for ever thinking that my life was somehow "less than," just because it was small and self-contained. I cried because she reminded me that I have so many blessings, that there may not be a really huge circle of people in my life, but the ones who are there are amazing and loving and loyal and I trust every one of them implicitly.

Teresa just handed out tissues and squeezed hands, and let us get it all out. And when Lynne was done, Teresa looked at us, soggy weeping messes.

"I'm really proud of you guys, I know that was hard. But here is what I like more. You love each other. You need each other. You have things to teach each other. Which means that you are going to get past this. Lynne, you are going to have to figure out how to accept Eloise and Shawn, because friends want their friends to have love in their lives. I don't care if you need to go talk to a shrink, or if you need to go talk to Shawn, or whatever, but one of your oldest and dearest friends is madly in love, and you don't get to shit on that, or make snarky comments, or wish them ill. Yes?"

"Yes. I promise. Really, El, deep down, I am happy. For both of you. It does sound like he has changed, and it makes me glad to know that he has shared with you that it wasn't all my fault. That shows a lot of backbone, and it makes me feel somewhat better. You both deserve to be happy and in love, even if it is with each other," Lynne says with a wry smile.

"Thank you."

"And, Eloise? You are going to have to give Lynne a break. She's clearly hard enough on herself, she doesn't need to feel like you are judging her every minute you're together."

"You're right. And truly, Lynne, I'm really proud of all you have accomplished, it's just amazing."

"Thank you."

"Okay. So. Before my insane boys get back from whatever sporting event they are at right now, let's have just the smallest bit of normal conversation, okay? Lynne, anything new to report?"

Lynne smiles a bit sheepishly. "Well, the matchmaker did set me up with someone I like, and we are having a second date this weekend."

"That's great!" I say.

"Who is he?" Teresa asks.

"He's a venture capitalist. Splits his time between here and L.A., and it turns out that some of my former clients there are people he knows. He's ridiculously well connected. Not my usual type, but smart and funny. Well dressed. Really nice. We had a bunch of good phone calls and a great first date, so we'll see what happens."

I push down the nagging feeling that pokes at me, the fact that she led with his professional credentials, hints at his wealth and success, his contacts. We've just agreed to think better of each other, so I'm just going to let it go. "That is so great, Lynne, I can't wait to hear how the second date goes." I put as much joy and hopefulness in my voice as I can muster.

"Awesome, Lynne, can't wait to hear more. What about you, El, anything new?"

I hesitate. Lynne looks at me. "It's okay if it's about Shawn, really."

I take a deep breath. "I met his parents."

"They're pretty great, huh?" Lynne says. "I always liked them. Just really lovely people. Please tell them I send my best."

"That's so nice, I will."

Lynne pauses. Then she smiles at me. "Maybe you should invite them to the party. It would be nice to see them again."

I feel bad about the nasty thoughts I was having about her motivations for dating this new guy. "Thank you, maybe I will."

"Well, not to be outdone in the love department, I am delighted to report that without any prodding from me, Gio has suggested we do a romantic weekend away, just the two of us!"

"Go, T!" Lynne says.

"Wow! Where are you going to go?" I ask.

"He's found some little place in Sauganash, a boutique hotel, and there are some good restaurants there, cute shopping, that kind of thing."

"That is terrific, Teresa, really," I say.

The front door slams open and Gio and the boys come flying in, a whirlwind of talking and laughing and telling stories over each other. Lynne and I greet everyone, give Teresa a big hug, and head out together.

We walk down the front stoop.

"Where are you parked?" she asks me.

"That way." I point up the block.

"I'm down there." She points the other way.

"I'm really glad we talked." Not really knowing what else to say.

"Me too, really," she says.

She reaches up, and I lean in to give her a hug. "Amazon," she whispers in my ear.

"Pixie," I whisper back.

And then we head off, in opposite directions.

# Twenty-two

look at chaos on my kitchen table. Piles of recipes and sketches. Versions of my resume. Photographs of food, lists, notes on napkins and Post-its and pieces of scrap paper. I've added and discarded dozens of recipes. I've redone sketches ten times. With the party only a month away, I'm definitely behind on my bet obligations. I mean, obviously I've killed it on the dating part. Shawn and I couldn't be better. We had a great time with his family for Easter—they're loud and raucous and fun, and it reminded me a lot of Christmas with Teresa's family. After Easter we went back to Cheryl and Darren's for pie and coffee, and Darren said that based on the chocolate cream pie alone, Shawn had better keep me happy or they might choose me over him.

Life is good, but the bet is weighing on me a little. I've completely slacked off on my socializing with strangers, especially since Teresa and Lynne informed me last week that I couldn't count Easter with Shawn's family, or meeting his friends, and that dates with Shawn to go to classes or things also don't count. So I essentially have to find four more opportunities for me to get out and meet new people in the next few weeks, which should be do-able. I finished the first drawing class and signed up for a second class, in lettering and graphics. I've been good on the exercising part: I work with my trainer once a week and Shawn and I are still doing the pool class on Wednesdays, and I bought some DVDs that I've been doing at home, much to Simca's bemusement. I definitely feel physically stronger, and while I know I'll never be fit the way I once was, it feels better to be more active.

But when it comes to creating, let alone sending out, the cookbook proposal, I'm stuck.

I read an article on pitching cookbooks, and it said the most important thing is to have a point of view, a story you are tell-ing, a clear vision. But what does that look like? What story am I telling? The story of "Here is a bunch of stuff Eloise, who you've never heard of, thinks is delicious"? The story of "Have some recipes, because, dinner"? I know, why don't I just call it what it is, the story of "I should never have told my friends that this was a dream because now they put it in a stupid bet."

I know that isn't entirely fair. The cookbook was my idea. I've always wanted to do one. All these years, testing and re-testing recipes, writing everything down, it always felt like it was leading to something. But I don't know what the hell I was thinking. I don't have a story, I don't have a point of view, and at this stage, I don't have a book proposal. All I have is a di-saster area on my kitchen table, and not the first clue how to even mock something up. I can't fake it for the bet, because Lynne decided that they need to see a copy of the finished proposal and that I have to blind-copy them on the e-mails for the ten submissions I'm supposed to send out for the bet, so that they have proof. So I can't just mock up something stupid, because they'll see it, and I have to send it to real people, and I do have enough pride not to send shit into the world.

I look at the table, at the work that needs to be done to get anywhere near being ready. Despite the fact I've set aside the day to work on it all, I feel paralyzed. I know I should hunker down, but for some reason I can't. I've already walked Simca, done my laundry, made a batch of blondies with pistachios and figs drizzled in white chocolate, and planned the Farber menus for the week. I sent Teresa all the e-mail addresses for the people I'm inviting to the party next month. I walk over to the table with complete resolve. And I pack it all back up into the large tub sitting on the floor and slide it back into the corner. I go to the counter and take a blondie off the rack I used to do the chocolate drizzle and bite into it. They have browned butter and a combination of dark and light brown sugar, which gives them a deep caramel tang. The pistachios have retained their crunch, and the figs are just slightly tart. The white chocolate takes the whole thing over the top, and I know that, if nothing else, I can cook.

"Saturday," I say to Simca, who is giving me the side eye. "Shawn and his partners have their strategic planning meeting all day, so I'll work on the proposal on Saturday." Simca tilts her head at me as if to say that she isn't convinced, and I don't really blame her. I sort of don't believe me either.

So, my darling girl, come sit with me," Lawrence says when I get to his place. He has iced tea made and pours me a glass as I greet Philippe and Liagre.

"You look perky," I say, taking in his pale pink button-down shirt and white jeans with lime green driving loafers.

"I am a bit perky, I have to admit."

"You look like the preppy cat that swallowed the canary. What gives?"

"I have news. Huge news."

"Barbra's doing another farewell tour?"

He smacks my arm playfully. "Cheeky minx. No, I bought a house."

I almost choke on my iced tea. "A house? A whole house? But you finally got this apartment the way you like it! And you've always said that you would never leave this neighborhood, and unless you've recently won a lottery I'm unaware of, you cannot afford an actual house within a square mile of this place!"

"Oh, no, lovey, not here—Palm Springs!"

"You bought a house in Palm Springs?"

"My friends Karen and Len called me last week. The house next door to them, the owner passed away. Family didn't want it, just wanted to unload it quick, no muss, no fuss, and asked them if they knew anyone, before it went on the market, since they are the closest neighbors. Karen called me, sent me a bunch of pictures, and hooked me up with their Realtor. Bing bang boom, I have a house!"

"I don't know what to say . . ." My head is spinning.

"I know! Can you believe it? I can barely believe it myself, it happened so fast. But you'll love it. It's darling. Little mid-century bungalow, sweet little saltwater pool in the backyard, two bedrooms, two and a half baths. You can come visit, pet!"

"Lawrence, it sounds amazing."

"Well, it will take some doing to get it organized—it needs

a total kitchen and bathroom overhaul, and of course there is the matter of furnishing—but I'm enormously excited. I'm going out there at the end of the month for the closing."

"So, when do you move?"

"Oh, sweets, I'm not moving there. Not full-time, not yet. I'm going to snowbird there, at least for now. This year I'm going to try going right after Thanksgiving, and then come back sometime early April, and see how that goes." He sees the look on my face. "I will be back for New Year's, don't you worry."

"Good Lord, Lawrence, I'm not worried about that!" But I have to say I'm a little bit relieved when he says it.

"You know, when I'm here, business as usual, yes?" He raises a white eyebrow at me.

"I'm here for whatever you want, for as long as you want it. You know that. And I'm thrilled for you. Truly. You always have such a good time when you visit your friends there, but I also know that you like your quiet and privacy. You are always deeply grateful for your friends who host you, but it isn't completely relaxing to be a houseguest. I think it's terrific that you'll have your own space."

"And you and Shawn will come visit?"

"Of course we will."

"To new adventures!" He reaches out his glass to me.

"I'll drink to that."

Wow. That is so cool," Marcy says when I call her with the news.

"I know, I'm really happy for him. Of all the places he goes to visit his friends, he's always the happiest there. He showed me pictures of the house, and it's super cute. He's going to have a blast decorating it. I just know he's already all over 1stdibs .com looking at midcentury furniture."

"Yeah, and you get a bonus day off, like, five months a year!"

I hadn't thought about that. "I guess so."

"Shouldn't you be a bit happier? If I got extra time off, I'd be over the moon!"

"Look, Lawrence is half a day at most, and not particularly complicated at that."

"Lucky girl. I'm just jealous. With the café opening next month, we are slammed."

"I bet."

"How's your stuff going?"

I'm too embarrassed to confess about being stymied about the cookbook proposal. "All good."

My phone beeps. Saved by the bell. "Hey, Marce, that's another call, can I get back in a bit?"

"Sure! Later."

I click over. "Hello?"

"Hey there!" It's Lynne. Which is weird. She never calls, she texts.

"Everything okay?"

"Better than okay. I'm headed to the West Coast for the weekend with Gabriel."

Lynne's matchmaker date has become something of a whirlwind romance. I'm trying, in the spirit of our new understanding, to be excited for her. But the conversations feel strange to me. For someone who is normally calculated and quick to find a small flaw that renders something dead in the water, Lynne seems to have thrown herself into this new relationship in a way that borders on manic. On the one hand, I certainly know how amazing it is to meet someone and suddenly want to spend all your time with him. On the other, this feels strange. Especially since she continues to rattle off his fine qualities with focus on who he knows and what he has instead of much about who he is. How he took her to Alinea, to a box at the opera, on a helicopter ride over the city. I just can't seem to help it, the feeling that she likes the idea of Gabriel possibly even more than she likes Gabriel himself. I'm hoping that she'll want to introduce us sooner rather than later, so that the reality of him in person will give me a sense of the human qualities he has that have Lynne so jazzed.

"That's great, Lynne. Should be fun. Are you doing something romantic?"

"Oh, yes, there is a party at Jon Favreau's house on Friday night, so that should be wall-to-wall celebrities. And then a charity gala for the Guggenheim Saturday night, full red carpet. Angelique is dressing me for both events, and Gabriel asked a buddy of his at Harry Winston to sparkle me up!"

Sigh. "Wow. Fancy. That sounds like fun. Will you get any time to relax?"

"Well, not a ton, but he does want to take me out on his sailboat for a little while on Saturday."

Of course he does. "Very jet-set. Will you get to see any of your friends while you're there?" Lynne always talks about her main pals being back in L.A.

"Not this trip, but hopefully, if things continue to go well with Gabriel, I'll be back there more regularly."

It seems weird to me that she wouldn't even try to sneak in a coffee or brunch or something with the ladies she calls her Westies, as in, West Coast besties. But who am I to judge her about that? I moved back to the States permanently and never reached out to Lynne and Teresa, so I can't really fault her for a sneaky weekend.

"It sounds just great, Lynne, can't wait to hear all about it."

"Thanks." She pauses, and then very deliberately asks, "How's Shawn?"

"He's good, thanks for asking."

"Well, you survived Easter at Jeannie's. I hear that is quite the event."

"Didn't you ever go?"

"I never did. Spring was always just too busy for me to travel—work is insane that time of year. But I've heard the stories. Is it true about Uncle Foster?"

"A thousand percent."

"I don't know why, but I sort of appreciate that. I always wondered if he exaggerated the details in an effort to pique my curiosity enough that I would have to see it for myself."

All I can think is that he was probably just trying to share his family with her, to encourage her to accompany him so that she could be completely connected. I think about the day we had, the amazing food, the heartfelt grace, the embracing and ballbusting, the funny family stories, the enthusiastic dancing. Lynne missed out on so much. But a part of me is grateful. Because I don't have to be compared to her with his family, the slate is clean. Mostly I feel bad for her. "Well, it's all true, and they are a great family."

"I bet. I do have an awkward thing to ask you, though. A favor."

"What's that?"

"Well, Gabriel is coming back in a couple of weeks and wants to meet you and Teresa. Have dinner."

"Of course. I look forward to meeting him."

"Just one hitch. Teresa is going to be bringing Gio—I didn't want Gabriel to feel like it was the tribunal or anything, and this way he'd have another guy there. But . . ."

Crap. Here it comes.

"But would you be horribly offended if I asked you not to bring Shawn, at least not to this one? They'll meet at the party, obviously, but that seems an easier thing, with all the other people there. But an intimate dinner with my ex is just, well, eventually, maybe, I hope, but not for a first meeting, not so early in the relationship, you know? Do you understand?"

As much as I think personally that it would be easier on all of us—maybe even better—to just pull off the Band-Aid and get it over with, for the two of them to meet small and quiet, to actually get to know each other a bit, instead of exchanging some small talk at a big event, I can't fault her. She's trying, I can see that. She insisted I invite Shawn's folks to the party, and she has been good about asking me about how things are going and making him a more open topic of conversation, so if she needs this, then I owe her that. "Of course. I understand and I'm sure Shawn will as well."

"Thank you for that. Really, El, I totally appreciate it."

"No problem." To get off the subject I tell her about Lawrence and his new snowbirding life change.

"That is fantastic. Are you going to bring in another client?"

"I doubt it. After all, he'll still be here over half the year."

"Yeah, for the first year. I guarantee you, it starts like that and then quickly becomes most of the year. They get excited about the new place and the new people, and then pretty soon they are just here from May through August, and then it doesn't make financial sense to keep a permanent place here when they're gone eight months a year, and then it's bye-bye."

It's sad to imagine, but it rings true. A lot of Mom and Aunt Claire's friends are now spending the majority of their time in Florida and Arizona; they've sold their Chicago places and just stay with their kids and friends when they come visit.

"Well, when that happens, I'll figure it out. But there's no rush, he hasn't even closed yet!"

"I'm just saying, you should keep your ear to the ground, keep your options open, right?"

"Sure, I guess."

"Okay, gotta go. I'll text you from Cali."

"Sounds good. Have a really great time, Lynne."

"You know it!"

I hang up just as my phone rings again. I'm terribly popular today. "Hello?"

*"Dinner at Jon Favreau's house!!!"* Teresa screams in my ear.

"I know, T, it's pretty cool."

"Did you see *Chef*? That man can cook."

I laugh. *Chef* is a guilty-pleasure movie—I've seen it a dozen times and it never gets old. Probably because it is one of those happy food movies that seems to understand how we really think. Plus, he did all his own cooking, and the man has legit knife skills. I fully appreciate that kind of commitment. "Of course I have. I own it on DVD."

"Lucky girl. I hope she gets lots of pictures."

"I'm sure there will be plenty of documentation."

"Guess what?"

"What?"

"I took my girlfriends from church to that Ethiopian place you recommended."

"Demera? How was it?"

"Amazing! I ordered all the stuff you said to, and it was

delicious. All the girls were so impressed, and eating with our hands was strangely fun. I really like that injera bread; it was more sour than I thought it would be at first, but kind of addictive."

"That is really cool, T, I'm proud of you."

"What else is going on with you?"

I fill her in on Lawrence's news.

"That is so great! Good for him. Ooh! When he is out of town, we should use your free time to hang out! Go explore more food places, and cook together, maybe make some dinners together for all of us."

I laugh. "Sure, Teresa, that sounds fun."

She fills me in on Gio and the boys. And then pauses. "Did Lynne talk to you about meeting her new guy?"

"She did."

"Are you okay with it?"

"Yeah, I get it. I'd probably do it differently, but let's be honest, what don't Lynne and I do differently?"

"That is true. But I'm glad you're cool about it."

"It's a first meeting. And they'll have a chance to connect at the party. If it becomes a thing after that, then we'll have to figure it out, but for this one time, I'm going to go with the flow."

I hear a crash in the background. "Crap. My beasts are up to something. I'll talk to you later."

I hang up and head over to the counter to pack up the blondies in a Rubbermaid tub, leaving a couple behind for Shawn and me for later. I'll take the rest to the Farbers tomorrow. I think Brad especially is going to love them; he's much less of a chocolate guy than the rest of his family.

While I'm layering them between waxed paper, I think

about the three of us, and everyone's reaction to Lawrence's news as it relates to me and my life. Lynne immediately saw career improvement potential. Teresa immediately saw an opportunity for more quality time with friends. And me? I didn't really see anything much at all. It makes me wonder. The whole point of the bet was to shake us up, to light some fires, and it has worked in a lot of ways. But can you really teach an old dog that many new tricks? It's strange—when I realized that I would have some extra time on my hands, I didn't think that I could take more art classes or meet new people or have more time for exercise. I certainly didn't think that it would give me time to work on cookbook stuff. I didn't imagine anything like what either Lynne or Teresa imagined. Deep down, now that I have a chance to think about it, I wonder how I will handle it when it actually comes. And while I'm not making any real plans until it happens, a part of me hopes that I figure out how to use it in some way that embraces the person that I'm trying to be, even though I clearly still have a ways to go.

# Twenty-three

S HAWN IS THE BEST!" Geneva yells, arms in the air, head thrown back. She's wearing a Cubs sweatshirt with the logo in pink sparkles and has chocolate all over her face.

"Yeah, thanks, Shawn, that was awesome," Ian says.

"Totally cool," Darcy says sheepishly.

"Rock star," Robbie says, reaching up for a high five, unable to actually connect with Shawn's hand until he lowers it halfway with a wink.

"Shawn, you've ruined my kids," Brad says, grinning. Shawn, having recently patched up an expensive rookie's ACL, took all of us to the game in a skybox, complete with being able to go onto the field after batting practice to meet and get signatures from the players, many of whom were on the World Series

Championship team in 2016. The highlight for the kids was getting to play round-robin catch with Jake Arrieta, and Joe Maddon coming over to coach them up while they did it. Ian had made a huge batch of homemade granola bars, packed with all sorts of high-protein ingredients, that he was able to take into the dugout, and the guys made them disappear in short order, all of them praising his skill and saying that if they won today, they would call them Ian's Secret Weapon Bars and he'd have to make more of them for tough games. He was beaming, and told them all about getting onto the show, and they said they would be rooting for him and watching the show for sure.

"Yeah, thanks a lot, buddy, how do parents top this?" Shelby beams at him.

"It was my pleasure, nothing better than a beautiful day at Wrigley, complete with a win! But yeah, you guys are screwed, because I'm going to do this to them for the Bulls, Bears, and Blackhawks later this season."

"WE LOVE SHAWN!" Geneva screams, hopped up on sugar and her own brand of almost-five-year-old mania. She spent at least four innings sitting in Shawn's lap and having serious conversations with him about anything and everything. Watching him with the kids melted my heart. He's a natural with all of them. I heard him talking to Robbie about colleges and telling Darcy about being a percussionist in the band in elementary school and how sad he was that he had to choose between football and music in high school. He confessed to her that, while he was really great at football, he was an enthusiastic but terrible drummer.

"I love you guys too. You made it a really fun day, so thanks for coming. Eloise and I would have been very lonely in that big box by ourselves."

"Well, we're always here for you," Ian says seriously, making us all laugh.

Geneva gets a very serious look on her face and waves Shawn down to her to whisper in his ear. He listens intently, and then gets a lovely smile on his face. "If it's okay with your folks, it's okay with me," he says seriously, and when he stands back up, I can see that his eyes are bright and shiny.

"MOM! CAN WE CALL HIM UNCLE SHAWN? HE'S SO MUCH BETTER THAN UNCLE GEORGE!" George is an old college buddy of Brad's, and something of a buffoon, the kind of guy who has no idea how to talk to kids and is always either talking down to them or boring them to death.

Shelby laughs, and smiles warmly at Shawn. "If he doesn't mind, we certainly don't."

"UNCLE SHAWN UNCLE SHAWN UNCLE SHAWN!" Geneva spins in a circle, and Shawn reaches for my hand and squeezes tight.

"Your fault, man, you said they could get anything they wanted from the dessert cart," Brad says, shrugging at Shawn.

"I'll take it," Shawn says.

We get to the parking lot, and after a lot more hugs and thank-yous, Shelby and Brad start loading the kids into their car.

"UNCLE SHAWN!" Geneva yells from the backseat while Shelby is buckling her into her car seat. "CAN I BE THE FLOWER GIRL WHEN YOU MARRY ELOISE?"

Shelby looks aghast, and Brad slaps his forehead.

Shawn laughs. "Absolutely. But only if you promise to wear a tiara."

"I'M A PRINCESS IN SHAWN AND ELOISE'S WEDDING!" She claps happily, while the rest of the kids grin and shake their heads.

Shelby winks at me.

We walk over to Shawn's car and he opens my door for me. "Tiara?" I ask.

"Well, I'd prefer you don't wear one, but c'mon, that face?"

I lean in to kiss him. "I love you. *Uncle Shawn.*"

"Uh-uh. Uncle is for the kids only, Miss Eloise. But you can call me Big Daddy if you want," he says with a wicked grin, slapping my butt lightly as I get in the car.

"As long as you don't call me Mommy!"

"Nope, only our kids get to do that," he says, casual as can be, as he closes the door, and I manage to shake off the happy tears before he makes it around to his side of the car to drive us home.

So, what, it's like a when and not an if? Or is it just play talk?" Marcy asks, biting into her enormous burger at the Orbit Room, juice running down her wrist.

I pop a tater tot into my mouth and chew. "Yeah, I sort of think it is. I mean, we talk about what we'll do, and he is really open about the kid thing. I think in part he started that because of what happened with Lynne—you know, he wants to be really up-front with me that he sees himself as a dad. But while we've never said the word 'marriage' specifically, it is sort of implied in a lot of our conversations."

"Wow," she says, dunking a lump of fried onion strings into ketchup and dangling them into her mouth. "Mama Eloise. I like it."

"I like it too, I have to say. The more time I spend with Teresa's family and Shawn's family, I just think it feels right." I'm still worried about whether I'll be as good a mom as I want to be, but Shelby made me feel better about that, and Teresa said that if I questioned my ability to be a good mom it was the ultimate insult to my own mother, who has been the best possible role model. Ever since she said that, I feel like she's right, and that even though I may not really know it, the tools are all there already.

"Damn, that will be a good-looking baby. Huge, but good-looking."

I laugh and waggle my pickle spear at her. "Careful, munchkin. I can squash you."

"True enough. How's the bet coming along? You've only got, what, three more weeks?"

"I'm in good shape," I say, lying through my teeth. "Three out of five are done, and I only have two more things to do for the social thing, and I've got one tomorrow night, a cookbook signing at the Book Cellar."

"Well, I've got another one, with a possibility for some ongoing connection," she says. "Why don't you come with me to my Dahms event next week?"

"Dahms? What the hell are Dahms?"

She laughs. "Les Dames d'Escoffier," she says in an exaggerated French accent.

"The Escoffier Ladies?" I ask, my rusty French kicking back in.

"Yeah. The Chicago chapter. I've been a member for a couple of years, and they are a great bunch of women. All areas of wine, food, and the hospitality industry, from chefs to food writers to culinary instructors to event planners. They raise money for scholarships for culinary programs and do community service and social programs. There's even a book club that reads culinary fiction and stuff. Ever since you've been getting more social, I've been thinking you could come to a couple of events and get to know the ladies, and if you like them, I could work on getting you nominated for membership."

"Wow. That sounds so cool. What is the event next week?"

"Thursday night. It's a spirits-and-chocolate-pairing thing hosted by Vosges and Mammoth Distilling."

"You had me at chocolate and booze."

"I really think you'll have fun."

"Why haven't I ever heard of them?"

Marcy pauses. "I never really wanted to mention. I mean, on paper, perfect fit for you, but . . ."

"But my antisocial nature?"

"I love you, honey, but these are super bright, fun women, and they have amazing big personalities. Yes, this is a way for them to give back, but it is also most importantly a way for them to network and connect. You really don't bring someone into the circle unless there is a part of you that thinks she might be a good fit for something bigger; after all, we are a charitable organization, and I never wanted to make you uncomfortable. I feel like last year, if I had taken you to something, I would have felt the need to really stick to you like glue, and that you would really mostly have just talked to me, if you had agreed to come with me at all. I don't get to go to as many meetings and events as I would like, so when I go I want to flit around and see all my girls."

"Didn't want the old ball and chain dragging you down." I hate how right she is, that in her position I would have probably done the same.

"Hey. I love you, you ridiculous giantess. You know that. And I'm super proud of how much you've changed in the past months. I never wanted to put you in an uncomfortable situation, but now I feel like you can come to this event and have a good time and meet some new people that might actually stick. I mean, wasn't the whole socializing-with-strangers thing supposed to be about broadening your group of friends? Meeting new people?"

"It was."

"Have you stayed in touch with any of the people you've met at any of these classes or tastings or events at all? Even taken someone's card?"

I think back to the things I've done and realize that, while I've had some good conversations and fun, I haven't really connected with anyone and, no, I haven't stayed in touch. "Nope."

"Okay, so here is a group of women you already have a lot in common with. That's a pretty good foundation. Why not make your last bet item one that might actually fulfill the idea behind the bet, instead of just checking something off the list? After all, you thought you were just dating for the bet to put a toe back into the water of a possible romantic life and you met your soul mate, for chrissakes!"

"I give! You're right, evil pixie. I'm in. Bring me to meet the Dahms. Is there hazing? Blood ritual?"

She winks. "You'll have to get nominated to find out."

"What the hell. It's the new me."

"Nope, it's just a slightly improved version of you, with all of the awesomeness that you've always been, just a bit shinier."

She raises her pint glass to me, and I clink it with my own, thinking that for the first time since the bet started, I'm actually looking forward to a social event, without a moment's uncertainty or the tiniest wish for a quiet night at home. This seems at once completely natural and totally monumental.

"So then you just have to mail out your cookbook things and you are all good!"

My heart sinks a bit, thinking about the dreaded tub, untouched for the past two weeks. Well, I am still a work in progress. I put on a big smile. "Yep!"

We finish our burgers and beers; she fills me in on the café opening plans, moved to the first week of June due to some unexpected construction delays. Her phone pings just as we're paying the bill.

"Hot date?" I ask.

"Nope, just Sophie and a bunch of people are meeting up with the Girl and the Goat gang at the Paramount Room for cocktails." She pauses. Then puts on a sly smirk. "Wanna come?"

I look her dead in the eye. "You bet."

snuggle back into Shawn's chest, and he kisses the top of my head. "How are you feeling about it?"

I've just gotten back from the meet-and-greet dinner at Spiaggia with Lynne and Gabriel, and I'm mentally worn out. "I feel like they are weirdly a really good match, for all the wrong reasons."

"Okay, so is that good or is that bad?"

"Are you okay with talking about this? I mean, I really want to talk to you about this, but I can completely understand if you don't want to."

"Lynne and I are ancient history, and whatever sadness I had about that failing has long been replaced with relief that I got out before I lost more time. Especially in the last seven months." He pulls me in tightly. "Yeah, do I wish she wasn't your friend? Of course. It's fucking weird, not gonna lie. But I don't ever want you to feel like you have to edit yourself or not talk to me about things because of our past. None of it is changing. So lay it on me."

"Okay, so he's one of those guys that you sort of know aren't really listening, they're just sort of waiting for their turn to talk?"

"Yeah, like you could be anyone, as long as you are a receptacle for their stories?"

"Exactly. And sometimes I feel like Lynne does that, so maybe neither one of them would care. He definitely wants you to know that he has a lot of money; it was all about the fancy dinner and expensive bottles of wine, and the truffle addition upcharge. And he made a very strong point at the beginning that he was treating, as if the rest of us would have been concerned about the cost."

"Ugh, that sounds shitty."

"I don't know, I mean, he did it in that blithe way like he really thought he was being a nice guy and a thoughtful host, but it just landed wrong. But the weird thing is, they really do seem to genuinely like each other, Lynne and him; they laughed a lot, and told us all about their trip to L.A."

"With an emphasis on famous people they rubbed elbows with?"

"Naturally. And his huge sailboat, and his enormous house in the hills, and his place at the beach . . ."

"Great."

"I mean, it's weird, it feels like they like each other and are happy together, but that part of it is because she sees herself living that life with that kind of man, and that he is the kind of guy who wants someone who is beautiful and accomplished, like he is disdainful of the guys who get the traditional younger, stupid-blond-bimbo trophy wives, so he is going to get someone smart and elegant; but she's still sort of a trophy, just a different type of trophy."

"But if that is what they both want, maybe that is part of the attraction?"

"Maybe. I mean, don't get me wrong—he seems genuinely nice, if a little self-important."

"Much like Lynne, if you don't mind my saying."

"I don't. You're right. I just wish that it felt like more of a love match than a business arrangement. They're certainly affectionate, but there's no real electricity, you know? They seem comfortable, but not sparkly."

"Not like us!" he says, nuzzling into my neck.

"Nope, we got all kinds of sparkle." I turn to kiss him, noting that the feel of his lips on mine are still on the super-insane-wow part of the electricity scale. I pull back, and shift so that I'm sitting facing him, and Simca takes the opening to jump up and snuggle into the warmth of the space I've left behind in his lap.

"But you don't think he's a bad guy? You didn't see some sort of red flag to cause you to want to warn her or not be supportive?"

"No, I didn't, which weirdly, is maybe worse? Because I think Lynne just checks off a lot of boxes for him—he looks at her like he has finally found the kind of person he deserves, instead of looking at her like he can't believe his great good fortune in finding Lynne specifically, and everything that means about her and who she is. And I can't say that it is any different on her side, so I can't really be anything but supportive, you know?"

"Well, for what it's worth, I'm glad. I don't really know if it is in Lynne to just go from the gut, from the heart, and leap into genuine love with someone. It sounds like she has found a decent guy who is everything she wants and needs, and has the same sort of attitude, so maybe they are truly perfect for each other. Ultimately, everyone has their own idea of happy, and if this is theirs, I think that's great. Maybe if she has what she believes she needs, she can fully open up to our love."

"That is a nice way to look at it. I'll try and adopt it."

"Despite your deep-down disapproval." He tilts his head at me.

"Argh, I know, I'm very judgmental." I keep trying to work on that, but it is a process, and some days are better than others.

"No, you just want more for her than she wants for herself."

"I think maybe because that was always her role for me, and over the last few months I've finally started to want for myself some of what she always wanted for me, and so now I wish I could do the same for her a little bit."

"You're a good soul, my love."

"I'm trying to be."

"How are you feeling about the party coming up?"

"Pretty good, I think. It should be a nice event, and I'm looking forward to your folks meeting Mom and Claire. I hope your superfan Geneva doesn't stick her foot in it with them!"

"Oh, I already told them about all my new nieces and nephews!"

"Oy, what did they say?"

"My mom said she couldn't wait to meet them, and that we should bring them all to the Memorial Day family barbecue."

"Seriously?"

"Mom doesn't play about the barbecue."

"Lord, can you imagine?"

"Oh, I can more than imagine—I can't *wait!*"

I laugh, thinking about the whirling dervish that is Geneva Farber and Shawn's family. We're going to have to take video.

"Well, I'll let them know the details. I think they're in town that weekend."

"What about the bet?"

"I'm good on everything . . ."

"Except the cookbook proposal," he says matter-of-factly. "I noticed the tub in the kitchen corner is getting dusty."

"Yeah, except that." I fessed up to him about the cookbook proposal problem when I recognized that I was really not just procrastinating but genuinely stuck.

"What do you think is the block?"

"The whole idea of having a story to tell with my food, I don't know how to pull that together."

"What about the *Love Plates* idea? I thought you had settled on that."

"Yeah, for a title, but what does it mean, really?"

"Baby, you have spent your life doing what you love, with love, for people you love. Didn't you always say that the thing that keeps you out of a restaurant is the need for the personal connection? That's what the title means to me when you say it. Loving the process, loving the product, and loving the recipient, even when the recipient is yourself. A celebration of how cooking is a pure act of love, and one of the most generous gifts you can give to someone. Right?"

"Sure, it sounds easy when you say it."

"Well, let me ask you this. Do you care at all about winning this bet?"

I think about this. "I did, sort of, in the beginning. But now I feel like I already did the most important part, you know? My body is a little healthier. My mind is a little clearer. My life is a little wider and more interesting. And most importantly, I found you, so I've already won so big."

"Well, thank you. So what if you thought of this cookbook thing as not part of the bet, but just part of this bigger, more open life you've embraced? Forget the deadline looming; forget needing to prove something to Lynne and Teresa, you've already proven it to yourself. Give up on using it to win the bet, but don't give up on the dream of it. I think you can't do the proposal because you haven't done the book. So forget about agents and publishers, and just do the book. The whole book. Delve into the joy of figuring out the chapters and culling the recipes and drawing your amazing sketches. Let it come to you the way it wants to, and once it's finished, then look at what you have and see how you want to handle it. Maybe you'll want to self-publish, and not go the traditional route at all. Who knows? But don't force it to try and win the bet, and don't let it go just because of losing the bet. Let Lynne and Teresa win the bet, and you win at life."

In one fell swoop, the tension in my shoulders releases, like a switch has been flipped. The idea of not worrying about how to describe the book and just delving into the actual making of the book, that seems freeing and like something that I could really do. "You are magic. Do you have any idea how much I love you?"

"I do. Because it appears to be as much as I love you, which is enormously much."

I push Simca out of the way and get back into Shawn's arms, knowing that for the first time in forever, I'm not just where I should be, but I'm who I should be. And while I'm no less content than I was last year at this time, I'm a whole lot happier. Which means that letting go of winning the bet?

Actually means I win the bet.

# Twenty-four

"The place looks great, Teresa! Thank you for doing so much hard work," I say, looking around the private room at Stella Barra. Teresa has put together beautiful flower arrangements on all the tables, from the walls she's hung silver Mylar ballons with *40!* on them in purple, and at each place is a cellophane-wrapped cookie with a photo of us from our eighteenth birthday party printed on it. There are bowls of retro candies on all the tables—our favorite stuff from our youth: Razzles and Nerds and Lik-m-aid packages and bowls of custom M&M's also printed with *40!* All around the room are photos of the three of us from high school printed on boards. She's outdone herself.

"It's terrific, T, thanks," Lynne says, winking at me. I know she thinks it's over the top and sort of ghastly, but I will say that she seems these days to be a little lighter, a little looser, and dare I say, maybe even a little more tactful. Maybe Gabriel is making her truly happy, in a way that lets her be more relaxed about life.

The waitress comes over with a tray of the official cocktail of the evening, the ELT French 40. It's a riff on a French 75, adjusted to suit us, with bourbon instead of gin, champagne, lemon juice, and simple syrup, with a Luxardo cherry instead of a lemon twist. "Here you go, ladies. As soon as your guests are here we will start passing hors d'oeuvres, but I thought you might want a little sampler plate before they arrive."

"That is great, thanks so much!" I say, knowing that in a half hour when people start to come in, we'll have a hard time eating and mingling. We accept the flutes and toast each other. The drink is warming and refreshing at the same time. The platter she has brought us contains three each of all the passed appetizers we chose: little lettuce cups with spicy beef, mini fish tacos, little pork-meatball crostini, fried calamari, and spoons with creamy burrata topped with grapes and a swirl of fig balsamic. There will also eventually be a few of their signature pizzas set up on the buffet, and then, for dinner, everyone has their choice of flat-iron steak, roasted chicken, or grilled vegetables, served with roasted fingerlings. For dessert, there is either a chocolate chunk or apple oatmeal cookie, served toasty warm with vanilla ice cream and either hot fudge or caramel on top, plus there will be their famous Rice Krispies Treats on the tables to share. We opted out of the huge-birthday-cake thing, since as usual, the three of us all prefer different flavors of cake. Growing up, we always did cupcakes for the birthday celebrations, and saved the big cakes for individual family events.

"Damn, these are good," Lynne says around a mouthful of fish taco.

"I could eat this whole plate," Teresa says, popping a calamari tentacle in her mouth.

"Well, I'm glad you approve of the choices." Teresa was in charge of décor, I was in charge of menu planning, and Lynne was in charge of paying her third and trusting us.

"So, enough chitchat. A little business before the festivities . . ." Lynne says. "And before either of you say anything, I have a confession."

"Yes?" Teresa says, raising an eyebrow.

"I didn't finish my list," Lynne says. "Apparently the whole nomination process for the DuSable Museum board is both rigorous and endless, and I'm still being vetted, and have not actually even been nominated yet, so I failed."

Teresa and I look at each other, jaws agape. Lynne was the hands-down favorite to win, and we all knew it, especially her, which was why she agreed to it to begin with. Lynne subscribes to the philosophy that you never ask a question you don't already know the answer to, and you never enter a competition you aren't sure you're going to win.

"That's okay, L, I didn't finish my list either. I've been working on the cookbook, but it isn't ready for me to send anything out that I'd be confident to share."

Teresa starts to laugh. "There is *no way* I won this thing!" She slaps her head. "I was just shooting for second place."

"Well, you totally won it, T, which is good since it was your idea anyway," Lynne says. "Anyway, since Eloise and I kind of tied for losing, what should we do about the checks?"

"I think all three of us do the same five grand," Teresa says.

"But you won—you're off the hook!" Lynne says.

"Yeah, but it wasn't ever really about that, you know? We were back together again, the Three Witches. We all had shit we wanted to accomplish that needed a push or two, and we needed to be back in each other's lives in a way that honored Mrs. O'Connor. She always taught us that we were stronger together. I think this was sort of her final gift to us, so our final thank-you should be even all around."

"I'm in," I say.

"That's sweet, T. I'm in too," Lynne says, pulling out her checkbook.

We all write our checks to the Helene O'Connor Scholarship Fund. We're going to give them to Glenn tonight. We agreed that this was just our private thing, so we aren't making a big deal about it; we're just going to tell Glenn that this is the way we wanted to mark our big birthday.

"To us," Teresa says, raising her glass. "The way we should be."

"To us," Lynne says. "For better or worse." She winks at me.

"To us," I say. "Better together."

And we drink.


I look around the room and can't help but smile. Over at the kids' section the Farber kids and Teresa's brood are laughing and having a great time. Geneva is teaching the younger ones how to make animals out of the Rice Krispies Treats, the older kids are tossing M&M's into each other's mouths, trying to see who can do the most in a row without missing, and I think Darcy and Teresa's youngest are quietly falling in twelve-year-old love. My mom and Claire and Glenn and Lawrence are all sharing a table with Shawn's folks. Turns out that Cheryl and Darren know Glenn from way back, as Cheryl and Helene did

some charity work together, so it was a bittersweet reunion.
Teresa and Gio are chatting with Lynne and Gabriel and some
of Lynne's coworkers. The food has been fantastic and everyone gave really funny speeches, telling all their best stories
about the three of us, and toasting us both individually and as
a group. There has been a lot of laughter, and everyone seems
to be having a genuinely good time.

"Hey there, beautiful. You having fun at your party?" Shawn
comes up behind me, handing me a Negroni.

"Thank you, lover. I am."

"Good."

"How are you? Too weird?"

Earlier there was something of an awkward moment when
Cheryl and Darren were saying hello to Lynne, and Darren
called her Linda. But Lynne laughed it off and greeted them
warmly, and then extracted herself gracefully. Later, she and
Shawn had a quiet moment, and then she introduced him to
Gabriel, who was all kinds of football-hero starstruck, and
while I doubt the four of us will be vacationing together anytime soon, I do think we can be at social functions together
without anyone coming to blows.

"Well, momentarily weird, but not awful. Plus, all I care
about is that my baby is happy."

"Being your baby makes me happy."

He leans in and kisses me.

"Gack. You two are *so gross*," Marcy says, swanning in.
"Sorry I'm so late, had to get the sweets table set up for the
wedding tonight before I could blow out of there, and we had
something of a croquembouche disaster."

"No worries. There is still plenty of pizza on the buffet if
you're hungry, or they can bring something fresh."

"I'm all good. Just going to grab a cocktail and make the rounds."

"She's a good egg, that one," Shawn says.

"Yeah."

"Think she'd be up for a fix-up?"

"You playing yenta?"

"Well, there is a cool new resident at the hospital that I just get a vibe about, think they might click. Maybe I could invite him to the party next weekend?"

Shawn and I are hosting our first joint dinner party. Teresa and Gio, Marcy, Shelby and Brad, Lawrence, two couples that are pals of his. I wish I could say that choosing a date when Lynne and Gabriel were going to be on the West Coast was an accident, but I'd be lying. We're better, but not perfect, and there is stuff I'm just not quite ready for.

"Sure, why not?" I smile at him, adoring that he wants to fix Marcy up. My mom once said that when someone is truly in love, all they want is for everyone else to be in love. I'd like to think that our happiness is what is inspiring Shawn to want to do that for Marcy.

Teresa comes over. "I think Glenn might be gearing up to head out. Should we do this?"

"Yeah. Shawn, I'll be right back."

We wave to Lynne, and she nods, extricating herself, and heads over to join us.

"Glenn, could we speak to you for a moment?" I say, pulling him away from his conversation.

"Oh, no, three gorgeous women want to chat with me? Now it feels like my birthday!" he says with a wink, following us to a quiet corner of the room.

"So, we wanted to do something special to mark this major birthday achievement," I start.

"And we realized that we wouldn't be here together if it weren't for Mrs. O'Connor," Lynne says.

"We owe her so much, so much about who we are, and why we make the choices we make. How much space we take up in the world," I say.

"That is so lovely, girls—the three of you were always special to her. I know she is here right now in spirit, and she's so happy."

"Thank you for that. Anyway, we decided that the best way to acknowledge our gratitude would be to make donations to her scholarship fund, in her name." Teresa hands him the envelope. Glenn takes it, tears in his eyes, and holds it to his chest.

"You are all so wonderful, and I know she's wonderfully proud of all of you. Thank you for this." He reaches in and we do a four-way hug, all of us wiping tears. "Now, let's get back to this wonderful celebration!" he says, and Teresa heads off to check in on her kids, and Lynne goes to say good-bye to Angelique Morris, who is headed for the door.

"A moment, Eloise?" Glenn says.

"Of course."

"I wanted to ask you a very important question."

"Sure, what's that?"

"Well, you know your mother and I have been spending some time together."

"Yep. I think it's great the work you've both been doing at the center. Those kids are so lucky."

"Well, I feel like the lucky one. In a lot of ways. When Helene

was sick, we didn't leave anything on the table, we said everything that needed to be said. And one of the things that she
said to me was that she would be very disappointed if I spent
the rest of my life alone. As long as I didn't date her friend
Holly, who was always getting drunk at parties and squeezing
my butt."

"I'd say that's a fair request."

"I said I would take it under advisement, but deep down I
never really thought that would be something I would be
thinking about."

"I sense a but coming . . ."

"But . . . then I reconnected with your lovely mother."

Holy shit. "She is the loveliest."

"Yes, she is. And I've come to really appreciate her company, and humor, and I find that I look forward to spending
time with her in ways that I hadn't anticipated."

"Glenn, are you asking my permission to date my mom?"

"Permission? No. But for your blessing, yes. If it wouldn't
make you uncomfortable, I think I would like to ask her on a
proper date."

I smile at him, feeling the small lump grow in my throat.
"Glenn, my mom and dad were very much like you and Helene
in many ways, a true deep love match. And I know my dad
would have never wanted my amazing mom to be alone either.
You have all my blessings, and what is more, I'm rooting for
you. My mom hasn't said anything to me specifically about her
feelings for you, but I can tell you that she certainly has seemed
happier and perkier since the two of you started spending time
together. I can't imagine anyone else in the world I would
rather see making my mom happy."

Glenn grabs me in a bear hug. "Thank you, darling girl."

"You're very welcome."

"Any advice?"

I think about that. "I think you both will need to make new memories. Don't fall into the old habits, don't go to the old favorite places you both used to go in your previous lives. Have new adventures together. Keep the start fresh."

"That is excellent advice."

"Also? She loves the opera."

"Really? So do I." He smiles.

"My dad hated it. I'm just saying."

He laughs. "So did Helene. She always said she could nap for free at home. Opera it is!"

He hugs me again, and then goes back to his place next to my mom. She smiles as she sees him approach, and it makes my heart bust open.

"You okay over here?" Shawn says, coming over.

"I'm more than okay. I'm perfect."

"That you are."

And maybe for the first time in my life? I believe it.

unroll the plans on the kitchen table. They look spectacular. The roof will get raised up a bit and dormered out, and the space is divided into a master bedroom suite, with his and hers walk-in closets, a huge master bath, and a small connected room, labeled *Nursery/Sitting Room*, which makes me smile. The basement will be dug down, and that space turned into two bedrooms, a large rec room, and a bathroom, in addition to laundry and mechanicals and storage. We're replacing the existing garage with a bigger one, and putting a deck on the top. Shawn and I talked about buying something new when we decided to move in together last month, but he knows how much I love this house.

"Besides," he said, "once there are kids, we are really going to want to be walking distance to Grandma and Great-Auntie Claire."

Couldn't argue with him on that, so we decided to renovate this place to make it more of a family-friendly home. He hasn't proposed yet, but based on the way my mom looks at him these days, I get the sense that permission has been requested and happily granted, and I just try not to have any expectations about when that question might get popped. Not that I'm lacking any joy after this summer.

The month I spent with Ian in New York was transformative for all of us. Ian got to the final two, and lost graciously to his new best friend Audrey, as happy for her win as he would have been for himself. The two of them were rock stars for the whole competition, and even when they were on opposite sides of team challenges, they were still supportive of each other. Producers said that the highlight of the season was during a bread challenge when Audrey accidentally dropped her whole tray of rolls, burning her hand. While she was crying and being attended to by the medics, Ian quickly knocked out a new batch of dough and left it for her on her station with a note that said "You can do it." Not a dry eye on the production staff. Ever since we got back, the two of them have been attached at the hip, Audrey coming over for joint lessons, and Ian going with her family to some of the fancy restaurants that they frequent.

Shelby and Brad alternated coming in for the weekends, and Shawn and I got to have three amazing weekends exploring New York together, and one fabulous weekend at home for his parents' fiftieth wedding anniversary party. I also got to really explore all of the culinary delights of the city, visiting markets and restaurants all over, and getting lots of inspiration for new dishes. Which couldn't have come at a better time. Because one of the people I met in the greenroom at the show on a taping day was Kelly Morgan. Cookbook editor for Penguin Random House. Apparently one of the prizes for this season was going to be a cookbook deal, and she would be the editor, so she wanted to spend some quality time on set watching and getting a sense of the kids. Ian told her about me in one of his interviews and mentioned that I was working on my own cookbook. She asked me about it and instead of just pooh-poohing it, I actually looked her in the eye and told her what I've been working on. She asked to see it, so I had Shawn bring a bunch of stuff with him the following weekend and gave her a look. She fell in love with it, and now she is personally helping me create the proposal, because she wants to see if she can buy it. She said she wants to be my Judith Jones. She's warned me that the odds are still against me, but that the odds were against Julia too, and look how that turned out. She loves my sketches, and some of the little anecdotes I've put in around the recipes, and she loves the title. She even introduced me to a literary agent who said that he would represent me in the deal once she and I get the proposal together.

The front door opens, and Simca goes scampering toward it. "Hello, my little love, how's my girl?" I can hear Shawn receiving his daily dose of furry affection.

"Hey, honey, I'm in the kitchen looking at the plans."

Shawn comes into the kitchen, Simca at his heels, and kisses me hello. "How's the nursery look?"

When we decided to move in together, we also decided to throw away my birth control pills. We aren't actively trying as much as we are actively not trying to avoid it. We both know that my age is a factor, but we wanted to just give nature a try. So I'm not taking my temperature or tracking my ovulation cycle, we're just living our lives without attempting to prevent it for a few months. If it happens, great; if not, we'll check into our options. We had a long talk about it, and we both agreed

that we'd like to try to have one of our own, and that then, if
we felt like we wanted more, we would explore both adoption
and fostering. I know Shawn feels like there are so many kids
who would benefit from a happy and loving home, and we both
know that family is what you make it.

"Looks good. They made all the changes we asked for. I
think it is pretty great."

He flips through the pages. "Looks fantastic. Just in time."

"Why is that?"

"I got an offer on the condo today."

"Really?"

"Yep. Full-price cash offer. And they're willing to do a quick
close."

Since we are mostly using Shawn's profits from his condo
sale, along with some of my savings, to cover the cost of the
renovation, we knew that we couldn't pull the trigger on construction till we had his place sold. "That is amazing!"

"Cross your fingers, we might be able to close end of the
month."

"Well, that is something to celebrate! We'll have to bring
bubbles tonight."

We are having dinner at my mom's with Claire and Glenn.
The two of them have had the most adorable, gentle courtship.
Somewhat formal in the beginning, and taking things very
slow. But then, right before I left for New York, a switch flipped,
and all of a sudden they were just giddy as teenagers. I mentioned it to Marcy, who immediately told me that they had probably finally consummated the deal, which at once made total
sense and completely squicked me out.

"Whaddaya gonna do? Love is awesome."

Marcy has been casually seeing Resident Mike since Shawn

hooked them up at our dinner party. Between their schedules I don't think either of them has time or energy to focus on something serious. I doubt they even see each other more than once a week, but I also don't know that either of them are seeing anyone else. They're super cute together—he's a very handsome guy, but maybe only three or four inches taller than Marcy, like the perfect miniature couple. There is a hilarious picture of the four of us from that party, and it always makes me giggle.

"You hear anything from Lawrence?" Shawn asks, digging in the fridge and coming up with half a piece of schnitzel from our dinner last night and taking a bite.

"Yeah, he got to Palm Springs safe and sound and promises to send pics of the renovation. He'll be back in time for the Halloween party."

"He'd better be. It is our anniversary, after all."

"I made him promise."

Shawn tosses the last bite of schnitzel to Simca, who catches it deftly and snarfs it in one bite. Then he looks over at me.

"What time do we have to be at your mom's?" he asks, a gleam in his eye.

"Seven thirty."

He walks over to me and pulls me into his arms. "Well, you're already barefoot, and you're in the kitchen . . ." He nuzzles into my neck. "I'm not saying, I'm just saying."

I laugh, and we head upstairs to maybe work on that third thing.

Delicious, as always, my dear." Glenn pats his mouth with his napkin and smiles at my mom. "I know where you got your cooking gene, Eloise."

She beams at him. "Thank you, kind sir."

The two of them are so cute it's almost disgusting. Claire rolls her eyes. "Good Lord, it's like you think you invented sex."

"Claire!" my mom says, faking shock.

"Seriously, old people, we're eating over here." I shake my head.

"Fine, different topic. What do you hear from the girls these days?" my mom asks.

"Shawn and I are having brunch with Teresa and her gaggle on Sunday. She's doing great. She learned so much with her financial class that now she's doing a class of her own at the church, mostly for the widows and divorcées. And she and Marcy and I are having a girls' night on Thursday."

"That's nice. Any news from Lynne?" Claire asks.

"She's delighted to be back in L.A., of course." Gabriel, true to form, decided he didn't love spending so much time coming back and forth to Chicago, so he decided to become an investor in Angelique's business, if she would move at least part of her operation to California. She agreed, and now Lynne is back in L.A. full-time, living with Gabriel and only coming back to Chicago for meetings now and again. She and Teresa and I do group e-mails and texts, and we have dinner when she comes to town. It's about all she can manage, really, and I'm okay with that. She's in my life, but not in a way that makes things difficult for anyone. I don't know that anything really changed much for her, reconnecting with us last year. Not really. But I'm not sad. She is who she is, and at the end of the day, I agree with Claire, there is value in having her in my life. We won't ever be as close as we were in high school, and we won't ever be as close as Teresa and I have become, but she's still my friend, and ultimately, I'm glad.

"Well, that sounds like just the thing for her, really. She was never fully happy here. I'm glad she's where she is most comfortable," Claire says.

"Me too," I say, leaving out the part where it's also the most comfortable for the rest of us.

My mom comes out of the kitchen with a tall coconut cake.

"Wow! Mom, that looks amazing."

"Is that coconut cake?" Shawn asks.

"Yep." My mom grins. "It's Cheryl's recipe. She mentioned to me when we had lunch last week that it's one of your favorites."

Glenn and Darren have started golfing together once a week, and when they do, my mom and Cheryl have been hanging out, sometimes with Claire. Two weeks ago Shawn and I popped over while walking Simca on a Sunday afternoon and found the five of them on the sunporch indulging in some of Claire's glaucoma pot, stoned to the gills and eating pizza. I swear, raising senior citizens is hard.

"Oh, Lord," Shawn says. "You spoil me rotten."

"Well, you spoil my Eloise, so that seems only right."

My mom cuts huge slices of cake for all of us, and Shawn brings out the bottle of champagne we brought over to celebrate his condo offer and the new house plans. We toast to family and home and the future, and the sheer joy of having sweetness on the tongue and bubbles in the nose, and so much extraordinary love and possibility around us.

# Recipes

Here are a few of the more special recipes mentioned in the book.

## Mrs. O'Connor's Macaroni and Cheese

### SERVES 8 AS A SIDE DISH

When Eloise's dad passes away, her former teacher starts showing up with comfort food just when Eloise and her mom most need it. This is one of those dishes, and it is not your everyday mac. This is your special-treat, soul-soothing mac, and I save it for very important occasions when someone really needs healing.

1 cup bread crumbs

3 tablespoons unsalted butter, melted

1 pound cavatappi or other pasta noodle

1 quart heavy cream

8 ounces Hoffman's super-sharp cheddar cheese,
    shredded

4 ounces sharp cheddar cheese, shredded

4 ounces smoked gouda (grocery store cheap stuff here,
    not fancy or aged), shredded

salt and ground black pepper, to taste

Preheat the oven to 400°F. In a medium nonstick skillet over medium-high heat, toast the bread crumbs in the melted butter until coated. Set aside to cool.

Boil pasta in well-salted water according to package directions. While water is coming to a boil, heat the cream to a light simmer in a medium saucepan over medium-high heat. Add the shredded cheeses and stir constantly until the mixture becomes a cohesive thick and creamy sauce. Taste, and adjust seasoning to your preference with salt and pepper.

When pasta is cooked al dente, drain and return it to the pot. Add the cheese sauce and stir well to combine. Put the mac into a casserole dish and cover generously with the toasted bread crumbs. Bake for 10 to 12 minutes to crisp the topping, and serve hot.

# Marcy's Cornflake Snickerdoodle Cookies

## MAKES APPROXIMATELY 1 DOZEN

Marcy's work with Sophie Langer (from my earlier novel *Wedding Girl*) is always fun and full of interesting baking problems to solve. So when Sophie decides she wants a cookie that tastes like the crispy cornflake topping of her grandmother's famous noodle kugel, Marcy is up to the challenge. This cookie is infused with cornflake flavor and then rolled in the same topping as is usually sprinkled on a kugel, for a whole new taste sensation. It goes without saying that they are really delicious dunked in milk!

COOKIE DOUGH:

- **2 sticks unsalted butter, at room temperature**
- **1½ cups sugar**
- **1 egg**
- **1⅓ cups flour**
- **¼ cup fine corn flour (You don't want cornmeal here; use corn *flour*.)**
- **⅔ cup cornflake powder (Pulse cornflakes in your food processor until you get a powder, and then measure out ⅔ cup of that powder.)**
- **¾ teaspoon baking powder**
- **¼ teaspoon baking soda**
- **1½ teaspoons kosher salt**

TOPPING:

> 1 cup crushed cornflakes (You want more of a crumble
>    here, as opposed to the powder in the cookie dough.
>    You can do this by putting the flakes into a Ziploc bag
>    and gently crushing it with a rolling pin to create
>    small crumbs.)
> 2 tablespoons granulated sugar
> 1 tablespoon cinnamon

In the bowl of a stand mixer fitted with the paddle attachment, cream butter and sugar together on medium-high for 2 to 3 minutes, scraping the bowl halfway through to be sure everything is getting combined. The mixture should be super fluffy. Add the egg and beat for 7 to 8 minutes until smooth.

With the mixer on low, add the flour, corn flour, cornflake powder, baking powder, baking soda, and salt. Mix just until the dough comes together, no longer than 1 minute.

Line a sheet pan with parchment paper. In a wide, shallow bowl, mix the crushed cornflakes, sugar, and cinnamon. Make generous balls of the cookie dough—about the size of golf balls. Roll the balls in the topping mixture, pressing so that each ball is well coated with the topping. Arrange them on the sheet pan. Press the tops of the cookie dough balls with the heel of your hand or the bottom of a drinking glass to flatten slightly. When all of the flattened balls are on the pan, cover tightly in plastic wrap and refrigerate for at least 2 hours, or as long as a week. Chilling is really important here. If you bake the cookies at room temperature, the butter will get greasy and the cookies won't have that perfect combo of crunch and chew! (This is a pretty good tip for most butter-based cookies, especially if you tend to have problems with them spreading too much or getting too thin.)

Preheat the oven to 350°F.

Rearrange the chilled dough circles so they're a minimum of 4 inches apart on parchment-lined sheet pans. Bake for 18 minutes. The cookies will puff, crackle, and spread. They should be golden brown at the edges and slightly paler toward the middle.

Cool the cookies completely on the sheet pans before transferring to a plate, since they will be tender and can break in half pretty easily if you move them too quickly.

~

# Ian's Winning Meat Loaf with Fig Barbecue Glaze

## SERVES 8

Ian knows that meat loaf is always a crowd-pleaser with his family, and Eloise has taught him how to elevate any classic family recipe to wow the judges on *America's Junior Super-Chef*. This is the recipe that gets him a callback for the competition. The spicy-sweet fig glaze is balanced by the crispy bacon topping. For me, it is the perfect dinner party dish, delightfully surprising in its hominess but still elegant enough for company. I would serve it with mashed potatoes enriched with sour cream and chives in addition to the usual butter and milk, and a steamed green vegetable.

GLAZE:

- 1 cup chili sauce
- 8 tablespoons fig jam
- 4 teaspoons fig balsamic vinegar
- ½ teaspoon red pepper flakes

MEAT LOAF:

- 2 teaspoons oil
- 1 cup finely chopped sweet onion
- 2 eggs
- 1 teaspoon dried thyme
- 2 teaspoons kosher salt
- 1 teaspoon ground black pepper
- 2 teaspoons Dijon mustard
- 2 teaspoons Worcestershire sauce
- ½ teaspoon red pepper flakes
- 1⅓ cups soft white bread cubes (crusts removed)
- ½ cup heavy cream
- 1 pound ground chuck
- 1 pound ground pork
- 1 pound ground veal
- ⅓ cup fresh flat-leaf parsley, chopped
- 1 pound thin-sliced bacon

FOR THE GLAZE:

Mix all of the ingredients in a small saucepan over medium-high heat. Bring to a simmer and cook for about 5 minutes to thicken slightly, stirring occasionally. Set aside to cool.

FOR THE MEAT LOAF:

Preheat the oven to 350°F. In a medium-sized skillet over medium-high heat, warm the oil. Add the onion and sauté until softened—about 5 minutes. Set aside to cool while preparing the remaining ingredients.

Mix the eggs with the thyme, salt, black pepper, mustard, Worcestershire sauce, and red pepper flakes. In a separate bowl, mix the bread cubes with the cream to create a paste. In a large bowl, add the egg mixture and the cream/bread mixture to the ground meat, parsley, and cooked onion. Mix with your hands or a fork until the meat mixture is evenly blended and does not stick to the bowl. If mixture sticks, add additional cream, a couple tablespoons at a time, until it no longer sticks.

Turn the meat mixture onto a foil-lined shallow baking pan. With wet hands, pat mixture into an approximately 9 x 5-inch loaf shape. Brush with half of the glaze, then arrange the bacon slices, crosswise, over the loaf, overlapping them slightly and tucking only the tips of the slices under the loaf.

Bake the meat loaf until the bacon is crisp and the loaf registers 160°F in the center—about 1 hour. Let it rest at least 20 minutes before slicing with a serrated knife. Simmer remaining glaze over medium heat until thickened slightly. Serve with extra glaze passed separately.

# Chocolate Cream Pie

REPRINTED WITH PERMISSION OF VALERI LUCKS

Eloise might be nervous about connecting with Shawn's family, but she is never nervous about her cooking skills, and she knows that the way to win them over is with this pie for Easter Sunday! I first tasted it at Palomino Bar in Milwaukee, and it haunted me so much I reached out to the chef for the recipe and asked if I could share it with all of you. Valeri was very kind, and I've made this a few times for friends and family, and everyone raves. If you ever have reason to be in Milwaukee, Palomino is a terrific gastropub with killer fried chicken and a whole case of extraordinary pies.

CRUST:

- 1½ cups graham cracker crumbs
- ½ cup sugar
- ½ teaspoon salt
- 8 tablespoons butter, melted

FILLING:

- 4 egg yolks
- ½ teaspoon salt
- ½ cup sugar
- ¼ cup cornstarch
- 2½ cups whole milk
- 1 tablespoon vanilla
- ½ to ¾ cups chopped dark chocolate or chocolate chips

2 cups heavy whipping cream, whipped to soft peaks

shaved chocolate or chocolate chips for garnish

(optional)

FOR THE CRUST:

Preheat the oven to 350°F. Whisk dry ingredients together in a large bowl. Pour melted butter over graham cracker mixture. Stir together until butter is incorporated (mixture should feel like wet sand). Press graham cracker mixture into a deep 9-inch pie pan. Use the bottom of a glass or a measuring cup to press crust together firmly in the pan. Bake for 8 minutes.

FOR THE FILLING:

In a large nonreactive saucepan, whisk together egg yolks, salt, and sugar until glossy and a pale yellow color. Slowly whisk in cornstarch until smooth and glossy. Pour in milk and whisk together. Put pan over medium-high heat. Cook, whisking constantly, until bubbles form and the mixture is thickened—about 10 minutes. Remove from heat and add vanilla. Mix chocolate into the hot cream. The heat from the cream will be enough to melt the chocolate; do not return to heat. Whisk until all the chocolate has completely blended into the cream.

Pour chocolate mixture over the bottom of cooled piecrust. Cover with plastic wrap and refrigerate 4 hours until cool. Top with whipped cream and decorate pie with some shaved chocolate or chocolate chips.

# Eloise's Lemon Chicken Pasta

SERVES 2 AS A MAIN COURSE
OR 4 TO 6 AS A SIDE DISH

When Eloise peeks into her fridge for inspiration, leftover roasted chicken isn't just fodder for chicken salad or a sandwich. This fast and delicious creamy pasta is the kind of thing that comes together in a flash but is also inspiring for Eloise, making her think about the kind of food she wants to celebrate in her cookbook.

1 pound linguine

1 tablespoon extra-virgin olive oil

1½ cups leftover chicken meat, shredded

1 egg yolk

¼ cup heavy cream

1 tablespoon lemon zest

½ cup finely grated Parmesan cheese (This will work best if you buy a chunk of good Parmesan and grate it yourself on a Microplane grater. Pre-grated stuff in the store often has cornstarch or other things in it to prevent clumping, and it can make your sauce grainy.)

3 tablespoons unsalted butter

⅓ cup fresh lemon juice

2 tablespoons chives, chopped

1 tablespoon parsley, chopped

salt and ground black pepper, to taste

Cook linguine to al dente in well-salted water in a large, wide-bottomed pot.

While pasta is cooking, heat the oil over medium-high heat in a nonstick skillet and sauté the chicken—just to heat through and crisp a bit on the edges. In a small bowl, mix the egg yolk, cream, lemon zest, and Parmesan cheese.

Drain pasta, reserving 1½ cups of pasta cooking water. Return the pasta to your pot, and over medium-low heat add the butter, stirring and tossing to coat all the pasta. Stir in the chicken. Then add ¼ cup of the lemon juice and mix well. Add the cream and cheese sauce to the pot along with ¼ cup of the reserved pasta water, and stir to combine well. The sauce should be smooth and velvety. If it needs to be looser, add more pasta water, ¼ cup at a time, until you get the consistency you want. The pasta should just be coated with the sauce, not soupy. Taste a strand of pasta to see if you want to add the remaining lemon juice—I usually do, but I like this really tart. Stir in chives and parsley, and season generously with salt and pepper. Serve with more cheese on the side.

# How to
# Change a Life

STACEY BALLIS

# Questions for Discussion

1. The goals that Eloise and her friends come up with are meant to be challenging and to push each woman outside of her comfort zone. What goals would you set for yourself? What goals would you create for your friends?

2. Eloise, Lynne, and Teresa have been friends since high school. How would you characterize their relationships? Do you think friendships can last beyond high school? Do you think that they should? Why or why not?

3. Lynne accuses Eloise of breaking "girl code." What do you think of Eloise's choices? How do you feel about Lynne's reaction? Use specific examples from the book to illustrate your points.

4. Discuss how the book handles race. Why do you think the author chose to feature an interracial couple? How did it affect your reading of the novel?

5. How would you characterize Eloise's relationship with her clients? Do you think that her devotion to other families has been beneficial or detrimental to her own happiness and achieving all of her life's goals? Use specific examples from the book to illustrate your points.

6. Eloise, Lynne, and Teresa each seem to play a specific role in their friend group. Discuss those roles. Do they change over the course of the novel? What role do you play in your own friendships?

7. Why do you think the author chose to include the character of Marcy? What does she add to the story? What do you make of her interactions with and feelings toward the other women?